A
Public
Murder

First published in Great Britain in 2020 by Black Crane Press

Black Crane
P R E S S

blackcranepress.co.uk

'The Door' by Miroslav Holub, trans. Ian Milner from *Staying Alive: Real Poems for Unreal Times* ed. Neil Astley, 2002, is reproduced with permission of Bloodaxe Books.

'Ithaka' by C.P. Cavafy, trans. Edmund Keeley and Philip Sherrard from *C.P. Cavafy: Collected Poems* trans. Edmund Keeley and Philip Sherrard, © 1975, 1992 is reproduced with permission of Princeton University Press.

Paperback ISBN 978-1-8382977-0-1
.ePub ISBN 978-1-8382977-1-8
.mobi ISBN 978-1-8382977-2-5

Cover design and layout by www.spiffingcovers.com

Printed by TJ Books Limited

For Helen
with love
Antoinette

Norwich
2020 xx

A
Public
Murder

Antoinette
Moses

ANTOINETTE MOSES

The author at Chiona in Crete

Antoinette Moses always wanted to be a writer, but didn't start writing until she was in her fifties. Since then she's published over twenty books and written seven plays. She enjoyed a long career running arts festivals, then went back to university, got a creative writing MA and a PhD at the University of East Anglia, and taught creative writing there for ten years. She lives in Norwich, but also spends time in Crete.

Antoinette's bestselling books of short fiction for foreign learners have won three Extensive Reading Awards, and *Jojo's Story* was described by one critic as 'a classic for all time.'

This is her debut novel and the first of a series of crime mysteries featuring DI Pam Gregory.

For

Vicky Holtby who first showed me Chiona,
and Eftychia Anaplioti who dreams
of finding the palace at Roussolakkos

Prologue

Brutus ... Mir Jafar ... Pizarro ... Pétain ... Dona Marina ...
Judas Iscariot ... Quisling ... Kim Philby ... Jason ... Simon
Bolivar ... Tokyo Rose ... Qin Hui ... Delilah ...

... Stephanie Michaels.

PREVIOUSLY

Tuesday 5th June

'I'm sorry, I'm so sorry, I was about to leave the office, then this student wanted to talk about her dissertation because she's left it all to the last minute and I missed the train. And I know I've been neglecting you...'

Jen Nichols stopped. Oh my god, she said to herself. I'm not just becoming one of those women who talks to her cat, I'm becoming one of those women who rehearses what she's going to say to her cat.

At least today nobody's locked their bike onto hers, stopping her from getting it out; one of the most infuriating things students do. Assuming it was students. What comes from teaching at a university, she thought, you blame them for everything.

Jen chucked her briefcase into the wicker basket and set off, ringing the bell to scatter the flocks of teenagers who insisted on cycling arms entwined, like flocks of birds, chatting to each other and laughing. Moderately pissed off with a world that seemed to be having a lot more fun than she was, she pedalled down Station Road and turned right. Road works again, she saw – the usual sequential game: it's June, so it's the turn of the gas company; July will be water.

Groups of people had already gathered, sitting and standing outside every pub, enjoying the evening. 'Wonderful,' she could imagine them saying, 'especially after all the rain we've had this year.'

The moment she got in, it was going to be a chair in the garden and a large glass of Sauvignon Blanc. At least there was a bottle waiting for her. Once her mother descended on her, she couldn't make that assumption. It would either be a meal cooked and a bottle on the table, or chaos everywhere and bottles emptied. You could never tell with Stephanie.

She was almost home when she felt it, a coldness creeping down her spine. Somebody was watching her. She turned her head, but there was nobody there, just some students sitting in a café laughing.

Imagination, she told herself. Nothing there. Nothing at all. Just go indoors.

'Puss cat! Skimble! Skimbleshanks! I'm home. Whiskas... OK... Sheba! All right, Waitrose special chicken! You're still punishing me for going to Sheffield last week, aren't you? Come on cat... supper!'

Jen threw her jacket on to a chair and walked into the kitchen. Where she stopped.

She registered the scene in a second as if it was on a screen: the blood on the walls which she'd painted a soft blue, last April, the blood dripping down the tiles she brought back from a holiday in Morocco, the blood covering the wooden worktop. It was much harder to recognize her elderly cat; the blood on his fur had already browned away his familiar colouring.

It took a great deal of effort to speak, but eventually she picked up her phone and said the word, 'police'. After that, she only managed to utter a few scattered words. Please, was one of them, and her address, and the words blood and everywhere. 'Please come,' she said, and burst into tears.

CHAPTER 1

Tuesday 19th June

'Advocaat.'

'Tequila.'

'Oh, thanks boss, another a. OK… absinthe.'

'Eau-de vie.'

'Nice one. Eggnog.'

'Isn't that the same as advocaat?'

'Yes. Except that it begins with an e.'

Pam sighed. 'Great. So, g,' she continued 'ginger beer.'

'That's not alcoholic,' her sergeant countered.

Pam could feel him smiling in the darkness. She groaned. 'That's unfair. I bet it can be. All right. Ginger wine. Hah,' she added, 'another e.'

'Eiswein.'

'That's a brand, isn't it?'

'Don't think so, think it just means ice wine.'

'So we're translating now?'

'Yes. Like translating brandy as eau-de-vie.'

'Very well. Negroni.'

'That's a cocktail. Cocktails aren't admissible.'

'Who said so?'

'It's the rules. Anyhow. Ice wine.'

'Now you're really taking the piss.' She sighed. 'What's the time?'

'It's half an hour later than it was thirty minutes ago when you last asked me. It's ten to five.'

'So what time do you think Pell will get here? If he gets here?'

'Can't see him coming anytime before seven. Mind you, if he thinks the kid has shat the drugs, he'll want to get them as soon as he can so he can distribute them to his own couriers. He might come at first light.'

'I just keep worrying the poor kid's lying there with one of the pellets having burst. He could be dying for all we know and we're just parked next door. I'll never forgive myself if that happens.'

'Would you be saying that if you were back at base supervising the operation?'

'I don't know. I might. The waiting would be just as bad. Are you criticising me, Josh, for being hands-on?'

'Never do that, boss. Besides, I know you too well. You're not that kind of DI.'

'As Superintendent Murton keeps reminding me. If I've had the general-not-a-foot-soldier speech once, I've had it a dozen times. Not that I'm going to change.'

'Can't see you ever changing.'

'I'm hoping that's a compliment,' she replied. But it was true. DI Pam Gregory was never going to become a desk officer. If there was a shout, she wanted to be a part of it, whatever the brass said. And this could be a significant arrest. It had taken months to set up, with a lot of assistance from the Met.

'Never thought we'd get Pell,' she said.

'It's somewhat miraculous the Met got the kid's mother to co-operate,' Josh agreed.

'Yeah. Been a great bit of co-operation. After all these years trying to get something on the Pell brothers. Which is why I keep telling myself not to rush in now. Because if we do, we won't get Pell, and God knows how many other kids are going to be force-fed heroin pellets..'

'It's tough though, I agree, boss. Especially with a kid in danger.'

There speaks a father, thought Pam. Josh had two of his own now since the birth of his second daughter last year. His wife, Barbara, who'd temporarily given up her job as a nurse, was one of the few people she knew who didn't mind being married to a cop. But then her own job was also one of shifts and unholy hours. Pam's ex, Richard, had never accepted that. Even though he worked in the Force himself, he used to accuse her of inventing excuses when she phoned home to tell him she couldn't make the dinner or meet him at the cinema. She was so much better off on her own. Perhaps she should get a cat. Or a goldfish. But she'd thought of getting a plant and then it had died from overwatering. She wasn't good with living things.

'Have you planned your holiday yet?' she asked her sergeant.

'We're thinking of going camping in France with Barbara's parents. There's this place which is really like a resort. It's got swimming pools and water slides for the kids and a golf course for Barbara's dad. And there'll be entertainment in the evenings as well as having live-in babysitters. There's even horse riding which Susan is excited about; she starts secondary in September, and we want to make this summer special for her.'

'That's nice,' Pam said absently. She couldn't imagine having a family and that kind of holiday. But Josh would come back fit and well, and that would be good. She guessed he wouldn't ask her the same question and he didn't.

'Have you heard the latest about Lorraine?' he began, naming one of the station sergeants who was notoriously tactless.

'No,' she replied, cheerfully. 'Do tell. Hold on...' she stopped him and listened intently. 'Is that a car?'

They both strained their ears, and moments later a car drove past them and screeched to a stop. Pam picked up the radio and ordered everyone out and to move to the barn silently behind her. They'd been lucky there was a children's nursery with a big shaded car park and a tall hedge just before the barn. It was a perfect undercover spot. After waiting so long, the officers all leapt out of their cars as smoothly as water and flowed in a dark stream down the road.

Pell got out of his car, unlocked the barn door and stormed in, leaving the door open behind him.

Right, thought Pam. If we can get him to incriminate himself, it's going to make the case a hundred times easier. Pell's very expensive lawyer had got him off half a dozen times previously. This time she was going to make no mistakes. Josh followed her with a camera, and together they approached the doorway. Pam nodded, and he began to film as they heard Pell's voice.

'Well,' he shouted angrily, 'have you got the shit out of you yet?' They heard him walk across the barn floor and pick up something that sounded like a metal bucket.

'Perhaps if I tipped this over your head and smashed it across your face, you might understand I don't like to be kept waiting. There's sixty thousand quid inside that skinny stomach of yours. In fact, I should just cut it open and...'

'And nothing,' said Pam walking into the room, a taser held behind her. Pell wheeled round to face her. 'You're not going to do a bloody thing, Mr Pell,' she continued. 'Now step away from the boy.'

Pell put down the bucket, thankfully, not throwing the contents over her. Its smell was appalling in the hot airless room. Even as she watched him, she was taking in the space. There was a folded tarpaulin in the corner covered in dust, a heavy wooden box that was padlocked, and a hoe hanging on one of the rows of hooks. Don't let him get to that, she thought. *Let's pray he doesn't have a gun.* She was wearing body armour, but her face was uncovered.

But it was a knife, not a gun and, as he approached Pam, it was already in his hand. Pam moved towards him.

'Police officer with taser!' she shouted. 'Put the knife down!' He ignored her and continued to rush towards her. 'Taser, taser, taser!' she yelled, sending several thousand volts into his legs.

Pell collapsed to the floor. Two officers ran in behind Pam and grabbed hold of him.

'Cuff the bastard, will you, Constable, and read him his rights, then get him back for processing.' She lowered the taser and approached the camp bed where the boy was lying holding his stomach. Oh shit, I was right. One of the pellets has burst. The boy cringed as if he expected her to taser him next.

She turned back to Pell. 'I've come across a few scrotes in my time and they're all pieces of shit. You're lucky I do things by the book. Otherwise I might just have tripped on that bucket of piss and knocked it all over you.'

Pell grunted. He could hardly do more than that as his face was being pressed into the ground. Pam turned back towards the boy. He cowered away from her, terrified.

'Hello, Winston,' she said and her voice was as gentle as she could make it. 'My name's Pam. I'm here to help you. It's all over.'

'You know my name? Did someone grass me up?' A strong London accent and a kid trying to sound streetwise. He tried to move again, but doubled up with the pain.

'Josh,' Pam shouted, 'Get an ambulance here right now.' She turned back to Winston. 'You're going to be fine,' she said. 'Just lie back till the medics get here. I'll get your mum to come to the hospital. She's been dead worried.'

'What?' he mumbled, confused.

'It's over,' Pam continued. 'We'll get this poison out of you, then you and I can have a good chat. You're not in any trouble. We know you were forced to do this.'

'You're not going to...?'

'Arrest you? No. We've had a word with the Prosecution Service, and they agree with us that you're not a criminal. So let's get you to hospital so you can get well. You and your mum are going to find a safer place to live, a long way from Tottenham. Like I said, it's over.'

She didn't know whether it was because of what she said or that he now believed that all this could stop, but the tears ran down his cheeks and he brushed them away angrily, as if he had no right to cry. Pam wanted to give him a hug, but that was for his mum. She just smiled at him and patted his arm, gently.

Twenty minutes later, after the ambulance drove away taking Winston to the hospital, Pam let out a huge breath.

'Good job, Josh. One large piece of excrement off the streets.'

'I hate the County Lines,' he replied. 'The kids just get younger and younger. That kid. He hardly looked much older than our Susan.'

'He's twelve,' said Pam. 'Should be in school, playing with friends, having fun. Not being forced to swallow pellets of drugs and sent here, there and everywhere. Vile.'

'Do you think one of the pellets had ruptured inside him? He looked terrible.'

'Probably. I'll know when I get down to the hospital later. Poor lad.'

'Good intelligence, though. And we were right to hold on.'

'Yes, we were, and you were right to stop me buggering it up,' she said, undoing her vest. God she hated wearing those things. 'Good intelligence and a good result.' She looked at her watch.

'Do you think we could treat ourselves to a bit of breakfast before getting back to the paperwork? I'd like to buy some pastries for the troops. It's been a long road getting Harry Pell, but we got him today.'

'Excellent work, everyone,' she called out to the officers who were photographing his car and putting tape round the barn.

'The Premier Inn serves breakfast from five-thirty,' said Josh. 'It's almost that now.'

'Nice thinking,' said Pam. 'I don't mind these all-night shouts when it's a fine summer day like this, but you can't work without coffee. I need a large injection of that before I tackle the paperwork.'

'And a bacon roll.'

'Now you're talking my language.' She smiled. 'With a fried egg and maybe a sausage on the side.'

'Thought you wanted to lose weight?'

'That's between me and my bathroom scales'. Pam smiled. 'I hardly ate anything last night. And doesn't working all night mean you need an extra day's food?'

'Not complaining, boss,' said Josh. 'I'm starving, too. Hope that poor little nipper makes it through, though.'

Pam knew she wouldn't relax until she knew Winston was safe.

CHAPTER 2

An hour later after they'd both demolished a hearty breakfast and Pam had allowed herself a second cappuccino and a blueberry muffin, they got back to their office on the fifth floor of the Cambridge Police Station with a bag of pastries for those who'd been manning the phones overnight.

'Why don't you ring the hospital?' Pam suggested. I have to check in with the guv'nor and then start interviewing Pell. He's probably got his hotshot lawyer from London coming up, so there's not a great hurry. And you need to process the film from this morning. Make that your priority. You got it all?'

'I did. Every word and gesture. And there's the knife in his hand at the end. He can't talk that away.'

'He certainly can't. And it will be interesting to see what else is in that car. I have a feeling that this wasn't his first pick-up of the morning. Forensics will let us know as soon as they've gone through it.'

Pam stretched. She was still stiff from sitting in the car for five hours. She should go for a swim. She'd made a start on the report she had to write for the CPS, but after fifteen minutes in her chair her back was killing her. As a DI, she could have delegated the paperwork to her Sergeant, but it wasn't one of Josh's major talents, and she preferred to do it herself.

It was still only six fifteen. In a couple of hours her boss,

Superintendent Colin Murton, would be in, and she could get him up to speed and let him know they'd finally got a result. But just as she thought this, her phone rang and she heard his familiar voice with its strong Birmingham accent. She couldn't say she liked Murton, but she'd known worse. He'd only been in the post for a few months, but already he'd managed to achieve the seemingly impossible task of balancing the demands of brass and their desire to scythe every department, and the morale of the staff, who saw their salaries and pensions shrinking. It was a job she never wanted to do herself.

'Gregory, good, you're back.'

'Yes, Sir,' began Pam. She was still elated. 'It was a successful shout. We arrested...'

'You can tell me all about that later,' Murton interrupted. 'Right now I want you to go straight to the Fitzwilliam Museum. We've got an unexplained.'

'What? In the Museum?' Pam asked.

'Not just in the Museum,' replied Murton, testily. 'Inside the new gallery. You know what that means?'

'Sir?'

'It means the Chief is going to be on it, not to mention the Met.'

'The Met, Sir?'

'In case you've forgotten, Prince Charles is coming to open that gallery in two weeks time. Which means that RaSP will be sniffing around like poncey dogs. Plus the media.' He made it sound as though it was her fault.

'Oh shit!'

Another bunch of bastards who thought they were better than anyone else, she thought. Just what I need.

'Are they still building that new gallery?' she asked. 'Was it an accident?'

'No, Gregory. The call came through about fifteen minutes ago. The victim was the archaeologist, Stephanie Michaels. The call was made to CID by the gallery director who'd just found her. Hawkswood rang me right away.'

Bloody Martin Hawkswood, thought, Pam. Always wanting to cover his back. She held the same rank as he did, though as head of EASOU, the new special operations unit for East Anglia, she was theoretically his superior, which wasn't something he recognised. They occupied different floors of Cambridge Police Station, though it might have been easier if they were in separate buildings. There had been talk of a new building in Swavesey, but it had never got off the drawing board.

'It gets worse,' continued Murton. 'It appears that somebody impaled her on one of the exhibits; to be precise on the horns of that golden bull she discovered.'

'What?' This sounded unreal, like something you'd find in a movie.

'I want you to be Senior Investigating Officer,' Murton continued, 'so start putting together a team and let's get this sorted quickly. I'm acting as though this is a Category One, but if it isn't, you can downgrade it at the scene. For the moment let's assume the worst.'

Pam put down the phone. The adrenaline and coffee sizzled inside her; she was buzzing. Until she got to know the victim, there was always this moment of elation, of feeling that this was the case that would define her career.

She had work to do, troops to organise. She stepped out into the office from her small room, which overlooked it and was hardly more than a cubicle. Josh was there along with Dave Butcher and Roberta Stills who were prepping their interview script for Pell.

'Listen up, everyone,' she called out in her shouting across-a-noisy-pub-voice. They stopped talking and she lowered the volume.

'I know you're all knackered. I'm knackered. But we've got a probable homicide. Stephanie Michaels. Yes, the archaeologist. The one we've all seen on the news. So, yup, this is going to be massive. And to make it worse, the murder is in the new Fitzwilliam Gallery which Prince Charles is due to open in a couple of weeks. As you can imagine, brass is going to make this top priority. Which is why Murton is already on it, and we'll probably have the Chief by the end of the day.'

'What the fuck?' asked Dave. He'd been a sergeant before she was, but if he resented the fact she'd been promoted and he hadn't, he didn't make a thing of it to her face. Though there were a few things she'd overheard him say that made her think about getting him to transfer, he was a solid member of the team.

'This doesn't mean we stop the work on Pell and the County Lines case. I'm handing that over now to you, Roberta. Dave will be your partner on that. Okay?'

Dave and Roberta nodded.

'As you'll have to work on this as well, I imagine it will be pretty much nonstop to begin with.'

'Overtime?' asked Roberta.

'Doubt there'll be any limits on that for once. You'll have a couple of months' mortgage payment at least.'

'Great,' said Roberta. She and her husband had bought a small house that was almost crippling them financially. But that was Cambridge.

'Right,' continued Pam. 'Roberta, will you ring the rest of the team and bring them in for a case conference asap. Josh and I are going to the Museum now and I'll ring back with a time for the meeting. But for the moment, let's say eight. That will give everyone time to get in.'

A few minutes later, she and Josh were driving down Fitzwilliam Street. It was hardly more than three minutes to the Museum, though it would be quicker on a bike. She glared at the traffic lights which held them at red even though there was no traffic.

'You know about Stephanie Michaels then, boss?' Josh asked her as the lights changed and he accelerated down Gonville Place.

'Well it's clear that you do, so tell me,' Pam replied.

'It's Barbara, rather than me. Huge fan of *Time Team* and all that. We had to watch this documentary the other night about the Golden Bull and all the things they found at Chiona...'

'Chiona?' Pam interrupted. This was a crucial time. She wanted to start filing away facts and get things clear in her head.

'The village in Crete. It's where Michaels lived. You know the story?'

'I haven't been living in a hole in the ground for the past year. I do catch the news.'

And you'd have had to be living in a hole or off grid to have missed it. An elderly retired British archaeologist deciding to dig up a dying olive tree in her garden finds an urn. The urn contains fine gold jewellery. An archaeological dig begins and there are more finds. So the entire village is demolished and underneath it they find a lost Minoan palace along with the Cretan Bull and a host of other treasures: a golden drinking cup in the shape of a curled snake and several brooches and necklaces and a gold dagger with a carving of bull dancers. All of it priceless. In the opinion of the public, and certainly the press, it was a fairy-tale story. Now that was about to change.

'You know what struck me,' Josh continued, ignoring her comment, 'it was how the money changed everything.'

'Go on.'

'Well on most of these programmes about digs, very little actually happens. They dig for a bit and find a bit of wall and, if they're lucky, a tile or a coin.' Then they stop because it's too expensive to go on. Digs are time-restricted. But this one changed because this billionaire stepped in and started throwing huge lumps of cash around. I mean huge. You really ought to watch the programme, boss.'

'I will in due course,' Pam replied. 'For the moment, just give me any details that will help.'

'Okay. So this billionaire, I can't remember his name,

but you'll find out because the gallery's named after him. Well he spent lots of money, not just on the dig, but creating a new village for the people whose houses were going to be knocked down. And then he built a new museum in the local town for the finds as well as the new gallery here, this new extension to the Fitzwilliam. He had to buy a large chunk of land from Peterhouse before he even started the building. Remember all that stuff in the papers last year?'

'Interesting. Though we don't yet know if any of this is going to be significant. Though it does sound like there could be all kinds of people who wouldn't be happy. Losing a home, being an archaeologist whose work doesn't get money thrown at it.'

'Enough for murder?'

Pam sighed. 'Well, we'll have to find that out. It may turn out to be personal. Murders usually are.'

Josh stopped the car in front of the railings that fronted the imposing classical building with its temple-like columns. As a child, visiting on a school trip, she'd just remembered it being huge and grey, now you could see it had been white. And it was more than one building. The gallery wasn't the first Museum extension.

A uniform was already standing at the gate which was firmly shut, Pam was glad to see. She'd worked with him before. What was his name? Yes, Bennett, Phil Bennett.

'Morning, Ma'am,' he said. 'Turn right into Grove Lane and there's a back entrance into the Museum and the Gallery. SOCO are there.'

'Thank you, Bennett,' said Pam.

They drove around the corner and into a yard where she saw the shabby white van of the Scene of Crime team and a red Golf convertible that meant that the senior pathologist Zofia Nowak had also arrived. Good. The sooner they had processed the deceased, the sooner she'd get answers.

CHAPTER 3

There was something about a homicide at the beginning of a case when everything was there to do and every moment counted. Pam leapt out of the car and turned away from the old stone building down the new path of white chipped stones… They won't stay white for long, she thought, and there it was, the new Fitzwilliam Gallery.

'Wow,' said Josh. 'That's quite something.'

It was a circle of glass and steel and the steel had been painted white so that you could look right through it. It lay on the grass as gently as a feather.

'Can we put your art appreciation on hold for a moment?' Pam said. Normally she enjoyed her sergeant's enthusiasms, but there was a time and place, and this wasn't one of them. Though even as she said this, she had to admit that she was impressed by this gleaming white building which seemed to almost float.

'It is beautiful,' she admitted, then put that thought aside; what was waiting for her inside wouldn't be.

There was another constable at the entrance of the gallery itself.

'Were you the first responder?' Pam asked him.

'Yes, Ma'am,' he replied. 'I made the place safe straight away as soon as I called it in and I've started the log. There's just the gallery director inside. He was the one who found the body.' He pulled out his notebook. 'His name is Mark Kitson and he arrived here at six. He knows this because he heard the chime of Great St Mary's just as he unlocked the door. Apart from him, there's just been Dr Nowak, and the Scene of Crime Officer, Larry Cuthbert.'

'And your name is?' asked Pam.

'Constable Barry Moorhead,'

'Thank you, Moorhead,' said Pam. A boy to keep an eye on, she thought, calm and collected. Could be one for the team in the future.

'Stay there until you're relieved, then write it all up, and email it to me.'

'Yes, Ma'am.'

There was no gateway into the gallery, just an automatic glass door that opened as they approached.

'We'll have to find out if this is the only entrance,' said Pam, 'and if it was locked. We need to know how the killer got in. And out,' she added, 'presuming it's not Kitson and there's nobody else here.'

Josh nodded. This was all standard practice, but his boss liked to rehearse things in advance to check that she hadn't forgotten anything as much as to tell him what to do. She was also snappy when a case began, but he ignored that, too. They walked down a short corridor with glass on either side and there in front of them was an entrance to the centre of the building and two corridors on either side circling away from them.

It was like walking into a kind of theatre, thought Pam. The centre drew you in and straight to the gleaming gold bull, golden, glowing, terrifying, that took your breath away. Had people worshipped it? It wouldn't have been surprising. Its two horns were like arms reaching outwards. Except now...

'Holy shit,' murmured Josh.

'Exactly,' she agreed.

The pure white gallery wasn't pure and white any longer. It looked as though someone had thrown something red on top of the bull and all over the floor. But a few steps closer and it came into focus. Lying across the horns of the bull, like a sacrifice, one horn piercing her chest, was the archaeologist Stephanie Michaels, her blood covering the marble.

'That can't have been easy getting her up there,' noted Josh, as they both put on the protective suits and blue plastic shoes that someone from SOCO had already placed on the floor inside the door.

'No,' said Pam. 'You'd have to be fairly tall to reach up there. Or use a chair.' She looked around the pristine white space, but there wasn't any chair visible or marks showing that there had been one there. Something to check later.

Right, she thought. *This is where it all begins.* She stepped into what she felt was an arena and joined the forensic team and the pathologist.

'Morning, Pam, my love,' said Zofia Nowak, stepping forward to meet her. Pam was extremely glad to see her here. They were old friends.

'You think they staged this just for me?' Zofia continued. 'You know how I love a bit of drama. Though you have to feel sorry for the poor lass.'

'Was she killed by the horns?' asked Pam.

'I won't know until I get her back into the lab,' said Zofia, 'but looking at the amount of blood on the floor, I'd guess she was stabbed first, multiple times, and then hoisted up. Those horns look lethally sharp and her weight alone could have caused one of them to go through her. But I can't begin an examination until we get her down, and your SOCO boys have to photograph everything first.'

'She was definitely killed by someone who wants to make a point,' said Pam. 'Sorry,' she added, 'Promise you that pun wasn't intentional. But you're right about the drama. It's what I was thinking. This isn't a murder that was meant to be secret. They wanted the world to know.'

'I expect they will,' said Larry Cuthbert, moving away from the back of the bull where he'd been photographing the floor. 'The media are going to be all over this, aren't they?'

'God, yes,' Pam groaned. 'I expect the Super will take

the first press conference, but he'll drag me into it if we don't get lucky quickly. And you all know how I hate the press.'

Time was everything. The morning was going to be crucial in getting the evidence they needed. At least having the death in this relatively empty building made it easier. Nothing left by other people to discount. It was all as clean and polished as an operating theatre. They needed to interview anyone who'd been near the gallery first thing and get hold of all the CCTV before it got wiped or lost.

'Well, once you do get a suspect, you're not going to have a problem,' said Larry. 'He stepped everywhere, assuming these were his footprints. And only one set,' he added. 'We're also finding fingerprints everywhere, but then several people had to get that bull into place. So you'll need to discount them. But there are fingerprints with blood on them and you won't want to discount those.' He turned to the waiting pathologist.

'Okay, Zofia,' he said, 'we've taken all the pictures we need of the body in situ. We can get her down.'

They lifted her down gently and placed her on some plastic sheeting so that she didn't contaminate the crime scene. Larry had trained his team well, thought Pam. If anyone could find a clue here, they would. Zofia made a quick initial check on the body and turned to Pam.

'Now you know that all this may change later when we have her in my lab, but rigor is pretty much at peak, so I'd say this took place nearly twelve hours ago. Certainly not this morning. And that's assuming this air conditioning was on all night.' Even at this early hour, it had been warm outside, and heading to be another blistering hot day, but the temperature inside the gallery was pleasantly cool.

'So she's been here all night,' said Pam. 'So much for the golden hour. There might have been people about in the Museum after that. Make a note, Josh,' she added. 'And ask about the air con.'

'On it, boss,' said Josh, whose phone was already out so

he could make notes.

'What about the guy who found her?' Pam continued, thinking about the footprints. 'Did he mess up the scene?'

'No. Didn't get close enough. Think it freaked him out to be honest. He was still shaking when we got here.'

'Where is he?'

'In his office. It's in the outer circle which you have to get to round from the entrance. If you go through there,' he said pointing to the passageway which led from the centre, 'you go round twice before you end up at the entrance. If this whole setup wasn't crazy enough, this building is a labyrinth.'

'It's a what?'

'A kind of maze. Well not actually a maze, they don't want the public to get lost. The director, his name's Mark Kitson by the way, started to tell me and I think he'd have gone on all morning if I'd let him.'

'Thanks for the warning. I'll go and speak to him. He may know who the next of kin is, and that's going to be my first job.'

She found Mark's office which was the fourth door after the public washrooms. There were no signs on the door and she'd had to knock and open all the others first. Mark's room was almost as empty as the other rooms she'd seen. There was an almost empty white bookcase, a single chair and a table on which a mass of architect's plans were laid out. No computer, she noticed. He didn't appear to work here.

Mark jumped to his feet as she knocked and entered. Was he the director? He looked like a schoolboy waiting for his A-level results.

'Mark Kitson?' asked Pam.

'Yes,' said Mark, nodding. 'This is horrific.'

'Yes it is,' said Pam. 'It must have been a terrible shock for you. I'm Detective Inspector Pam Gregory, and this is Detective Sergeant Josh Phillips. You don't make it easy to find you, do you?' she added.

Mark made as if to shake their hands and then realised

that might not be the right thing to do, so sat down again.

'Make it easy?' he asked.

'This building. Your office.'

'Oh,' he replied and relaxed slightly. He was clearly more comfortable thinking about the gallery than the fact that someone had just been killed inside it. Mark pointed to a design that had been loosely pinned on to a cork board hanging on the wall.

'The design makes sense if you're visiting the gallery', he said. 'It takes you logically round the exhibition so that you end up in the centre. Then there are the two arms which contain later works from the permanent collection. Or will do. Of course, nothing's here yet. That's all happening this week. That's when we'll get signs on our doors, too.'

'Maybe not this week,' said Pam. 'This is a crime scene now, nobody's going to be allowed in.'

'But you can't...' began Mark jumping up again, 'we're opening in two weeks and...'

'Is this a plan of the gallery? asked Pam, interrupting him. She thought it highly unlikely that the gallery would open in two weeks, but didn't want to get into an argument about it. This wasn't the time.

' Can you make me a copy and email it to me?' she asked. 'That would be useful.'

'It reminds me of a drawing of the inner ear,' said Josh, examining it. His elder daughter, Susan, had had ear trouble recently and they'd looked at pictures together. She liked knowing how things worked.

'Yes,' agreed Mark, smiling, 'that's because both are spirals. The spiral is one of the most ancient symbols that we have and the shape of the Cretan labyrinth draws on that.'

'Yup,' said Pam. 'And it has emergency doors I imagine. Can't see health and safety, not to mention fire regs, not making sure of that.'

'Oh, we've had all of that,' said Mark. 'We've ticked

all their boxes and passed all their tests.' He pointed to the drawing.

'There is an entrance door for staff here, just next to my office. That's where I came in this morning. I like to walk here across the Fen.'

'And it was locked when you arrived?'

'Yes. Absolutely.'

'And the other doors?'

'They're hidden within the panes and are on all the other sides. They light up and open in the event of an alarm going off. It's all automatic. The building looks as if it's made of glass columns when all the doors are open. It's an extraordinary design.'

'Good,' she said, briefly. 'We'll have to inspect those in due course. But they can't be accessed from outside?'

'No. Not at all.'

'So your locked door and the main automatic door are the only ways in and out?'

'Yes. And I had to unlock the automatic door to let your people in.'

Pam and Josh looked at each other. Had the killer been in the building all night?

'After you let yourself in the side door, did you lock it behind you?'

'No. I don't when I'm working here. Are you thinking that the killer could have still been here? I could have been alone with him?'

'I think you'd better sit down, Dr Kitson,' said Pam, kindly. He looked as though he'd topple over any moment. 'I'm not thinking anything right now, I'm merely ascertaining facts.'

The new thought had made Mark decidedly shaky. He needed a cup of tea, thought Pam, but couldn't see where he could get one. There didn't seem to be a kettle in his office. In fact there was very little of anything in his office. Mark saw her looking around.

'My things are all in my old office in the main building.

I haven't properly moved in yet. I haven't had time to be honest. This has been such a crazy time with so much to do and fretting that we'll never get it done. The opening's in two weeks, and with Prince Charles coming it's all been a bit frantic. Stephanie and I have both been worrying ourselves sick about whether any of the artefacts will get damaged in transit and how they'll look in their cases.'

'You'll have to tell Sergeant Phillips all about her,' she said.

'Yes. But to be honest I really don't know much about Stephanie,' replied Mark. 'I wish I'd talked to her more now. All we ever talked about was the exhibition and the gallery and where each object should go. Perhaps it was because she'd begun working as a site photographer, but she had a brilliant eye. I never asked her about herself. I'm not even sure whether she lived with anyone. She never mentioned a name, anyhow. But you probably know all that from her interviews. I liked her,' he added. 'She came over a couple of times for meetings. Actually, she reminded me of one of my aunts. They shared a taste for gin. I can't believe I'll never see her again,' he added, sadly. 'I can see her now, floating around the gallery in her long skirts and floaty scarves. She looked as though she was always in motion even when she was still. Not that she kept still for long. She was always getting in the way of the workmen. But then she made them laugh. I can still hear her laughter.'

Larry was right. You couldn't shut this one up, but he was clearly still shaken. 'You probably have a lot of information that will help,' she said.

Which I will have to get someone to read and summarise, she thought.

'She lived in Greece, yes?' Pam continued.

'Yes. On Crete. In the new village of Chiona. Her old house is of course at the centre of the site.'

'Where's she staying while she's over here then?' asked Pam. There might be clues in her luggage. Probably a nearby hotel.

'Sorry, I should have said. She used to live in Cambridge

and still has a house here. It's where her daughter lives.'

'Her daughter?' Next of kin in Cambridge. That was useful.

'Yes,' replied Mark. 'Jen something. I think she's an academic, something Stephanie said but...' he broke off realising that this wasn't what the police officers needed to hear. 'But I've got her address and phone number,' he added. 'I'll write it down.'

Mark checked his phone and wrote down the details on a notepad.

'Here you are,' he said, tearing it off and handing it to Pam.

'Thank you, Mr Kitson,' she smiled at him. This would save her a lot of time.

'Now we'll need to know who had access to this gallery and who has been here over the past twenty-four hours. Was it you who closed the gallery up last night?'

'No. Actually I was in my old office in the afternoon and I'd left Dr Michaels doing drawings. Actually, she didn't call herself that. It was an honorary degree and she felt she hadn't earned it. Mind you, he added, I always feel odd when people call me Dr Kitson, after all I'm not a medical doctor... No, she insisted that everyone call her Stephanie. She was a bit of a hippie, a free spirit.'

He really would talk the hind leg off a donkey, this one. But he'd clearly liked Stephanie, thought Pam, unless he was a very accomplished liar. But somebody hadn't. Somebody had hated her enough to kill her and display her body to the world.

CHAPTER 4

'So what time did you leave?' Pam asked him.

Mark Kitson cast his mind back to the previous day. He'd been in his old office from about five-thirty, checked that the catalogue deliveries were on time and then gone through the media lists with the Fitzwilliam marketing department. It was almost seven when he left. He'd assumed that the gallery had been empty. He told Pam that. 'I don't know what time Stephanie left,' he added.

Stephanie hadn't left at all. It still hadn't sunk in.

'Right,' said Pam. She turned to her sergeant. 'Josh, I'd like you to stay with Dr Kitson and get the details of all the builders and museum staff who had access to this gallery. And the names of the security people who were on duty last night. You know what we need,' she added.

'There's one of the tilers still working on the floor,' said Mark. 'There was a team of four came to lay it from Greece.'

'Don't we have any tilers in this country?' asked Josh.

'It's a specialist team. You see the floor tiles are Parian marble. They cost two hundred euros each; they have to be laid in a special way.'

'Two hundred euros... and how many?' began Pam. The entire floor of the gallery was marble. They had to be at least ten tiles in this office. Which meant...

'I've learned it's better not to think about the money,' said Mark. 'It's so far beyond of anything I've ever been involved with before. But, yes, the tiles cost about half a million pounds. Everything in this building costs ten times what you'd expect. I'm just glad it's not me who's responsible.'

'And that person is?' asked Pam.

'Well, basically the architect and her assistant, George, who is one of the two project managers, the other being ...'

A sudden high-pitched scream stopped him mid-sentence. The building didn't just look like a theatre, thought Pam, it echoed sound in the same way; the scream went right through them.

'Oh my God,' said Mark. 'I think that may be Anna. You'd better come and meet her.'

Pam grabbed her bag and ran out of Mark's office and down the corridor, which, thankfully did not disappear into another circular maze, but led directly back to the central atrium. Here she found Larry holding a woman at arm's length from him and trying not to get kicked by her stiletto heels. If it wasn't the scene of a recent violent death, she'd have burst out laughing. It wouldn't be too long before one of the team re-enacted the scene in the pub.

The woman was now shrieking. It reminded Pam of the chickens when a fox got in. She looked like a kind of bird too, with jet black hair and a slash of purple lipstick.

'What the hell is going on?'

Larry dropped the woman carefully on to the floor away from the blood spill, where Josh stepped in and quickly took her arm in case she ran back.

'She was about to contaminate the scene, Pam,' Larry said. 'I had to stop her.'

'Get away from me,' the woman screamed to Josh. 'Do you know who I am?'

It was a phrase that never failed to irritate Pam. She crossed the room and stood in front of this skinny shrieking woman.

'You're Anna? she asked. 'The architect? I need to talk to you.'

Anna looked down at Pam scornfully. 'You cannot do this!' she shouted at Josh, who looked remarkably unfazed by her behaviour. But then he'd heard worse outside the Jenny Wren pub. Just as well it had closed. 'I'll report you.'

'You can do what you like, Ms...' she paused, what was her name?

'Karanaki,' said Mark, who'd followed them out of his office.

'Thank you, Mark.' She pulled out her warrant card and held it out to the architect.

'Well, Ms Karanaki, as I said, you can make a report if you so wish, but this is the scene of a serious crime. I am Detective Inspector Pam Gregory, and the officer in charge here. We have laws in this country and one of them is that you do not contaminate a crime scene. Which I believe you were doing. In fact, you have no business here at all. If you take one more step, I will be forced to arrest you. Do you understand?'

Anna folded like a puppet whose strings have been cut. Pam was quickly losing her patience as Anna began to wail. How the fuck did the woman get in?

'Where's that bloody Constable, what was his name? Why did he let her in?'

'I'll find out,' said Josh, seeing that Anna no longer needed to be restrained.

'I'm sorry,' said Mark. 'It's my fault. I messaged Anna and told her about Stephanie's...'

He stopped, unable to say the word.

'And who else have you told?' asked Pam. She should have asked him this already.

'Just Eleni,' he answered.

'And she is?'

'I suppose you could say she's the organiser. She's... I don't know if she has an official role, but she's the person who liaises with Mr Leotakis. I have to make regular reports to him about everything. He's very hands on. Eleni worked with Stephanie on the whole project from the moment she made the first find.'

'Useful,' said Pam. 'I'll probably want to talk to her, then. Do you have a number for her?'

'Yes,' replied Mark, but she's in Athens. She's due to come here next week to prepare for the opening.'

'At least she won't be contaminating the scene then. Anyone else I need to know about who might try and get in?'

'No, no. I'm sorry,' said Mark. 'Nothing like this has ever happened before. I was just thinking about the exhibition. And what we have to do to make the gallery ready.'

'You should have told me,' said Pam. 'As for the gallery opening, that's something quite different, and we shall have to see when we can let you or anyone else back into this building. As of now it's a scene of crime. So you need to remove any papers you need from your office and work from your former office. This gallery is closed.'

'But the exhibits. They arrive today. Stephanie was here to help me unpack them and put them in the cases.'

'I don't care. They'll have to wait.'

'You don't understand...' began Mark.

'No,' replied Pam, turning to face him. He was beginning to piss her off, too. 'It's you who doesn't understand. Like I said to Ms..' She'd forgotten the name again. 'Like I keep saying, this is a crime scene.'

'But we can't have the pallets sitting around in the yard. It would be a security nightmare. Each piece is worth millions. In fact they have a security escort.'

'Well, you will have to find somewhere else in the Museum to house them until we re-open this space. I presume the Museum has security.' She paused and looked round for cameras. There weren't any visible, yet there must be security here. Josh had come back and she could see him screwing up his eyes as he studied the beams looking for hidden cameras.

'And now, Mr Kitson, I want you to go with Sergeant Phillips and tell him who was here and when, and when I can see some CCTV footage.'

'We'll talk in your other office, Sir,' said Josh. He turned back to Pam. 'I had a word with Constable Moorhead. Apparently Ms Karanaki told him that she'd been asked to come in. He assumed that you'd asked him.'

'Hmm. Very well,' said Pam. 'He'll know for another time.' *How come that Josh can remember her name and I can't.* It was a familiar complaint.

'By the way, there won't be any footage,' said Mark, who seemed to have regained his confidence. 'The building is basically empty apart from the bull and we didn't expect anyone to steal that, it's only a gilded copy and it weighs a ton. It's going to be part of our permanent display; the real one is still in Crete. We've tested the cameras, of course. They were going to be switched on today.'

Bloody wonderful, thought Pam. She made shooing movements with her arms and Josh led Mark out of the building. Pam turned to Anna, *what was it? Yes, Karanaki.*

'So, Ms Karanaki. You designed this gallery.'

'I did,' said Anna, getting to her feet. 'It is my masterpiece. This is why I cannot have it..' She stopped, not knowing the word she wanted in English. She looked for an alternative, '*vromiko...* made dirty.'

'That's not what we want either,' said Pam. *We don't like our crime scenes made dirty because we need to find evidence here that will help us find the person who committed this crime. That's why you can't stay here.'

'My floor. My marble floor,' wailed Anna, looking at where the blood had dried in the cracks between the tiles.

'It's only blood,' said Larry cheerfully. 'It will come out.'

'But the marble...'Anna continued, 'it was perfect.'

'Look,' said Larry, as Pam raised her eyes to heaven. The DI looked as though she was on the verge of exploding. 'It really is only blood and it will come out,' he continued. 'All you need is some hot water and baking soda. I ought to know, I've cleared up a few sites over the years.'

'Then let me start now,' Anna pleaded. She stepped to the side and her hand flew to her mouth and she screamed.

'What the hell..?' began Pam.

'I was about to tell you about this, Pam,' said Larry. 'It seems as if chummy wrote a word for us. I can't make it out though.'

'What does it say?' asked Pam, stepping carefully around the bull and then taking a quick photograph. She tried to make sense of the flowing letters. They weren't English. Greek presumably. 'There's a B. Bevtet something. What does it mean?'

'The B is a V,' said Anna, 'and what looks like a v is an n. It says vendetta.'

'I thought that was Sicily not Crete,' said Pam, 'the Mafia. Vendetta?'

'Cretans invent everything: plumbing, baths, printing, vendetta,' said Anna.

Pam sighed. 'I am sure this is very interesting, and we can discuss it another time, but for the moment we have a killer to find.'

'Who writes Greek,' added Anna, sounding rather pleased with herself.

'Yes, strange as it may seem, I'd processed that. Which is why I do want to talk with you later. But not now. Stephanie had a daughter and I think she deserves to know that her mother is dead.'

'I am so sorry. I'm not thinking. Jen. Oh *Kriste mou*, Jen. She will be destroyed.'

'Do you know the daughter?' asked Pam.

'Jen? I go there last week to have dinner.' She paused. 'She is not like her mother.'

'How?'

'You will see. Her mother was, how you say, everything is out. She tells you everything. She never stops talking.'

No longer, thought Pam.

'Jen. She is closed. And tidy. Like me. I liked her. Very

much. And her house, it is beautiful. Her father is an architect. Stephanie said he gave it to her as a present, a blue and white house full of light. So much glass. And for that time. It was extraordinary. The whole house is a triangle. It was in one of your English magazines last month. With an interview with Stephanie.'

Which means that the journalists who wrote that would know where it was. And that information would leak out into the rest of the media. Damn, she thought. They'll be camping outside like vultures with microphones. I need to get to the daughter asap...

'Really,' said Pam. 'that's also interesting. But now, as I said, Larry has to work here and you have to leave.' She looked at Anna more closely, an immaculate white shirt with a long pointed collar and stiff cuffs that showed underneath a black silk jacket. It screamed designer, and not simply because the belt had a gold buckle with the distinctive letters CD. This wasn't a marketplace copy, she could see, this was the real thing. But then the kind of person who ordered hundreds of marble tiles that were worth more than she'd earn in her lifetime was exactly the kind of person who could afford couture clothes. She also looked amazingly clean and tidy for someone who had got up quickly.

Pam looked at her watch. It was still only seven in the morning. It was going to be a very long day.

'We're both leaving,' she said. 'This is where we hand over to the experts.'

'The experts should have initial reports for you later today,' said Zofia, getting to her feet and putting away her thermometer into its case. 'Larry,' she added raising her voice. 'You might want to look around outside for a BFO.'

A blunt force object, thought Pam. That would mean that Stephanie could have been knocked out before she was stabbed. She hoped that would be the case for her sake. She might have been unconscious and not known about the stabbing.

'I think we may already have found it,' said Larry. 'There was this chunk of marble in the corner. I was about to examine it.' He went to the side of the room and picked up a rough piece of marble tile about the size of a mobile phone.

'Yes. There does seem to be matter on it,' he observed. 'I'll bag it and take it to the lab.'

Pam wanted to get a close look. She wanted to get hold of the tiler and start questioning him but restrained herself. She needed to get back to her office and begin to set up her team. She had to organise and send out the troops; she wasn't one of them anymore.

The trouble was she didn't enjoy sitting around waiting. She hadn't joined the Force to sit at a desk all day, and she wasn't the best person in the world when it came to computers. Which reminded her that Peter, the tech guy on her team, had just left to go into insurance and she hadn't yet replaced him. That was something she had to do fast.

Pam put her arm around Anna's shoulders and gently led her down the white corridor and outside. She looked around for Anna's car, but couldn't see it.

'How did you get here?' she asked the architect.

'I ran,' Anna said. 'I stay in the Hotel du Vin. It is convenient. I was up early. Mr Leotakis demands perfection. It is not easy.'

'I can imagine,' said Pam, although she couldn't. How could you cope with such pressure? But then the rewards must be tremendous along with the perks of staying at luxury hotels. The Hotel du Vin was virtually next door to the Museum. She'd had a birthday lunch in its Bistro restaurant with Zofia and her wife Grace a couple of months back. It was not the kind of place she normally went to, but Zofia had insisted and it had been a wonderful evening. She was relieved that Zofia was on the case. She was both meticulous and good at giving out information.

'I do need to talk with you later,' Pam told Anna. 'Perhaps this afternoon. Can you wait at the hotel?'

'I will go there later,' said Anna. 'Now I need to tell Vassili. He is the tiler,' she added.

'How many tilers were there?'

'There were four. They are specialist of Parian marble. Which now comes from Naxos because there is not enough pure marble on Paros for this. They are almost finished and now there is just Vassili. I meet him here.'

'Can't you message him?'

Anna shrugged.

'I suppose. But if he leaves, then the floor will not be ready for the opening. And he liked Stephanie. It is nicer to tell him person to person, yes?'

'Yes,' agreed Pam. 'But I can't promise you will be finished that soon. You may not be able to open in two weeks.'

'It has to. Mr Leotakis will demand it.'

'Even Mr Leotakis has to obey the law.'

Anna looked at Pam thoughtfully. 'No I do not think that is so. For people like Mr Leotakis the law is an inconvenience. You find a way round it.'

'I don't think that applies here.'

'You think I mean Greece. No. America, England. Where there is enough money there are no laws. You will discover this. And maybe…'

'Maybe what?'

'Leotakis. He is also Cretan, like me. And, of course, he has many enemies. Before, I work on the Stavros Niarchos Cultural Centre and I hear things. They are all dead now, but Onassis and Niarchos that was the big quarrel… and Niarchos, Livanos. They all fight, but cannot keep away from each other, but above all these men hate Leotakis. Who still goes on living. Almost a vendetta, you might say. Mr Leotakis was called The Pirate, you know; he is a very strong man.'

'You think this might be an attack on Mr Leotakis?'

'It is possible. Because why hurt Stephanie? Yes, she also had enemies, but she was a good woman. You will ask her daughter.'

'I will be doing that. And I need to tell you not to contact her yet. I have to be the one to inform her.'

'It is not something I would want to do. You do this?'

'Yes, but thankfully not very often.' But every one of them was seared into her memory: the mothers, the fathers, the sisters, the husbands and the wives. A road traffic incident or a fight that got out of hand, the grief was the same. At least today she wasn't going to have to inform Winston's mother as well. And it could have come to that. If she'd have known that one of the pellets had burst, she'd have broken into that garage earlier. Collar or no collar.'

'I could not do that.'

'That's not your job. You make beautiful buildings. Today isn't the day for admiring architecture, but even someone like me was impressed when I first saw the gallery.'

'Thank you. Now I look at you, I can see that you have soul.'

Pam laughed. 'I don't know about that.'

'You must never deny your soul, Inspector. You have to let it sing. And you must come to Crete.'

'One day maybe,' said Pam. 'I've always wanted to go to Greece.'

'Not Greece, Crete.'

'What's different about Crete?

'You will discover. Crete is where the world began. It is the birthplace of the Mother. Stephanie knew that, and now I must tell Vassili she is dead. He will be very sad.'

'Can you give me his number?' asked Pam. 'I'll need to talk to him.'

'He does not speak much English,' said Anna. 'You want me to translate?'

'No thank you,' replied Pam. 'We have translators.' If we can get them, she thought. 'So you have to tell bad news, too?' she continued, wanting to draw out the woman.

'Yes. Often. But usually it is merely to builders that their work is not good enough and they must do it again. They do not like to hear this from a woman.'

Pam smiled at her. That was something she'd learned herself as she rose through the ranks.

'It is the same everywhere for women who have power,' continued Anna. 'Goodbye Inspector. Forgive me for my behaviour earlier. I was not thinking. It was all very shocking.'

'It is not a problem,' said Pam. 'We'll talk later. In the meantime, I have to ask you not to leave the hotel. And do not contact the media. We cannot reveal information that could stop us finding the killer. You do understand that?'

'Of course. I promise. I want you to find who killed lovely Stephanie.'

Pam got back into her car. She had readjusted her thinking about Anna, but at the same time was aware that the woman had told her what she wanted to hear. She was clever. And she mustn't forget that this architect was also a suspect. Though while Anna was clearly not strong enough or tall enough to have lifted the body on to the horns, she could have done it if she'd had help. If she'd had an assistant. And she did have an assistant, Mark had said.

One for the whiteboard.

CHAPTER 5

Yea, mine own familiar friend, in whom I trusted which did eat of my bread, hath lifted up his heel.

Raise me up that I may requite them.

Do not spare them, but kill both man and woman, child and infant, ox and sheep, camel and donkey.

Next comes the daughter.

CHAPTER 6

The room at the end of the corridor on the fifth floor looked as messy as usual, its pale hospital-green walls splodged with white where blue tack and Sellotape had removed the paint, its blinds either stuck at the top or half-way down, several at acute angles like sad drunks. At one end was a large whiteboard although it was hardly white; its surface had been stained a faint pink with the constant rubbing-out of marker pens not meant for whiteboard use.

Now, as the hub of a major enquiry, it was transforming into something else. It had an electricity within it that made you forget the shabbiness of the surroundings. While Pam and Josh had been at the Museum, work had already begun to set it up as the Investigation Room. Pam saw Roberta and Dave already moving around along with a couple of Civilian Investigation Officers, known officially as CIOS, but unofficially as civvies. And somebody, almost certainly Roberta, had brought in a large coffee-making machine which a civvie was filling up with water. Good thinking, thought Pam. They'd need a lot of coffee on this one.

As head of EASOU, Pam had a large number of detectives from around the whole of East Anglia who she could call on. The unit worked best where there were crimes that crossed borders, and some did, but when it came to a local investigation like this one, she only had her own local team. And despite it being a relatively small unit, she rated it highly;

she'd worked hard to get here and she was proud of them. It was a world away from the murder squads of the Met in London, she thought ruefully, beginning to make notes. They had teams of squads with up to twenty-five bodies including over twenty detectives. She currently had six detectives. She was going to need more; this could be a long investigation.

Josh had driven her back to the nick and then returned to the Museum to continue questioning Mark about the CCTV and the air conditioning. He should be back soon and they could work on the case conference together.

Pam started to make lists of what she needed while she watched the additional computers and phones being brought in. There were rows of desks at one end for the extra staff who would be needed to run the inquiry. Beside the whiteboard the easel held a fresh flip chart pad, and on one of the three aluminium-framed grey felt notice boards someone had already pinned a photograph of Stephanie.

She'd have to get permission from the Superintendent to bring in additional people from Hawkswood's team. And she needed Martin to be happy about it or there would be all kinds of problems down the line. So much of her job these days was organisation, and while she knew she was good at it, it wasn't the aspect of policing she enjoyed.

It was now half past seven; she had thirty minutes before the case conference began. She began to load some pictures on to a PowerPoint. There were many pictures of Stephanie taken to accompany all the articles written about her over the past year. She'd have to read some of them when she had a moment. Or better, get a civvie to read them and give her a summary.

Delegate, woman, she told herself. Remember. She looked at the picture of Stephanie on her screen. She had that look many elderly academics had of wearing a lot of colourful flowing things. She was the opposite. In any case, in her job the last thing she wanted was something that could snag on a fence or be grabbed by someone. She preferred functional black trousers and polo shirts. With jackets that could be thrown on when and if she needed to look a bit smarter. Although she was no longer in uniform, she realised that she still wore a form of uniform; she couldn't remember the last time she wore a skirt. She had the feeling that Stephanie Michaels had only worn skirts. She'd probably been dressing the same for decades.

She looked down at her list. She needed to brief the Super and then get his permission to talk to Hawkswood. She needed to do that first.

As if on cue, Superintendent Murton appeared outside her office and Pam waved him in. He sat down, frowning, and tapping one knee as if in time to some unheard music. Pam resisted the urge to tell him to stop. He always reminded her of a Jack Russell, his reddish hair, now going grey, and his tendency to snap.

' I have to tell you I don't like this one bit,' he grumbled after Pam had told him a few basic facts. 'I've had to tell Seaworthy, of course, and the Chief Constable was more than a bit put out. Spoke as if it was our fault. Even told me his wife a had bought a new hat for the gallery opening. Though we haven't said yet that they'll need to postpone it. But I can't see us opening up the place in time, can you?'

Does anyone still wear a hat? wondered Pam, thinking of the crimped blonde curls and the over-made-up face of the Chief's wife. She was another doggy one. Like a pug. Which she also happened to breed.

'No, Sir. It's very much a live crime scene.'

'It strikes me as the work of a total nutter,' he said. 'Vendetta? Isn't that the Mafia? And he's left footprints and fingerprints? Nutter, has to be.'

Appropriate language not sunk in there. 'Seemingly,' She nodded. 'I'm waiting for Larry to give me an initial verbal report.'

'Do we have a next of kin?' he asked.

'A daughter, Sir. I asked family liaison to send an FLO

to the address – it's only five minutes' walk from here, by the way – and she's reported back that there's nobody at home. So I've asked her to stay at the house for the moment. I hope that's okay with you?'

'Well, we need to find the daughter to do the formal identification. Do you have a number for her?'

'Only a landline. I've left a message asking her to call me.'

'Sounds as though you're on top of it. I'm glad to say we sound a lot further on than we usually are this early. I think significant progress is the phrase I'll use for the media.'

'Are you doing the press conference, Sir?'

'Yes. Along with Seaworthy. He's suggested this afternoon.'

Pam's eyebrows disappeared into her fringe. The Chief Constable was known only to do media once a case had been solved. This was a first.

'I imagine he'll dish out the platitudes and expect me to come up with the facts and answer any questions,' continued the Superintendent, whose feelings about the new fast-tracked Chief were well known. 'Do you want to brief me?'

'If you don't mind, boss, I'm holding a case conference at eight. If you'd like to come along then I can put you in the picture along with the team. It will also give you the opportunity to see what needs doing and decide how many other bodies we need.'

Murton nodded. He appreciated the clarity of the DI's thinking. Of course she did still rush off and do too much herself, rather than delegating tasks, but as long as it resulted in arrests as it had this morning, he wasn't going to complain. Pity that it looked as though he was going to have to disband the unit to meet the next round of cuts.

'Good,' he repeated, 'good, good. And the County Lines case? When can I see a report on that?'

'Pell has been arrested and we have compelling video evidence against him. He's lawyered up, of course. His brief is coming up from London so we can't talk to him yet.'

'Actually I do have more news on that front for you, said

Murton. 'Had a call from your opposite number at North Area CID. Seems a solid chap.'

DCI Jeff Ellsworth, the skinny, bike fanatic who ran a case-heavy and high-profile area of North London would laugh at that description, thought Pam.

'He's a good man,' she agreed. 'And shares info. Unlike so many of them.'

'Indeed he does. Which is why he rang. Oh, he wanted to say well done, by the way. As of course I do. Not sure if I've said that yet.'

You haven't, but I wasn't holding my breath.

'Well they've got a new computer man, IT geek, ex GCHQ as it happens, and he's managed to get into a whole lot of stuff that your man Pell would like to keep hidden. It's all dark web stuff. Do you know what that means, Pam?'

He's beginning to relax a bit, she thought. Even calling me Pam. Bet he isn't even aware of it. Like his tapping.

'Only vaguely, Sir. Basically it's what you've just said. It's where you find sites on the internet that people want hidden for various reasons.'

'All criminal, I expect. There ought to be a way to stop it.'

'Can't see that happening any time soon. It's global, isn't it?'

'Yes. Complications. Our world has become far too complicated in my opinion. but, luckily for us, this computer man in London has got hold of all Pell's emails, which he'd tried to hide. And there had been a previous case like ours when the boy died.'

Pam thought of the skinny boy, Winston, cowering on the couch a few hours earlier.

'It still could be a homicide. The boy, he's only twelve, is in theatre right now. I'm waiting for an update.'

'Let's hope he pulls through. Keep me posted. But in your absence, and I trust you don't mind, with this new evidence I had a chat with CPS, and they've agreed to up the charges to attempted murder. Thing is, Pell knew he was making them swallow too many capsules. Just didn't care. The timeline is clear. He had an argument online with one of his subordinates who thought he was putting the mules in danger. And that was before he ordered our boy's delivery.'

And you wait to the end to tell me! That was huge and made the case against him so much stronger.

'That's excellent news,' she said, trying not to punch the air. 'Thank you, Sir.'

'Well, see you at the briefing,' he began to stand up.

'One more thing before you go,' Pam said. 'I don't think I can stay on the Pell case while I'm running the Michaels' murder. Do you mind if I ask DI Hawkswood to come on board and supervise? It's not that the sergeants working on the case aren't doing a good job, it's just that we don't want his smart London lawyer finding any holes in our paperwork.'

'Fine,' said Murton. 'Do you want me to ask the DI or will you?'

'I'll do it,' said Pam. 'I'd like him to feel it's coming from me. And I may need some of his detectives if this gets complicated.'

'Not a problem. The Chief Constable wants us to prioritise this. If Hawkswood isn't happy, tell him to come and talk with me.'

He'll love that, thought Pam. I think I might try a bit of diplomacy first.

'Right, then,' said Murton heaving himself out of the chair. 'I'll see you in the briefing room at eight.'

At a quarter past eight, Stephanie stood facing the team, fuming internally. How dare he hold up her meeting? As if time didn't matter. She was going to start anyhow, she wasn't going to hang around all day waiting. She smiled at Josh, who was sitting in the front row. He said he'd got some useful information and she was looking forward to hearing it.

'Good morning everyone,' she began. 'Now I don't need to tell all of you that what we discuss today is even more confidential than usual. There is going to be a lot of media interest in this, and some of the lowlife who work for the tabloids will be offering any number of inducements in brown paper envelopes. Which for those of you struggling to pay mortgages is tough. But when it's put beside the fact that leaks can jeopardise cases, I know none of you will give in to the temptation. Nor will you leak information to anyone else in this building or elsewhere. We have to keep a lid on this if we're to find our killer.'

There was a low murmur of assent, but Pam knew that there would be junior officers and civvies who'd be tempted. Money was money.

'I also want to thank you all for coming here this morning so quickly. I know a few of you have been up all night.'

'So have you, boss,' called Dave.

'Yes, Dave, thanks for reminding me. Hard to believe it's still only eight. Feels to me as if it has to be lunchtime. But while we wait for Superintendent Murton who wants to sit in on this briefing, I'm happy to tell you all that thanks to Josh's video evidence, we've got enough to put Pell away for a long spell. Plus...' she waited for the cheers to die down. 'We've got new evidence from London that puts chummy in the loop for attempted murder. And the CPS have agreed he should be charged with that.'

'Yes,' shouted Dave, punching the air. He'd been in on the case since the beginning and had done much of the initial compilation of evidence.

'Oh, if we're talking about the Pell case,' said Roberta. 'I was about to tell you. I've just had a call from one of the nurses at Addenbrookes.'

'Oh yes? I rang them a bit earlier.'

'She said you'd want to know that Winston's operation went very well. None of the packages, which we're pretty sure were full of heroin, had ruptured and they were all removed safely. They'd caused a blockage. Forensics are on their way down there to pick up the pellets. Apparently the kid had been forced to swallow forty-five of them. But they're certain he's going to make a full recovery.'

'Thanks, Roberta,' said Pam. 'That's excellent news.'

And almost physically, she felt that layer of stress, as thin as a child, float away. Winston was one less thing to worry about. She could concentrate on the job ahead.

'Normally, folks, after a great collar like this, we'd all go off to the pub and then go home and collapse. Unfortunately, we can't. We've got a serious, and somewhat bizarre, murder on our hands.'

She stopped as Murton came into the room. He took a chair at the front and waved at her to continue. That's considerate of him, thought Pam. Though it was also out of character for him to be even a minute late; he was fanatical about time-keeping.

'Okay everyone. So let's begin. Just to put you in the picture, Sir,' she said turning to Murton. She wasn't going to let him off the hook that easily. 'I have warned everyone about the nature of this case and the reason why confidentiality is more important than ever.'

'Good,' said Murton. 'And can I add to that? It's the reason I'm late. I've just come off the phone from the Chief Constable who has received a call from the Prime Minister.'

'What?' exclaimed Pam. The PM getting involved in a crime? This didn't happen.

'Yes,' continued Murton, as if voicing the collective surprise of the room, 'I'm afraid that we have a number of complications regarding this case. It is not simply because of the mass of recent publicity regarding the upcoming exhibition at the new Fitzwilliam Gallery, nor the publicity about Dr Michaels herself. I'm sure most of you are aware of her and how she discovered a Minoan palace in her garden.'

'Why do I just find old dog bones and rusty cans?' interjected Paul.

Pam smiled ruefully. Even the presence of the Super can't shut Paul up, she thought.

'Thank you, Constable,' said Murton. He cleared his throat. 'That would be enough to make this a problematic inquiry, and one which meant all of you and DI Gregory would be conducting it under intense media scrutiny.'

Thanks for that, she thought.

'There is also the factor that Prince Charles is due to come here in two weeks' time to open the exhibition. And we very much have to prevent there being anything which would impinge negatively on the Royal Family.'

Paul was about to say something else and Pam glared at him. He wasn't the only member of her team who had republican leanings, and also wasn't the only person who thought finding a killer might be slightly more important than upsetting the Prince's calendar. It pissed her off, too.

'Yes,' continued Murton. 'If this complication wasn't bad enough, we also have to contend with the fact that the patron and funder of the gallery, a Mr Leotakis, is a close friend of the Prime Minister. He rang her just now. He's currently staying at his country house in Dorset.' He turned to Pam, who was shaking her head in frustration. 'You haven't contacted Mr Leotakis yet, have you?'

'No, Sir. He's on my list as someone who might be able to throw light on this killing, but so far this morning I've only telephoned the next of kin, the daughter.'

But someone had rung Leotakis. Mark? she wondered. No. Oh God, it had to be the woman Mark said was the organiser.

'I think the person who rang Mr Leotakis must be the Greek woman who has organised the exhibition. Because she is currently in Greece, I haven't had time to speak to her. But I did speak to the architect, who Kitson also told and who arrived at the scene, Miss Karanaki.' She'd remembered the woman's name this time. 'And I warned her not to speak...' she continued, but was interrupted by Paul, who was looking at his phone as he often, irritatingly, did during briefings.

'I think you need to put on the TV, boss. I've just seen a picture of the golden bull flash up on *Good Morning Britain*.'

Josh turned on the computer and the wall screen, and the

image of Stephanie Michaels smiling at them filled the screen. Her long grey and white hair flowed over her shoulders escaping from the turquoise scarf she'd bound round her head and matched her long cotton dress and the crescent of blue sea behind her. Pam longed to leap into the sea right now; it was baking in the room. The two fans, though they were sending the tied cotton strips waving, were doing precious little else.

'Look at that sea,' sighed Roberta.

'And that was where I made this initial find,' Stephanie was saying. 'In my own garden over there.' She pointed to a bit of what looked like rubble behind her. 'And the combined international schools of archaeology who have since excavated this site made the other wonderful discoveries.'

The picture clicked off to be replaced by the presenters.

'That was Stephanie Michaels, who has been found dead today in the new gallery which Prince Charles is due to open in Cambridge this month,' said Piers Morgan, the bags under his eyes reminding Pam of one of the Chief Constable's wife's pugs.

'I believe we have the architect of that gallery on the line,' interrupted his co-host, Susanna Reid, smiling. Piers nodded at her.

'Good morning, this is Piers Morgan and you're on *Good Morning Britain*,' he said.

The camera stayed on the presenters as Anna spoke.

'Hello, I am Anna Karanaki. I am the architect of the Nikos Leotakis Gallery of Classical Art, yes,' she said and Pam could hear the pride in her voice. She was not going to miss this opportunity to promote herself.

'And did you find the body of Dr Michaels?' asked Susanna.

Oh my God, they're such ghouls, thought Pam. I'm going to hang Anna by her thumbs from one of the struts of her bloody building. She promised me she wouldn't speak to the media.

'I did not find the body. But I saw it, yes. She was placed

on the bull. As if it had, how you say?'

'Gored?' suggested Piers, helpfully.

'Pierced her,' finished Anna. 'As if she was a sacrifice.'

'This must be so distressing for you,' cooed Susanna, who was clearly not upset at all. This had all the ingredients of being the juiciest kind of story. A sacrifice, for God's sake. Pam caught Josh's eye as they both groaned.

'It is terrible. Terrible,' continued Anna.

'Thank you very much, Miss Karaki,' interrupted Piers. He can't remember her name either, thought Pam.

'Breaking news,' continued Piers, 'the death of the famous British archaeologist, Stephanie Michaels. We shall bring you more on this brutal killing tomorrow.'

'It's so sad,' said Susanna. 'She was such a lovely woman. Who's going to want to see the exhibition now?'

'I imagine thousands,' said Piers. 'People don't have your sensitivity, Susanna. An exhibition that is also a crime scene. They'll be packing them in.'

'You are such a cynic, Piers,' she said coyly. There were a few vomit sounds in the room which mirrored Pam's own feelings.

'Experience, Susanna. Now the rest of today's news. It's going to be another record-breaking hot June day. And for the latest on the Brexit talks.'

Josh switched off the computer.

'Oh holy fuck!' said Pam.

Murton looked as if he were about to condemn her use of language, but then decided against it.

'As DI Gregory warned you earlier, there will be an unprecedented level of media interest. You've already seen it. Moreover, as I told you, the PM is taking a personal interest in this case. I think it is now appropriate for me to tell all of you that she suggested to the Chief Constable that we might like to work alongside the NCA on this case. However, you'll be glad to hear that he told her that we have a crack investigative team and did not need the assistance of the

National Crime Agency.'

'Unaccountable bunch of ...' began Paul.

'Indeed,' said Pam, firmly, before Paul could say another word.

'So,' she addressed her team. 'One reason to be happy. The Chief believes we are a crack team. Now all we have to do is prove it. And we're going to have to solve a murder with the world looking on. And it's going to be a shitstorm. But if we do our jobs quietly and efficiently, we shall discover who killed Stephanie Michaels.'

She wished she felt as confident as she sounded.

CHAPTER 7

'Let's start with the facts, with what we know,' began Pam. She nodded to Josh, who clicked the keyboard and a picture of the archaeologist filled the screen. Pam and Josh had spent fifteen minutes before the briefing putting the pictures and a summary on to the PowerPoint.

'Dr Stephanie Michaels, seventy years old. Born in London, and lived for a short time here in Cambridge, but spent most of her life in Greece. Much of it in the village of Chiona on the island of Crete. Archaeologist.'

She paused. This was the moment she enjoyed. When she could present a clear picture of events and then get their insights. It was when the team began to cohere.

'You may think that this sounds irrelevant, but it may be that the discoveries that she made, which as you have seen, are national news, are at the heart of this case. But we don't know that yet.'

She nodded to Josh, who clicked up the picture of Stephanie as Pam had discovered her earlier that morning. She took a sip of water.

'So what do we know?' she asked the room. 'We know that Dr Michaels was assailed with a blunt instrument and then stabbed repeatedly. Following that, she was hoisted up on to the bull. This is the initial suggestion of Forensics, but of course they will let us have a full report later.'

'How tall is that bull?' It was Paul again.

'I haven't got the precise measurements yet, but I'd say from the ground to the top of the horns is a bit over two metres, wouldn't you say, Josh?' Josh nodded. 'Seven feet for those of you who prefer the old measurements.'

The team looked at Dave and laughed. 'Those of us who think in the old money' was one of his favourite phrases.

'So you'd have to be tall to put up the body?' he asked.

'Unless you used a chair?' offered a DC from the back of the room.

'But you'd have to be strong,' continued Paul. 'Dr Michaels isn't some frail wispy girl. Not judging by that film and the picture.'

'We can speculate on this once we've had the details from Forensics,' said Pam. 'But this is good thinking. If there was a chair, I'd imagine that there would be a trace of it. If you look at the blood spatter, it's all round the bull with no breaks. And I think you're right about the strength. You'd need considerable upper body strength to hoist someone up that high.'

She smiled at them. 'For the moment, let's begin by thinking about what kind of murder this is.'

'Dramatic,' said Dave.

'Precisely. This is a very public murder. Somebody wants to make a point. As you know, what we usually do at the beginning of a murder inquiry is ask who and how. Well, we know who already, and we know how. So, for once I think we do have to ask why. And there is another reason for my saying this. The perpetrator left behind a mass of footprints and fingerprints. Which will make it much easier for us to remove people from our enquiries,' she added.

'This makes me feel that our killer doesn't have a record, or at least not in this country. But we will, of course, share this information with our Greek colleagues as it is possible that our perpetrator came from that country.'

Murton nodded.

'I can help you facilitate that, Detective Inspector. The

pressure from the PM's office goes two ways. We can bulldoze any bureaucracy that would hold us up.'

'Thank you, Sir. That's very helpful.'

'Generally murderers don't want to get caught,' agreed Pam. 'They don't leave traces of themselves behind. The exception to that is terrorists.'

'You think this is a terrorist...' interrupted Josie, one of the younger DCs.

'No, I don't, Josie. But there is a sense of someone who has that kind of mindset. As if they don't care whether they are caught or not.'

'A nutter,' said Paul.

Murton nodded. 'My thoughts precisely, DC Collins.' Paul grinned until he caught Pam's eye.

'Sorry, guv,' he added. 'But it is bloody odd. Has to be some kind of weirdo.'

'Your medical vocabulary is as unrivalled as ever, Paul,' continued Pam. 'But we do have one other initial piece of evidence. The perpetrator – and I think we can safely assume it was the perpetrator and not a random passer-by or the victim – wrote the word *vendetta* in blood. Only it was in Greek.'

'OK, simples,' said Paul. 'Greek mafia.'

'There's no such thing,' said Roberta. 'It could just mean a feud or something like that.'

'Actually there is a Greek Mafia,' said Sue. 'I used to go out with a DS who worked around Green Lanes in London, which is a big Greek and Turkish area. Basically, the villains there are your average organised crime lot. You know, drugs, weapons, people trafficking, all the nasties. They're linked with the Russian and Albanian mobs.'

'There is nothing in this case to suggest these are the kind of people we are looking for apart from national identity,' said Pam firmly. 'I don't want to escalate this. Let us please keep it within the bounds of probability. There is quite enough to keep us occupied without that.'

'What about Mr Leotakis?' asked Paul.

'What about him?' asked Murton, snappily. 'He's the philanthropist who funded the gallery. And a friend of our Prime Minister you need to remember.'

'I'm sorry, Sir, but Paul is right to mention him,' said Pam. 'Not in any way as a suspect,' she added quickly before the Superintendent got any more red-faced. 'But it was something the architect Anna said to me that made me feel that we do need to think that he may be linked in some way to this death.

'As we've seen, it was clearly dramatic. And if it wasn't the frenzied attack of someone who has mental health issues, then we have to consider whether it was a statement. Anna also said that the usual laws did not apply to Mr Leotakis and suggested that he was a man with many enemies, so I'd like to share a train of thought with you all.'

Pam looked round the room and saw they were all listening intently. 'Dr Michaels made the initial discovery that led to the finding of the Chiona treasures,' she continued. 'But – and it was Sergeant Phillips who pointed this out at the very beginning...'

She smiled at Josh who reddened slightly.

'Leotakis brought in the money. And when I say money I mean a lot of money.'

The picture of the billionaire filled the screen.

'Josh, I think you've done an initial skim on Mr Leotakis. A very influential man. The kind of man who can call on the Prime Minister at an instant. Probably Prince Charles, too, for all we know.'

Pam turned and looked at the photograph behind her.

Leotakis had been snapped looking away from the camera at something to his left. His face reminded Pam of some ancient coin, or one of those pictures of Roman emperors she'd studied at school. Not that she could remember their names. The large nose and the hair, collar-length at the back, swept off his face. It would be a hard, cold face if it hadn't been for the network of lines that made him look as if he was about to laugh at any moment. He had plenty to laugh about, she thought.

'Nikos Leotakis was born in Crete in 1936,' began Josh. 'He made his fortune in shipping, hotels and real estate.' Josh stopped reading from his phone and addressed the room. He'd have preferred to have given Pam this information privately, but knew that the team would find it useful. 'I've only looked at a couple of entries online, but it seems that from the outset there are all kinds of questions about where he first made his money. He wasn't born with any money, but by the time he was twenty-five he owned five oil tankers. After that, his company just grew and grew. Along with the nickname The Pirate, from which you can all draw your own conclusions. But for the past thirty years he's basically been a philanthropist. He was married to an English woman who was the daughter of two Cambridge academics, and has said that England is his second home. Thus he gives a lot of money to British institutions and organisations. And when I say a lot, I mean a lot.

'Nobody knows exactly how much money he has, but according to the Forbes list of billionaires he's up there with Bill Gates and Jeff Bezos. Possible estimate is eleven point two billion.'

'What exactly is a billion? asked Roberta. 'I mean we all use the word, but I've never been sure. Is it a hundred million?'

'No,' Josh replied. 'It's a thousand million.'

The mass inhalation of breath in the room was followed by a mass gasp of laughter.

'Jesus, I mean,' began Paul.

'Yes,' continued Josh. 'You could spend a few hundred million and not feel it. Leotakis didn't leave his money in shipping. He put a lot into the tech business as it began. Like Microsoft and Google. So every time I look up his name I'm probably making him just a little bit richer. Though not as rich as the founder of Google, who Forbes puts at having a fortune of around forty billion.'

'I can't even begin to imagine that kind of money,' said Roberta.

'No. Don't think any of us can,' said Pam. 'A DI salary isn't to be sniffed at but...' Several DCs smiled ruefully knowing it was almost twice theirs.

'If he gets just one percent of his fortune a year,' announced Paul, 'that would be a hundred and twelve million a year, or over three hundred thousand pounds a day.'

Pam let the team buzz for a moment as they tried to come to terms with what that kind of money meant. Then she called them back to attention.

'While you may think I've gone way off track with this, I think it is relevant. And not just because Mr Leotakis is already taking an interest in this case. He threw vast sums of money into building this gallery.'

'Yes,' agreed Josh. 'And not just this gallery. He's put millions into a new museum in Crete in a place called Sitia, which is the city nearest to Chiona. He's behind a massive hotel development there, and the expansion of both the port and the airport. And all of this is based on the finding of the Chiona treasure. In a time of massive unemployment. The article I read suggested that locally he was a hero.'

'Goodness knows how much he gave to Peterhouse to buy the land for the gallery,' added Murton, now interested in the billionaire as a possible witness. Perhaps he might have the opportunity to meet him, he thought.

' Yes,' said Pam, as an idea hit her. 'I bet a lot of you remember all the controversy about it in the local press at the time. Which suddenly all stopped and there was nothing but praise for the project.'

'You think the press was paid off?' asked Paul.

'That's way, way above my pay grade to make any such assertions, Paul. And there are subtler ways to influence the media. I don't think Mr Leotakis interests us as a possible suspect, but a man like that has to have enemies. This murder could have been an act to smear him.'

'Wasn't there a feud between Onassis and some other tycoon?' asked Dave. 'Years back. Isn't that how that lot are?'

'Let's hope it's not, otherwise we could find ourselves treading on some very sensitive toes. But it's just something we have to be aware of. That will hopefully make it easier to see what this murder is all about and who is behind it.'

She picked up her tablet and began to read her bullet points.

'The body was found by the director of the gallery, and while there doesn't seem to be any evidence linking him to the murder, we do of course, have to make him a suspect until we can dismiss him from that list. Having fingerprints will most certainly make that easier. There was also a Greek tiler working at the Fitzwilliam Gallery that afternoon and we will need to question him. With a translator.'

She looked at Murton, and he nodded and made a note.

'The other principal people we know so far who were also in the gallery on the day of the murder were the architect and her assistant. They are also Greek. The architect, Anna, who you heard just now, is around my height and somewhat less than half my weight. I think it unlikely that she was physically tall or strong enough to have committed the crime. At the moment we know nothing about the assistant except his name which is...' she paused and looked at her notes.

'Ah yes,' she continued. 'George Dimitriakis. We believe he speaks excellent English and will need to talk with him as soon as possible. Along with the English project manager.'

She wrote down the names on the board.

'I asked Sergeant Phillips to discover what CCTV coverage there was. Josh, can you fill us in on that?' Josh took out his phone and started to read from it, paraphrasing as he went along.

'The director of this new Fitzwilliam Gallery is Dr Mark Kitson.' A picture of Mark flashed on to the screen.

'He doesn't look old enough to have left school,' said Roberta.

'He does look that young in person, too,' agreed Pam.

'Actually Dr Kitson is forty,' said Josh.

'That's quite young for a senior post like that,' interrupted Paul. ' Do you think his appointment might have pissed someone off?'

'That is another possibility,' said Pam. 'But let Josh finish.'

'Actually, I asked Dr Kitson that and he agreed that a lot of people had wanted his job. Apparently, it wasn't just the prestige, but thanks to Mr Leotakis, and I'm quoting him here, he had 'a budget for exhibitions and new acquisitions that would make even the Getty blink'. There were a few curators round the world, he thought, who wouldn't have minded if the new gallery wasn't the success it promised to be. But mostly he'd just had lots of good wishes. The kind of things he'd got from his colleagues were jokey suggestions that he might like to find them another Greek billionaire. But he'd certainly not had any threats.

'As to his movements, he left the gallery at approximately five thirty, and went back to his study in the main building of the museum. He met with a couple of colleagues. I've got their names.'

'Good,' noted Pam, 'we'll need to interview them to corroborate his story.'

'According to Dr Kitson, Stephanie Michaels was still in the gallery making some sketches when he left and she said she'd be leaving at around six to go and have a drink with someone. He didn't know the name of this person, and didn't think she'd mentioned it.'

'Interesting. I wonder who that was,' said Pam. 'Maybe her daughter, Jennifer, can fill us in when we locate her. I haven't mentioned her because we haven't yet had the chance to talk with her. She wasn't at her home earlier. We are, however, assuming that she's the next of kin and we have an FLO outside her house in case she comes home. Sorry, Josh,' she added. 'We all keep interrupting you.'

'No problem,' said Josh. 'Okay, the good news is that

the gallery was locked from the outside. There are two doors and both were shut first thing this morning. There's a small door at the side with a conventional lock and an automatic door at the front which can be fixed open or shut. When it is shut, you can press a button inside to open it to let you out. Additionally it can be locked. When it's locked it can't be opened from inside or outside without a key. Only Dr Kitson and the Fitzwilliam Security office have that key.'

'So a key question is: was the door locked before or after the murder?'

'If it was locked before,' said Murton thoughtfully, 'that means the killer stayed in the gallery all night.'

'Yes. It does,' said Pam. 'But what kind of person does that?'

'I've set up a meeting for later with the person who was the security officer on duty last night, boss,' continued Josh. 'I haven't got his name yet. I'll find out what time he locked up.'

'Thank you,' said Pam.

'Now CCTV,' continued Josh. 'The bad news is that the CCTV for the gallery has not yet been switched on. It was due to be activated today when the artefacts arrive.'

'The treasures are arriving today?' asked Murton.

'Yes,' said Pam. 'I suggested to Dr Kitson that they be housed securely within the Museum until we can hand the gallery back to them.'

'Excellent,' said Murton. 'At least they'll be safe there.'

Josh put up a map of the area on to the screen.

'If you look at this map, you'll see why we have a problem with CCTV. The new gallery backs on to Sheep's Green and Coe Fen, and there are any number of footpaths leading there and no nearby cameras.'

'I wonder whether Peterhouse have any at the back,' said the Superintendent.

'We can ask,' said Josh. 'There are plenty of cameras along Trumpington Street in front of the Museum, but none at the rear. There is one covering the yard of the Museum, but it doesn't go wide enough to cover the new entrance to the Gallery. That will be covered by the new system of cameras.'

'Which will be turned on today,' groaned Pam.

'Yes. That's about the nature of it,' agreed Josh. 'Oh and one final thing, the air conditioning was on all night.'

'Good,' said Pam. 'Can you call Larry and Zofia and let them know that.'

'Will do,' said Josh.

'Right,' continued Pam. 'Action points everyone.'

There was a quiet bustle as everyone got out their phones. Everyone apart from Dave, who got out a new notebook and a pen. He always had a new notebook for every case; he had a stash of them in his desk.

'The first thing we have to do is to eliminate people from this inquiry. We have to think of all those who had access to the gallery. And that means all those who work at the Fitzwilliam Museum. I want to take all their fingerprints, so we can compare them with the ones we have of the perpetrator.

'I'll talk to the Museum Director and get her approval – there's bound to be a few who will say it's an infringement of their personal liberties, we all know what Cambridge is like with that – but if I need to do it I'll wave the Leotakis card. As Superintendent Murton says, pressure from the top goes both ways.

'Josh, you now know your way around there now. I'd like you to put together a small team of say three people to go to the Museum and do this. I'll ask Larry for a member of his SOCO team to make examining them a priority. If the tiler turns up, we can get his dabs as well. Ditto the project managers. And you can combine that with your interview of the security person. I don't want to start the investigation with a huge number of people on our list who can be quickly eliminated.'

She stopped as a name flashed up on her phone.

'I'm sorry everyone, I need to take this. It's the FLO.'

'Diane?' she asked.

'Yes Ma'am,' said the liaison officer.

'I'm here at the nick with the team,' said Pam. Do you mind if I put you on speaker?'

'No, that's fine,' said Diane. 'Hi everyone,' she added. 'Well, I'm here in Flower Street with Dr Nichols, Dr Michaels' daughter.'

Everyone's a doctor, thought Pam. But that's Cambridge. You couldn't lob a ball without it bouncing onto an academic.

'She's just come home to water her plants because she's staying with a friend. The thing is she thought I was here about her cat.'

'Her cat?' asked Pam incredulously.

'Thing is, her cat was killed here two weeks ago. Someone got into her house and stabbed it. Then they spread the blood all over the wall. Which is why she's staying with a friend. She was understandably freaked out by it.'

'Have you broken the news about her mother?'

'I have. Yes. I'll let you know my impressions on that later. But basically I think she's still more upset about the cat. It was a particularly vicious killing.'

CHAPTER 8

Pam walked past the black gates of the Box Café, her favourite. But no bacon rolls today, and not just because she'd already had a giant breakfast. Today there was not time for anything except this case.

Flower Street wasn't far, fortunately, and the walk helped clear her head. Normally, she'd have taken Josh, but he was going straight back to the Museum. Murton had agreed to make the call to the director to get the permissions. Paul was following up on the architect's assistant and getting hold of a translator, and Dave and Roberta were preparing their interview with Pell. Roberta had also offered to do the paperwork on that case, which she'd gratefully accepted. All the notes were up to date, and Roberta had been with her on it from the outset. Just because there'd been a murder didn't mean she'd let up on that collar. She wanted Pell off her streets and put away for a very long time. Which reminded her of the boy, Winston. Thank goodness she didn't have to worry about him anymore.

Sorting all this out in her head, she almost walked past the house. The only thing that stopped her was the large blue number painted on the white door. The whole building was hardly wider than the door which had a knocker in the shape of a hand. Another Greek touch? This case was full of them.

She knocked on the door and the liaison officer, Diane, answered it straight away. Pam found herself facing a long corridor lit by a series of overhead skylights. The corridor led down into a large room with a wide glass wall at one end. On the right of it was another room, also leading to the same glass wall. Light flooded the house and everything in the room was white and blue.

No children, thought Pam. And it must have been a very clean cat.

Pam studied the woman who sat on the sofa, nervously twisting the tassels of a white throw. She looked about her age, or a few years younger. Pam had had her fortieth birthday the previous year, not that there had been a lot to celebrate. A failed marriage and very little life outside her job. Yet while she often complained about the job and the hours and the pay and the sexism, she mostly loved it. Now, running her own unit, she thought there was nothing she'd rather do.

Even when it involved smashing into the lives of people like the elegant and rather contained woman who looked as unlike Stephanie as you could possibly be. Dr Nichols had thick dark brown hair, cut just below her ears, which swung as she moved her head. Pam had always dreamed of having hair that did that. Glossy, the magazines called it. Hers was fine and frizzy and never managed to look polished even after a long session at the hairdresser's. And after a hectic day of her running her fingers through it, it looked more like she'd slept in it. This woman probably had bed hair that looked as though she'd been to the hairdresser's.

'My name's Pam Gregory, I'm a Detective Inspector for the East Anglian Special Operations Unit,' began Pam. 'I'd like to offer you my condolences for the death of your mother.'

'Was it a car?' Jen asked. 'She said she didn't know,' she added, pointing to the FLO. 'Mum's spent so long in Greece she always looks in the wrong direction.' The daughter sounded more irritated than heartbroken, but Pam knew that grief showed itself in any number of ways. Sometimes the brain took time to process it.

'I'm afraid she's been murdered,' said Pam.

'How? When?' asked Jen. 'They'd had threats, you know. Mum and Anna and the gallery guy. I can't remember his name.'

'Mark Kitson?' asked Pam.

'Yes, that's the one. They didn't like the exhibition being here,' she said. 'And they said the exhibition should be in Greece. And the marbles in the British Museum should be in Athens. There was a lot about the Elgin Marbles. Mum just laughed. But then she would. She said she was going to be out last night, and I only found out she hadn't come home when I got back here just now. And Diane told me.'

She smiled at the liaison officer. Diane was clearly good at getting on with people, though that did have to be a fairly basic requirement of an FLO. But now she'd rather not conduct the interview with the officer hovering behind her thinking that she was just as qualified as Pam to ask questions and wondering why was she being side-lined.

'Forgive me,' said Pam, 'but your mother was only discovered a few hours ago and I still know very little about her. It would be really helpful if you could tell me what she was like.' She turned to the FLO. 'But before that, I wonder, Diane, whether you could do me a favour?'

Diane nodded. Pam walked back down the corridor and outside.

'We've sent the paperwork to the Coroner's Office, but I wonder whether you'd go back to the nick to see if the order has come through to do a post-mortem. If so, can you come back and then escort Dr Nichols to the mortuary for formal identification? I'm going to have a chat with Jennifer now ...'

'She calls herself Jen, actually,' interrupted the officer. 'Nobody calls her Jennifer, apparently. She told me her mother liked the Donovan song at the time. Do you know who Donovan was?'

'No idea, Diane, but I'm sure someone back at the nick will know. They'll probably play you the song.'

Diane nodded and kicked herself. She was hoping to put

in for a detective upgrade, but she wasn't doing very well at impressing the DI so far.

'I also need you to look after Dr Nichols,' continued Pam. 'I don't think we can run to a twenty-four hour surveillance yet, but it may came to that.'

'You think she's a possible future victim?'

'It seems unlikely, but let's just make sure, shall we?'

'Yes, guv, I'll make sure she doesn't go out unaccompanied.'

'Good. I don't think she should. I need to have a quiet chat with her now, so take a break and get back here in about an hour. Oh, and Forensics will be coming here later. So you probably need to prepare her for what that means.'

'A lot of mess in a very white house.'

'Yes. I think she'll be reaching for the bleach after they're done.'

'No, problem, Ma'am,' Diane smiled and went back and picked up a large handbag. I bet that contains a lot of useful things, thought Pam. A woman who comes prepared.

'Right, I'll pop back to the nick and see you later.'

Pam watched her go and walked back inside where it was cool and welcoming.

'I could do with a cup of coffee,' she said. 'I don't suppose you have any, do you?'

'Filter?' asked Jen. 'Diane kept offering to make me tea, but I do prefer coffee.'

'I don't think the police force could operate without it,' replied Pam.

'Let's go into the kitchen, then.'

Pam followed Jen into the room opposite, which smelled as though recently painted. The walls were what she thought of as duck blue, a colour she'd recently painted her own bedroom except the tin had been called Lulworth Blue and she'd only bought it because she and her parents had gone to Dorset for a summer holiday when she was nine. It was a rare happy memory.

Like the main room, which was a dining room and a sitting room, the kitchen had a long wall of glass looking out over the strip of garden. Jen noticed her looking.

'The house is a triangle. My father designed and built it on this odd patch of land that nobody else could do anything with. It was his present to Mum. It's still her house. I rent it from her. I love living here. Or I did until'

'It must have been very hard,' said Pam. 'You don't have to talk about it.'

Jen took down a white jar from one of two thick oak shelves which ran above the worktops. The wall beneath them was tiled with turquoise and white tiles. I'd love to photograph that, thought Pam. Zofia would adore it, but this was hardly the time. All the plates and glasses were neatly lined up on the shelves along with several white jars. Pam wondered how she knew which was which. She must keep them in order, the thought. It amazed her that someone could be that tidy.

Jen took a paper filter from a drawer under the worktop and put it into a gleaming silver filter machine.

'The only Porsche I'm ever likely to have,' said Jen running her finger down the brushed aluminium. 'I've had it for twelve years and it's brilliant. The jug is a vacuum flask. Gives me hot coffee all morning while I'm working.'

'Oh, I want one,' said Pam.

Pam looked out of the window while the machine chugged and hissed happily. The garden was just a small yard enclosed by the walls of neighbouring houses. Nobody could break into there, she thought. It was totally private. So if someone had broken in, it had to be through the front door. The machine hissed itself to silence and turned off, and Jen carried the tray with the coffee jug and two mugs and a small jug of milk back into the sitting room, having ascertained that the detective didn't take sugar. She liked the fact that Inspector Gregory hadn't spoken while she made the coffee. She felt more comfortable with her than she had with other one, Diane. She felt that Diane had been waiting for her to break down and cry so she could comfort her. It had had the opposite effect. If she had tears to shed for her mother, they had been blocked a long time ago.

Pam sat down on a white-painted wicker chair that had two blue and white checked cushions in it. It was surprisingly comfortable. She took her phone out of her bag and placed it on a low glass table in front of her. There was a white sculpture of a dove on it and blue and white coasters where she now placed her mug. This was a home where order was everything. Somehow, already it didn't match the picture she had of Stephanie. The daughter was very different from her mother.

'First of all, can I just confirm your name. Is it Jen Nichols?'

'Yes,' said the woman pleasantly, but with the air of someone who has had to explain this too often. 'My mother used her maiden name.'

Jen got up and crossed the room to the line of neat bookcases which lined one side of it. On the other side was a large blue tapestry and photographs of the sea. She took a card from a small plastic box and handed it to Pam.

Pam read it. Dr Jennifer Nichols, Senior Lecturer, Film Studies. Pam wondered what film studies meant. Did they just watch films and talk about them? Seemed like a nice job if you could get it. She never had the time to go to the cinema, and when she watched films on the box, she invariably fell asleep. It was one of the things that had annoyed Richard most. Mind you, everything about her had annoyed him before their marriage finally broke apart.

There was nothing in the room connected with cinema. It all seemed to be all pictures of Greece. Somewhere she'd always wanted to go and Richard hadn't.

Pam shifted her weight, and the chair complained with a creak. I must go back to the gym, she thought. Or when it's a bit warmer I can go swimming in the open-air pool on Jesus Green, so much nicer than the indoor Parkside one.

'Do you mind if I record this?' she asked. 'It will save you from having to say the same thing again later at the station. Although I may, of course, need to ask you more questions down the line. The more I can find out about your mother the sooner I can find out who killed her.'

'In films they always say: is there any reason why someone would want to kill x?' said Jen.

'Yes they do, and while it's a good question, but not one I often ask. The questions we tend to ask are: what, where, and how. That's all. Why is for fiction and films. It's not something we necessarily can provide, although it's certainly what families need to hear. All we want is enough evidence to make an arrest.'

Why am I telling her this, she thought. Is it because I've just told the team and it's still in my head?

'Isn't that unsatisfactory, not knowing the motive?'

'Not really. My job is to take criminals off the streets and protect the public. It's not about understanding them. But that's what my job normally is. And I most certainly want to find the person who killed your mother, but I sense that in this case I do need to know why. Partly because the death was how it was.'

'Can you tell me that?'

Pam sipped her coffee. She didn't want to divulge too much, and it was always possible that Jen would prove to be a suspect, although she felt this was highly unlikely. But a little information from her might prompt a lot more from this quiet, contained daughter.

'I will, she said, 'but I don't want it to go outside this room yet. I have a nasty feeling the press will be on to the story very soon. The thing is,' she paused, how should she frame this? 'I'm afraid your mother was stabbed and then placed on top of the statue of the golden bull in the gallery.'

'Stabbed? Like Skimble?' burst out Jen. Interesting that she ignored the bull and the gallery, thought Pam.

'Skimble?' she asked 'Was he your...'

'Yes, he was my cat,' said Jen.' Somebody stabbed him. Then they spread his blood all over the kitchen wall.' Her bottom lip quivered and she was trying not to cry.

'When was this precisely?'

'Just over two weeks ago. I'd got back late. I teach in London, and I'd been held up by one of my postgraduate students who wanted to ask about a reference. I remember I was rehearsing apologies in my head for being so late as I cycled back from the station and laughing at myself for being so stupid. I mean not just talking to one's cat, but imagining a conversation... Do you have a cat, Inspector?'

'I'm thinking of getting one.'

'You should. When they snuggle into your neck and purr, there's nothing like it. I'd had Skimble for thirteen years. I miss him so much.' She began to cry. 'You must think I'm a horrible person, crying for my cat and not my mother. But my mother and I weren't really that close.'

'Tell me what happened to your cat. If it isn't too painful.'

'Well, as I said, I came back home...You have to understand, Inspector, that my subject is documentary cinema. For twenty years, I've sat and watched scene after scene of horror and violence. I've seen murder, rape, war. I've seen people shot and heard the testimony of children who've been tortured. I've sat in the comfortable darkness of cinemas around the world watching these things and then critically analysing the way that film-makers showed them. And how they react to death.'

She took a deep breath and Pam let her talk. Jen was processing her mother's death as information. At some point it would become real.

'In fiction people always scream but, as you probably know, in real life they don't. In the films I saw they wailed and sobbed. Nobody ever told me that you could freeze at the sight of death, that your blood supply iced up, that you stopped breathing. That was how I felt.'

Pam nodded. She wanted to know about this stabbing. It didn't sound like a coincidence. And, in any case, she didn't believe in coincidences.

Jen took a sip of coffee and continued her narrative.

'He was a wonderful old cat, but I could hardly recognise him he'd been stabbed so many times. And my kitchen. You see how lovely it is, but it was spattered with blood. Everywhere. On the wall and on the worktop. I rang the police straight away.'

'I'll look into it,' said Pam. 'There'll be a report.' There had better be a report, she thought, or I'll put someone through the mincer.

'The police came but...well, they were sympathetic and quite shocked actually, but sort of just shrugged. The thing is there wasn't any forced entry. Somebody had unlocked my front door and then locked it behind themselves afterwards.'

'Did they take any fingerprints?' asked Pam.

'No. They seemed to think it must be somebody I'd upset.'

'Had you upset anyone?'

'No. Not that I'm aware of,' replied Jen. 'And you'd know, wouldn't you if someone was that angry with you?'

Yes, thought Pam. You would. Which means that Stephanie must have known why someone would want to attack the cat and kill her.

'Did you tell your mother about it?'

'Oh yes. I rang her straight away. She was shattered. She loved Skimble. She thought it was about her, and I sort of ignored that at the time because Mum thought everything was about her. But it probably was, wasn't it?'

'It does seem likely,' Pam agreed. 'Did you tell the police that the house belonged to your mother?'

'No. I didn't. I didn't think of it.'

That might have woken somebody up, thought Pam. If anyone was thinking.

'Do you mind if I send a forensic team round?' asked Pam. 'You have changed the locks?' she asked quickly.

'Oh straight away. And I've installed a burglar alarm. I didn't tell my dad, but I knew he'd tell me to do that if I insisted on staying here.' She paused. 'Actually I wanted to. I've had the horrible feeling someone was watching me, but I expect they were watching the house. That's why I've been staying with my best friend. That and the... well you can imagine.'

Pam could.

'Very sensible. However under the circumstances, this may now become an extension of our crime scene and I think it might be best if you do go away for a while. Could you go on staying with your friend?'

'No. Not really. She's got a teenage son and I've been usurping his room. But I could stay with my father in London. Since Oliver and Luca left home – they're my half-brothers – he and Caroline have got stacks of room.'

'This is going to be difficult, but I have to ask it. Did you take your cat to the vet for cremation?'

'No. I buried him in the garden. It's not illegal is it?'

Pam shook her head. Jen stood up and pointed through the window at the garden. There was a circle of beds in the centre with herbs and lavender. Like the rest of the house, it all felt very designed, very controlled.

'He's there. Skimble. Under that little rosemary bush.'

Pam looked at the small herb. She was going to have to dig up the cat and give him to Zofia. It was possible that Stephanie's killer had used the same knife. She felt that it was most unlikely that these two stabbings were unrelated.

'You're going to ask me whether you can exhume him, aren't you?' Jen's voice quivered. 'The answer's, yes. As long as I can have him back.'

'We'll bury him again and replant the rosemary. We'll treat him with dignity,' said Pam. And Zofia would. She was a deeply kind person.

'He was a very dignified cat,' said Jen and began to cry again.

Pam offered her a tissue. Like Diane, she always came supplied on occasions like this.

'Now,' continued Pam, 'and I understand how hard this will be, I need to talk to you about your mother.'

'That isn't so hard,' said Jen wiping her nose. 'My mother was a very difficult person, Inspector, and not always a very nice one. I can think of any number of people who would want her dead.'

CHAPTER 9

Pam sat silently and waited for Jen to continue. This was interesting. Mark and Anna had presented Stephanie as this charming loveable woman, but now it seemed there was another side to her. Or it could be that the daughter had a personal grudge.

Was this relevant, or was she wasting valuable time here? She was dying to get back to the station and get everything moving. There was already a lot to do. The cat stabbing could be a game changer. But she wouldn't know whether the killing had been done by the same person until Forensics had been here. They had to exhume the cat and see if there were any traces left of the intruder in the house. But if he hadn't broken in, that meant he had had access to keys. Something else she needed to ask. And if it was the same perp, that would certainly limit the number of suspects. Mark Kitson and Anna, for example, wouldn't have keys to this house.

'When it comes to my mother, I'm probably not the best person to talk to,' said Jen. 'Over the last few years I've hardly seen her. She's stayed here when she had meetings about the gallery, but we didn't really have time to talk even then. I still go to Crete to visit her most summers, but I tend to combine it with a bit of island hopping. A few days with my mother is usually all I can manage. Sorry that sounds terrible,' she added.

'It sounds honest. But you got on? I think you had the architect over for dinner one evening?'

'Yes. Have you met her? God, she's a weird woman. And her assistant George is even stranger. He hardly spoke. To start with I thought he didn't speak English, but actually his English was as good as hers, and that's almost perfect. She actually worked for two years for a London firm and George was with her then. But yes, Mum and I were always polite to each other, and I enjoyed her company until she started to mess up the house. She's incredibly untidy. The house looks like this I think because as a child it drove me mad that I could never find anything.'

'Does she have the keys to the house?'

'Yes, she's always had them. And given out copies to all her friends. I thought of this after Skimble was killed.'

'And your father has a set?'

'I expect so. I've always given a set to my neighbours. Though I haven't got round to it yet with the new keys. Nobody has these except me.'

'Probably wise to keep it like that for the moment,' said Pam, thinking of how her life had just been complicated again. Keys everywhere. And anyone who had access to Stephanie's bag could have made copies.

'Maybe if you could just tell me a bit about your mother and her life. Just so I can get a picture of her.'

'When it comes to pictures, you'll find lots on her iPad. You've got that? It was in her handbag.'

Pam nodded. Though where was her bag? And were her keys in it? Wouldn't Larry ring her if he'd found it? One thing at a time, she told herself. One thing at a time. Don't waste time by trying to run down too many things at once.

'Obviously there are people like Henry and Popi who can tell you more,' continued Jen, but this is what I know.'

'Sorry to interrupt,' said Pam. 'Henry and Popi?'

'My godparents. My mum's oldest friends. Popi, that's with one p and an i. She lives in Crete now she's retired. She's very tied up with politics, close friends of the last President. The Greek one, that is. She's always ticking Mum off for not being active enough. And Henry. Henry Cox. He's a bit older than Mum, I think about seventy-five. He's known her for ever. They were in Athens together in the early seventies and then Mum moved to Crete because Henry had a house there in Chiona.

'So Henry was one of those who had to leave his old house?'

'He must have hated that. All his books and papers. Actually he rang a couple of days ago. He's in London doing some research at the British Library. Said he was digging up some names and really needed to speak to Mum. I gave her the message, but don't know whether she got back to him. Henry had the keys to this house, by the way, because he stays here sometimes when he needs to study at the University Library. It's usually in the summer when I'm away.'

'We'll ask him whether Stephanie rang him back. Do you have a number for him?'

'Not a mobile, just the landline of his house in Crete. It's the same one it always was. I do have an email.'

'Can you send it to me, please?'

Pam took out her card and wrote her own mobile number on it. She handed it to Jen.

'Sure. Oh God, I'll have to tell him and Popi.'

'Unless you'd prefer me to do it.'

'No. I've known them all my life. I want to do it.'

'Can you give them my phone number. They might want to ask me questions,' said Pam. Though that was not actually the truth, what she wanted was to ask them a host of questions. Henry being in England certainly helped. Unless... Could an old man have done it?

'Henry? Is he physically fit?' she asked.

'Oh yes. He's as strong as an ox. Swims every day. And climbs the hills behind the village. He can out puff me for sure.'

'So. Let's go back to your mother. You said she was in Greece in the seventies.'

'Yes. She'd gone there on holiday in 1973. Her dad had died, and she wanted to get away. So she did what everyone did back then. You know, Leonard Cohen and all the poets.'

Pam loved the everyone. She thought of her own parents living in their small house on the outskirts of March. Her mother thought Cambridge was another world, even though it was only an hour away, half that on the fast train. She'd never been abroad and never wanted to travel.

'So Mum is island hopping and ends up on Crete. Where she meets Henry. And Henry introduces her to Laurent and that turns into the great romance of the century.'

'Laurent?'

'He was French, an archaeologist and was working for the French School in Athens. It's a sort of institute I think. They were exploring a site in Eastern Crete. I don't know if you know, but the sites are run by different countries. So the British have Knossos, etcetera, and the French had this tiny site near Vai.'

Pam let the information wash over her. She didn't feel that any of this was relevant, but was there an old feud between Stephanie and this Henry?

'So Mum and Laurent fell in love,' continued Jen. 'Laurent moved out of Henry's house and he and Mum rented a little house in Palaikastro for the summer. Then they moved to Athens. Henry had a flat there, too, where he spent the winters. And Mum and Laurent lived together for over two years, but just as Mum agrees to marry Laurent, that was in 1977 – I know all this because Mum and Henry talked about it so often – there was this huge rainstorm and Laurent was drowned. He'd actually gone to Henry's that night to tell him the good news because the phones were down and he wanted Henry to be the first to know. It's a story my mother told me so many times. And I think it became the most important moment of her life. That and the Polytechnic.'

'The Polytechnic?'

'The student massacre in November 1973. Henry can

tell you all about that, he's writing a new book about it. I think it will be the third. It's all he ever thinks about.'

Pam determined that she would find a way to not let Henry tell her about it. Academics could win an Olympic medal in boring when it came to their pet subjects.

'Go on,' she said.

'So after Laurent died, Mum decided to become an archaeologist herself. She came back to England the following year, came here in fact and started studying archaeology. And that's where she met my Dad. In 1981. They got married really quickly because I was on the way. And Dad built her this blue and white house because he knew she missed Greece. But it didn't really work out. Mum kept disappearing. On digs she said, but Dad always knew there were other men. Though he didn't tell me that till long after I was grown up. And there were all kinds of dramas. My mother could create a drama out of anything.'

And died dramatically, too. Was that connected?

'One of the major rows was about her dissertation. Which another student said she'd stolen from him, though it all got hushed up. I don't know if it was true, but Mum could be very lazy, so it seems perfectly possible.'

'Do you know the name of the student who made that accusation?'

'I don't, but Dad will. He used to send abusive letters.'

Vendetta, thought Pam. An archaeology student would probably be able to write in Greek, too. This could be something. It could have had a significant effect on that student's life.

'And so Mum and Dad got divorced. That was when I was six. I lived with Mum in Greece for two years, because she went straight back there, but she didn't really want a small child around. She'd met this drunk poet and was with him for a couple of years. So I came back here to live with Dad. And by that time he'd met Caroline and they got married.'

'And you lived here in this house?'

'Yes, though Caroline always hated it, felt it was Mum's house, which I suppose it is. And she missed living in London. So when Dad was offered a partnership with a firm in Putney, they moved there. He's got a big house near the river, what Caro always wanted. And Caroline was pregnant with Ollie.'

'So your mother got the house?'

'Mum, being Mum, refused to allow Dad to sell it, so she somehow found the money to buy him out. She's always had a bit of money from when her Dad died. It's what she's lived on all her life. She never needed to work. I often think that's why she's the way she is. I mean was.'

Jen shook her head as if she didn't want that idea to enter it. It's going to hit her later, thought Pam.

'Do you know where the money for the house came from?'

'I never asked. I expect Henry would know.'

Henry again. She needed to talk to him soon. He was now at the top of her list.

'I lived with Dad and Caroline in London and Mum let this house until I was eighteen when I asked her if I could rent it. And she agreed.'

'So you pay rent to your mother?'

'Yes. Though it's pretty much a peppercorn rent. I pay her five thousand a year.'

'So you didn't live with your mother growing up?'

'No. After the divorce she wanted to go back to Greece. There was a big row I think because Dad understandably didn't want to lose me. But that's more about me. You want to know about Mum'.

'You said earlier that you could think of any number of people who might want to hurt your mother. Were you thinking of the student whose work she allegedly stole?'

'Yes, him. And then Henry himself. I mean I love him and I can't imagine him hurting Mum, but they have had some monumental rows over the years. Of course, he usually forgives her, but for two people who aren't a couple, it's a pretty volatile relationship.'

'Anyone else you can think of?'

'A few,' said Jen sighing. Who hadn't Stephanie annoyed or betrayed? She wished she could feel upset, but it was more like a kind of general regret that she and her mother had never been able to recapture the close relationship they'd had when she was very young.

'There are probably a few wives out there who weren't delighted at the way Mum openly had affairs with their husbands, but primarily it would be the people who are furious with her for taking all the credit for the Chiona find. And Tim who's spent his entire life looking for the palace and writing about it and who doesn't get any credit now at all for Chiona.

Pam noticed that Jen pronounced it Shona. Anna and Mark had pronounced the name of the village as if it began with a breathy 'y'. And she'd first thought it began with a 'k'. She'd never been good at languages and all this Greek was well, Greek to her. It just gave an extra layer of complication to everything. Like a b being a v.

'But your mother did make the initial discovery?'

'Yes. She found a bit of the palace in her garden and the first urn, which did contain two brooches. But then the whole site was handed over to the archaeology people. They're based in Palaikastro which is a rather bigger village near Chiona. And they organised the dig, and did all the work and made all the finds. Including the golden bull. That discovery in fact was made by a Greek archaeologist working there. Petros, his name is. Petros Manoussis.'

'So why do you think it was your mother who became associated with the finds?'

'Because Mum brought in the money. Or rather she got Leotakis to bring in the money.'

Which is exactly what Josh had noted at the start, about the way money had poured into this project.

'The dig would never have happened the way it did if Leotakis hadn't poured some of his squillions into it,' continued Jen, echoing Pam's thoughts. 'And my mother and Mr Leotakis became very close. You'll probably need to speak to him.'

Oh Lord, and won't that be fun? Pam thought. She already had the feeling that dealing with this Greek billionaire was going to be a total nightmare.

'He became the force behind it all, with the help of Eleni – she's Leotakis's fixer supreme, and a friend of Popi, which is how Mum met her. They organised all the publicity and made sure it was Mum who was interviewed. I imagine that nobody who actually did the work is very happy about that. Especially Petros. But that was Mum.'

'I did see a clip of your mother being interviewed,' said Pam, 'and she did say she just made the initial find.'

'But did she mention the name of the archaeologist who made the major finds or suggest they interview him? She'd sound as though she was deflecting the praise, but it always had to be her in the spotlight. And she's not even a proper academic though she pretends to be.'

You really did dislike her, thought Pam.

'When she was with Laurent she used to hang about sites taking pictures and doing drawings. It's what she's actually good at. And then she came here and did an MA. She never actually got a PhD.'

Unlike her daughter.

'She got an honorary degree from a University in Crete, and ever since then she's started calling herself Dr Michaels. So now I couldn't outrank her, that's what she said.'

'The dissertation that she may have stolen was for her MA?'

'Yes. The way she's shrugged it off over the years made me think that she'd got away with it and was rather proud of herself. She always thought she knew better than anyone else. She loved all the publicity about the exhibition. You'd have thought she'd personally dug up all the artefacts and designed the gallery. She had a massive row there recently with whatshisname... Mark.'

'Do you happen to know what that was about?'

'I do. She told me. Rather proud, as if she'd got one up on him, though I don't know how. The thing is the Fitzwilliam's a prestigious gallery. It's based on research that is linked to scholarship. The kind of stuff you don't get in the papers. When it came to the catalogue for the exhibition, and quite rightly in my opinion, Mark went to the head of archaeology in Crete, and he and his colleagues wrote the catalogue. Mum was furious. She wanted to write it.'

'But Mark didn't let her?'

'No. They had a tremendous row, she said.'

Interesting, thought Pam, and not at all what Mark Kitson had told them. She needed to have another word with him. The list of people she needed to talk to just got longer and longer. The inquiry had only just begun and already she felt exhausted. But this interview had been revealing for many reasons, not least for the way Stephanie's daughter talked about her mother. There was some real animosity there. And if her daughter felt like that, how many others might?

Her thoughts were interrupted by a trill on her phone. She glanced down. It was Larry.

'I'm sorry,' she said to Jen, 'I need to take a call. May I go into your garden?'

'Of course,' said Jen, getting up and sliding the doors open. Pam rang Larry's number and he replied instantly.

'Well, DI Gregory, do you want the good news or the good news?'

'All of it. Right now and keep it coming,' said Pam. 'This case is already swamping me. It's just going everywhere at once. It's like kicking a basket of snakes.'

'Very appropriate Greek simile, Pam. They worshipped snakes in Crete. One of the exhibits coming to the gallery is an incredible snake vase. There was a picture of it in the Guardian.'

'The only thing I know about snakes is that you shouldn't get bitten. Which means you have to be careful when you lift up old stones. This is all about old stones and memories and snakes. I don't like it.'

'Well I'm not sure whether what I'm going to tell you will make you all that much happier. But here goes. First, we've found the victim's handbag.

'Where?'

'It was in an unlocked locker in the gallery. I imagine she had just put it there out of the way thinking nobody would be going through empty lockers.'

'Makes sense. Is her phone in it?'

'Everything. Doesn't look as if it's been tampered with. There's her phone, her wallet, her iPad, and more good news, she didn't use passwords. No problem opening the iPad or her phone. Also in the bag were her spectacles. Actually two pairs of spectacles. Tissues, tickets, cough sweets…bits of paper, chocolate wrappers, her wallet, and her passport. Jesus, she was messy!'

'Sounds like the average woman's handbag to me.'

'That's one thing. And the other is your killer didn't just leave his dabs on marble, though Zofia will tell you after she's done the autopsy whether it was the blow that killed her or the stab wounds. Which look to me as if they were done when she was unconscious. What I can tell you is that he left behind a set of bloodstained plastic overalls.'

'What?'

'Yes. Unbelievable. It seems that after killing Stephanie, our man went into one of the gents toilets and removed them. They're the kind builders wear if they're dealing with asbestos or something. Have feet and a hood. You can get them in any big DIY place. He then spent the night there. We've got DNA and prints just about everywhere.'

'So when did he leave?'

'My guess is he waited until Dr Kitson arrived and walked out when he went into his study to call your lot.'

'But anyone could have seen him.'

'But did they? Anyway, it does give you a new timeline

for your enquiries.'

'That's so cold. Being there all night. What kind of person does that?'

'Over to you, kid. I'll get all this back to the lab and let you have the full report later.'

Pam walked back inside the house. Jen was looking at a picture of her cat, tears running down her face.

'If it was Mum who was responsible for someone killing Skimble. I'll never forgive her,' she cried. And suddenly it was real. Her cat was dead. Her mother was dead.

'Oh, Mum,' she said, wiping her face with her sleeve and then broke down and sobbed like a small child. Pam patted her shoulder.

'I'm so sorry.'

Pam handed her tissues and Jen wiped her face and blew her nose.

'Do you think I'm in danger?' she asked, the idea suddenly coming to her.

It was probably not the moment to tell her about the word vendetta, there was no reason to make her panic. But she'd already thought someone was watching her. The sooner she got out of Cambridge the better.

'We don't have any evidence of that,' Pam told her. 'But it does makes sense for you to move to London for a while. We need you to be safe.'

'I don't want to be here now either,' said Jen. 'I can easily stay at Dad's until you arrest the man who did all this.'

As if it would be that easy. And that quick.

CHAPTER 10

He's late. Again. And he can't be late again. But if he can get the tram, it'll take him to the airport. Except he doesn't have a passport with him, and the tram is going in the wrong direction, and if he looks out, the girl is standing there holding a gun. And he's reaching out for her and he mouths 'I love you', but she's turned away and now it isn't the girl anymore, it's Stephanie. 'Go on,' she says. 'You know you want to.' Then the gun is in his hand and he's pointing it at her and shouting. And she's laughing and he runs towards her and she isn't there anymore.

Mike Petersen sat up, sweat pouring down his face. He'd had that dream again. First time for ages. He looked at his phone. Six. It was almost light outside, and he jumped out of bed, pulled on his swim shorts, and ran down the twisting path to the beach. The sea was still, the early morning calm before the day's breeze ruffled the surface, and cold. He dived in but, as he ploughed his way out to sea as if trying to outrace the voices of his dream, the sun began to rise in front of him. Just the merest crescent of fire, it soon became a circle surrounded by a red and yellow sky. He stopped swimming and trod water, watching the colours filtering into the sea, first grey, then turquoise and the surrounding hills turning from black to a hazy grey. His tension began to leach away into the water. 'I'm sorry,' he whispered to the girl from the dream. 'I'm so sorry.'

He swam slowly back to the shore, thinking about how Henry so often commented on this easterly sunrise, how glorious it was to wake up and see the sun rise out of the sea in front of you. Like being born new each day. Except that what Henry actually said was 'Without taking part in this diurnal nativity I think I would be shrivelled and dead by now.' Where on earth Henry had learned to talk like that? As if he'd read some book when he was young and identified with it. As if he belonged to a previous generation. Probably why his books were unreadable, Mike decided, as he shook the water off him like one of the stray dogs now running along the beach, their arched, fronded tails wagging in unison.

He showered off the salt and began to think about breakfast. Eggs today. The fresh eggs from Electra's productive chickens with the bread he'd bought at the bakery in Sitia, freshly squeezed orange juice and good coffee. The one meal he could produce perfectly himself and enjoy on his own.

He put on a CD of Kula Shaker. Something about the bands you loved at uni always being the first you turn to. Nick Cave and Kula Shaker being his. He remembered how Stephanie had laughed when she heard it. 'My God, that's so sixties,' she said, 'they could have sung that at Woodstock.' She should be coming back in a few weeks after the exhibition opened. He wondered if she was nervous or just excited. A few of the other archaeologists from the dig were due to fly out soon, but a few were also notably boycotting it. Ah well, that was inevitable under the circumstances.

His phone rang and his jaw clenched as he saw that it was an unknown English number. Who the fuck? Not someone from his old job? The dream he'd begun to forget formed itself again in his mind. If only he could put it away from him permanently, if only he could go back and change time. Change his life.

He picked up the phone. 'Petersen,' he growled.

'Michaelis,' the voice unmistakeable. Mike had never had a call from Leotakis when the billionaire was staying in

England. Perhaps he wanted him to do some work on his house, though it was more like a palace, and Mike couldn't think of anything that needed to be done. He'd first got to know Leotakis through Stephanie and had been invited to go out on his yacht.

'This boat's far too big for a day out fishing,' he recalled Leotakis grumbling. 'You've got a little boat, we should go out in that.'

Mike leaned back on the semicircle of silk cushions that surrounded a low table of the rear deck of the exquisite, double-masted yacht. 'Whenever you like,' he said, trying to imagine the immaculately dressed eighty-year-old in his own tiny wooden boat that he'd rescued from its derelict state and cobbled together with bits of old wood and weeks of work. He'd bought the oars from a fisherman who had a spare pair, and a fifteen hp outboard that he'd picked up second hand for under five hundred euros.

Three coats of white paint and two lines of blue above and below and a pale turquoise blue to cover the inner wood, and he had his own, small and perfect caique. And he'd been wrong about Leotakis. The billionaire did want to go out in his boat and spend a few hours pottering around the nearby islands pretending to fish. Two weeks following that conversation, there they were, the old man sitting on the wooden decking, drinking cold beer from the bottle.

'You look happy,' Mike told him.

'I am happy. This is all a Greek needs for happiness. A boat, a beer, and a line to catch fish.'

Mike laughed. 'That sounds like one of those stories they tell foreigners like me.'

'You're no foreigner. You're related to half the village. So which story is that?'

'It's set in a small village. One day a villager, let's call him Yannis, comes back from America where he's made money. He walks down to the shore where an old schoolfriend is mending his nets. The men hug each other and sit down and have a coffee. "You work so hard," says Yannis. "Every day you go out in your little boat and you're not getting any younger." "This is true," says the fisherman. "You know what you should do?" asks Yannis. "You should go to the bank and borrow money. Then you could buy two boats and catch more fish. And then you could borrow more money and buy more boats and you could become rich." "Rich would be nice," agreed the fisherman. "So imagine being rich. What would you do?" "I'd buy myself a small boat and go fishing."'

'That sounds as though you've just summarised my life. Just exchange fishing boats for oil tankers.'

'Nikos, I'm sorry I didn't mean…'

'No. Don't apologise. It's a good story even though it's total bullshit. Everyone wants enough money to provide for their families. That contentment is the fantasy. As you say, it's the story to tell foreigners!'

'Yes. And it conveniently excludes the long winters and what happens when the banks call in loans. It's the summer painting.'

'Which today we can enjoy. A small boat, a cold beer and a few fish.'

'We haven't caught any fish yet.'

'These seas are becoming a desert. It worries me. I talk to the Minister, but it is not only Greece. The Mediterranean is dying.'

'It feels like it. Soon there will be nothing but a few sardines and jellyfish.'

'We need to bring back the tuna and swordfish. Without predators the whole ecosystem fails.'

'How do we do that?'

'We let them breed. We stop fishing. We set up more marine reserves, conservation areas. I attended the last World Conservation Congress. I am funding a new reserve, but it takes time. The French are doing good things. We have Alonissos, but we need to do much more.'

He swigged his beer.

'You know about the environment, from what you say today and other days.'

'I was with an animal rights group for a while,' replied Mike. 'I read all the leaflets.'

'But I thought... ah. You were a policeman at the same time.'

'It's not something I usually talk about.'

'Because something very bad happened?'

Mike nodded.

'You don't have to tell me. Stephanie told me a little. She needed a gun.'

'It was your gun?'

'Yes. Thinking now, I realise I must have trusted both of you. Especially you. When she gave you the gun, you could have killed her.'

'I would never have done that.'

'That's what she said. Of course I didn't know you then. But I trust her judgement. She is a wise woman. A little like your aunt.'

'They both terrify me.'

'They are like the Fates. Stephanie is more Greek than most Greeks. She needed to come here to survive.' He sighed. 'But she is ill and she will not save herself.'

'The drinking?'

'Yes. She is never drunk, and she is never sober. It is the worst.'

'She saved my life.'

'Do you want to tell me?'

Mike took another beer out of the cool bag and knocked the top off against the rowlock. He took a swig. Could he tell Nikos this? Did he trust him? And yet the old man, without knowing him, had trusted him enough to give him a loaded gun.

'There was this animal rights group that was planning a lot of violent things: bombing laboratories, killings. MI5 were concerned about them as well as the Met, but there was a policy then (they've abandoned it now) of putting officers into these groups long-term. I was in it for four years.'

'Four years! That's total immersion.'

'I fell in love – as you do. No, I can't talk about that side of it yet. But there was a major cockup and my cover was blown and the girl died. The Met, for some reason, thought I'd be less likely to tell the story to the press if I stayed on the payroll. One of those decisions from the top. Which is why officially I'm still an active officer, but nobody expects me, or wants me to go back. I was just cut off and thrown away. So I stayed with Aunt Sofia. I hardly got up, I hardly washed. I was over fifty pounds heavier than I am – that was actually part of my cover; and stayed fat, all I ate was rubbish. And I drank raki. Bottles of it. Aunt Sofia did what she could, but she knew I wanted to die. I believe she and Stephanie talked together.'

'They did. Stephanie told me.'

'So one day, Stephanie comes to the room where I was staying just outside Sitia. It was a bit like a shed for animals; it was a cottage waiting for the owners to restore it. There was a well for water and a cracked sink. The floor was stone and mud. I was living like an animal. She virtually dragged me out of the house and together with Spiro, the fisherman, pushed me into his van which he drives to the harbour.

'I'm so drunk I hardly know what's going on. But we get into Spiro's boat, and he takes us out, not far from here, on the south side of Dragonada, below the little chapel of Saint Antonio. And Spiro throws Stephanie's bag onto the beach and she jumps into the water. I follow her. It was in April and the water was freezing although it was a calm day. We swim to the beach and Spiro goes. I turn to her and ask her what the hell is going on and she's pointing a gun at me. And it's cocked, ready to go off.'

'I showed her how to do that.'

'Thanks. It scared the bloody life out of me.'

'She tells me that Spiro is coming back in fifteen minutes and I have that time to decide. Either I kill myself or I sort myself out. Because if I don't, next time she will shoot me. And then she hands me the gun.'

'She never told me that. She's quite something, isn't she?'

'She is.'

'How long did it take you?'

'To decide I didn't actually want to die that day? About a minute. But I sat there with the gun for at least ten. I didn't give it back to her until I heard Spiro's boat coming back. After that, I had a lot of long conversations with her. And with a friend of hers called Popi.'

'Popi Filotaki?'

'Yes. You know her?'

'Everybody knows Popi. Even the former President talked with her.'

'She's astonishing. After all she went through, she's still fighting.'

'Every day. She is all fire, that one. I have known her almost forty years. When I see her coming I know it will cost me a lot of money. But every euro will go to help someone.'

'She helps victims of torture, doesn't she?'

'Yes. Perhaps only those who have been tortured can really understand the pain of others.'

'You've been?'

'I did not expect that question?' Leotakis looked up, surprise in his still clear blue eyes. 'Nobody has ever asked me that. What words to share on such a perfect day. But yes. A very, very long time ago. I was young and doing crazy things in the Caribbean. I got caught. It is a miracle I survived. They threw me to the sharks, cut and bleeding, but it was one day when the sharks were somewhere else, and a fisherman happened to see the blood on the water and came to investigate.'

'You and I have been close to death and chosen to live.'

'Popi also.'

'Glad to join the club!'

Leotakis threw back his head and roared with laughter. 'I don't think we need a club tie, though, do you?'

It was under two years ago that conversation, just before Stephanie found the first bit of the Chiona treasure, and everything changed. Mike wondered whether she had asked Nikos to ring him to persuade him to come to the gallery opening. The answer was still no. He wasn't going back to England yet; there were too many people there who wanted him dead.

'Nikos,' he began now. 'How good to…'

'Stephanie is dead,' said Leotakis. 'She was murdered in my gallery and I need you to help find her killer.'

CHAPTER 11

'So. In addition to the death of Stephanie Michaels, we now have the brutal killing of her daughter's cat, Skimble. The cat's blood was smeared all over her kitchen wall,' Pam continued. 'According to PC Marsh, who attended, it was and I quote,' she continued, reading her notes: '"like something from a fucking Tarantino, excuse my language, Ma'am, but I've seen my fair share of violent crime over the years, on the Arbury, and the odd knifing at weekends, and the mess of multiple vehicle pile ups, but nothing remotely like this".'

'That's disgusting,' said Roberta. 'No wonder the poor woman's upset.'

'I'd bloody upset if it were our cat,' said Josh.

'You've got a cat, Josh?' Pam thought she knew everything about his family, the daughter who was doing so well in science, and the toddler who still wasn't sleeping nights. She didn't remember a cat. 'You never said.'

'No, we've got a Labrador. Just got him the other day from the Blue Cross. But it's still a family pet isn't it? It sounds like the killer really hates Dr Michaels. I mean kill her cat? I mean I'm thinking he thought it was Dr Michael's house, not her daughter's.'

'Yes. And it is still Dr Michaels' house although her daughter rents it from her. But, you're all right. Nasty. Poor Skimble.'

'What kind of name is that for a cat?' asked Paul.

'Skimbleshanks,' said Roberta

'What?' Paul looked confused.

'Cats,' Roberta replied, 'the musical and the poem. It's the name of the cat. Skimbleshanks, the Railway Cat. I learned the poem when I was a kid.'

'If you say so,' said Paul. 'Skimbleshanks! What's wrong with Ginger?'

'He was a tabby,' replied Pam. 'Now shall we move on? As I was saying. The person who attacked the cat deliberately spread his blood around afterwards.'

'A cat has only a quarter of a litre of blood,' said Paul. 'I Googled it.'

'That's a large glass of wine,' replied Pam, imagining one in front of her right now. 'You can make quite a mess with that.'

'I know,' said Paul, 'a girl once chucked...'

'Thank you Paul, may we get back to the briefing?'

It was just past twelve; Josh had returned from the Museum earlier saying that the fingerprinting was going very smoothly and nobody had refused to be checked.

'There were a few grumbles about police powers and totalitarian state etcetera,' he reported. 'But mostly they're all deeply shocked that a death like that could happen in the museum. The worst thing that's ever happened there before was when a man fell over his shoelaces on a staircase and smashed some priceless vases. I heard that story a few times today. That had shaken them, they said, but a murder? That kind of thing didn't happen in a museum.'

'Sadly, it can happen anywhere.' Pam was glad to have Josh back as a sounding board as she prepared a more detailed case conference with a list of names of the people who needed to be investigated.

She'd sent out for some sandwiches; Murton was going to have a large bill for pizza, Chinese, pastries and doughnuts by the time this case was closed. Assuming it would be. She always believed she would find the perpetrator of every crime she investigated, yet there were always the ones that got away. However long ago it was, they still hung in the air reproaching her. She never forgot them. That young girl, Nicola, who'd never been found; she often thought of her.

At least Pell was a tick on her list. Despite the efforts of his lawyer to have the emails and video evidence withdrawn, and his 'no comment' interview, Pell had now been charged and remanded in custody prior to his trial.

Which had been one of the things on her mind when she paid a visit to Martin Hawkswood. She'd gone round the corner to get a bacon bun from the Espresso Library, which she'd heard was his personal addiction. She needed all the ammunition she could muster for this one.

'You know, prestige murder, money no object. Thought you could benefit from our largesse.' She handed him the bun with a smile.

Martin gave a small laugh, but his eyes remained cold. He was another man who reminded her of a dog. In this case a bull terrier, dark little eyes and a large mouth ready to snap.

'Very kind. So what do you want? Bodies, I imagine. Saw the telly earlier. Bit of a mistake letting that witness speak to the press.'

Pam forced herself to give a kind of chuckle, although it sounded hollow even to her.

'Much as I'd enjoy locking all our witnesses and possible witnesses in a soundproof box, health and safety wouldn't go for it.'

She plumped herself down on a chair without waiting for him to invite her to sit. She wasn't in the mood for games. Not that she ever was when men like Hawkswood wanted to play power games.

'You think that was the worst of my day so far...'

'Seemed pretty bad to me...'

'Yup, but not as bad as a personal call from the Prime Minister to the Chief asking if Cambridge would like the NCA to take over the case.'

Light the blue touch paper and stand back. She knew that Hawkswood loathed the National Crime Agency, and particularly hated the fact that unlike the police, they weren't accountable. Except directly to the Home Secretary. And May had been Home Secretary when she founded them. She let the detective fulminate on the absurdity of a British FBI and nodded along.

'Happily,' she told him, when he stopped swearing, 'the Chief told her that we in Cambridge have – and I quote – a crack team.'

'No pressure then!' He was looking really cheerful, thought Pam. Now's the moment to strike.

'And you're right. I want a favour, but it's actually you I'm after, though I may come to you later if I don't have enough troops for my crack team.' She put the phrase into inverted commas.

'You want me to join your little band of heroes?'

'Not exactly. I need your expertise and experience. It's about the County Lines case.'

'Oh yes. Good result. You should be pleased.'

'I should be home asleep. But life doesn't work like that.' She rolled her shoulders, feeling the tension and the tiredness locked in them. 'No, I'm delighted CPS has upped it to attempted murder. He's utter scum. Thing is I don't have the time to do the paperwork on this one, and have delegated it to two of my sergeants, Butcher and Stills. They're good. But they haven't prepared a case for trial on their own before.'

'And you'd like me to guide them?'

'If you would.'

'Sure,' he nodded. 'Happy to do that. 'You've only got to get one fact wrong or one bit of paperwork missing and the defence team can get the whole case thrown out.'

'Don't I know it. Had that on one of my first cases. Bastard abused his wife and his kids and walked. Never again.'

'Completely agree there.' He took out a crumpled tissue and wiped the remains of sauce from his lips. 'It's good to collaborate, Pam. You know I'm always happy to do that.'

'Thank you so much, Martin. I knew I could rely on you. You're the best.'

Push the right buttons, get what you need, she thought happily as she walked back upstairs to let Roberta know. She'd be relieved, rather than cross that Pam didn't trust her to get it right. One of the many good things about her sergeants, they cared more about results than their egos. It also meant that she could bring Roberta on to the murder team. Virtually all the Pell work had been done.

She played Josh the tape of her interview with Jen and they worked on the briefing together. He wanted to prioritise Anna's assistant George, who hadn't yet come forward, but Pam had begun to develop a feeling about Stephanie's friend, Henry.

'The fact he's here in England right now. He's close to her, but capable of major rows. There is something about the way she died that feels personal. It wasn't an assassination, Josh, there's nothing cold about it. Same with the cat.'

'I'm coming over to the Super's view of it being a nutter. The cat rather clinches it for me.'

'Mad or driven mad,' agreed Pam. 'So we also have to think about people who feel that Stephanie ruined their lives.'

Josh nodded and together they put together a list and created a short handout.

'What I'd like to do first,' Pam told her team, 'is to take us through the possible timeline. One solid thing we have in this case is forensics,' she continued. 'I've had a call from the pathologist who says that time of death is looking like seven o'clock yesterday evening or just before. Rigor was sufficiently advanced for her to make a quick judgement on that, especially knowing the precise temperature of the gallery. So, once we've fingerprinted all the museum staff and those who were in the museum, after it closed to the public, we can discount a lot of names. Including Mark Kitson.'

'He doesn't look strong enough anyway, Ma'am,' said one of the constables, looking at a picture of the gallery director.

'No,' she agreed. 'But looks can be deceptive. Now let's think about what happened and when.' She began to make a timetable on the whiteboard.

'Four thirty pm. Mark Kitson and Stephanie Michaels are in the gallery. He talks to her about the exhibition, which was due to be installed today, and they discuss which pieces they will unpack and display first. Five thirty, Mark says good night to the tiler, Vassili, who was working on one of the final tiles near the women's cloakroom, and then Mark goes back into the main office. Six pm, the tiler leaves. Have we spoken to him yet today to confirm this?'

'Yes, boss,' said Josh. 'He was one of the first to come forward. He's been printed, but he's also short. About five foot five, I'd say. And he went straight to The Olive Grove where he's become friendly with one of the chefs. I've got a uniform checking out his alibi.'

'So not a likely suspect. Good. Thank you. Okay. At six thirty, the security guard begins to shut down the museum, apart from the offices. Josh, you talked to the man who was on duty?'

'Yes.' Josh pulled out his phone and read his report.

'His name is Dan Roberts, and he's been working at the Museum for five years, though not for much longer after this I imagine. He said that as he toured the museum, he met Dr Kitson in the corridor of the main building and Kitson told him that he wasn't going back to the gallery that evening. Roberts therefore assumed the building was empty and Kitson himself had also assumed that Stephanie had long gone. As I reported earlier, she told Kitson that she was meeting someone for a drink. But she didn't give him a name.'

'Hold on a minute,' Josh said Pam. 'Have we received the plan of the gallery from Dr Kitson?'

'Yes, boss,' he replied.

'Good. Well let's put it up on the screen now. We need it to understand how this all happened, since the building isn't any normal kind of building with corners and walls.'

Josh nodded, went over to the computer, and the image filled the screen. They all turned in their chairs to view it.

'That's weird,' said Roberta. 'I mean that's not like a proper building.'

'No,' agreed Pam. 'It's a... whatsitsname... a labyrinth. Anyone hot on their Greek mythology?'

'Yup,' said Paul surprisingly. 'A labyrinth is a kid of maze and your Minotaur, the half man, half bull monster, waits in the centre. Minotaur – the Labyrinths of Crete. Fave game when I was, what? Twelve?'

'Kill your enemies. Kill your friends' enemies. Kill your friends,' said a civvie, laughing.

'Must have passed me by,' Pam sighed. She'd never been much of one for video games.

'Plus that film Minotaur,' the civvie added. 'That was excellent. Really scary.'

'And had Tom Hardy,' added Sue. 'Fit or what!'

'So you're all aware of the mythological background to this gallery?' Pam knew that any moment they'd start listing Tom Hardy films if she didn't stop them. 'Good. And the fact there is a bull in its centre is therefore significant.'

'Do you think Stephanie's death was a sacrifice then?'

'I'm not thinking anything yet, Sue,' said Pam. 'What the killer wants us to think is, for the moment, neither here nor there. I think if we're to follow leads based on movies and video games, we could waste a lot of time. However, there is quite likely a Cretan connection since Dr Michaels lived most of her life on that island.

'It's also worth thinking about how the murder was committed. It does seem to be a very theatrical murder; there was no attempt to conceal the body. On the contrary, the killer wanted her to be found. But now let's continue with the timeline shall we? Back to the gallery.'

'It's really confusing, isn't it?' said Paul examining the plan. 'I can see the public getting lost.'

'I imagine there'll be a signed route,' said Pam. 'Not our

problem. But what you can see is that it's a series of circles, and if someone is in one circle they can't be seen from another.'

'May I, boss?' asked Josh

'Please. Go ahead.'

Josh got up and walked to the screen. 'Now,' he said. 'This is the centre of the gallery and where the bull is. There are arrowed windows all around here, that's what those marks are. And if you come through the corridor to the end past the desk, you're facing the centre and the bull. Which means is that if Roberts had got that far last night he would have seen Stephanie. But, he didn't. Roberts walked half-way down the corridor and called out: Is anybody there? And got no answer. So he turned round and went back outside and locked the door. So from that moment, it could not be opened from the outside or the inside.'

And if they'd found the body last night and the investigation had begun then, it was possible that the Pell job could have been postponed. Pell could have got away, and Winston could have died. On such small details, lives are saved.

'Thank you, Josh.' She smiled at him. He was doing well with this case so far, taking his time to be thorough.

'And this is where it gets unusual. According to the initial verbal report I've got from the forensic team, it appears that after committing the murder, our man, and for height reasons I think we should probably be looking at a man, stayed inside the gallery. Which is what we wondered at our earlier meeting. So, having found that he couldn't get out, he doesn't break out, he goes into the men's lavatory, takes off his bloodstained overalls – which SOCO are examining as we speak – and has a beer and a sarnie.'

'That's creepy,' said Roberta.

'It is,' Pam agreed. 'And two weeks ago, the person who killed the cat let himself into Dr Michaels' house and locked it behind him when he left. And while this does mean that they appear to have a set of Dr Michaels' keys, it seems that there were many sets of these around. Anyone with access to her handbag could have borrowed them and got new keys cut.'

'He's cool, isn't he?' Paul was making notes on his handout and frowning. 'Everything we're hearing about this man shows that same sense of purpose. He lets himself in and out of Dr Michaels' house. And surely he must have watched it prior to the attack to know when the daughter was out.'

'Good thinking, Paul. CCTV around there? We've got Anglia Ruskin University right there and a few offices. Josh. Get uniforms to check the streets around Flower Street. For that Tuesday and the preceding week.'

'On it, boss.'

'That is all the timeline we have. But I did have a fruitful conversation with Dr Michael's daughter, Jen Nichols, who does not have a glowing opinion of her mother, and came up with a number of possible suspects who might be said to have a reason to kill her.'

'Bloody hell. Her daughter said that?'

'It seems that Stephanie Michaels has more than one skeleton in her cupboard. There are actions that the daughter has described that could have had serious consequences and certainly destroyed other people's lives or reputations. But there is no point in examining them unless we can prove they were in Cambridge last night. So anyone who was in Greece can be safely...'

Pam stopped as she saw a uniform enter the room and make signs at her.

'Yes? We're in the middle of a case conference.'

'I'm sorry, Ma'am.' The young man looked as though he'd prefer to swallow his words rather than deliver them in front of everybody. 'It's just that we have a woman at the desk who's insisting you see her straight away.'

'She'll have to wait until we're finished.'

'It's the architect of the new gallery,' he continued. He's probably had to withstand Anna's screams, thought Pam almost feeling sorry for him.

'She'll still have to wait,' she said. 'Tell her I'll see her at two. She can wait in an interview room or go away and come back.' She looked round. The constable was still standing there. 'Go on. Tell her.'

'Yes, Ma'am, I will. But she wanted you to know that George was missing, and he'd left a message saying he'd seen a ghost. She thinks he's left the country.'

'Well if he has, there's nothing I can do right now, so please tell Ms Karanaki to wait.'

Pam turned away from the constable and sighed.

'Sue, get on to the Hotel du Vin and see if George's room has been cleaned yet. If not, let's get the room fingerprinted.'

'On it, boss,' said Sue. She took out her phone and went into the corridor as she began to search for the hotel number.

'Now, where was I?' continued Pam. 'As I was saying. Once we've eliminated those who've been fingerprinted, we do have a number of possible people of interest.'

She stopped again as Sue returned to the room.

'Sorry, boss. His room's been cleaned, and he left nothing behind.'

'Damn,' said Pam. 'I don't like that one bit. Sue, can you go to Cambridge station and get the CCTV footage for the morning.'

'He checked out of his hotel at six thirty' said Sue. 'That's right after...'

'Yes. Timing is definitely suspicious. That's thirty minutes after Mark Kitson got to the Gallery, and presumably allowed the murderer to leave through the now open door. Oh, and see if any local taxi picked him up, too,' she added. 'And check airlines. See if he's left the country.'

'On it, boss.'

Pam returned to the rest of the team.

'Well, that's one name to put up on the wall. Let's see who else needs to be investigated. Let's see who wanted to kill Stephanie and, more importantly, had the opportunity.'

CHAPTER 12

The harder the task, the greater the honour. Her family must die so that mine shall not be dishonoured.

CHAPTER 13

After the briefing, Pam and Josh talked through the list over a sandwich in her room. Anna Karanaki may have been waiting, but Pam hadn't eaten since her dawn breakfast and she was starving. If George had done a runner, there wasn't a great deal she could do about it.

'Talk through the list with me in case I'm missing something.' There was this nagging feeling there was something obvious she'd overlooked.

'The person who'd arranged to meet Stephanie for a drink…' she began.

'Could have been her old friend, Henry Cox,' Josh commented. 'As you said in the briefing.'

'We need a number for him. He also rang Stephanie. What did he want? Where does he stay when he's in England?'

'One to ask Mr Nichols,' said Josh. 'They might still be in touch.'

'Yes,' replied Pam. 'Top of the list. And Paul is looking into our Henry. As far as he can. We need a replacement for Peter asap; we really need a good IT person right now. Remind me to ask Murton later, will you?'

Josh nodded and keyed it in. 'Then there's the student who accused Stephanie of stealing his work,' he said, looking at his notes.

'If it was true, and we only have the daughter's word for it so far, it could have changed his life. Another question for Mr Nichols.'

'Mr Nichols could be very useful.'

'Yes. I'd like you with me tomorrow if that's all right. Who knows? While we're in London, we may even have found other possible leads we can speak to. The student, the friend.'

'Maybe that's where George has gone, too.'

'Wishful thinking, Josh. I'm pretty certain that one's out of the country already. But why? Maybe Anna will throw some light on that.'

Josh chewed a cheese and pickle bun. The pickle was homemade and was just how he liked it, both spicy and sweet. If it wasn't for his morning runs, he'd put on kilos, the amount of carbs he ate. That they all ate, though not all of them ran. Dave, for example never ran further than the pub. And it showed.

'The ex may also know about a possible will,' continued his boss, making more notes as she talked. 'I don't know whether money is an issue here, but we have to look into it.'

'Who benefits by her death?'

'The daughter, I imagine. That Cambridge house must be worth a small fortune.'

'You think the daughter?'

'Not on her own. Too short. But if she had an accomplice. We'll need to check her bank statements. But between you and me I'm not liking her for this.'

'You said she didn't show any emotion when she heard about her mother.'

'She did later. Grief is unpredictable.'

'And she was keen to put forward other suspects.'

'Okay, okay, I'm not eliminating her yet, Josh. Alright?'

'What about the vendetta thing?'

'Yes. I need to look into that. Do they have vendettas in Greece? Would be useful to have a bit of input there. Ms Karanaki said they did, but we need to check.'

'You said Ms Karanaki also mentioned the billionaire and a possible feud between rivals.'

'Yes, she did. But the discovery of our man also killing

the cat, makes me feel that this is highly unlikely. They might kill Stephanie to bugger up the opening of Mr Leotakis's precious gallery. But kill a cat? No. That feels personal.'

'So not an Elgin marbles person then.'

'Exactly. The same argument. It doesn't feel right for that. But I will check with the British Museum about any new threats relating to the Elgin Marbles and why they should be returned to Athens. Stephanie had had threats. That was something else Jen mentioned. And, finally, we come back to George. Who've I missed?'

'The archaeology people.'

'Yes. Good thinking, Josh. That's what I haven't been thinking about.'

'While I was at the Museum earlier I kept thinking about the Chiona treasure.' Josh put down the remains of his bun and licked his lips clean of pickle. 'The Fitz is full of amazing finds and most of it is pretty old. I sometimes take the kids there and we talk about it, but the stuff they found at Chiona was Minoan. That's way before all the Greek and Roman stuff. We're talking about 3,500 years ago. We're talking pre-Stonehenge. Bronze age.'

'Got this from Barbara, did you?'

'I haven't spoken to her yet. It's going to infuriate her that I'm involved with something that really interests her and I won't be able to tell her about it.'

'Well, you can after we've nabbed our killer. So go on, what are we missing?'

'Well finding this treasure has to be massive in terms of a career in archaeology, yes? It's a find not just of a lifetime, but of the century.'

'Yes?'

'And although Dr Michaels made the first find, she wasn't the lead archaeologist on the site. She didn't find the bull.'

'The bull. Of course. The man who found the bull. Jen gave me his name. Oh yes. Petros Manoussis. Jesus. It's been staring at us all along. She was laid out on the bull.'

'We need to know whether he's in the country.'

'Yes. Good. That's it for now. Let's go and find out about this George.'

They made their way down the stairs. It was often quicker than waiting for the lift. Pam hated waiting, but surprisingly, waiting seemed to have calmed Anna down. She was writing on her tablet when they entered and seemed much more subdued than earlier. Even her clothes looked less fresh, as if she'd slept in them.

Pam switched on the recorder and gave it their names. 'So tell me about Mr Demetriades,' she began. She wasn't in the mood to mollify the architect, not since she leaked the story to the media.

'George. *Yiorgos*, in Greek. He is my oldest friend, Inspector. I know him since we are students. Twenty years. We work together many times. He always tells me everything.'

Nobody tells a friend everything, thought Pam. We all have secrets.

'Which university was this?'

'The Polytechnic University in Torino. It is the best.'

Everything that Anna had done was always the best, decided Pam.

'They have a specialist in the passive cooling of buildings. This for Greece is important. George and I, we both study this. We are friends. Like brother and sister.'

'But he was happy to be a project manager on the Gallery, not the architect?'

'George is always happy to learn from me. He is my details. I am the imagination. He would never walk out on me. And before we open. Never,' she told Pam. 'Something terrible has happened to him.'

'So talk me through it,' said Pam.

'So after you and I speak, I am very upset. Nothing like this ever happens to me.'

Actually, it happened to Stephanie, thought Pam, but

don't let that get in the way of your self-importance.

'I ring his number and it is turned off. So I ring his room number and it does not answer. I think he has gone for a walk. Or for breakfast. So I ring again and still no answer. Then I take a pill because I am still very upset and I fall asleep. When I wake up, it is already eleven and there is no message from George. So I ring again and he is not there. So I ring the reception and they say he checked out this morning.'

'Yes. He left at six thirty. What time did Mr Kitson call you?'

'It was six ten. I shower and dress and run to the Museum.'

'And what time did you ring George?'

'I did not say I rang George.'

'No, but you would, wouldn't you? He's your assistant, your right-hand man. You'd want him to know straight away.'

'Yes. I rang him. After Mark phone me.'

'And?'

'And nothing. He does not answer.'

'But his phone rings?'

'Yes. It rings and it goes to message and I leave a message he should ring me.'

'And he calls you?'

'No. That is what is so strange. That is why I keep calling him. But…'

'Go on,' God, this woman took her time to give out information.

'While I am waiting for you now I discover something new.'

'Which is?'

'I check my emails all morning and nothing. Then now I look in my *fákelos anepithimita*, how you say that? My rubbish folder?'

I wouldn't be able to say that at all, thought Pam. This was a language of tongue twisters. 'Junk mail?' she asked.

'If you say so. Yes. And I find one from him.'

'And it says?' Pulling teeth would be quicker.

'It says, "Sorry. I must go. I have seen a ghost." What does he mean?'

'I have no idea. What do you think it means? You know him.'

'Yes, I know George. I know George who never sleeps until he is happy that the work is good. I know George who is so excited about the new Gallery. I do not know George who sees ghosts and runs away.'

Anna showed Pam the email and she photographed it. Along with her text messages to George. Pam used the brief moment she held the phone to check whether Anna had sent a picture of the crime scene to anyone. She hadn't. But that didn't mean she hadn't taken one. Had Anna had her phone out when she first saw Stephanie? Pam didn't think so. She'd hustled Anna away before she had a chance to take a shot of the body on the bull.

She could apply to get Anna's phone, but that didn't seem to be a priority right now and she wasn't convinced she'd get the necessary permission.

But the more she encountered the Greek witnesses and associates, the more she realised she'd have to get a translator on board. She asked Anna a few more questions without getting any more information and then sent her away with a stern warning about not contacting the press.

'Perverting the course of justice is a serious crime in this country and the maximum penalty is life imprisonment,' she told the architect.

Anna burst into tears.

'We are not taking any action this time,' Pam continued. 'But please take this as a warning.'

'I'm so sorry. I never meant... You see I was so upset and I think maybe the gallery will not open, and the Prince will not come, so I text my friend who writes about architecture, and then I get a telephone call from a woman who says she is a researcher for television and she wants to allow me to tell the world about my building. And so everyone will want to come and see it. And she says it will help the police.'

'I'm afraid the media lie about these kinds of things. They'll do anything to get a story.'

'I do not speak again. And they are not interested in my gallery.'

'No. They're not. And it's good you realise that.'

Research, thought Pam. That reminded her once again that she needed to get a new tech specialist on board quickly, too.

She looked at her watch. 'Two twenty,' she said to the machine. 'Interview terminated.' The press conference was in ten minutes. She'd go and see Murton after that. He'd want her to congratulate him. She needed him on her side more than ever.

The timing of the press conference had allowed the London media to shoot up the M11 to join the locals, and the new conference room on the sixth floor was packed with eager-looking reporters, fluffy microphones held out like baby chicks wanting to be fed. They exuded hunger, all of them; they wanted the story, the details, and the gorier the better. Gold, treasure, death, and a bit of mythology. It would stay on the front pages for days. Pam joined the team in the Investigation Room as they watched the live news coverage.

Behind the desk, the two senior officers in their crisp dress uniforms did their best to look serious and efficient. Pam had been on a training course on how to present oneself to the media. How is the public going to perceive you? she was asked. In a few days she'd almost certainly be up there beside Murton being asked why she hadn't yet got a result. And she wouldn't be getting back-up from the brass. She was mightily relieved she hadn't had to join them today.

'Good afternoon, everybody.' It was Gordon Seaworthy, the Chief Constable. He always looked as if somebody had polished his skin. She could feel that he was enjoying the spotlight, but at the same time trying to demonstrate a sad face. Not a man people would trust, she decided. She said the same to Josh, who nodded.

'Too slippery by half, boss,' he replied.

'Ladies and Gentlemen, thank you for coming here today. My name is Chief Constable Gordon Seaworthy, and this is Superintendent Christopher Murton. We will make a brief statement, but we will not take questions today.'

He nodded to Murton who leaned forward to the microphone as if concerned that it wouldn't pick up his voice. Murton took a deep breath and began.

'I am sad to report that at approximately six am this morning the body of the British archaeologist Stephanie Michaels was discovered in The Nikos Leotakis Gallery of Classical Art of the Fitzwilliam Museum, here in Cambridge.'

'See he's getting billing already, your billionaire,' muttered Paul.

'Before going into further detail,' continued Murton, 'we would like to express our deepest condolences to the family and friends of Dr Michaels. This is a terrible and tragic death of a distinguished British scholar.'

Pam could imagine Jen and a few others snorting at this.

'We are at the beginning of this investigation, but the police do have a number of people to whom they wish to speak, and we will report back to you as soon as more information becomes available. The investigation is being led by Detective Inspector Pamela Gregory, head of the East Anglian Special Operations Unit, and she will speak to you in the future.'

'And bang, she's thrown under the bus,' said Pam. 'Dave, can you get an intercept put on my calls.'

'On it, Ma'am,' said Dave. 'The vultures have landed and they smell blood.'

'We believe, however, that Dr Michaels was killed yesterday evening, and we are therefore asking anyone who was in the vicinity of the gallery at that time to come forward. If anyone has any information about this murder, they can contact us by ringing 101 or anonymously through Crimestoppers.' Murton stopped and a babble of questions were shouted at him. Seaworthy looked at the press as if they were a class of irritating small children. He ignored their questions and smiled.

'Thank you, Superintendent.' He turned to the media. 'It is clear from your presence, and I see that many of you represent the international media, that there is considerable interest both national and international in this tragic death.' He took a deep breath.

'Whatever he's about to say, he's looking forward to it,' observed Josh. 'This is his moment in the spotlight.'

'Another message from the PM?' wondered Roberta.

Seaworthy smiled again. 'His Royal Highness, Prince Charles, who is due to open this gallery in two weeks time has sent the following message...'

He paused for a moment to allow any hack who wasn't already making notes to begin. Then picked up a piece of paper as if it had a Royal association and was valuable.

'It says: "Camilla and I would like to join all of you in sending our condolences to the family and friends of Dr Michaels. Her discoveries in Crete have changed the way we understand the ancient Minoan culture, and her death at a moment when her finds were about to be unveiled to the British people is particularly tragic."' Seaworthy paused again.

'Christ, he's milking this,' said Paul. 'It's as if the Prince himself had rung him!'

'I would also like to say that the Prime Minister has also sent her condolences to the family of Dr Michaels, and has emphasised that all necessary resources will be made available to those who are undertaking the investigation.'

'Like sending us the National Cunts Anonymous,' Paul growled, and even Pam couldn't help laughing. There was no way she'd willingly let the NCA muscle in on her case whatever the handbook said about collaboration.

'One final point,' finished Seaworthy. 'We would ask the public and the press to please stay away from the gallery and its vicinity, and please bear in mind that this is a university city and there are still students taking examinations at this time. Thank you.'

Seaworthy and Murton both stood up and left the room to the echo of unanswered questions. The programme then returned to their own journalist who paraphrased what had just been said and asked the obvious question: Who could possibly have done such a terrible thing?

'And the bastards get paid for that,' muttered Paul. 'Bunch of wankers.'

CHAPTER 14

Pam gave the Super a few minutes to get his breath before ringing his office.

'Thought you were spot on, Sir,' she said.

'Thank you, Pam,' he replied. 'Something of a nightmare these media things. Though never seen quite so many as today.'

'Could you spare me a few minutes,' she continued. 'There are a couple of things I need to ask you.'

'Come right now if you like,' he replied.

Pam picked up the folder carrying her notes. Glanced at the mirror. Oh great, her hair had its electric shock look; she must have been running her fingers through it all day. She took a brush out of her handbag and tried to bully it into submission, then walked down the corridor to his office.

Murton's room was almost as bare as when he first moved in apart from two framed signed football shirts and a photograph of him and his wife standing on top of a mountain.

'I'm just having a cup of tea. Would you like one?'

'I'm fine, thank you, Sir,' Pam replied. What would she put in an office if she had one large enough? She wasn't a big one for pictures or photos. Any photos of her and Richard had long been burned. She couldn't think of anything that really represented her apart from work. She didn't have the graduation picture because she'd never been to university, and wedding pix, well, that was a joke now. Pictures of her parents? Even they didn't have pictures out; it had never been a thing in their house. Not even of the dogs. Besides, her mother disliked clutter.

The superintendent had taken off his jacket and was now loosening his tie.

'Christ, it was hot in there,' he said. 'Surprised some of them didn't faint. Do sit down,' he added. He picked up his personal water bottle, which Pam noticed was in his team's familiar yellow and green colours. 'I have a feeling I know what you want,' he continued.

'Been rubbing the old crystal ball have you, Sir?'

'I expect you could use one.'

Pam laughed. 'Without glancing into one, Sir, I can tell you that we will now have any number of members of the public who swear they know such things, and can tell me exactly who killed our victim because they've been told by an ancient Egyptian spirit guide. I've got an intercept put on my phone, by the way.'

'Good,' he replied. 'Okay, well without celestial intervention I can predict you came here because you need a tech replacement for Peter. Bloody nuisance him leaving us this week. Why would a man leave the police for insurance?'

'Evenings and weekends?'

'Don't you have them? You know what I think about work life balance?'

'I know what you think about budgets and getting results, Sir.'

'Easier said than...' Remember you're management now,' he continued. 'Anyhow, you certainly need a good IT man.'

Or woman, thought Pam.

'So happens, I think I've got one. Remember the guy this morning who found out about the Pell emails?'

'The guy at the Met who was ex-GCHQ? Yes, does he know someone?'

'Not someone, him. His super suggested I call him, and he wants to come here. His wife's just got a research post at John's College, and he'd be happy to move to Cambridge.

Name's Stuart Weir. He's coming here next week, but if you need anything urgently, he says do email him. He'll commute until they find a place to live.'

'Much as I'd like a brilliant IT guy, Sir, I am rather wary about having an ex-spook. They break the rules and you know me, I work by the book. Nobody on my team breaks the rules.' Though we may bend them a bit when it comes to my getting stuck in.

'I've discussed that with him, and he says that's fine. According to him, he's signed so many Official Secrets Act papers, that if he broke the rules, they'd probably drag him to the Tower.'

'Well, if he understands that, then I'm delighted. Having a really good IT bloke on board will be wonderful. We really miss Peter.' She sat back and smiled. That would make a huge difference and take a lot of work off the others' plates especially if he was, as he said, willing to check stuff straight away. 'Now, the other thing,' she began.

'Is the Greek connection.'

'You have been polishing that crystal ball, Sir. Spooky! Well, it's not so much a connection that's really needed as a good translator we can call on.'

'I think you can have both. The chief is not the only person getting calls from on high. I had a call from our ambassador in Athens.'

Pam raised her eyebrows. 'Really? If this goes on it will be the Archbishop of Canterbury next, followed by the Pope.' Murton laughed. It sounded more like a cough, as if laughing was something he hadn't practiced enough.

'So what did he say, the ambassador?'

'She. The ambassador is a woman.'

'Right, I stand corrected,' Pam smiled. 'Excellent. And what did she say?' Pam thought for a moment and groaned. 'Don't tell me, she had a call from Mr Leotakis.'

'It seems they are friends, yes. And she was looking forward to coming over here for the opening of the Gallery.

A major piece of Anglo-Greek co-operation as she put it. And Mr Leotakis reminded her that someone helped out the previous Ambassador a year or so back. Something sensitive, it sounded like. And this chap sorted it out and made sure it didn't leak.'

'That's always a plus. I saw Miss Karanaki, the architect, earlier and put the fear of God, or at least the English justice system, into her. I don't think we'll get any more leaks from her. I checked her phone, too, in case she'd taken a quick snap of the crime scene. So who is this man? It is a man, I take it?'

'It is. His name is Mike Petersen and he lives in Crete.'

'In Crete? So he's not attached to the embassy?'

'Not officially, no. It seems that Petersen, or to give him his correct title, DS Petersen, is actually Met.'

'What? In Greece?'

'On long-term, and I think you can read into that permanent, medical leave. But the ambassador did say that Mr Leotakis said he was a brilliant investigator. He's half Cretan, knows the locals near where Stephanie lived and speaks the language. Anyhow, Pam, he's willing talk to you anytime, and will translate any documents you send him.'

'Sounds odd if you ask me, but I suppose he could be helpful.'

'Good. Here's his phone number. Don't forget that everything is a priority as far as this case goes. The existence of your unit depends on it.'

What?? What the holy fuck? Her unit was in danger of being axed and he chooses this moment to tell her? Pam tried not to show how shocked she was and instead took a deep breath and smiled at her boss. And she'd bloody trusted him to support her.

'Is this the moment to ask for a new whiteboard that we could actually read?' she asked him.

'Yes. I can order that.'

'Thank you, Sir. New window blinds that actually work? Or better fans?'

'Don't push it.'

Pam returned to her office, trying not to think about the possibility this could be her unit's last case. Maybe if she got a quick result, they'd decided to keep it going. The heat of the afternoon was making her room uncomfortably hot, and she was finding it hard to stay awake. Time to go home, she thought. And send Josh and the others home, too. They weren't going to achieve anything tired.

Perhaps she should just give this Petersen guy a call first. Everything did keep going back to Crete. The standard knocking on doors and asking neighbours colleagues, etcetera, that helped build a profile of a victim wasn't available. The doors, neighbours and colleagues were all in Greece. In Crete, to be precise, where the DS now lived. The number Murton had given her was a mobile and it gave the long heartbeat-like ring of a number ringing in Europe. It rang a few times and then stopped.

Oh, for fuck's sake, don't tell me he's turned off the answer thing. She put down the phone irritably. Who the hell was he anyway? On permanent medical leave? What did that mean? Maybe she should call one of her new friends at the Met and ask them. Or maybe she shouldn't. Maybe his partner had got killed on the job or he'd been injured. Either of those things could bugger you up. She imagined how she'd feel if Josh died. She'd never forgive herself. Yes, she wasn't sure she could go on working after something like that. Better not to probe. Her phone rang and she saw the number she'd just called come up.

'Hello? I think you just called me?' A deep voice, a good voice.

'Yes. I'm Detective Inspector Pam Gregory, I was given your number by my superior officer, he...'

'Kate rang him, didn't she? Sorry, I should say Madame Ambassador, I suppose, but she's too intelligent to be hung up on titles. Yes, I'm Mike. May I call you Pam? Sorry I didn't answer your call but I was just pouring in some cement, and that's something you can't stop halfway.'

Cement? And not boss or guv. He'd clearly put the job behind him.

'Certainly,' she replied calmly, drawing circles on the sheet of paper in front of her. If this was a charm offensive, she wasn't buying.

'It's about Stephanie's death, isn't it? You have no idea how upset everyone here is.'

'Did you know her?'

'Oh yes. I helped build her new house. And Henry's. I live in Chiona at the moment, and they're neighbours. And friends.'

'So you know Chiona well?

'It's pronounced *Hyona*,' he said 'like the ch in loch. And yes, I know the village really well. Stone by stone, you might say. I helped build all the new houses. It's what I do here, building work. And a bit of fishing. I keep a small boat here in the little harbour.'

'Sounds idyllic,' Pam said.

'Well, maybe you'll be able to come and see for yourself.'

'I doubt it. Budgets and all that. And please don't tell me that Mr Leotakis would foot the bill.'

'No.' He laughed. Unlike Murton, he sounded like a man who laughed a great deal. 'Though he would. He was a close friend of Stephanie's.'

That's interesting, Pam thought. How close?

'Let's facetime later and you can show me any Greek writing you need translating.'

'That would be very helpful, Mike. Thank you. Do you have Skype?'

'I do.'

'Excellent. Then I can share your information with the team.'

'No problem. Sounds sensible. The more you all know about Stephanie's life here, the sooner you'll be able to discover who killed her. Actually, I could give you a quick guide to the handful of people who live here if that would be useful.'

'It would, definitely. Thank you. No names that jump out at you? Nobody who happens to be in England?'

'Actually no. Apart from Henry. In England that is. No, I can't think of anyone here who is isn't genuinely mourning her death. She'd lived here for well over thirty years; she was one of them.'

'Yes. I don't feel that she had any roots here'.

'She didn't. She always said that England felt like a foreign country.'

'Good. Now give me a moment to put my head under a tap and change my T-shirt. Oh, by the way, just so you don't get a shock, I'm black. Saves me having to watch people do a double take.'

'Do they do that? That's awful.'

'Oh yes. Apparently, I don't sound black.'

'I wouldn't know what that sounded like.'

He laughed again. 'No. Come to that nor would I.'

Pam thought for a moment. If the team who'd been up all night were as tired as she was, it would be better to do this the following day..

'Actually, can we make it tomorrow? Half my team and I were up all night on an obs, and then this happened. I think they'll be fresher tomorrow.'

'You sound remarkably on the ball for someone operating without sleep.'

'On automatic pilot. You know what it's like, adrenaline kicks in.'

'That was another life ago. Can hardly remember what that felt like.'

Well, bully for you, Mr Petersen. Some of us have to work for our living rather than swanning around in the Med on sickness benefit. He sounded just that bit too pleased with himself, she thought. Still, he knew the area and she didn't. And that could save a lot of time.

'Good to talk with you, Pam,' he said, 'We'll speak again tomorrow. What time's best?'

'Shall we say nine am our time?'

'That works for me.' He switched off the call without a goodbye.

And goodbye to you, too, she thought. Another rude Met officer who didn't think manners mattered.

Pam walked out of her office into the Major Incident Room, where everyone was busy on their computers. She'd be getting quite a few reports by the morning.

'Sorry to interrupt your work,' she said. 'Listen up. You know how everything is leading to Greece. Well, we've got a man on the ground now. Name is DS Mike Petersen and it so happens that he lives in Chiona.'

'In the village itself? What's he doing there?'

'Building it, as far as I can make out. When he's not taking his boat out to sea fishing.'

'That sounds cool. Can I transfer to that division?' asked Roberta, laughing.

'He's Met,' replied Pam.

'I may be wrong,' said Paul, 'but when I last looked, Piccadilly wasn't on a Greek island.'

'Off the job for the moment, I gather.'

'Out of the box then,' said Dave. 'PTSD?'

'I didn't ask, Dave, strange as that might sound'.

'Sorry, boss. Just curious.'

'Well please keep your curiosity for those who knew Stephanie.'

'Doesn't that now include our new friend?'

'It does, but as he's in Crete, I don't think we need to add him to our list, do you? In any case he's Skyping us all at nine am tomorrow. Anyone with specific questions that have arisen from your work today, please give them to me first thing. We'll meet here for a briefing at eight. And those of you who should have ended your shifts at ten this morning, please go home now. I'm going, myself. We're not going to break this case if we're too tired to think. As Superintendent Murton reminded me, we have to get our work-life balance right.'

Pam waited for the laughter to die down.

'Yeah. Well see you all tomorrow. Let's hope we have a bit more evidence and not merely a lot of questions.'

She stopped as Josh picked up his phone and signalled her.

'Now what? If it's that bloody billionaire, tell him he can speak to me tomorrow. I've already had it with his interference.'

'It's Henry Cox, boss.'

'Put the call through to my office, Josh, please.'

'Think he wants to confess, anyone? No. Me neither. Paul, you've been researching him, let's catch up when I get off the line.'

'Thought you were going home, boss.'

'So did I, Paul. Never quite works out like that, does it?'

CHAPTER 15

'What's that?' Jen pointed to a pile of folded plans on the side of her father's desk.

They were sitting in his study upstairs, a light room, overlooking the tree-lined road, and only partly shaded by the wisteria, which grew up the front of the house. 'What a pity you weren't here a few weeks ago!' Caroline had exclaimed as Jen wearily dropped her cases inside the hall. 'It's been one of the best years ever. The scent was gorgeous.'

A few weeks ago my mother hadn't died ,Jen did not say.

'Lovely, Caroline,' she murmured. 'Which room am I in?'

'Thought you'd like some peace and quiet, though actually I don't know why I say that. We hardly see Ollie since he and Eleanor moved to Bristol, which means that I don't get the chance to play adoring grandma as often as I'd like. And now Luca's got this new job in Leeds, we probably won't see him except at Christmas. Hardly need this vast old house any more for us two ancients. If it wasn't for the dogs, I'd be going doolally. At least your father was here today when the press all turned up. Don't know how they made the connection so quickly, but there they were. You probably saw them.'

Jen nodded. Press here and press outside her Cambridge house.

'You're not working, Caro?' she asked her stepmother.

'A bit here and there, but to be honest I get rather tired these days. Now do go up, you know where it is.'

She's right, thought Jen. This house is too big for the two of them. But it will be a wrench to move. Unless they go to Bristol to be near the grandchildren. There were two of these already and Oliver's wife Eleanor was thinking of having a third, Caroline told her later over coffee. Within minutes of arriving at her father's house, Jen discovered that the move to Bristol was a rumbling furnace of a row, Caroline wanting to be near Oliver and Colin refusing to move until he retired.

'And he's got no plans to retire at all,' wailed Caroline, later, pouring green tea into National Trust mugs.

Jen sympathised with her stepmother, who she could see was lonely. She'd also lost a lot of weight. Her blue cotton sweater looked way too large for her and there were deep hollows under her eyes. Had her father noticed? He must have done. At least thinking about this distracted her from thinking about her mother, or 'the horrible thing about your mother', as Caroline called it, as though Stephanie had been responsible for her own death.

This, as it turned out, was pretty much her own father's view. 'Stephanie didn't care who she annoyed,' he told her, but Jen could see he was hurt and disturbed by the murder.

'Stay here as long as you like, Jumps,' he said, using her childhood name, based on the Jennifer Juniper song that had inspired their choice. 'I won't worry so much if you're here, and Caroline can keep the press away. Her and Boots, though Boots is such a softy, he'd probably run into the press pack wagging his tail and wanting tummy tickles.'

'There were journalists outside my door at lunchtime,' Jen told him. 'Don't know how they tracked me down so fast. Diana, she's my family liaison officer, was great though. Threatened them with parking tickets, obstruction of the highway and everything else she could think of. Nice of her to drive me here, as well.'

'Doubt if it was about being nice, Jen,' her father frowned. His eyebrows were going white now as well as his hair. In a couple of years, he'd be seventy. Maybe he'd retire then. She hugged her father. If her stepmother was losing weight, he wasn't. He was as solid and comforting as ever. She told him so.

'Yes, I'm as fit as a fiddle,' he told her. 'It's Caroline's health that's really worrying. She's got Addison's.' He explained about the disease and its symptoms.

'Why didn't you tell me?'

'I didn't want to worry you. But now it's been diagnosed, she's so much better. Just gets tired. But she is beginning to put the weight back on. Slowly.'

'Good. Another time either of you gets ill, will you tell me?'

'Another time will you tell me if you're in danger? The police probably drove you here because they're worried about your safety.'

'But whoever killed Mum is hardly going to come for me, are they? It's not as if I've ever lived in Greece. I'm sure this is all about the Chiona treasure. I really don't see why they think I should stay here and not go to the university.'

'Can you at least wait until after your mother's funeral?' Pam had asked her. 'Just until we know a bit more about this case.'

Jen sighed. Already the university and her students had agreed for her to take time off and only do distance teaching, which, she had to be honest, was not a problem. There were only a few MA students she had to work with at the moment. All the undergraduates had finished their exams for the year. She could give the first and second years lists of books to read and films to watch and they could email her.

She could stay here and write. There was stacks of room, and Caroline was only too happy to cook for her and bring her coffee at regular intervals. But although she was deeply fond of them both, the idea of staying here made her feel restless. She wanted to be either home or in Crete. In fact, the more she thought about it, the more the idea of travelling to Crete appealed to her.

Maybe there she could find out more about what her mother had been doing in recent months. Although she knew that it was up to the police to find the killer, she felt she just had to know the truth.

'I can't stop thinking about it,' she told her father. 'Who'd want to kill Mum?'

'Any number of people I'd imagine.' He sighed. 'It's not your job to find that out.'

'I know. But being pissed off with someone isn't the same as actually killing them, is it? It's not just saying, "I hate that bloody woman," but being angry enough to pick up a knife and stab her. And Skimble!'

'As far as I can see, the person who'd do a thing like that to your cat has to be insane. I really don't know why you didn't call me at the time,' he repeated.

'You know perfectly well why I didn't. Because you'd have told me I had to come and stay with you, and I didn't want to leave Cambridge.'

'Well, I'd have been right. Just think. If the madman who killed your mother had done so in your house and not in the gallery, he might have attacked you, too. I couldn't bear anything happening to you.'

'Oh, Dad, I'm sorry. It didn't occur to me.' Jen paused and thought for a moment. 'Actually, Dad, I don't think they did want to kill Mum in our house. They wanted to make a statement. Pam rang me up to tell me the press had got some details about the killing from the architect. She wanted me to hear it from her first.'

'That's Anna Karanaki,' said her father. He reached up and pulled down a magazine.

'If you say so.'

'She's good. There's a piece on her here. She worked with Renzo Piano on the Niarchos Cultural Centre. You must have seen pictures of that.'

'Dad. Not everyone is as absorbed by new buildings as you are. No. I haven't seen pictures of that centre. I don't read architecture magazines. But Anna also leaked the story of Mum being gored by the bull to Piers Morgan. And I'm pretty furious about that. I expect the police are, too. So, don't expect me to celebrate her skills as an architect right now.'

'Placing your mother's body on the bull. So bizarre. Vile. Caroline and I were horrified when we heard. To be honest, it's very Greek. Theatrical. Very like your mother.'

'So tell me. You know Mum better than anyone. Who do you think killed her?'

'I haven't been in your mother's life for thirty years, Jen. I've no idea.'

'So who might know?'

'Henry, I imagine. And Popi. And anyone else your mother has become close to.'

'Popi was devastated when I rang her, but I haven't spoken to Henry yet. I don't have a mobile number for him, and I can't ring him at home as he's in England. Did I tell you that he rang Mum the day before she died?'

' No. Why? What's he doing in England?'

'I don't know, Dad. I haven't spoken to him.'

'Henry and your mother had a huge row that lasted a couple of years. I think you have to be careful about Henry.'

'He's my godfather.' Jen pulled the magazine towards her and began to ruffle the pages.

'He's something of a fanatic. No I'm being serious,' Jen don't look at me like that,' he continued. 'There was this reviewer who wrote a bad review of his last book and Henry's reaction was quite excessive, irrational even. He started to stalk him at his work. He was staying in London at the time. Stephanie found out about it and asked me to intervene. Must have been about 1992 because I remember I was working on the house in Orpington when your mother rang me. You don't remember?'

'I was only ten, Dad.'

'Ah yes. Well, I went and had a word with him and he calmed down. But I saw another side of Henry that day. He can blow up, and then I don't think he's responsible for his actions. In that state, I think he's capable of anything.'

'Well, I still don't believe he'd kill Mum. They go back too far.' She paused. 'You're not going to tell that little story to the police, are you?'

'I think I have to. They need to know.' Colin got up and paced in front of his study window. There was a blue tit outside, upside down on a ceanothus bush. He watched it for a moment. If only he could wrap up his daughter and keep her safely in the house until the lunatic had been put away. He hated the fact that she was an adult and would no longer do what he told her. Mind you, she'd always had an independent mind.

'Well, I'll see him at the funeral. But that can't happen until they release Mum's body. Actually, though I'd rather not think about it, Mum's post-mortem's going to take place on Thursday. But this means the Coroner should release her body on Friday. Then we can have her funeral. I don't think I'm going to be able to mourn her properly till after that.'

'Where's Stephanie's funeral taking place? Cambridge?'

'In Crete, of course. Where she lived. I'm going to fly out there the day before. I've discussed it with Popi. It seems we're all going to be staying with Mr Leotakis. The funeral is in the chapel on his estate, near Chiona. There isn't a cemetery in Chiona or Sitia, for people who aren't Christians, apparently.'

'You are not going to Crete. Not until the murderer is found.'

'Don't be absurd, Dad, I have to go my mother's funeral.'

'Then I'm coming, too. I'll find a hotel. Not sure Caro will be up to it, though.'

'Good. I want you there.'

Jen walked across and hugged him again. Here in this comfortable old house it didn't seem plausible that there was somebody out there who might kill her. The feeling she'd had of being watched now felt like something she'd imagined.

'So. You were thinking about who might have killed Mum.'

'Was I? Yes, I was. I can't really imagine anyone. Except perhaps that poor guy whose work she stole, what was his name. Kieron someone. Yes. Kieron James. That was sad.'

'I thought he drove you mad.'

'It wasn't surprising. He didn't have any evidence that he'd shown Stephanie his work or that it was his original research. He had the list of books, but then so had she and she'd submitted them. So when his dissertation read much like hers, he was accused of plagiarising her work. And when he made a fuss, the university didn't want to hear about it. They took Stephanie's side. It was just her word against his. And so Kieron got drunk and accosted his tutor in a pub and of course got sent down without a degree, and there goes his career in archaeology. It's a small world, as are all professional worlds when you come down to it. No idea where he ended up, but not with an MA and a career. If he's still angry...'

'Did Mum steal his work?'

'She said she stole his references. She was even rather proud of herself. She could be frighteningly narcissistic at times. That's why I think she's upset someone with this Chiona find. Taking credit for work that isn't hers.'

'Yes. She did exactly that. She found a bit of the palace and an urn but she didn't find the bull. That was someone else.'

'Well, if I was the police, I'd want to interview that someone else. Do you know their name?'

'No. Mum never mentioned him. Do you think the police are having conversations like this?'

'Doubt it. They're probably just examining evidence and timelines and things. It's all CCTV these days, isn't it?'

'Don't ask me. All I know is what I see in films.'

'What's she like, the police officer you talked to?' her father asked her.

Jen thought for a minute. She hadn't really taken her

in. 'I think she's all right. She didn't say a lot, but I got the sense she was thinking. She looked frazzled, but then she apologised and said she'd been up all night on another case so that's hardly surprising. Probably about my age, or a bit older, so I guess she's bright or she wouldn't be running this special crimes thing she's in charge of. Yeah. She understood about Skimble, too.'

'Do you think she's up to the job?'

'Dad, that's such a male question. Would you ask that about an officer if they were a man?'

'Probably. Sometimes you sound just like your mother.'

'Good.'

'Anyhow she's nothing like Diane, who I didn't like at all. She kept starting sentences with I expect. "I expect you feel a bit lost right now…" "I expect you'd like a nice cup of tea". When she said that I told her to make herself a cup, but I was having a glass of whisky.'

'Now you really sound like Stephanie.'

'I do miss her. Already. I miss the sense she's not here. Like going down the road where you lived, and your home's been pulled down. The emptiness. The nothing being there where something should be there.'

'I missed her terribly when we broke up.'

'I didn't know that.'

'You were tiny. She made life fun. She drove me mad. There were times I could have strangled her, not least for making love with every young man she met on a dig – she couldn't understand fidelity. She was faithful to the person she was with at any one moment. It was wearing. But when you were that person, she could make it all worth it.' He sighed. 'I bloody hope your detective is as good as you say. I want the bastard who did that to your Mum to pay. I want to see him found guilty and put away for ever.'

''I just wish I could do something.'

'Jen. You can't do anything. Why don't you get another coffee and go and sit in the garden? It's a glorious evening.

Read a book.'

'What are you going to do?

'Work on these for a bit.'

Jen eyed the pile of architect's plans spread over the father's desk. She couldn't remember a time when there weren't such plans around.

'My latest project. You want to see?' And for the first time that day Colin's eyes lit up.

Jen found herself smiling in spite of herself. This was home to her, sitting on one of her father's favourite Scandinavian woven leather strip chairs, which were much more comfortable than they looked. This was the only room in the house that was purely him and to which Caroline hadn't added cushions, curtains or ornaments. It had white walls and white shelves full of books on architecture and design, and framed plans and elevations of houses by Corbusier, Frank Lloyd Wright and Gehry. She thought the new Fitzwilliam Gallery plan might join them, although perhaps that building would now be forever tainted for him.

'Did I ever tell you of my dream to create stilt houses as a means of preparation for floods?' he began. She nodded and listened as he told her, as he had many times, how, despite the increased risk of flooding, no local councils would accept his new ideas and he could only create such a house for a private client. Which he had done several times. There was a beach house on the Suffolk coast and a house near the river outside Norwich. But now there was a council in Suffolk interested.

He showed her the plans and she understood how he couldn't possibly retire now. It was the culmination of his life's work.

'Dad,' Jen began. 'Just thinking about how one fulfils one's dreams...what if finding the Minoan palace at Chiona had been someone's life dream? How would they feel when Mum stumbled on it?'

'I don't know,' he replied. 'But for them to act like that, you'd have to be more than a frustrated archaeologist.'

'Yes,' she agreed. 'You'd have to be unhinged.'

'Oh, I think that whoever did this to your mother is definitely unhinged. That's why I worry about you, pusscat.'

'But not while I'm here.'

'Not while you're here. You've got Boots to protect you.'

Later, Jen sat in the garden on a many-cushioned bench leafing through a glossy architecture magazine when it sprang out at her. The Leotakis Gallery. And an interview with the architect, Anna Karanaki. She knew all about the gallery, of course, but she hadn't actually studied it before. She slammed the magazine shut. She didn't want to think about the building or read about it She wanted to get away from it all. She wanted to go to Crete. Crete was safe, and she could swim, lie in the sun and remember her mother in her own way.

And Crete was also Mike Petersen. She'd only met him a few times on her most recent visits to her mother, but the thought of him inevitably gave her a tiny thrill.

Yes. She must go to Crete.

CHAPTER 16

'Now this is the nearest main town, Sitia.'

Mike Petersen clicked the key on his laptop, and the map of Crete was replaced by one showing the east of the island. Lasithi. The place he now called home, and where he'd finally begun to feel at home.

He wasn't sure why he'd expanded what could have been a very short Q&A session into a kind of semi-academic briefing. Perhaps the irritation that Steph's death was being investigated by a bunch of regional officers who'd never met her, and almost certainly hadn't a clue about what the Chiona discoveries actually meant in terms of understanding Minoan culture. They also knew nothing about Crete. Just another place where you can find long chairs, long drinks and read long books where fantasy cops solved unlikely cases.

It was a quick, and he knew simplistic, version of the island with a few pictures on a PowerPoint he'd thrown together late the previous night. He'd been tempted to have a couple of drinks while he was doing it, but he owed Stephanie the benefit of a sober presentation, even if hers might not have been. Almost certainly wouldn't have been. So far he'd told them that Crete was one of the largest islands in the Mediterranean, a hundred and sixty miles long and packed with the kind of history that made you understand why so many archaeologists hung out there. It had been the centre of Europe's first advanced civilization, the Minoans.

'When people talk about Greek civilisation it's all Athens and the Parthenon and the kind of columns you see in your Fitzwilliam Museum...' Might as well bring it home. 'But this was a lot earlier.'

'Yes,' agreed Pam. 'One of my sergeants was saying we had to think of Stonehenge for this period.'

'Yes. Not that I can give you the date of Stonehenge!' Mike laughed. It was good they were thinking about this. It was like being back at university when you find a student who's really interested. Centuries ago in my own life, he thought wryly.

'The Minoan civilization was incredibly successful. They were traders, lots of trading with Egypt, and they had plumbing and made the most beautiful things. And decorated their everyday things, like jars for olive oil. Forgive me if I go on about them, but you have to understand that here in Chiona, I hear little else. Anyhow, before the island was partially destroyed by a major earthquake and then invaded, they had a good thing going here on Crete, and it lasted for over a thousand years. It also may have had a matriarchal government.'

'You see,' Pam told the people behind her. He wished he could see them, though he could at least hear them. 'When women rule, good things happen,' she added.

'Apart from Thatcher,' said a voice.

Mike smiled. 'Moving on then.' And then it was the briefest mention of the various invaders and occupiers and how that had included over four hundred years of Venetian rule, which had ended when the Turks took over.

'Crete was first an independent island on its own but became a part of Greece just before the first World War. It was and is, however, still fiercely independent. To understand the Cretans,' Mike told Pam and an unseen room of detectives, 'you have to remember they've fought to keep their own religion and language and culture for literally thousands of years despite successive invasions. You think history is about the classroom, but here it's still lived. Grudges rumble on through the generations. Who sided with whom during the Civil War in the forties, for example, or under the Junta in the sixties and seventies. Or even earlier.'

Why was he saying this? They didn't know Greece had a Civil War or about the Junta. They weren't going to be interested. But he was. He always had been. Which accounted for his politics degree. It was about family. In Crete it was always about family.

Mike replaced the map with a picture of a small port. Small red, blue and white fishing boats were reflected in an improbably indigo sea. He could imagine how they'd all want to go there. It was how he'd felt when he lived in England and whenever he saw a picture of Greece. It set up a longing. Now it was just home. Though there were still days when he could step back and look and be thrilled.

'Sitia is a working town, not just a tourist resort, and if you're thinking it all looks very new, that's because the old city was destroyed three times, once by the Turks, once by an earthquake and once by the Venetians. Now there's about nine thousand people living and working there, about half the size of St Ives.'

It had taken him ages to find the right town on Google that could give him a local comparison. He hoped they were appreciating all the work. The DI hadn't mentioned a fee. But seeing how he was still getting his Met pension, they probably thought he'd help them for free. Would she at least ask?

'Though of course numbers soar in August when all the tourists arrive, our most recent invasion. The carnage after a night out in Malia could make you think it's one of the bloodiest.'

Somebody laughed. One of the men. 'Our son went there after his A-levels,' he told his colleagues. 'Came back with massive sunburn and a broken ankle. Said everyone was off their face the whole time.'

'Major problem for local police as you can imagine.' Mike

smiled. 'Now we come to Chiona,' he continued and put up the slide showing the sprinkle of white cottages around a bay of turquoise and blue sea. He'd worked flat out helping build those after the old ones got compulsory purchase orders from the National Archaeological Service and were demolished in order to facilitate the dig.

'No wonder Dr Michaels liked living here,' said Pam. 'Her daughter said she couldn't imagine living anywhere else.'

'Yes, it's lovely, especially in spring,' agreed Mike. 'But it wouldn't suit everyone. It's incredibly isolated and very bleak in winter, which is basically the first three months of the year. The nearest large village, Palaikastro, is about two kilometres inland.

'Did she live there year round?' asked Pam. 'What did she do? 'she added.

'Stephanie usually stayed in Chiona till Christmas. The weather is good for walking and Steph loved walking. She also took lots of photographs, she was thinking of doing a book on village faces in Crete, so she drove around a lot. This is just in the time I've known her, which is only two years. But I think she spent winters in Athens before then. Or sometimes Cambridge. You'd have to ask Henry. As for what she did? She basically lived like many older people do here. Would you like me to talk through Stephanie's routine, as far as I saw it?'

'That would be helpful.'

'Okay. Well, she'd get up and swim every morning about eightish. Depends how much wine she'd drunk the previous evening. She did have the capacity to put it back, though, from what I've heard, nothing like she'd previously done. I think she'd had a bit of a health scare a few years back. After the swim, she'd have breakfast on her veranda and do an online crossword. We have good WiFi here as you can see from our connection right now.'

'Yes, better than some bits of Cambridgeshire,' agreed Pam.

'It's pretty good all over Crete, but then it's something

the tourists all want.' He smiled again. 'Everything here adapts itself for the tourists; they're our industry. Right... Stephanie's day,' Mike continued. 'Several days a week she'd walk into Palaikastro and have coffee with friends and do a shop, and some days get the bus to Sitia. We have a bus here twice a week, but there are four buses a day from Palaikastro and it takes about thirty minutes. She didn't have a car, by the way, though she did sometimes hire one. I think money was tight.'

'Well, we'll be looking at her finances of course,' Pam told him.

Of course they would. But they'd need local help getting them from the Bank of Piraeus where he knew she had her account. Though probably Nikos would unlock those in a moment if they asked him. Mike wondered how Pam would get on with Leotakis. It would be a mistake to keep him out of her investigation, but then a lot of the police he'd known weren't the brightest.

'So then Steph would have lunch somewhere,' he continued, thinking about his own lunch. He had a nice bag of freshly-caught sardines in his fridge. He could take them over to Dimitri and they could cook them over charcoal for lunch. He deserved it after this. 'And two or three glasses of wine,' he continued. 'She'd have it here or in Sitia or Palaikastro. After that she'd probably have a siesta. Then another swim, though in the spring and autumn this might be a walk, and then a drink with Henry or me or someone, and we'd all meet up for supper in the taverna. At least three or four times a week.'

'Is that your routine, too?' Mike wasn't sure whether it was the drink she wanted to know about or just what it was like when you leaped off the treadmill.

'Without so much alcohol. My aunt lives in Sitia so I go there a few times a week and meet up with cousins and we go out to eat or watch the football on Sky at one of the cafes. Or stay at home and watch stuff on Netflix. Simple life.'

'Sounds bloody brilliant,' muttered another male voice.

A bit older. 'If you don't have to work and you get the State to pay for you.'

'Did Stephanie work?' asked Pam quickly.

'Not so much. She didn't have a UK pension as she'd never paid any National Insurance, but during the summer she used to have archaeologists staying in her house and they paid for room and meals. She also occasionally ran workshops on fabric dyeing. She used to pick plants and experiment with natural dyes. She made all her own clothes and got the odd commission to make them from people who came in the summer. And I think she might have got some kind of sum from Mr Leotakis as compensation for having to move. Again Henry will know. You should ask him.'

'I'll do that,' said Pam. 'Could I ask about Mr Leotakis? His name keeps coming up, and of course it was his new gallery where Stephanie was murdered. I believe he has been involved with the dig ever since Stephanie made her first discovery. Has that been popular locally? He paid for the dig, I believe.'

'He paid I've no idea how much for the dig. Only one I've ever heard of that brought together so many international archaeology schools working together. It was like a small city here at the height of the work. The whole district had work housing and feeding and ferrying them around as well as digging. But much more importantly, locally, he put pressure on the Archaeological Service to pay a decent price for the houses they purchased and demolished. He may have put some of his own money into that. He doesn't say. And it meant that all the villagers including Stephanie and Henry Cox had more than enough to build their new homes. It was Mr Leotakis who actually first bought the land where they are and paid for an improved road and electrics and water. And now he's put money into the new Sitia museum – that's where the treasure will go after the Cambridge exhibition, and into the airport, and he's building two massive new hotels in Sitia. Which means that as far as unemployment goes round here, it's become negligible.'

'All that must make him rather popular? Or not?'

'It has, but he always was popular. He lives locally, though he grew up in Western Crete. He's actually a delightful man as you'll discover.'

Mike noticed how her eyebrows raised at that, doubtingly.

'And that must also mean that Stephanie was generally popular.'

'God, yes. Things have been really tough in Greece these last few years. This has been a godsend. Before the discovery, Stephanie was just another English eccentric, and there are a few around, but afterwards she became a kind of local hero. Everyone in the village is devastated by her death.'

'How many people live in Chiona?'

'Apart from the two restaurants by the beach which are only open in the summer, there are eighteen houses. Ten of these, one of which I'm renting right now, are summer homes. Owners live elsewhere in Europe. We've got two Swedes, three Italian families, two German, one French and two English.'

'None of them had any noticeable rows with Stephanie?' He noticed she'd switched from Dr Michaels to Stephanie. She was beginning to feel she knew the victim. That was always an important moment.

'Steph had rows with everyone when she'd drunk too much. And then made it up the next day. She spoke first and thought later, so she could really upset people. But enough to kill her? That's a stretch. Enough for people to cut her in the local shop for a few days, but then she'd do something kind and we'd all forgive her.'

'You're including yourself in this, I notice.'

'Oh yes. When I was building her house, she drove me mad. Kept changing her mind. Told me once she'd do better doing it herself than having some failed cop pretending to be a builder. I told her to find one and left. She came round to my aunt's the next day with one of her paintings (she wasn't bad, by the way) and abject apologies. And that was that. She actually consulted me more after that. She knew how far she could go. She had legendary rows with Henry, which had rumbled on for years, according to my aunt.'

'Your aunt sounds as if she knew Stephanie for many years.'

'Oh, my aunt knows everyone. Aunt Sofia is a kind of institution in Sitia. She thinks our family have been there for ever. Very little escapes her. And the ladies who have coffee with her – they could out-Stasi the Stasi. She's tough, too. If she sees somebody stepping out of line, she's on it. One-woman police force.'

'Would it be possible to set up a link later to talk with her?' Pam asked.

'Sure,' replied Mike, though he didn't know how the two women would get on. Pam really should come out here if she wanted to discover what Stephanie was really like. 'I can translate. She doesn't speak much English. But I've wandered off track. I was telling you who lived where. Would it be useful for me to draw a map and write down who lived in each house? Then you could see how Chiona works. We're all only a few metres from each other. It's a friendly place. The locals here grow olives and let rooms to tourists in the summer. And to the archaeologists.'

'Thank you very much, Mike. That gives us all a much clearer picture of Stephanie than what we had. One more thing, could I show you a couple of emails?'

Pam held up a printout of the two pages of phone text. Mike wondered why she hadn't just put them on the screen. Not very computer literate, he thought to himself as he read them. The writer sounded frantic, a woman? He wondered who she was and who the George was she was messaging.

'It says, "George where the fuck are you? I need you." Then, "George why aren't you answering your phone?" Then, "George will you please get back to me something terrible has happened and I need you." And the same repeated.'

'Thank you. That ties in with what we were told.'

'Sounds as though George is in trouble.'

Pam smiled. It was clear she wasn't about to divulge any more than she needed.

'One final thing before you go,' she said. The fee? No. She wouldn't do that in front of her team.

'Yes?'

'We believe that there is the possibility of this murder being part of a vendetta. Is that likely?'

'Likely in terms of knowing Stephanie recently, no. A vendetta in Crete, yes. But it's a local thing, it involves whole families and if there was one smouldering round here, I'd have heard about it by now. Mostly they've happened in the west of the Island – there's one village that virtually wiped itself out – but here we're about as east as you can go without falling into the sea and I've never heard of any vendettas.'

'Thank you. But perhaps you can tell us all what vendetta means in Crete?'

'Remember what I was saying about history? Well it's part of the same thing. Cretans have very long memories, and if they feel they or their families have been wronged, they take revenge. That's actually what the word means. Generally in Crete you get a vendetta when a member of a family is murdered. And then a member of that family takes revenge. Like you get with the gangs in London, only over generations.'

'And this still goes on?'

'In very rural areas, yes. You have to understand that it's all about honour. They don't see it as killing, it's something to be proud of.'

'So the person committing this act wouldn't hide the body. They'd want people to know.'

'Is there something you're not telling me, Inspector?' This was beginning to get interesting in terms of how they were going to work together. Everyone knew she'd been impaled on the bull, but was there something more? He saw Pam bite her lip. She's making a decision, he thought.

'What I am about to tell you is strictly confidential and

not to be shared with anyone else,' she began.

'I'm good at secrets, Inspector. You can trust me.' He gave her his best smile and she smiled back.

'After Dr Michaels was killed, as the press has already revealed, her body was placed on the golden bull in the new Leotakis Gallery. What they don't know is that the word 'vendetta' in Greek was written in blood on the floor.'

Mike tried to show he didn't already know this, or that Nikos hadn't told him, having heard it from Anna.

'I can see why you don't want that to get out. To be frank, it sounds like someone who believes that they are carrying out some kind of revenge killing, but it is most certainly not the Cretan way of doing things. That tends to be a simple gunshot. They don't go in for theatrics.'

'Yes, it was extremely theatrical,' agreed Pam.

'I imagine then that your inquiry is following the lines of the mentally disturbed who had come into contact with Stephanie.'

'Your assumption is not incorrect.'

'If it was a Cretan vendetta, then of course Stephanie's family would be in danger. But I expect your psych people are advising on that.'

Pam bit her lip again. Oh, they haven't got a forensic psychologist yet, thought Mike. Good old austerity. But with a case like this she'd be wise to use one.

'Did Stephanie have any family apart from her daughter?' she asked him.

'I think there was a brother, but she hadn't spoken to him for nearly fifty years. Yes. I remember, there was. She called him the unspeakable Jeffery. Jeffery Michaels. If it was a vendetta, then I'd say that both he and Jen are in real danger.'

CHAPTER 17

'Well that was fun,' said Roberta, after the phone link had been cut. 'One important thing, boss, when are you arranging a group trip to Chiona? Preferably taking a week.'

'As if,' said Pam. 'Okay, everyone. Let's come back from our summer holiday fantasy, shall we? Now, firstly...'

'Firstly can we admit that that hunk has no right to be in the police force,' said Paul. 'I mean give us a chance! Yes, Shona, I did notice you fanning yourself. You owe me a drink for that at least.'

Shona laughed, and Roberta smiled. Shona was one of the civvies, and everyone knew she and Paul enjoyed a friendship with benefits. Roberta pondered whether that relationship would ever develop further than that. It seemed to suit them both at the moment, but it was unlikely to stay the same. One of them would want more. Or less. Shona's reaction to Mike, though, was hardly surprising. 'Hot or what?' She'd mouthed to Roberta during the briefing. She and Shona often joked how unnaturally attractive cops were on TV, but this one, thought Roberta, actually looked more like a film actor than a real cop. His hair had a long buzz cut and his beard was a similar length, and his faded blue T-shirt didn't hide the fact that he was remarkably fit. All that building work, she thought. Just as well she wasn't looking for outside enjoyment or she'd be on the first plane out there.

Being with someone you loved and not on the treadmill of relationship hunting was such a relief, and Roberta couldn't imagine being with anyone other than Simon. She'd got lucky when she'd met him while visiting a school all those years ago. Yes, he was losing most of his hair and could comfortably lose some weight, but nobody could be kinder than her husband. Or give better foot rubs after a long day. No, she wouldn't swap Simon for a sexy hunk like DS Petersen. And how come he still was a DS and living in Greece? It didn't make sense. Medical leave, as far as she knew, had very tough cut off dates. She wondered whether the boss had found him attractive. If so, she'd showed no signs of it. It was ten years since Pam's divorce, and you had to have something more than work. Well, *she* did.

'You don't need me to remind you that a woman has been brutally killed and a daughter is without her mother.' Pam paced in front of the whiteboard with list of names, its tacked images of Stephanie, the crime scene and an interior plan of the Leotakis Gallery. 'I know we're only in day two, but we need to be motivated and focused. We'll have a short briefing now, so we can all get up to date and then let's crack on.'

'Yes, boss,' they chorused. Mike Petersen was forgotten.

'Let's do a quick rundown and then concentrate on Henry Cox, the friend of Dr Michaels,' she began. 'We need to prep for our interview with him this afternoon. Paul, sorry I didn't have time last night to go through your notes with you.'

'You were knackered, boss. I was knackered. Just as well we all left early.'

'Yes. I was just too tired to think any more. That was the longest day I've ever known. Anyhow you all look more rested today. Josh, you look as if you've actually slept for once.'

'I did,' Josh confirmed. 'Amazingly.' After a young constable dropped him off home the previous evening he'd been too tired even for speech, and prayed that Barbara wasn't in one of her chatty moods. But she wasn't.

'You look utterly exhausted,' she said, as he sleep-walked into the kitchen. 'Well, Bella slept through the night last night. Eight hours, can you believe it? So tonight's your turn. There's some lasagne in the fridge, if you want a quick snack, and then Susan's offered to sleep with me, so I've made up her room for you. And the girls know that Daddy mustn't be disturbed this evening. So you can say goodnight to them and just crash. You know you shouldn't be driving when you're that tired.'

'I wasn't. Pam made me accept a lift.'

'Can't say I always like your DI, she tends to think you're at the end of a piece of elastic she can pull in whenever it suits her, but she's not stupid.'

'She's kind, too,' added Josh.'

'Well, that counts for a lot,' admitted Barbara. 'I'll leave you to your tea.'

Josh heated up the lasagne in the microwave and then crawled upstairs to his daughter's room. It was extraordinarily pink, he thought, before unconsciousness hit him. It even smelled pink. Like jelly-babies.

Eleven hours later, he woke up, feeling as though molten lead had been poured inside him. But after a coffee and a very quick run in the nearby Cherry Hinton Park, he felt more alive and energised than he had for weeks. No, months. He gave Barbara a huge hug, enjoying the familiar scent of her floral perfume. Issey Miyake. She'd always worn it. After this case was over he would take them all for a long weekend away, maybe to Wells. Or park the children with the in-laws and take Barbara away. She'd love that.

Josh shook himself back to the present. The boss looked more tense than he'd ever seen her, but that was hardly surprising. This was a crime with so much pressure. The press were all over Cambridge, trying to get quotes from the police as they came and went. Well, they wouldn't get anything out of him or Pam.

Pam, at that moment, was thinking about her phone call with Henry Cox. He'd rung, as he told her the previous evening, the moment he'd heard the news. Yes, from Jen as it happened. He'd been in the British Library all day. He presumed she might want to talk to people who had known Stephanie well.

'I'm coming up to water the plants in Jen's garden tomorrow,' he said. 'Since it's so hot and she's in Putney with her father. Would it be convenient to talk there?'

More than convenient, she thought, though rather odd. All that way to water the plants when her best friend lives nearby. It didn't make sense. There had to be another reason. But that was for later. Back to her briefing now the team were refreshed and concentrating.

'So,' she began again. 'Thanks to having a killer who has given us his fingerprints, we've been able to eliminate all the staff at the Fitzwilliam Museum. We're a lot further on than we usually are on day two. We know the victim and have clear prints.'

I must write a personal note of thanks to the Director there, she reminded herself. She'd been very helpful.

'And we've also eliminated the English project manager, what was his name?

'Jon Hodgson,' said Josh.

'Yes. And the tiler, Vassili...'

'Vassili Papaconstantinou,' added Josh reading his notes.

'They do have some names,' said Dave.

'He's in the clear, as is the architect, although she was never in our sights, personally. Also, glad to say that Dr Mark Kitson has been removed from the list of suspects. So where does that leave us?' She looked at the names on the board.

'We've got the angry student...'

'We have a name for him,' said Sue. 'I rang the ex-husband, Colin Nichols with your questions, boss. He was more than helpful and is happy for you to visit him Friday afternoon.' Pam nodded, and made a note.

'First, the ex-student's name is Kieron Jones and he lives in Ipswich. I've now got an address and a telephone number. I've checked Holmes,' she continued, citing the data base named the *Home Office Large Major Enquiry System* after the fictional detective, 'and we don't have a record for him.'

'Fine,' said Pam and wrote his name on the board. 'Roberta, I'd like you and Paul to visit him this afternoon. If you think he's a possible, then have a word with the neighbours. See whether he has a car. See whether you can get his fingerprints.'

'Sure, boss,' said Roberta. She liked working with Paul. They made a strong team.

'And Stephanie Michaels did have a brother,' continued Sue. 'Mr Nichols gave me his name, Jeffrey Michaels, and said he lives in Weybridge, and again I've got an address and a phone number.'

'Not sure whether he can add anything if she hadn't been in touch for fifty years, but we do need to ensure she hadn't been in touch recently. And would he be a recipient of a will? We can't rule out conventional motives however bizarre this case may feel. I'll telephone him later. I don't think we need to visit him at this stage of our enquiry.'

'Regarding the will, boss,' continued Sue, 'Mr Nichols also gave me the name of a Cambridge solicitor that Stephanie used for her divorce. He thought it likely she'd continue to use them. They've got an office in Hills Road.'

'That will save a lot of time if she did continue to use them. Dave, would you like to follow that one up, please? Find out if she was still in touch and who the beneficiary of the estate is. And any anomalies.'

'Will do. Actually I do have a couple of bits of news myself.'

'Fire away!'

'The archaeologist who found the bull and never gets credited, Petros whatshisname, is currently working in Athens. I rang the British School of Archaeology, and they said he was due to come to Cambridge for the opening along with several of their own members but was currently in Athens. He'd actually dropped by their office yesterday, as soon as Stephanie's death was made public, to offer his condolences. Like everyone, he was shattered to hear about it, they said.'

'Another name to remove then,' commented Pam. 'Good,'

'I also contacted the British Museum about the Elgin Marbles nutter,' continued Dave. 'The office there were incredibly cagey, so I told them that they should speak to you. Their words were – hold on let me find it – "there have been many requests over the years with regard to the Parthenon marbles now exhibited to the world in the Museum, but they have no knowledge of any threat and would like to know where the source of this information comes from. There are, of course, always a number of people with strong personal views who believe the works should be returned to Greece." I told them that the info came from Dr Michaels, and they did admit getting online threats. But they have no idea of his or her name. It's all been emails. This is where we need Peter,' he added.

'We have a new Peter,' Pam told them. 'His name's Stuart Weir, ex-Met...'

'Not another one...' interrupted Paul.

'And ex-GCHQ,' Pam finished.

'A spook?' asked Dave. 'Is that a good idea?'

Pam shrugged. 'If he's good and doesn't mess up, that's fine. I've said my piece to Murton about doing things by the book. But one good thing, Stuart's also willing to start making some searches now before he gets here. Paul, if I give you his email, can you put together our list of possible suspects and anything we know about them. And run it past me before you send it.'

'Can do, boss. He might start with the Elgin Marbles man.'

'Definitely. Oh, and what have you found out about Mr Cox?'

'Very little, boss. And virtually nothing since 1992, which was when his last book came out, except one photograph. And thank the Lord for thorough caption-writers. It was a dinner in Chiona two years ago in an article about Stephanie. Here it is. I've scanned it.'

The picture showed a table on a concrete promontory, as close to the sea as being on a boat. The team sighed in unison as they compared it to the airless, stuffy room they worked in. The table was covered with a checked tablecloth, half covered with a white paper one, and on it were the remains of a lunch, fish bones and heads, a couple of chunks of bread in a woven basket and two empty bottles of wine.

'Why can't we have lunches like that?' asked Sue.

'Because Cambridge isn't on the Mediterranean coast when I last looked,' replied Pam.

'I expect there are people here who live like that. Picnics and wine in Grantchester Meadows and by the pool on Midsummer Green.'

'Yeah. Students,' said Paul.

Pam studied the picture. Around the table sat Stephanie, facing the camera and smiling, opposite her the man they knew was Mike Petersen. He had a glass of water in front of him and was having a discussion with an unknown man on his right. Beside Stephanie, and watching Mike, was an elderly man in a rumpled cream linen jacket. He had a thatch of white hair and his dark glasses had been thrust into it, pushing it off his face. A decrepit panama hat was on the table beside him and a dog-eared book that looked as battered as he did. It was clear that he was a tall man. But could he have put on a pair of overalls and then had a beer and a sandwich after the murder? It seemed highly improbable. But nothing so far about this death seemed credible. Henry looked like the kind of man you'd run into on a summer's day on Jesus Green or in one of the colleges.

'Looks like your standard Cambridge academic,' said Roberta, echoing Pam's thoughts. 'How old is he?'

'Not sure,' said Paul, 'but a few years older than Stephanie, so maybe seventy-four or seventy-five.'

'Would he be strong enough to lift her on to the bull?'

'Jen told me he swam every day of the year,' Pam replied. 'That would give him upper body strength. And she thought he was seventy-five.'

'He doesn't look like a murderer,' said Sue.

'Few do,' said Pam. 'Anything more, Paul?'

'He's published two books...' Paul flicked his notes to another page. 'One was called *1974: How one year defined Greece in the 20th century*, and the other *Constantinos Karamanlis: A Life in Three Acts*. Karamanlis, apparently, was a Prime Minister of Greece,' he added. 'Oh, and the reviews weren't good. Got one example here. "Henry Cox is a knowledgeable and thorough historian, an expert on Greece in the 20th century; it is a pity that his florid style makes this book unreadable."'

'Ouch,' said Roberta.

'The bio in his books says that he went to Winchester and Emmanuel College, Cambridge. Of course he did.'

'Careful, Paul, your prejudices are leaking,' said Sue.

'Okay, but as far as I can see, he's never bloody worked. No posts at schools or universities. Which is odd, isn't it? He's lived in Greece since 1970. And that's it. Who is he? It feels as though something is missing.'

'Not a lot to go on. But useful. Thanks Paul. Anything else, anyone?'

'Are we following up the idea that it was an attack on Mr Leotakis?' Dave was making notes on the board.

'Not for the moment. Not unless we have any evidence. You don't involve someone that powerful without a strong case to back you up, and all we've got is some gossip from our somewhat flaky architect. It certainly wasn't Mr Leotakis himself, as he was in in his mansion in Dorset. And of course on the phone to the Prime Minister, the British Ambassador in Athens and probably God. No. For the moment we steer clear of Mr Leotakis.'

'It doesn't feel like a professional job, does it, boss?' observed Josh. 'I mean, if a rival shipping guy or someone with a grudge had hired a professional, he'd do a professional job, surely? And Stephanie Michaels' murder doesn't have any of the hallmarks of a professional assassination.'

'No, it doesn't,' agreed Pam. 'Plus the savage killing of the cat which has all the hallmarks of someone who is very disturbed.'

'Talking of which, boss. After what that Mike guy said, do you think we should get a pysch in?'

'I don't know. I'll think about it. Maybe a bit later when we've interviewed our first possibles. Right now let's all follow the leads we have. I'm hoping we can get the handbag back from Forensics today along with Stephanie's iPad and phone. Josh, I want you to take the lead on studying those. See who called her on Monday evening.'

Josh nodded and made a note.

'Good, and now Josh, you and I can prep for our meeting with Mr Cox.'

They began by listening to Pam's interview with Jen.

'Several things from that, boss,' said Josh, reading his notes. 'The phone call he made to Jen. Why was he ringing?'

'Yes. And was he the person she was going to have a drink with? And what about the rows he had with Stephanie? He had his old house knocked down.'

'Yes. How did that affect him? I mean it's not easy to move when you're old. My gran always says that wild horses wouldn't get her out of her old place.'

'Yes. All good. And we should also ask him if he knows where she got the money to buy the house. Actually, also feed that question to Dave. The solicitor might know if he's still around. It might be in her files.'

A few hours later, Pam and Josh knocked on the door of Stephanie's house, and Henry Cox let them in and ushered them into the garden. In addition to a curved wooden bench, there were a couple of director chairs that Henry must have put out. There must be a cupboard somewhere hidden away, thought Pam. Chairs and a watering can. He knew his way around. She found herself glad to be back in this house. It was surprisingly restful for a place that was a scene of crime. Once again, she could understand why Jen loved living there. Anyone would.

Henry Cox looked remarkably like the photograph she'd seen earlier. He was wearing the same rumpled jacket, and the same panama hat sat on a low table in front of him. He did seem a most unlikely killer, but you never knew what went on in people's heads.

'Would you like a coffee? asked Henry. 'Jen told me to make myself at home and I just about know where things are.'

'No, that's fine, thank you,' said Pam sitting down on one of the chairs. Josh followed her example. He took out his phone and put it on the table.

'You don't mind if we record this, do you?' Pam asked him. 'We are so keen to learn more about Dr Michaels and...'

'For a start, you don't have to call her Dr Michaels,' interrupted Henry. 'It was only some honorary degree and she never used it.'

That's not what Mark and Jen said, thought Pam. But maybe she didn't dare with someone who'd known her for so long.

'I'm sorry for your loss,' she said more gently. 'It's hard to lose an old friend.'

'I couldn't speak yesterday. I just wept. That's why I didn't call you until late. There were times when I thought we might lose Stephanie because she was very ill about five years ago with hepatitis, but this. Who could possibly do this to her?'

'That is the question we have to find an answer to.'

'Yes. That is what I assumed you would need. If it is satisfactory with you, I would like to begin with some notes I made on the train coming down here.'

I thought it was up to Cambridge, thought Josh, or was

that just the university? The expressions that people like Henry used baffled him.

'That's fine,' said Pam.

'Good.' Henry put on his glasses and began to read. 'First, I'll explain very briefly who Stephanie was. What kind of person, and how that might have led to her death.'

If there was solid content, that would be very useful, thought Pam, but at the same time it brilliantly deflected any inquiry into him.

'Before you begin, though, I do have to ask you a couple of personal questions regarding the murder.'

Henry put down his glasses and turned to her in surprise. His eyes were pale blue, but bloodshot, though crying might account for the latter.

'That was one scenario I did not expect,' he said. 'It never occurred to me that I might be one of your suspects.'

Really, thought Josh, or are you just being very clever? And I do think you are an extremely clever man. Is all of this an act put on for our benefit? He had the feeling that Henry had spent a lot of his life hiding the truth from people. Paul could have been right, there was something about this man which did not add up.

'You telephoned Stephanie on Sunday and said you needed to speak to her,' began Pam.

'I did.'

'May I ask what it was you wanted to say?'

'It sounds so trite now. I read the Greek papers everyday and Steph never does. Never did. Did.' He took out a folded handkerchief and wiped his eyes. 'It's going to take a while to get used to that.'

I didn't notice his eyes watering, thought Josh,

'There was a piece in it about the coroner's report of a recent suicide in Athens. The man was the great-nephew of a man Stephanie had tried to help during the Polytechnic butchery back in 73… it's an area I've been researching for my new book. And that his father had also taken his own life. I thought Stephanie would want to know.'

And if you believe that, you'll believe anything. Josh glanced at the DI and she shook her head slightly. She doesn't think that either, he thought. I wonder what Henry really wanted to talk to Stephanie about?

'I also have reason to understand that Stephanie was meeting a friend for a drink on the night she died,' continued Pam. 'Was that you?'

'No, that wasn't me,' he replied cheerfully. Pam noticed his change. He was much more relaxed about that question.

'And I'm sorry to have to ask you this, but where were you on Monday evening?'

'You mean do I have an alibi? As it happens I'm afraid I don't. Although I didn't ring Stephanie to have that drink, I did want to talk to her as I've just said.'

'So where were you?'

'Here.'

'Here in Cambridge?'

'No. Here in this house. I was waiting for her, to talk to her, but she never came home, nor did Jen, and so I gave up. I'm only in England for a short while and there is a lot of work I need to do in the British Library. So I slept here, and in the morning I walked to the station, though I did have a short meander in Mill Road cemetery first, there are some rather remarkable Victorian tombs there; it has always been a favourite place for an idle promenade. I wake up at dawn most days.'

Pam took deep breath to stop herself laughing. An idle promenade. Maybe she could adopt the phrase.

'Do you know what train you got?'

'Indeed I do. I probably still have the ticket somewhere. It was the six something to St Pancras. Perfect for me, being virtually next door to the library.'

Could he have walked from the Fitzwilliam to the Station in time to get that train? If indeed he did get it.

'You didn't wonder why Jen wasn't here? You didn't ring her?'

'I did wonder, but then thought that if she were with

some young man in London, the last thing she'd want was her old godfather interrupting the evening.'

'You didn't ring later to tell her? Where did you sleep?'

'On the sofa. I gave myself a whisky and then fell asleep. After which I couldn't be bothered to go to bed. So I put that rug, the one that's draped over the sofa, over me. I tidied up before I left. Unlike Stephanie, who could make a room look as if it had been visited by a hurricane, I am known for liking order.'

'And you haven't told Dr Nichols since.'

'Of course not. I was about to tell Jen when she called me to tell me about Stephanie's death. Under the circumstances I hardly thought she'd be interested.'

We need to check CCTV, thought Josh. We need to see whether his story pans out.

'So now let me tell you a little bit about Stephanie,' continued Henry. If the questioning had troubled him, he showed no signs of it.

Pam nodded and Henry leaned back on the bench. He crossed his legs and prepared himself for his speech. This was why he was here, it was his last gift to an old friend.

CHAPTER 18

'When I thought about what I should talk about,' began Henry, 'it came to me that you're at the beginning of your journey. This is something that as a historian I fully comprehend. Therefore, if you will allow me to talk a little without further interruptions, perhaps I can help you understand, if not your route map, at least some aspects of the landscape.'

God, he was pompous, but given there was always the possibility that he'd trip himself up, he might as well think he's in control here. Pam gave a brief nod and he continued.

'I want to start with the first time I saw Stephanie, in a restaurant called Les Bohèmes.'

As he talks, he's back there. It's 1973, and he's sitting at a table inside the small taverna in Kolonaki, the smart district of Athens that swathes the base of Mount Lycabbetus, though there is nothing fashionable or expensive about this place which is run by the cynical, bear-like Costa. The taverna flouts all the regulations and laws despite its proximity to the police station and the number of officers who eat there. And, despite its name, there is nothing French about it. The walls have posters of Japanese temples and the music Costa plays is traditional American jazz and the banned and exiled Theodorakis. There's also a group of foreigners who eat here every evening, including the drunk English actor, Tony, whom Henry dislikes, and the poet Cathy, who is witty when she is not drunk. She is the only person he has ever seen fall face-first into a plate of beans. However, he enjoys Costa's company and gossip and his heavy meat stews.

Today, Costa tells him, there's a new addition to the regulars and she's doing the cooking. Her name's Stephanie, and according to Costa she's an expert on French cooking and told him he should have at least one day serving the food the name of the restaurant suggests. In fact, Henry will learn later, she's not a trained cook, but can follow a good cookbook and has one. She's doing the cooking in return for being able to eat for free every night. And she's not even intimidated by the ancient stove which judders like a steam engine and shoots flames into the air. It will explode a few years later and burn down the restaurant, but by then Stephanie will be in Crete with Laurent.

'It was a Thursday and the Junta were in power,' Henry continued, then briefly explained to the police officers that there was a ruling far-right junta from 1967 to 1974 which imposed any number of bizarre and inexplicable laws in addition to those of oppression and control.

This latest decree is that restaurants must not serve pork on Thursdays. Costa tells him it's to help the farmers up North. He laughs because he has just given Stephanie pork chops to cook that evening. It is late, the usual crowd are into their second litre of retsina and Stephanie is still grilling meat when the pork-checking police officers arrive.

Henry summarised the background and continued. 'The police officers walked into the kitchen and began to poke around in the dishes. "What's this?" they asked Stephanie, "isn't this pork?" "No, no, it's lamb," she told them. "It's just very pale. It's white lamb. Look," she said to the policemen, and she was relaxed, completely at ease even though she might have been arrested at any moment. She pointed to a bowl and told them it was mint sauce and that you never make mint sauce to eat with pork – you only eat it with lamb. "I'm English," she said. "We never eat pork with mint sauce. We eat it with apple sauce. And look, there's no apple sauce here."'

Henry laughed at the memory. 'Stephanie always spoke with such conviction. She could make you believe day was night.' Yet the two officers, Henry had thought, watching their polite smiles, were probably not taken in. He realised later that Costa had almost certainly done a deal with the officers – paid them off with food or cash or even information. That was the reason the taverna was allowed to stay open and Costa could behave as he did, was because he gave them reports on us all.

'That was Stephanie,' he continued now. 'She had chutzpah and bravery. The latter very evident later that same year when she tried to help a student who'd been shot at the Polytechnic – the incident I mentioned earlier. And from that evening onwards we became friends.'

Pam made notes and smiled quietly to herself. Normally she'd have interrupted this rambling story, thought Josh, but she must think that it's worth listening to this man for some reason. Unless she was simply enjoying the quiet of a morning in a peaceful garden. But that did not sound like his DI.

'Now let me tell you another story,' continued Henry. 'A much more recent one and you will begin to understand the layers of Stephanie's personality. This is about when she first made the discovery of the urn under the olive tree in her garden. Of course it was not something that she could keep quiet about. The local young men who'd been helping her with the olive tree – I think it was Vangelis's son, Andreas, and his friend Lukas – well they'd tell everyone, as indeed they did. But the first thing Stephanie did was to find me. Our houses then were virtually next door to each other.'

Again he's back there. He's checking dates of a demonstration in Paris in 1968, checking the names of journalists who had covered the events, and she bursts in. She's hysterical, he decides, but not drunk. She hasn't drunk much since her attack of hepatitis a few years back. She's not making sense, but he follows her back into her garden and sees the unmistakable curve of the faded terracotta.

'When I saw it I felt both excitement and dread. I had a presentiment that this was the beginning of something tremendous. I told her she must ring Irini, she is the director of archaeology in Palaikastro, and she would come and look at it. But when I said that, she gave me a strange look, and when she nodded I knew she would do something quite other. As indeed she did. Yes she did ring Irini, and so should you, Inspector. She's a quite brilliant young woman and certainly worth your talking to. And her English is perfect.'

'Thank you', says Pam making a note.

'However,' Henry sighs and shakes his head. 'That was not the first number she rang. Before she rang Irini, she rang Nikos Leotakis.'

'So she knew him before the discovery? I've heard they were quite friendly.'

Which could mean almost anything.

'She liked the highlife from time to time. So yes. She knew him. She knew him very well. They'd met somewhere. Leotakis has always taken an interest in local archaeology, after all, he lives nearby. I think he bought some of her drawings.'

'He lives near Chiona?'

How well did Stephanie know this man? Josh wondered.

'Just outside Sitia. He bought an entire promontory and built himself a small estate. His stately pile is about fifteen minutes by car from Chiona and Leotakis arrived before any archaeologist. The rest is history.'

'Why do you think she rang Mr Leotakis?' asked Pam.

'So that he would take charge and make her the heroine of the hour, as indeed he did. Without him, there would have been a small dig. It is possible that the Archaeology Service would have wanted to excavate beneath our houses, but that would have taken years to organise. They don't have the money these days. And I'd have lived out the rest of my days in my own home.'

'You resented having to move?

'Wouldn't you? I had been in that house for nigh on fifty years. I wore it like a comfortable coat. Or, indeed, a second skin. It tore my flesh to have it ripped off me. And then to watch it being demolished. Yes. You can say I was very angry.'

'But wasn't there anything you clould do? You couldn't refuse to move?'

'I did make a protest, but there was too much money involved. The other villagers smelled it, and were happy to move away into their new houses.'

'What were they like the new houses?

'They were very nice. Not the usual instant steel and cement. Then I could have had grounds to complain. No. They were made in the old way with stones which were then limewashed white. A new village made to look old. I have to confess that I cannot complain about the construction. It was done with taste and care. As only money can buy.'

Paul would get on well with Henry, thought Josh. They could attack the rich and bewail the ills of capitalism.

'You don't like Mr Leotakis?' he asked Henry. Henry raised his eyebrows and threw up his hands in horror.

'Like him? I loathe the man. You know what his name used to be? The Pirate. And don't imagine some romantic Johnny Depp bandana-ed version of the name. This was corporate piracy, learned from his mentor and later rival, Onassis. No,' he repeated. 'I don't like him. I fundamentally disapprove of the kind of money that thinks it can buy the world.'

Amen to that, thought Pam. Hope I don't have to meet this man myself. She cleared her throat and prepared the next level of questions.

'So what you're saying is that while Stephanie could be brave and even praiseworthy, she did her own thing.'

'And she didn't mind who got hurt along the way. Yes. That is exactly what I am saying. And yes, she was exasperating and difficult and sometimes behaved very badly indeed, but we all forgave her. Because she was also generous and funny and thoughtful and kind. We got over it.'

'Somebody didn't,' Pam commented quietly.

'No. Somebody let their anger fester and build. I mean you would have to be simply seething to stab a cat. Poor Skimble. I miss him.'

Are you describing yourself, thought Pam watching him. Has all this been to distract us from thinking about you as the killer?

'Can you think of anyone who might still be that angry?'

'This is what I've been writing down on the train today. There was a student whose work she was said to have stolen. But that's really Colin's era. You will have to ask him.'

'Yes. We know about him.'

'Ah. Then there's Petros. He's furious the way the media have made out that this excavation was Stephanie's. Apart from finding the urn, she didn't run the excavation at all. That was Petros and Irini. They co-ordinated the international teams and ran the site. Brilliantly. And Petros, himself, found the bull. The Greek press have credited him, but here it is all about Stephanie. As if she's a new Arthur Evans. He was the archaeologist who uncovered the famous site at Knossos, by the way. Which today is made up of cement and a disturbed imagination. Pleases the tourists though.'

'Petros was in Athens yesterday.'

'Ah. Well that leaves Tim Bayers.'

'And he is?'

'He's the man who spent his entire life looking for the palace of Roussolakos, as the site at Chiona used to be called. Retired now, but had a nervous breakdown I heard when it was discovered. If any man wanted to kill Stephanie, I would say that it was him. He was fanatical about the palace, sure it existed. As indeed it did, but further north and east from previous excavations.'

'And where does he live?'

'Somewhere in England. Irini would know. I'm sure he still sends her emails.'

'You don't have Irini's contact details, do you by any chance?'

'No. I don't, I'm afraid. Probably on my rolodex back home. Still, it will be on Stephanie's phone if you have that.'

'Of course. Thank you.'

Josh nodded. His next job, he thought. Get all the names from her phone.

'Just one more question, Mr Cox?' Pam was at her most relaxed. She's letting him think he's merely a useful witness, thought Josh and not a possible suspect.

'I wonder whether we could talk money. You've known Stephanie all these years yet it doesn't appear that she ever had what might be called a proper job.'

'But she still could live. You're right. She never earned anything very much even from her latest projects. Her fabric workshops.' He stopped. 'Do you mind if I get a glass of water? It's very hot here today even though we are in the shade.'

'Of course.'

'And would you, both?'

'We're fine, thank you.' Pam, however, took advantage of his absence to take a quick swig from the water bottle in her bag. Just as well I didn't put on a jacket, she thought. She and Josh were both in short-sleeved shirts.

Henry came back with water into which, Pam notices, he'd dropped some ice and a slice of lemon. He most certainly did feel at home in this house.

'Stephanie had talent which I believe was never fully realised. I think she could have been an artist with the right encouragement. There were things in Stephanie's past. Her mother above all – her father had died when she was young. He left Stephanie a small amount, and when her mother died, she got the rest. I think her mother died rather conveniently around the time of the divorce. It enabled her to buy this house from Colin.'

'Right. That's very helpful.'

'Not unlike my own story. You are almost certainly

wondering how is it that an eminent historian like myself did not choose to become an academic. I did, naturally, consider it. I came here to study as a young man in 1963. My parents died when I was a small child and my father, who had been a teacher, had also been a follower of the stock exchange. He had put a small nest egg in a company that became IBM and it had grown substantially. That was what I inherited. I didn't care for things like the stock market, I still don't, but I did like this City and thought I might well live here one day. Property then cost very little here. I bought up a small terrace of three run-down houses and let them to my own college as student or staff accommodation. That has provided me with a comfortable income my entire life. Today, it is more than comfortable, it even allows for small luxuries.'

He smiled and Pam was about to thank him when he continued his rambling monologue.

'Why didn't I stay here or take a post at another university? I will tell you. When I was at school, I realised early on that my passion was for my own sex. At school, such things were not only acceptable but expected. And here, too, in Cambridge among students. Yet this was, back then, an illegal act. I felt the danger and it made me shrivel. So I, along with many of my generation, moved to Greece where foreigners were exempt from personal scrutiny as long as these things happened discreetly.'

'Basically, we were a group of fairly happy buggers. I was shy, unlike some. But I met one or two men, and fell in love with one of them,' he concluded. 'But that is not a story for today.'

Henry sat back. He had said what he wanted to say. He waited for the response. No further questions he thought, applause, thank you, good afternoon.

'Thank you, Mr Cox,' Pam said. Strange how she thought of him as Henry. Perhaps because that was how he had been introduced to her by Jen and then Mike. Was the one he'd loved Laurent, the man Stephanie had been engaged to? It seemed likely. But Henry was right. This was not something she needed to question today.

'Since you were in Cambridge the night of the murder, could I ask you to come by the station later and give us your fingerprints so that we can eliminate you from that side of our inquiries?'

Henry smiled graciously. 'Certainly, my dear. I will treat myself to a cold beer at the Free Press,' he said. 'And after that I will come by the Station. Is there anyone I should ask for?'

'If you think you've forgotten anything that might be useful, do ask for me,' said Pam giving him her card. 'But I shall leave a message with the sergeant on duty at the front desk and someone there will take your prints. It only takes a moment.'

'Then that is what I shall do.' Henry jumped up and walked them to the front door. He had a stiff way of walking, but walked in long strides as though he was used to walking long distances, she thought. He was strong, she thought, and he was also a most eloquent liar.

CHAPTER 19

The traffic began to pile up after they left the A14 and began to crawl into Ipswich. They were behind a red Golf whose driver believed that the way to drive in heavy traffic was to hit the accelerator, leap forward and then jam on the brakes. Paul ached to get out and tell him how to drive. He could feel the tension build between his shoulders and wondered whether Shona was up for a back massage later that evening. She wasn't the brightest in the bunch, but he enjoyed her company in small doses.

'I like Ipswich,' commented Roberta, 'it's a real town. Not a giant university with a few locals allowed.'

'You sound like me.'

'Well, occasionally you talk sense. I get sick of being talked down to in Cambridge. Went to a party once – one of Simon's friends – and this woman, face like a squeezed lemon, comes up to me and first question is which was my college. When I told her I was a police officer, her 'oh' went through the octaves. Like I was some lesser species she'd never encountered before. Or shit on her shoe.'

'Snobby cow,' agreed Paul. 'Hate them. Brass can be as bad.'

'At least there's nothing of that with the boss.'

'No. Not in the least. Don't we turn left somewhere here?'

'Yes. Another two streets, and then it's left and then right.'

Paul slowed down, and prepared to make the turn when his phone rang. He pulled in between a couple of parked vans and answered it.

'Paul?' said Sue. 'Seems that your bloke Kieron has had a few enforced stays in St Clement's, which was the local mental hospital before they decided to make it into luxury housing. I'm repeating what our new IT man, Stuart, just rang through. He thought you might find that helpful.'

'Very much so,' said Paul.

'Very useful,' agreed Roberta.

'Hi, Roberta, enjoying the glorious sights of Ipswich?'

'Not so much,' said Roberta. 'I was hoping for a cocktail on the Waterfront, but we're the other end of town.'

Sue laughed, and they drove on down past a couple of garages, a DIY store, and through a twist of roads of mixed flats and terraces until they found themselves in a small road with a couple of houses and several bungalows. Towards the end of this was one whose owner clearly didn't share the gardening skills of his neighbours. The overgrown grass was interspersed with ivy, cow parsley and brambles. A few dandelions offered a touch of colour.

'This looks like chummy, let's see whether he's home,' said Roberta, leading the way. They'd decided to go for a soft approach and let her take the lead. She knocked firmly, but not aggressively, and after a short time the door opened very slowly.

'Yes?' The man facing them filled more than the doorway. He must be about twenty-five stone, thought Roberta, and that track suit looks as though it hasn't been washed since the millennium.

'Mr James?' she asked. 'My name is Detective Sergeant Roberta Stills and this is Detective Constable Paul Collins. May we come in?'

'Why?' Kieron James's face was red, as if he'd been rubbing it, and clusters of spots showed between a fuzz of his hardly-shaved beard. He glared at them as if daring them to arrest him.

'Because we think you could be a very valuable witness. We're investigating the death of Stephanie Michaels, and believe that you are someone who knew what she was really like.'

The former student's face changed from suspicion to pleasure. He smiled at them and opened the door fully, allowing the smell to hit them as they followed him inside. Stale sweat, cigarette smoke and urine. Please God, Roberta thought, almost gagging, I hope we don't have to sit on a sofa.

'If those overalls were normal size he'd never have got them on,' Paul whispered.

'No. Don't see him as our man. Doubt if he ever goes out, but we might as well use him for background now we're here.'

'The thing you have to understand about Stephanie is how plausible she was.' Kieron was off almost before they'd had time to sit down. 'She could make you think she was your best friend, someone who mattered to her. But then she'd use you and discard you. Behaviour like that isn't a one-off. She totally fucked my life, but I'll bet you the lottery win I'll never get that she's done the same to somebody else.'

'I'm certain you're right,' said Roberta trying to push the chair cushion to one side. To her horror, it was wringing wet as if he'd poured sweat into it. 'Maybe you could tell us what happened.'

Kieron James hesitated for a moment as if uncertain which version of his story to tell and then he got up from his couch with considerable effort and waddled over to a bookshelf on the other side of the room. Roberta had no idea how long he'd been living in this house, but there were few signs of anything personal. It could have been any dosshouse that he'd been using. The cream woodchip wallpaper was peeling and there were black mould stains under the window. The only exception to the impersonality of the room was a bookcase crammed with box files. He removed one and opened it.

I do hope he's not going to expect us to read his dissertation, thought Roberta. But Kieron handed her a photograph. It showed a slim young man with thick brown hair and a happy smile. It took her a good few minutes to realise that this had once been the fat man in front of her. He was, how old, fifty-seven, but looked a good ten years older than that.

'I didn't always look like this, you know. So I want you to think about me as I was then and not how I am now. This is what a nervous breakdown, mental illness and a lot of prescription drugs do to you.'

And a lifetime of junk food, thought Paul, vowing to give up his takeaway Chinese and go running again.

'I was studying archaeology in Cambridge, and Stephanie was in my seminar group. She was about ten years older than me, and had so much more field experience than any of us, apart from the lecturers of course. And she had all these drawings from a dig in Crete. That's what she used to do, drawings of objects. But she never came across as someone who knew it all, the opposite in fact. She was all, "I've just been lucky". But then she always was a lucky cow.'

Roberta almost expected him to spit. He was clearly angry enough to have killed Stephanie, he just didn't look physically able to have carried it out. Unless he'd got someone else to do it for him. That was one for the new IT guy.

'It was one of the words she used all the time. How so much archaeology was a matter of luck. Most people thought it was study and hard work. But then they didn't find the Chiona treasure.'

'Lucky' was how Stephanie had described her Chiona find in an article he'd just read, thought Paul. She'd been lucky all her life. Until she suddenly got very unlucky.

'You clearly were someone who believed in the study side,' Roberta smiled at Keiron and he smiled back, clearly unused to flattery.

'I was. I was set to get a First. All my papers and essays had got top marks. And there she is, coming round with a bottle of red and asking whether she could look at the work I'd done on flora designs in Greek pottery. That was my dissertation. How the medicinal use of Greek herbs was suggested in their representations. And she'd brought me copies of her own drawings for me to use in an appendix. I thought that was so kind of her. So, had no problem giving her a carbon copy of my bibliography. All my references with the quotes needed for my dissertation.'

'And that's what she stole.'

'Every bit of it.'

But not his actual dissertation, thought Roberta. Not what he's subsequently accused her of stealing. Rather different.

'So then what happened?' asked Paul.

'She gave in her dissertation. And got a First. Just happened that I had an extension. I hadn't been well that term. No. Time to be honest. I went a bit off the rails, drinking too much. Cambridge isn't easy when you've got a working-class background like mine. But I got myself together and submitted. That's when they accused me of plagiarism. Said all my citations...'

'Citations?' asked Paul.

'Quotes. You have to back up your opinions and facts with evidence. Like you lot do. So you have to put in lots of quotes from other sources. As I did. Only madam had got in first with all the ones I'd shown her. Thing is, her opinions based on them were rubbish compared with mine. But the university refused to take that into consideration. I accused her, and she denied it. They believed her and not me and I got sent down. She became an archaeologist.'

'No wonder you were angry.'

'It was so much more than angry. Stephanie Michaels destroyed my life. I knew I'd never be able to work as an archaeologist after that. And it's all I'd ever wanted to do. I've been on sickness benefit ever since. Actually been hospitalised a couple of times.'

'I'm sorry,' said Roberta.

'And now the bitch is dead. And no, I didn't kill her though I'd buy a drink for whoever did. Probably one of her own kind who got jealous.'

'You mean another archaeologist?'

'No. I mean another Jew. You did know she was Jewish?'

Oh shit, I don't like where this is going, thought Roberta, catching Paul's eye. I have to stop it.

'I have to warn you, Kieron,' she told him, 'that any expression of hatred toward someone on account of their race is regarded as a hate crime, and I'd suggest that you say no more on that subject.'

'You're all the same, aren't you?' he replied, spitting out the words. A very different man from the one they'd previously witnessed. 'All part of the same fucking Zionist plot. Not enough you kill Princess Diana, the greatest pure Englishwoman who ever lived, you have to protect all the bloody...

'Stop it right there, Kieron!' Paul stood over him. 'Do you really want us to arrest you?'

Kieron shrank back into the sofa, which sagged beneath him.

'Fuck off! Fuck off the both of you. You know shit about shit. It's all out there. Like the way the Jew Duveen took over the art market and destroyed the Elgin Marbles. They've been building up all the world's wealth for centuries. You lot don't even want to know. You should read what Adrestia says about that. She knows all about the marbles, all about the plots to steal the world's resources.'

'We'll let ourselves out,' said Paul.

Roberta nodded to Paul and walked quickly back to the car.

'Yuck,' said Roberta, reaching in her bag for a packet of wet wipes. She pulled one out and wiped her hands with it. 'Let's stop at the first service station we see so I can wash my hands. This isn't doing the job.'

'Fine,' he agreed. 'And I could use a strong cup of tea to get that stink out of my nose.'

'Seems that Kieron's not our guy.' Roberta stuffed the

dirty wipe into an evidence bag to dispose of later. 'That's another to take off the board.'

'Unless he fired up one of his nasty group. What about... did you get the name?'

'Adrestia, I think. Could be a useful lead. I don't think he meant to tell us. But certainly one for IT.'

'Yes,' he agreed. 'I'll jot it down.' Paul pulled out his phone and wrote down the name.

'You know, Paul,' she said as Paul efficiently did a three-point turn and started back towards Cambridge. 'We seem to be eliminating a lot of suspects very quickly. I mean we got a lot almost immediately, but we're ticking them off one after the other. God knows what we'll do next if they all turn out to be clear.'

'Not the kind of case you want dragging on,' agreed Paul. 'Did you know that there's the likelihood of the brass closing down our department?'

'What! No. No I didn't. How come you know?'

'Contacts,' he said. 'Charm.'

'Charm? No. You've been bugging the Super's office.'

'That would be fun. No. But the leak did come from him. Conversation he had with the Chief Constable, or rather the other way round. And the Super, all pissed off about it, slips this information to Julia when she's typing up one of his reports.'

'And Julia murmured this along with other sweet nothings across the pillow.'

'Not quite. I did take her for a drink. She likes the boss and thought it was awful. Everything the boss has worked for is now wrapped up in this case, Paul. She'd probably get another posting, maybe even promotion, but..'

'But not run a team like this? Don't see her wanting another straight DI post, back doing the nitty gritty. Or even a DCI. She'd hate it. She's worked so bloody hard for this.'

'Do you think she knows?'

'I don't know. Possibly. Have you seen how tense she is?'

'Yes. Thought it was just the case and the publicity. But

come to think of it.'

'We'll just have to solve the case then, won't we?'

Paul began typing the moment he got back into the office. He typed up the notes from the interview with Kieron James, and then paused when he came to the name he'd mentioned at the end. Adrestia, was that it? He typed it into Google.

'Roberta, come here a moment,' he called.

Roberta looked up from her own day's notes and came across to his desk.

'Remember that name, Adrestia?'

'Yup. Why?'

'Look at this. She's a Greek goddess of retribution. Her name means "the one from whom there is no escape" Does that sound like revenge?'

'Retribution, revenge. Like a vendetta. We have to tell the boss about this.'

'Tell the boss about what?' asked Pam breezing into the room with a box of doughnuts.

Roberta opened the box and sank her teeth into the sugar and jam. Just as well that she never put on weight.

'Retribush...' she mumbled. She swallowed. 'Paul will tell you.'

'To sum up our afternoon, boss. Kieron James isn't our perp, though he is a kind of poisonous slug. Must be well over twenty stone and can hardly walk. Everything he does is online.'

'Like the Elgin Marbles man.'

'Except that the Elgin Marbles man might be a woman. Something slug man slipped out just at the end of our interview. And they may be meeting online. He was boasting about those who might want to kill Dr Michaels and gave us this name Adrestia and look...'

He showed Pam the description.

'Could be something. So scrub Kieron as the perp, but let's keep an eye on him online. Can you pass this on to Stuart, Paul. I'll be glad when he's actually here working for us full time. Looks like online communications are going to be vital again. Oh, and ask him if there's anything that jumps out about Henry Cox.'

'You're liking Cox as a perp, boss?' asked Roberta.

'I don't like being lied to, and I'm absolutely certain that what Josh and I just witnessed was a brilliant smokescreen. And he was in Cambridge on Monday night.'

'Monday night?' echoed Paul. 'Where was he?'

'According to Mr Cox, he was asleep on the sofa of Dr Michaels' house, after which he returned to London first thing the following morning. His timeline makes it completely feasible that he was our killer. So we need to delve further. Right,' she turned to the room in general. 'Have Forensics sent down Dr Michaels' bag and contents?'

'On your desk, boss,' Sue told her. Josh followed Pam into her office where she sat down and opened the large, sealed plastic evidence bag containing Stephanie's handbag. The bag was more of a basket made of a woven kilim-like material, lined in cotton and with a strong zip. Pam could imagine having one as a beach bag. It was big enough for a towel, but you could also zip away your purse. She shook out the rest of the contents of the bag onto her desk.

'Okay,' she said, opening a drawer and snapping on a pair of latex gloves. 'I think the used tissues and chocolate wrappers can go straight back into the bag. Good taste in chocolate, though,' she added. 'Charbonnel et Walker. Expensive.'

Apart from the used tissues and some stray euro coins, two ancient cough sweets covered with the fuzz of time, three pens, two pencils, and a couple of small paintbrushes, there was a small hairbrush, two lipsticks, a stick of mascara and crumpled receipts and torn pages from a notebook. There was also an iPad in a battered leather case, a phone, a green leather wallet and Stephanie's passport. Pam returned everything except the paper, the wallet, the receipts, the iPad and the phone to the bag and sealed it again in the evidence bag.

'We can use the receipts for a timeline,' she told Josh. 'If you can make a start on that, I'll write up the phone messages. And ask Roberta to go through the emails. They may be on the phone or on the iPad. '

'Or both,' suggested Josh.

'Doesn't matter if they are. The more brains we put on this the better.'

She gave Josh a fresh evidence bag for the receipts and notes and he took it back to his desk. She turned to the phone. As Larry had told her, it didn't have a password. She began to make a list.

'This is where you live, Stephanie,' she told the dead woman. 'People think it's in people's memories and recollections, all of which are unreliable, but here this is you and your world, and it's highly likely that one of these people killed you.'

She looked down the list. Not a huge number of contacts for a long life. And not many calls on the day she died. But there was one incoming call. A number, not named as a person, a Cambridge number. Worth a quick check, she thought, as she typed it in.

The result came back instantly. It was one of the old public phone boxes in Silver Street. She got up and called Josh.

'Can you add Silver Street at three pm, to your list re CCTV. I have a feeling that this was the call from the person she was going to meet. She rang Jen shortly afterwards. Let's find out whether there's a camera nearby. Don't see the point in getting dabs, they'll be far too many and we have his fingerprints.'

'But if his prints are there, then we'll know it was his call.'

'Good point. Can you ring Larry. Oh he's going to love us!'

She went back inside her office and returned to the phone. A few numbers here and there. But there was one person in Stephanie's life who was most definitely there. Nikos Leotakis. There were five numbers. Nikos mobile; Nikos,

Dorset; Nikos, Sitia; Nikos NY; Nikos, Paris. Just numbers Stephanie needed to keep in touch with him or more? What had Henry said? Very friendly.

Pam knew that thirty-three percent of women killed in the UK had been murdered by partners or ex-partners. Normally, the first place you looked was the home. Was the bull thing simply a distraction? Could Leotakis have organised Stephanie's death? It didn't make sense, not least because it had tainted his gallery, and that seemed to mean a great deal to him. So someone wanting to get at the billionaire? Someone who knew they were close and hated him? Or hated that fact? Someone who was jealous?

She needed to talk with Nikos Leotakis.

CHAPTER 20

'Anyone need some ointment?' Pam asked, holding out a jar of Temple of Heaven. 'It's like Vick, but doesn't stink so much afterwards.'

Derek, the police photographer, nodded gratefully, and Pam passed him the jar.

'You'll want to wash your hands after that,' laughed Dave. 'Just in case...'

'Think Derek has other use for his hands right now, Dave, unlike an older wanker like you,' Larry interrupted, seeing Derek blush.

'This your first? Pam asked him.

'No,' he said. 'But my first murder. Last one was a car crash.'

'Just concentrate on thinking of it as a job, thinking that your pictures make it easier for us to catch the bastard.'

'Thanks, Guv,' he replied, going over to the small sink, and washing his hands thoroughly.

The mortuary at Addenbrookes Hospital needed more than a fresh coat of paint. They'd been talking of updating it for ages, but on the principle that the dead didn't care and weren't going to complain on social media, it always dropped down the list. Nobody could ever do anything about the smell, though. Pam was wearing jeans and a T-shirt that could go straight in the wash afterwards. She'd come here straight from home after, what was for her these days, an amazingly long sleep. Six whole hours from eleven to five which was when she'd got up and continued her constant note-taking. Somewhere among all the different facts was the one piece of information that would lead to the killer. There was always that sense she was missing something.

Lists. And more lists. Keep on top of it all. And a whole chunk of this morning was Stephanie's autopsy. She'd phoned round the previous evening to make sure that everyone knew the time. But there they all were, sitting on those uncomfortable plastic chairs, waiting to go through and join Zofia and her anatomical pathology technician, or APT, who would do most of the actual cutting.

It was one of those things that puzzled Pam on the rare occasions when she watched a TV detective programme. Why did they always show the forensic pathologist working alone? Or solving crimes for that matter. It was like the way the paperwork was swept away. If only she could, she reflected, having spent three hours the previous evening writing up the latest stages of her logs that had to include links to the transcripts of her briefings and all initial intelligence reports. It wasn't surprising that lawyers used suitcases to bring case notes to court. One day, somebody should write down how many trees were cut down to provide the paper for a single homicide. Still, it felt safer than just having everything online. She had a permanent nagging fear than one day everything they had online would crash and disappear into the ether.

Being a homicide post-mortem rather than the usual coroner-requested autopsy, the full team had to be there. Josh could have taken her role as deputy SIO, but she always felt she owed it to the victim for her to be there to make sure nothing got missed. But with Zofia in charge she knew that was highly improbable.

As they waited, Pam made notes from the notes she'd made the previous afternoon. Possibles, she'd written: Henry – there was something this man was hiding, could it be that he was jealous about Stephanie's friendship with Leotakis?

Then there was the archaeologist, Tim Bayers, she needed to talk to someone about him. Ring Irini, she wrote now and circled it. George. Yes. Why had he run away? Was it related or had he just freaked out? Talk to Anna again and get Josh to have another chat with Mark Kitson. And then there was this Greek marbles woman with a name that meant revenge. That would be for Stuart to investigate. And he needed to check on Kieron's online activity, too.

Nikos Leotakis. She couldn't ignore him now. She pulled out the sheet of paper where she'd copied the list of Stephanie's contacts. Later she'd ask Mike to ring all the Greek numbers Stephanie had rung over the past two weeks that didn't have names attached to them. She suspected they'd all be in Crete and that would save her a lot of time, as well as having to bring him in as translator. That meant she had to trust Mike. She stopped for a moment and doodled a couple of question marks beside his name. He was a police officer, even if no longer working. But he also had links with Leotakis, who'd conveniently brought him on board. But if the people he spoke to were all in Crete, it couldn't affect the case that much, could it?

She didn't want to have that conversation with Murton, but she might discuss it with Josh. End of the day, though, it was her decision.

She sighed and went back to her list. Stephanie didn't have a huge number of recent calls which made the job easier, but she'd been surprised to see her brother Jeffrey's number on the list. And so, almost out of curiosity as well as everything else, she'd rung him.

His wife had answered the phone with a perfunctory 'Hello', and Pam instantly had a feeling that this was customary, this man didn't answer his home phone. In the background she heard an irritated golf-club voice asking who it was.

'It's a Detective Inspector someone for you,' the woman replied curtly, and Pam heard a clunk as she put down the receiver. They had an old-style telephone to match their behaviour.

'Yes?'

'Is that Mr Jeffrey Michaels?'

'And you are?' he replied.

'I'm Detective Inspector Pam Gregory of the East Anglian Special Operations Unit,' she began.

'Yes?' He sounded bored, as if she'd announced she was selling some dodgy financial product.

'May I ask? Are you the brother of Dr Stephanie Michaels?'

The man sighed. 'I thought one of your people might contact us regarding this recent unpleasantness. I imagined it would be a senior local officer who had the courtesy to drop by, not merely a phone call.'

'I was actually ringing to ask whether it would be convenient for a member of my team to drop by and talk.'

'Really? Well, the answer's no. It would not be convenient in the least. As far as I'm concerned, my sister stopped existing some fifty years ago.'

'Does that mean you haven't spoken to her within the past fifty years?'

There was a long pause. He's wondering whether lying over the telephone to a police officer is against the law. She wished it was.

'Well,' he cleared his throat and she could hear a lifetime of smoking. 'As it happens I did speak to her a couple of weeks ago.'

'Can you tell me what it concerned? This is a murder inquiry,' she added.

'Well it was nothing to do with that. It was this new gallery. My wife saw that Prince Charles was going and... well... you know what women are like. I telephoned a young man at the Museum and asked whether he could put my wife and me on the guest list.'

'Would that be Dr Mark Kitson?'

'It might have been. Can't recall. In any case, it never happened. I got a telephone call from my sister and I have to say she was extremely rude.'

I bet she was. Pam was beginning to develop a sense of Stephanie; she wouldn't have minced her words.

'Was there a reason why your sister's feelings towards you might have been negative?'

'No real reason. You have to understand that Stephanie was a spoilt child who became a spoilt adult. And she nursed grudges in a most unpleasant way. Apparently she held it against me that I'd stopped her from going to art school. Can't think why she wanted to go, anyway. As I told her back then, her mother's money would not be well spent on someone who was all artistic temperament and no ability. I was quoting her mother back at her, you understand. It was what she used to tell Stephanie.'

'However, Stephanie did inherit your mother's money on her death?'

'Nothing I could do to stop that. Her solicitor made that clear. Fifty-fifty, me and her. Even after everything she'd put our mother through. The drugs, the drink. Running off with some Frenchman. The lawyer said no court would even consider it. But that's lawyers all over.'

So he tried. Interesting. Was it worth looking at his bank accounts? But why would he write in Greek? And the theatricality of the posed body; that didn't fit.

'She hardly ever talked with our mother, but there it was,' he continued. 'She got half the estate. Straight down the line. Talking of wills, I suppose Stephanie did leave one?'

'I am not at liberty to discuss that, Mr Michaels, but I can tell you that we believe she did employ the same solicitor and I am sure they will be able to give you the details.'

Jeffery Michaels responded with a sound that could only be described as a harrumph. Where did these people come from? No wonder Stephanie cut all ties with them.

'Is there anything else you can tell me about your sister?' asked Pam.

'Nothing at all. So don't waste the taxpayers' money on petrol coming down here. As I said, my sister and I inhabited different worlds, and I am not merely speaking geographically. I had nothing to do with her while she was alive, and I have nothing to say about her now she is dead.'

He paused for a moment.

'Is that all?'

'For the moment, it is. Do you wish to know when the funeral will take place?'

'That won't be necessary. Goodbye Inspector.'

The funeral. She hadn't thought about the funeral? Normally a few officers would go to observe as well as pay respects. But where would it take place? In Crete? Why hadn't she thought of this before.

Sitting in this bleak waiting room beside the mortuary, Pam began to think about the men in the Stephanie's life. Her father had died when she was young and her mother had been, by all accounts, a cold narcissistic woman. The brother who could have offered her affection was a domineering bully. So where had she found love? Laurent, the Frenchman, who'd introduced her to archaeology, but died the day they got engaged. Colin, who'd built her the beautiful house. To whom she'd been unfaithful, if Jen was to be believed. Were there others? Leotakis? But surely not at their age.

She turned over the page of her notebook and wrote: 'Questions for Colin Nichols.' She and Josh would be driving to Putney on Friday, and she didn't want to waste the meeting. A pity she couldn't combine it with an interview with the archaeologist, Tim Bayers. But they still didn't know where he lived. Which reminded her she had to ring Irini. Which she'd just circled.

That was enough. She was going round in circles herself. There was too much information, too many people, but no clear facts leading to the murder and no forensics that were any use.

She gave a deep sigh and caught Dave's eye.

'Early days, boss,' he said. 'Too early to start beating yourself up.'

A few minutes later, the APT came through and told them that Zofia was ready. Like the pathologist, she was fully masked up in scrubs, apron, wellington boots, protective face mask and gauntlets over her gloves. She handed Derek a full set of protective clothing and they all waited as he covered himself in the thin blue plastic. The police team, apart from Derek, merely wore overalls and shoe covers as they were the other side of the glass screen from the mortuary examination room.

The procedure was always the same.

'How does an autopsy begin?' a pathologist asked at a lecture Pam once attended. 'You don't begin with the scalpel, you begin with the deceased. You begin with the paperwork.'

And so it always was. Zofia read the request she'd received from the coroner and then from her own scene of crime report. This was followed by the APT's notes. The name of the deceased, Dr Stephanie Michaels and her height, weight, any scars, or visible identification marks. Stephanie was five foot five inches and weighed ten and a half stone, but it would have been more, Zofia told them, before blood loss. There was a small scar on her right index finger, possibly a recently-healed paper cut and a dark mole on her back.

'If her doctor had seen that, he'd have been requesting a biopsy,' said Zofia. 'Comes from living in the Mediterranean. I'll examine it myself for the record, of course.'

Pam tried to tune out as the autopsy continued. She only wanted to concentrate on the things that were relevant to the inquiry. The state of Stephanie's liver – thickly covered with fat and showing signs of significant alcohol use – were not surprising. Everyone had said that she drank.

'What the liver shows us is non-alcoholic fatty liver disease, which, contrary to its name, is a condition that is caused by drinking as well as other factors. She may have had hepatitis at some point, too. '

'She did according to her friend, Henry,' said Pam.

'If you look here, you can see the fibrosis, where persistent inflammation has created scar tissue around the liver and nearby blood vessels, but it would appear that she continued to drink to excess and there is now clear evidence of cirrhosis. This happens after years of inflammation, you can see how the liver has shrunk. It's extremely scarred and lumpy. I would say from looking at this that Dr Michael's liver would have given out within the next six months. She was extremely unwell. And now, to what did kill her.'

Zofia moved around to the head and pointed out the abrasions. 'As you can see here from the depth of the wound, there is clear evidence of blunt force trauma. She was struck by a hard object which, from the fragments,' she picked up a minute particle of stone with tweezers, 'appears to have been stone.'

'For the record, it was a piece of marble tile,' said Larry. 'We've recovered it along with fragments of the victim's hair, blood and skin.'

'Thank you, Larry. This matches what we have here. As you can see from where the wound was, here on the side of her head, and how the wound penetrates the brain, this would have been a fatal head injury. Dr Michaels was already dying when she was stabbed. The killer was behind her and I would estimate that he or she was significantly taller. Probably at least six foot.

'There was a quantity of blood on the floor,' said Larry. 'If she'd shut down, wouldn't she have stopped bleeding?

'Yes, if she was dead. But I would estimate that as she was stabbed, she was dying. Almost certainly unconscious. But as to the extensive blood spatter, after the stabbing there was an open arterial wound. I imagine this cut to the chest. And this would have spurted everywhere as the killer lifted her up and placed her on to the bull.'

'There were little drops, big sprays and pools all over the floor,' confirmed Larry, 'which all tie in with an arterial bleed. Very Tarantino.'

The second time that director's been mentioned in relation to these killings, thought Pam.

The pathologist moved around the body and pointed to the many lines of incisions. There were eight stab wounds. All done within a few seconds of each other.

'I would suggest that the actions were frenzied,' commented Zofia. 'The killer stood over the victim, who was on the floor, and stabbed from this angle.'

'The murderer had put on a chemical haz suit which he discarded later in the cloakroom,' noted Larry.

'That is interesting,' replied Zofia. 'If you are asking me whether he had time to put this on between hitting her on the head and beginning the stabbing, while allowing that she remained alive, I would say that if he was quick, yes.'

'It doesn't seem likely that he'd have walked in wearing it, does it?' said Pam.

'There are no signs of any struggle,' agreed Zofia. 'No bruises, which one might expect if she had fought off an attacker. The evidence would suggest he was standing beside her when he attacked. Now for the wounds themselves.'

It had been a partly serrated knife, the kind you can buy in any camping shop, Pam learned, and as Zofia had previously examined the cat, she could confirm that the blade was almost certainly the same.

One killer. That was a relief. And a planner.

'That's what I keep thinking,' said Larry, as he and Pam joined Zofia in her office afterwards for a welcome coffee.

'Have you talked about the case with Grace?' asked Pam. Grace, Zofia's wife, was a clinical psychotherapist, and Pam would have welcomed the opportunity to discuss the case with her. Unfortunately, if she wanted to bring in a forensic psychologist to do a profile on the killer, it would be the current man who was already on the police payroll.

Anything rather than consult Adam, she thought. He always thought he knew everything and never listened. It was one reason Pam had not yet asked for him to join her team.

'Of course we have,' replied Zofia. 'The whole of England is discussing this case.'

'Please don't tell me that,' Pam groaned. 'And they all think they could do better than me.'

'I couldn't tell her much, naturally, but we did discuss the way the killer had attacked both the cat and Stephanie, and she said you should look for a recent trigger.'

'That's helpful,' replied Pam.

'She also was interested in the way the body had been displayed.'

'What did she think?' asked Larry, who also had a high opinion of Grace's perception.

'She said it reminded her of one of those Greek tragedies. You know, Euripides.'

Larry nodded. Pam remembered a play that Zofia had taken her to in one of the colleges. She hadn't really understood it; there had been lots of wailing and shouting. Battles between gods and families, she thought.

'Families destroyed because it was the will of the gods,' she suggested. Zofia gave her a warm smile.

'You've nailed it,' she said. 'That's your case.'

'Well, that makes Pam's life easy,' said Larry. 'All she has to do is find a Greek god.'

Pam laughed. 'Just drop by Mount Olympus and make a quick arrest.'

Zofia joined in the laughter, but she watched Pam carefully. Her friend was unusually tense; this case was taking a great deal out of her.

'Sure,' she said. 'Now think metaphorically. Think of how this murder was enacted. And it was. Grace put her finger on it. It was acted out. Your killer planned this. He brought the haz suit and the knife, just as he had somehow obtained the keys of Stephanie's house when he let himself in.

Now, normally, when you have a killer who is calculated and cold and plans every detail, you're thinking of an assassin. Someone who assassinates a president or a king. It's cold. It's forensic.'

'And this was planned, clearly,' agreed Pam. 'There's a lot that's odd about this case, like leaving fingerprints behind and sleeping in the museum. Presuming he did sleep.'

'That's something Grace mentioned. You don't sleep if you're still angry and pumped up. If he lay down and slept...'

'It certainly looked as though he did,' Larry commented. 'We know he laid down, he left traces. Whether he slept or not...'

'Then he must have felt he'd done what he had to do,' finished Zofia.

'It was a staged murder,' said Larry. 'He wanted the world to know what he'd done. As for his dabs, they're not on record, and I'm pretty certain our perp knows that.'

'Grace also said there was something almost triumphant about how he placed Stephanie. As if killing her was something to be celebrated. Like the death of a tyrant in a play.'

'But from everything I'm learning about Stephanie, she was difficult and annoyed a lot of people, but that doesn't sound like her. People seemed to like her.'

'The killer really hated her,' warned Zofia. 'The furious way he stabbed her was anything but cold. He was in a frenzy.'

'Like those Greek plays,' said Pam thoughtfully. 'Vendetta. Now Mike,' she told them, 'that's the cop we're using as a translator who lives out there – though I'm not sure if he is still a cop – talked about families destroying each other. Just like those plays. And talking of Greek gods...Oh, my god. I'm so stupid!'

'What?' called Zofia as Pam picked up her bag and ran to the door.

'I need to make some phone calls,' she replied.

CHAPTER 21

It was something along the lines that a person meets his destiny on the road he took to avoid it. Mike couldn't remember where he read it. Perhaps it was stuck on the wall on one of the hippy houses where they used to go to smoke dope during those years undercover. They inevitably had copies of Desiderata and stuff like that pinned up on a kitchen noticeboard.

Mike felt close to punching the wall, but decided to go for a walk instead. He thought he'd come to Crete to get away from police work, but here he was again investigating a crime. Only this time it was murder, he wasn't part of the team and he'd been very close to the victim. He was surprised they'd allowed him on to the case and could well understand the initial hesitancy of the DI, even though she tried not to show it. Though as far as the Cambridge cops were concerned, he wasn't on the case. Just facilitating their work and doing a bit of translation. But that wasn't what Leotakis wanted.

Nikos had phoned him within two hours of Stephanie's body being found and Mike hadn't been able to say no. He had, at least, refused to take any money for his work, he knew instinctively, that he didn't want to be on Nikos's payroll, but if he was honest with himself, he wanted to find out who killed Stephanie just as much as Leotakis did.

As far as DI Gregory was concerned, it was clearly just another murder and he'd felt irrationally angry about that.

He'd even put down the phone without saying goodbye, which wasn't like him. He'd find a time to apologise later. But she didn't know how the whole thing made him feel. The last thing he wanted was to have to think of himself again as a cop. Which raised the question why he went on taking the money. Because they owed him big time for their total fuck-up? Because if he ever breathed a word of it, there would be an almighty public row? Not that he would. He couldn't bear even thinking about those last days in England. No. Better to shut that door.

But he owed Stephanie, and Nikos, too, to a lesser extent. And he liked them both. Actually he'd come to love Stephanie, even though she drove him mad at times. He'd have done anything to prevent her murder. It was an unthinkable way for someone like her to die.

So here he was, with less than a clue, and a Cambridge cop who knew diddly squat about Crete. Though at least she hadn't shut him up when he'd given that pretentious little lecture. Maybe she was interested. Maybe this case did feel different, even for her. But her problem was that she was in England and this had to be a Cretan narrative. But a vendetta here in Chiona? His aunt didn't believe a word of it, she told him, when he asked whether she'd ever heard of such a thing locally.

'This is not how we are in Sitia,' she'd told him. 'Go to Heraklion!'

'But that's not where Stephanie lived. I don't know whether she knew anyone there. Apart from her friend Popi.'

'Popi Filotaki has too much sense to be mixed up in that kind of garbage, but you are right about dear Stephania, God rest her soul, she was never involved with Greek stories or politics. She thought she lived like a Greek, but she didn't. She was a permanent tourist. She floated over the space, she wasn't rooted.'

'Though discovering the treasure means she'll always now be a part of Chiona.'

'Yes. That's true. And her death makes her even more famous, sad to say.' She crossed herself and muttered a quick prayer. Then she looked sharply at her nephew. He was looking well, not like he had two years before. But she didn't want him dragged into some murder inquiry. 'Why are you asking me questions?' she said. 'You aren't police here.'

'I'm just helping the English police with Greek translations,' he replied. 'And I'm as curious as I know you are. Don't tell me that when you and your friends sit round drinking coffee and eating *koulourakia* after your morning swims, or should I say chats in the water, you don't talk about Stephanie's death.'

His aunt snorted and then let out a hearty laugh. 'In which case you have to promise to tell me all the latest information.'

'You want me to tell you things that the public doesn't know?' he asked, and her eyes lit up. 'Very well,' he continued, unable to deny the aunt who'd become his new mother, and told her about Stephanie being placed on the bull and the word vendetta written in blood on the floor.

'It sounds like something you see on television,' she said. 'It's absurd!' Mike knew that she would now tell all her women friends and the news would get out. Which wasn't a bad thing because if there was any local vendetta, then she'd definitely find out about it.

'Can you tell me about the vendettas in the west of Crete. What do you know about them?'

And it seemed that his aunt knew a considerable amount, despite her assertions that this wasn't how Cretans behaved. One interesting fact was that years or even decades could pass between killings.

'There was this shepherd, some years back, who killed a hospital porter in Heraklion and that turned out to be a vendetta. It was in revenge for the death of the porter's uncle and he'd been killed nearly thirty years before that, before the shepherd had even been born.'

'But there's no Cretan or even Greek link with any of Stephanie's ancestors,' said Mike. 'She told me she was the first member of her family to go to Greece.'

'Then it's not a vendetta. Somebody's playing games here. You'll see.'

But would he see? He began to feel sympathy for DI Gregory. It was a bugger of a case. Could it just be a disgruntled archaeologist? If so, the Chiona find must have tipped them completely over the top.

He needed to talk to Henry, but Henry was in England. And that was interesting. Henry hated England these days, always said he felt like a foreigner. Didn't know the country anymore. So why was he there?

He walked along the Sitia port, which felt to him like a harbour waiting for a missing fleet. There should be so many more fishing boats, so many more fishermen getting a living from the sea. But it was just as Nikos had said, the Mediterranean was dying, and the problem of course was people. People fuck up the world, as the group used to say. The planet would be better off without us. Which was true, but there was more than simply air and earth and water. There was thought and music. And once he'd have said love.

He sat in the cafeneion near the beach where Yiannis was once again moaning about his controlling mother and how she drove him to distraction. But it was just as clear they both loved each other. Families, he thought. Stephanie's case felt like one of those ancient Greek stories: quarrelling families, a sacrifice, a brutal death.

He'd wondered at first whether Nikos had wanted him to find a scapegoat to cover his own actions. But if he'd wanted to kill Stephanie he could have done it in any number of silent and invisible ways. And Mike believed that the old man had genuinely cared for Stephanie. But could it be his son, Antony? Nikos never mentioned him, but nor did anyone else. Whenever his name came up in a bar or elsewhere, it was batted away with a 'don't go there' gesture; he wasn't somebody anyone wanted to talk about. He'd asked Henry once out of curiosity, but Henry had just said that however much he disliked Leotakis, which was a lot, he felt sorry for him having a son who was totally evil.

'Just a very nasty, crook, Mike,' he'd said. 'Better not to talk about him. And pray he doesn't come back here to Crete when the old man dies.'

Henry. He kept thinking about Henry. He sipped the coffee and wondered whether he should have a look in Henry's house. He had the keys, Henry had given them to him when he was helping build the place. In fact, he'd basically designed it.

Henry had been so angry at having to move that he'd wanted nothing to do with the new village, but Mike had gone round there with a bag of figs and a bottle of his favourite white wine from the nearby Monastery of Toplou. They'd talked politics and books for a while and then Mike had begun the tricky business of getting him involved in the creation of his new home.

'It strikes me that what you want is a library and writing room with bits attached for sleeping and cooking. How often do you have people round to eat in winter?'

'These days, practically never. Steph drops over occasionally, but I'm more likely to go to hers. She likes cooking.'

'So all you need in winter is a small table in the kitchen. And a larger table on the outside terrace for eating and writing etcetera in the summer?'

'A library?' Henry asked. 'Explain.'

So Mike had got him to get out a piece of paper and he'd begun to make a rough sketch. It was that simple with so much money. Tell the site architect what you wanted and then build it the old fashioned way, with Mike and the team doing the work.

'The key thing is,' Mike told him, 'you want it to feel as if it's always been there. Now...' he began to draw. 'You want to ask for a narrower and longer plot like this.' He drew a rectangle on a scrap of paper. 'Now let's begin on the left hand side. You need a terrace which is covered but open and faces the sea.'

Henry nodded. 'I like that.'

'So let's make that about five metres, if we're thinking metrically.'

'Which I'm not.' Henry smiled for the first time.

'I can convert it for you later, but everyone's plot size is three hundred square metres, which makes it easier to cut into chunks. But how you want it is up to you. Stephanie is making hers into a house with a central courtyard and no terrace, but if you want a long library, I'd suggest making it a longer, narrower plot like this. Say six metres across, which is about eighteen feet, room for your outside table and a door.'

Henry nodded.

'Right. Remember we're going down the left hand side. We begin with the terrace and then the first room on the left is your library and the bookcase goes all the way down to the end of the house which is just over a hundred feet. And the last bit,' he drew another line across, 'is your bedroom. Then there's an open space at the end to park your car and where you can grow a few vegetables if you want to.'

Over a hundred feet of bookcase and room for a huge table for his papers was all it took to convince him. After that, it was easy to build it and for him to move in. And there had been space for all his books and papers. And he could still watch the sun rise.

'Think of it like a bespoke suit. A house designed to fit you,' Mike had said.

'My father used to have suits made for him,' Henry reminisced. 'My first suit was made by a tailor in London. Lasted for years. Mind you, most of my clothes are decades old.'

Mike had been tempted to say that they looked it, but held his tongue. Instead he asked about Henry's new book.

'I'm finishing my November 17 Terrorist Group book,' he'd told Mike, 'but after that I'm writing a memoir. And some poems. Names that matter so deeply can be forgotten in a moment. I don't expect anyone to remember me, but I'd like someone to know about Laurent. It's what divided Stephanie and me and what brought us together. He was the love of both our lives. It's why we will always need each other because there is nobody else who knew him. I've written about him and his ideas – which I jotted down in a notebook at the time – and of course his absurd and terrible death.'

'Stephanie told me a bit about it.'

'That rainstorm, the worst in my memory. The phone lines were down in Athens, but he wanted me to hear the news from him and not anybody else. He was soaked through when he arrived at my apartment. I had to get him to undress so I could begin to iron his clothes dry. I told him he'd get a death of a cold.'

Had they made love that night, Mike wondered. One final farewell.

'He insisted on going back to Stephanie. He didn't want her to worry. I shouldn't have let him go. We rowed about it and he left.' Henry took out a large white handkerchief and wiped his eyes.

'If I'd have known how bad the flooding was I would never have let him leave, even if it meant knocking him out. I should have thought. Athens is shaped like a cup and so all the water flows in and the level rises. One of the avenues, Leoforos Olgas, near the Zappeion Gardens, became a torrent. Laurent was washed away under a car where he hit his head and drowned.'

'I'm so sorry,' said Mike, thinking about the loss of the person you love. He'd tell Henry his own story one day. He'd understand.

'There's never been anyone else since,' Henry finished. 'I've never wanted anyone since.'

There's want and want, thought Mike. Thinking about Stephanie makes him think about her daughter Jen, whom he's met only twice, but who clearly found him attractive.

And they'd be together sorting her mother's house. She wasn't a woman with whom you could enjoy a passing fling. And, like Henry, he was never going to be able to fall in love again. Or to let himself fall in love again. He'd have to keep his distance from Jen.

CHAPTER 22

Pam ran into her office from the carpark. She wasn't sure why this phone call felt so urgent, but talking with Larry and Zofia suddenly made her realise she'd been almost deliberately closing down the Greek side of the inquiry. Especially anything relating to Leotakis. Was it that he'd got in there first with that call to the Prime Minister? He might think he was one of the gods, but he wasn't. Nobody was above the law. She needed to set up an interview. She felt certain he had key information that would open up her inquiry.

'Boss,' Sue was standing in the doorway with a notebook in her hand.

'Shoot, but make it quick, there's a phone call I need to make.'

'Sure. Just thought you'd want to know about the will.'

'Yes, I do. Anything strange?'

'Yes. And you're not going to like it. She actually went there a week ago to write a new will, which they did on the spot and she signed it. The solicitor is a Mr Ian Coules, and he was super helpful, unless it was just my charm.'

Pam laughed. 'Almost certainly.' Sue did have a way of making people feel she was approachable. It made her an excellent interviewer; suspects relaxed and revealed more than they wanted to.

'Apparently Stephanie told him she'd be too busy later

with the Gallery, and wanted it settled before she went back to Greece. She said her Greek doctor gave her liver another six months, and she wanted Jen to feel safe.'

'That ties in with the post-mortem findings. If the killer had known, he could have waited.'

'Her Cambridge house with all its contents goes to her daughter. Her books and paintings are to be shared between her daughter and her friend Henry, but the Chiona house in Crete – you're not going to believe this...'

'Goes to the ex-husband, to the local dogs' home... come on, spit it out!'

'Mike Petersen!'

'I don't fucking believe it! What! Well, that takes him off the case. He's now got a conflict of interest. Damn, I'll have to break the news to Murton.'

'But he's not a suspect, surely? He was in Crete.'

'I don't know. It's dodgy ground. I'll have to get advice on that. But why? He never indicated they were that close. Oh shit! Any other bombshells?'

'No. Just cash to her friends Henry and Popi, a book of Donne poems to Nikos Leotakis and some money to her two stepsons. Mr Coules also talked to me about the funeral. Dr Michaels told him she'd been thinking a lot about this because of being ill. Apparently you can't be cremated in Crete, their Church doesn't allow it, but since she wasn't a Christian she couldn't have a Greek Orthodox funeral, and didn't want to be buried in some Anglican corner of a Cretan cemetery miles from her home. Fortunately, her friend Mr Leotakis has promised that he'll look after it. He has a private chapel on his estate and she can be buried there.'

'Thanks, Sue. Excellent work....Yes? There's something you want to say.'

Sue fiddled with the pens on Pam's desk.

'The poems she's left to Leotakis. He wrote love poems, didn't he, Donne?'

'Did he? You're thinking they were close. So am I. This

just adds to everything else I've heard the over the last few days. I think they were extremely close.'

'You don't think that…? I mean, she was over seventy!'

'Sue, it does appear that people over seventy have sex, however yuck that might sound to you at your age. I have no idea whether in this case. Actually I don't think it even matters. It's the fact that Stephanie was in a close relationship with a man who is rich enough to do whatever he wishes. And, because of that, must have more enemies than most.'

'And friends who would put us all out of a job if we upset him.'

'You said it. That immediate phone call to the PM. He took instant control of this inquiry with that. If we do something he doesn't like, we're off the case and it's hello NCA.'

Sue grimaced. 'Great. Oh, great. This case is impossible. Anything else you want me to do?'

'Just chase the CCTV. I want every bloody camera in Cambridge station and on every street between the Fitzwilliam and the Station examined.'

'Didn't Josh tell you?'

'Didn't Josh tell me what?'

'They were all down. Half of them weren't working, and for the past two weeks the Council has begun repairing them. The whole system has been off.'

'You are joking?'

'Sorry, boss.'

'If I wasn't in such a rush, I'd get on to the Council and tell them exactly what I think of them. The whole bloody system. That's another thing to bring joy to Murton this morning. Oh, god. This whole case is a total nightmare. Witnesses disappear, nobody's prints match. Suspects can't have done it. Talking of which, Henry… Did anyone check whether Henry Cox finally came in last night to give us his prints?'

'He didn't.'

'I'll call him. Thanks, Sue.'

The list of Stephanie's contacts was on her desk in front of her. There were two numbers for Henry. A number that looked like a landline and a mobile. She rang the mobile. There was a pause and then came the ring, the extended sound that meant Europe. Pam slammed down her phone and stormed into the Investigation Room.

'Can you bloody believe it! Henry Cox has bloody legged it, too. Murton is going to crucify me. Two runners. This is not happening. Somebody please give me some good news, preferably yesterday.'

'Don't know whether it's good news, but the IT guy Stuart has just rung and says can you call him back.'

'I've been through most of the emails and there's nothing odd,' said Josh. 'Mostly Stephanie asking friends in Greece if they want anything brought back, lots of people wanting invites to the opening and the rest is all about the exhibition. Lots of too-ing and fro-ing with Mark Kitson. She did have a massive row with him about the programme.'

'We know that. Odd that he didn't mention it. Josh, go and have another chat with him. I've got a feeling there's something he hasn't told us yet.'

'I'm on it. One other thing, boss. I'd like to go through her photographs. Do you need me in London tomorrow?'

'No. It's not as if the ex were a suspect. More a friendly chat with him and the daughter. Just see what other information they have. And making sure she's staying put. I'm still very concerned about her. The more I hear about Greek vendettas being about families, the more I worry.'

'Won't she be going to Greece for the funeral?' asked Josh.

'Damn. Yes. Of course she will. I'll have to find a way to get the local police to help us.'

'And Mike?'

'Possibly. Did you hear he's inherited the house in Crete?'

'Don't see him going back to work in London after that,' said Dave. 'Little house, little boat, maybe a nice little Greek girl. What else does a man need?'

'Football?' suggested Paul.

Pam left them to their laughter. Perhaps Mike did have a girl and Stephanie had given him the means to marry her. Perhaps she was seeing problems when there weren't any. She shut her office door and groaned at how untidy her desk was. There were notes and papers everywhere. She took an empty box file from the bookcase and piled all the papers inside. She'd sort them later. At least she had space to think now.

Then she remembered that one of the bits of paper was her list of Stephanie's phone contacts. She took it out and put it on her desk beside her notebook. Paper. Why didn't she just put everything on her computer like Josh?

At least she'd stored Stuart's number online. She looked it up and rang him.

'Thank you for getting back to me, Pam.'

Pam? What rank was Stuart? Had Murton told her? She couldn't remember. She made a note to ask him later.

'Happily I've managed to sign off everything down here so I've been able to concentrate on your case.'

'That's the best news I've had today.' It was only two days, and they'd achieved a great deal, but she'd been increasingly aware of how much she needed someone exploring the online traffic.

'I've got quite a bit of news and I'm not sure you're going to like it.'

'It can't be worse than everything else that's happened in the last twenty-four hours.'

'Anything I should know about?'

'No, not specifically. Just another suspect who's left the country before we can eliminate him from the inquiry. If we can. One I'd asked you to have a look at, actually, Henry Cox.'

'Ah.' Stuart gave a wry laugh. 'He's one of my bits of news.'

'Tell me. There's been a previous murder and he was a suspect, but never arrested.'

'Nothing like that. Just that there's a number attached to his name and it has a trigger which alerts our friends in Vauxhall.'

'Not our friends, particularly, Stuart. Cambridge might have produced more spooks than any other city in England, but we don't tend to have any dealings with them here in the Force. Are you telling me that Henry works for MI6?'

'I can't tell you that without going into areas I've promised you I wouldn't. Actually even I wouldn't want to try to get past their firewalls. After I triggered his name, I got a call from a guy called Christopher, and I rather think he'll call you today.'

'Thanks, Stuart. Actually, that might be good news. Could be why Henry didn't want to give us his dabs.' Pam put the phone into her other hand while reaching for a pen. Another note to add to the file.

'And what's the other news?' She had to admit that Stuart was a lot quicker than Peter had been. Years of training, she imagined. Or ways to access information that was not officially allowed. She hoped very much it wasn't the latter.

'I've managed to track down Adrestia. Not too hard, he's the kingpin of a group of people who basically moan and threaten. They don't operate on the dark web, as far as I can see, and from a preliminary sweep, and a quick call to an old colleague, they're not perceived to be a danger. All mouth and no trousers was what she said. Adrestia himself is...'

'He...?' interrupted Pam. She'd been imagining a woman.

'Yes. Despite calling himself after a Greek goddess, he's a man. He also happens to be Greek. Lives in Athens in a district called Nea Smyrni. My friend read me bits from his file. He went to school in Athens, went to university here, in Manchester, where he studied electrical engineering. Which would be useful if he was a bomb-maker but there's no indication of that, but I guess that could be why they're keeping a close eye on him. He does have a thing about the Elgin Marbles and sent threatening emails, but hasn't come to the UK for a few years. I have a feeling that there's somebody in Intelligence reading his emails regularly, though, just in case.'

'Interesting. Is that the kind of thing you used to do? Sorry, I shouldn't ask that.'

'No, you shouldn't,' laughed Stuart, 'and I wouldn't tell you. But obviously anyone who might be thought to be a danger to British people or our institutions is watched closely.'

'And our chap is.'

'You could say that. I can tell you that we do know when and where he uses his phone, and he's been using his phone in Greece every day for the past week. So, he wasn't in England and isn't your murderer.'

'Thanks, Stuart, that is incredibly useful.'

'Also had a long look at your man Kieron, who is a totally revolting specimen of the human race, but apart from being a fan of Adrestia, he isn't attached to any cell that is planning anything. Just follows a lot of mad groups. Again, it's all threats and collective invective.'

'My officers said he was a rabid anti-Semite.' Pam shivered as she remembered Roberta's description of the cushion. Disgusting in every way, thought Pam, but not their perp.

'Oh,' continued Stuart. 'He also believes in lizard people. That they rule the world and our Royal Family are lizards.'

'Loony tunes,' said Pam. 'Can't get my head around people like that. How could you really believe in that shit?'

'You've no idea what people believe in,' Stuart told her, happily. 'Over twelve million Yanks believe that lizard people control the world and over fifteen percent of Americans believe that the big pharma companies invent diseases to make money.'

'Jesus. Fifteen percent. It's the internet. It encourages them.'

'Sadly, it does. Kieron is a nutter and a slug, but if he commissioned a killing, he didn't do it online. Do you want me to check his phone calls?'

'No. We don't have any evidence to suspect him and can't do that until we can get a court order. We do things by the book, remember? I'm not really liking him for this. He's mad enough and angry enough, but the whole bull thing. More and more, I'm thinking this is Greek in some way. I don't suppose there's stuff on Nikos Leotakis?'

'I imagine there are filing cabinets full of stuff on Mr Leotakis. You do know who he is, don't you? He has half the Cabinet to stay with him regularly and that includes the PM.'

'I'm not thinking of him as a perp, Stuart. More as the actual target. Seems he and Dr Michaels were close. Just possible that the killing was done to hurt him.'

'Well, I think you'll have to ask him that. It's really not an area I could begin to explore.'

'I can see that. Thanks, Stuart. I'll get back to you if there's anything else we need.'

'Happy to help.'

Pam put down the phone and went back to her lists. She'd ring the archaeologist Irini first, and then Eleni. But before she rang Eleni, she really should begin to find out who Leotakis was. Why hadn't she researched him? It was almost as though he was a name, like any other of the names attached by colleges to donors and philanthropists.

She turned on her computer and began to read up on him. There were thousands of entries, but Wikipedia was as good a start as any.

Nikos Leotakis, she read. Born in Crete in 1936; eighty-two, they'd written in brackets in case you couldn't do the maths. He'd been married to Maria Gonzalez – oh not Greek, she thought, interesting – from 1950 till she died in 1962. One son Antonio, born in 1951. He'd have been eleven. Tough. Married to Alison Richards, 1965 until she died in 2016. So they'd had a golden wedding. If her father was still alive, they'd have been celebrating one in a few years. Instead they'd only been together thirteen years when her father died.

Pam skimmed Leotakis's early years: school in Crete, no mention of university, parents died in 1947. Then he's in South America. Not much detail given. Became a shipowner, how did he do that? Owned a fleet of oil tankers. Then became a property magnate. Bought the Palace chain of hotels in Europe. Lives in London, Paris and Crete. Becomes a philanthropist.

The biography felt heavily edited, she thought. There was nothing much there at all, not even the reference of his being called The Pirate that Josh had found. She skimmed down the most recent newspaper articles which were all interviews about the new gallery. A few pages further on she came across an article from The Guardian. 'Nikos Leotakis: how the Pirate became the Patron. Chris Brook, who is currently working on a book on the Greek billionaire, reveals how our knowledge of the shipping magnate has some notable omissions'.

Pam clicked on the article and printed it. She'd read it later, and share it with the team if it looked interesting. Meanwhile there were calls she needed to make. She picked up the phone and rang the number she had for Irini, the woman who'd been one of the lead archaeologists and whom Stephanie had never allowed to be credited. How did she feel? Pam wondered.

After a few minutes of friendly conversation, Pam discovered that the woman was remarkably calm and accepting.

'You have to understand that without Stephanie and the money she persuaded Mr Leotakis to give us, none of this could have happened and I would never have been able to oversee this miraculous find. It has moved on our knowledge of the Minoan civilisation at this moment in time to an extraordinary degree. There is enough material here for so much future study. And we have a new museum and I have all the funds I need to have a team to do the in-depth analyses we require. No, I am not angry with Stephanie.'

'But somebody was.'

'It is terrible to have to admit that, Inspector.'

'The name Tim Bayers has cropped up. Do you know him?'

'Of course we know Timothy. He is with us so many years. So sad now the arthritis he has.'

'He has arthritis?'

'Very bad. Last month he came to visit as he does every spring, though many of us wonder whether that was his last visit. His hands and legs are so painful. You know he cannot even hold a cup anymore in one hand. It is a very wicked disease.'

'So he could not have lifted Stephanie up on to the bull?'

'Tim cannot stand without his stick, Inspector. And I do not think he could hold a knife. Yes, he was angry about Stephanie making the find he felt should have been his. But his anger was aimed more against the gods than her. He railed against the Fates for a while, but he told me that now, since he can see that the cloth of life they have woven for him is coming to an end, he is peaceful.'

'Thank you for that. It's very helpful. So there is a general sense of acceptance among the archaeologists?'

'I think that is the correct word.'

'What about Petros Manoussis? I've heard he was angry that his find of the bull was attributed to Stephanie and not to him.'

'He was furious yes, but then he's Greek. We explode and then it's over.'

Apart from those involved in vendettas, thought Pam.

'Could I ask you a favour?' she said. 'Do you have a photograph of all the archaeologists you could email me. Just so that I can put faces to the names. It would help me create the picture.' It would also help me discover whether there were any names I had missed, she did not say.

'I will do it today,' said Irini, who Pam had warmed to enormously, She had promised, too, to give Pam a detailed personal tour of the site if Pam did come to Crete.

'But you must,' she said. 'You cannot understand Stephanie unless you are here.'

I think you have hit the nail on the head, Irini, Pam said to herself after she concluded the call. I do have to go to Crete. But first she had to make contact with Mr Leotakis. Or at least his so-called fixer, Eleni. She reached for the phone with one hand and her list with the other, as the phone rang. It wasn't a number she knew and it hadn't gone through the station switchboard.

'DI Gregory,' she announced, praying it wasn't a journalist who'd circumvented the system.

'Good afternoon, Detective Inspector.' The voice reminded her of the politicians she heard on the news. 'My name is Christopher Gray.'

Or that's your name today, thought Pam. She imagined what the team were going to say about the injection of MI6 into their inquiry. It's all going to be Bond and *Spooks*. No, that was MI5. Not that she knew exactly where the boundaries were. Stuart would. She'd ask him. Or Paul. He was a big fan of *Spooks*.

'Mr Gray. I believe you may be phoning in connection with Henry Cox.'

'That's correct. But before we say any more I have to tell you that the nature of our conversation is restricted and should not be repeated outside of your office.'

'I will need to inform my team if what you're saying has any bearing on this case. This is a murder inquiry.'

'Understood. Which is why I am calling you as a courtesy.'

'We do appreciate courteousness in the police force,' Pam replied. Don't let him get under your skin, she told herself. Just because he thinks that he is so much more important than you are.

'Do I understand from this that Mr Cox is connected with your agency, and you do not wish me to make the necessary enquiries I would have to do for anyone who might be considered a suspect. In other words, are you telling me that when it comes to Henry Cox I should back off?'

'I think you have it in one.'

'Even though he may be a possible suspect?'

'Oh, I think that's most unlikely.' Christopher Gray laughed. 'I've known Henry for twenty years. The idea he'd kill anyone is totally laughable.'

'Oh, I thought that was what you chaps did do.'

'You've been watching too many movies. What we do is gather intelligence and prevent crime. We would be most displeased if Henry was impeded in his work.'

'I shall bear that in mind, Mr Gray.'

'I think you have to, DI Gregory. With such a clean record as yours it would be a pity to damage it.'

CHAPTER 23

The bloody nerve of the man. Threatening me with my career. Pam picked up her box file and hurled it at the wall. It burst open and papers flew everywhere. Her door opened and Roberta put her head round.

'Boss... is everything?'

'Go away,' shouted Pam. 'Just leave me alone.'

Roberta came into the room and shut the door. She started to pick up the papers and placed them on the desk.

'When was the last time you had a decent night's sleep?'

Pam sank back in her chair, 'I don't even know what that means.'

'Is it because they're already threatening to close down this unit?

'You've heard that? My God, does everyone know?'

'Only me and Paul as far as I know. He has ways of finding things out.'

'Make a good spook. Talking of which, I've just had a creep from MI6 on the phone telling me that he'll destroy my career if I go on investigating Henry Cox.'

'What! You have to go and talk with Murton.'

'Oh, I'm going to. Except he'll probably find a way to make it my fault.'

She closed her eyes and wished she could be anywhere else but here in this baking hot cubicle called an office trying to unpick a case that seemed to have a ghost at its centre and rings of people surrounding her small team willing them to fail.

'Do you sometimes worry why you do this job?'

'All the time and then something happens and you know exactly why. Remember Winston?'

'It was only two days ago. Jesus. I think these have been the longest days of my life. I feel as if I've aged ten years since the weekend.'

'Well, boss, remember how it felt rescuing the boy?'

'I do. It's just this bloody case. I feel that the everything is stacked against us.'

'Why don't you call a briefing and we can all pile in and see where we are.'

'I know why I do this job. It's because I get to work with people like you. Yes. A briefing this afternoon is a good idea. What's the time, two o'clock…?'

'Did you have lunch?'

'No. Had a coffee with Zofia and Larry a few hours back.'

'Right. I'm going to get sandwiches in for everyone and then shall we say three thirty for the briefing?'

'Sounds perfect. Go to Espresso Library and put it on the account.'

She had begun to organise her thoughts into lists when Roberta returned with lunch. Pam bit into the overflowing baguette, which immediately sent a jet of hummus on to her shirt collar.

She wiped it off with a wet wipe and hoped it hadn't left a stain. She had to see Murton later and it was just the kind of thing he'd notice.

While she ate, she read the Guardian article on Leotakis. It seemed that there was a great deal that Chris Brook wasn't saying, which was probably on account of the fact that, as he noted, the billionaire was famously litigious. A lot of it was posing questions about his early business affairs in South America. How was it that he was able to buy all these ships when he began with no money? And why was it that he had acquired the title, the Pirate?

It seemed that once he had become rich, there was nothing particularly scandalous. He had refused to work with the Junta in Greece in the sixties, and had thus managed to work closely with the following democratic government, which had allowed him to buy a lot of land that previously had belonged to the military or the State. It was here that he had built his first hotels which he had then sold for many millions.

There was little else of interest, but Pam was sure there was a lot this Chris guy knew that wasn't in the article. Perhaps he could tell her. After all, she would be in London tomorrow. She looked up a number for the Guardian and picked up the phone.

Some minutes later while, as she discovered, Chris looked up the number for the Cambridge police station, asked for her, passed her intercept and got back through to her, they began to talk.

'I have to be careful,' he told her. 'You could have been anyone wanting to know what I knew and then taping a call to use against me.'

'Have you come across a lot of that?' She was intrigued. Were there things that Leotakis didn't want revealed?

'Quite a bit. Goes with the territory. Actually I don't ever say much on the phone, even when talking to a verified police inspector.'

'Maybe we could meet then,' she suggested. 'I'm coming down to London tomorrow. If you could spare the time.'

'You're the SOI on the Michaels' case, aren't you? That must be a tough one if it means you have to start digging into my world.'

'I'm just beginning to realise how tough it is,' she admitted.

'It's all about the past, I imagine. These things often are with people like Leotakis. Skeletons rise up from unmarked graves.'

'You may be right. I've had more history lessons in the past two days than for the past ten years.'

'Is that a problem?' He sounded faintly amused.

'Actually if I wasn't under so much pressure, I'd welcome it. There are so many holes in my knowledge of history. No, that's not right. I have one large hole when it comes to history with a small smudge called the Romans and another one called the Tudors. As for modern history, nothing.'

He laughed. 'Sounds like England's famous national curriculum.'

'I'm meeting a relative of Dr Michaels tomorrow afternoon, just after lunch. May I ring you when I get there and arrange a time and place?'

'Tomorrow's good,' he told her. 'I've just filed a piece and am researching a new one, but it's not due for a few days, so I'm relatively free.'

'What's it about?'

'Brexit, what else?'

It was odd perhaps how little they talked about Brexit on the job. Her mother was obsessed with it and couldn't wait for all the foreigners to leave. She felt that Dave felt the same, though he hadn't said so in her earshot. Josh was fervently against leaving Europe, and when she did think about it, which wasn't that often, she agreed with him. She'd voted to remain in any case, and was glad that Cambridge was a Remain city. March and the rest of North East Cambs had been almost seventy percent Leave. No wonder her mother fitted in so well there.

Half an hour later she walked down the corridor and knocked on Murton's door. She certainly didn't want to have to expand the inquiry overseas because God only knows how long that would take. Murders can't be solved overnight, she said to herself. However much everyone would like them to be, however much the press, still camped outside the police station, thought they should be. It was time she briefed the Super and asked for permission to go to Crete.

'Once again you drop by, just when I am about to ring you, Inspector.'

She hoped that was not as ominous as it sounded. She also prayed that he wouldn't notice the greasy stain on her collar she hadn't managed to get out yet.

'Did you get a call from MI6, too?' she asked.

'What? MI6? No,' he replied. 'Why?'

Pam told him and even told him how Grey had threatened her. She might as well, Murton was officially her line manager, though she rarely felt as though he had her best interests at heart.

She was gratified to see that he was nearly as angry as she was. Though she also thought that he was particularly annoyed that they'd gone directly to her and not through him.

'Bloody outrageous behaviour!' he shouted. 'Who the hell do they think they are?'

'I think a lot of people ask that from time to time, Sir,' she answered. 'The problem is that Mr Cox has the opportunity to have committed the murder. He was in the vicinity at the time and we only have his word that he'd come up to Cambridge, slept the night on Dr Michaels' sofa and then returned to London on an early morning train.'

'What does CCTV show?'

'That's another problem. Both the station and the City are working together to update their CCTV this week, and a lot of it's been down.'

'I should have been told that.'

'As for street CCTV, we have some footage, but haven't been able to pick him out. But there are so many small streets without cameras. I've got a couple of constables walking round all the possible streets and seeing if they can see any cameras. But nothing so far.'

'So who do we have in our sights apart from Cox, who we've been warned off? Mind you, if he does look like the perp, you can most certainly follow that up. Spooks or no bloody spooks. This is a murder on British soil.'

'Yes, sir. Our suspects are thinning out, to be honest. It seems that they are being eliminated one way or another.'

'What about the Marbles man?'

'Kieron James? He's just an internet nasty. Twenty odd stone, and can hardly walk. Got the information from our new IT guy, Stuart – and I have to say that was a good choice of yours, sir – he's leapt onto the case already and is being incredibly helpful.'

'Glad to hear it.'

'By the way, what's his rank? Just so as I know.'

'Didn't I say? He's a DI. One of these fast-track ones.'

Nice to get there without the slog, Pam thought. But at least he's an expert, not just an attitude in a suit.

'Stuart's been looking online in case Kieron got someone else to do the job, but there doesn't seem to be anything. Unless, of course, Kieron commissioned the murder by phone or in person. Stuart and I discussed that and he's now going back through earlier emails in case there's a chance that he met someone and invited them to phone or visit.'

'Good. We need to keep him on our list.'

'He's certainly angry enough. But he seems to be angry with the world. Thinks it's been taken over by lizards.'

'Oh, one of those nutters. Who else?'

Pam told him that the archaeologists had all come off the suspect list, which was now looking sadly empty.

'There's still the Greek project manager who did a runner on Tuesday after saying he'd seen a ghost. George. DS Phillips has had a word with HR at the Fitzwilliam where some payments were made to him directly. They had a photocopy of his passport and his address in Crete. He rang it, but there wasn't an answer. Phillips has also been in regular contact with his colleague and friend, the architect Anna Karanaki, and she said that his parents haven't seen him either, but she wasn't sure whether they were telling the truth. I'd love to be able to question them.'

'We can't interview foreign nationals in their own

country, but the Greek police can. Which is something I have been thinking about.'

'I wonder whether DS Petersen has a link with the local police in Crete. It might help bridge the gap.'

'That liaison going well?'

'Yes. He lives in Chiona and does seem to have excellent local knowledge. Lots of stories about the past.' She paused. 'Did I tell you that the project manager said he'd seen a ghost from the past. Our killer is beginning to feel like a ghost coming out of the past wanting revenge. It's all about old history.'

'Then you'll have to dig into that history and find him. This isn't looking good, Gregory. What with the brass and the press, we do need a speedy result on this case. In fact I think it could be said that you have remarkably little new evidence but a great deal of vague conjecture. I am beginning to wonder whether your team is the right one for a case this serious.'

This was so unfair that Pam found herself unable to speak. She shook her head.

'There is of course the possibility the murder was done to hurt Mr Leotakis, himself.'

'That's absurd. Do you realise who you're talking about? He's a friend of Mrs May.'

'Is it absurd? He has a fairly dark past as I'm beginning to discover, and every day people are telling me how close he was with Dr Michaels.'

'You mean they were romantically involved?'

Another one who can't imagine sex in the over seventies. Mind you I can't imagine sex with you and Mrs Murton and you're not even sixty.

'Yes. It is looking that way.'

'In which case, Gregory, it would seem that he has an even stronger reason for wanting us to find the killer. You are not to contact Mr Leotakis. And that is an order. You are to follow the leads you have.'

'I agree. Which is why I would like to go to Crete and

liaise with the police there.'

'Out of the question. If there are inquiries that have to be made in Greece, we will send a formal request by the usual channels for the Greek police to follow up.'

Which could take months, she thought. And all the while Jen would be in danger and the press would get more and more persistent. She wasn't sure that her team would last that long. This is all about cuts, she thought. Maybe you've already started to work on disbanding us and you'll hand the case to Hawkswood. Had he suggested this to Hawkswood from the beginning? Was this why he was so nice?

'There is one other thing. Although I said that our liaison with DS Petersen was satisfactory, there is a possible conflict of interest.'

'Why?' Murton barked.

'Because Dr Michaels has left him her house. I've just got the details of the will.'

'Good God.' Pam thought she'd never seen Murton look so surprised. He got up from behind his desk and began to pace.

'You know, Pam, whatever may happen in the future, I don't want you to think that I don't respect you as an officer. But I really think that this case should be handed over to the Greek police. It would take a lot of pressure off this department. In my opinion this case…'

'Basket of snakes.'

Yes. And they're not British snakes.'

'No,' she said. 'Ours generally don't have a fatal bite.'

CHAPTER 24

We cannot avoid the will of the gods. Honour above all things.

CHAPTER 25

How much time did she have? It was two days since the murder had been discovered and the brass were about to take her off the case already? Why had they given her the case in the first place, she wondered. Was it merely to give her a reason to fail?

Everything pointed to Crete, but she wasn't allowed to go there. Surely she should be at the funeral? She couldn't remember any funeral in a murder inquiry where there wasn't a police representative. Or would they simply send someone from the British Embassy? Perhaps this case was too complex for her?

No, it bloody isn't! she said to herself, looking at her neat list. In two days they'd achieved a great deal. She picked up her personal phone. This was something she couldn't ever remember doing before; she was going to disobey her boss and ignore his order. She pulled the list of Stephanie's contacts towards her. Eleni, that was the name of the woman who Jen had described as Leotakis's fixer supreme. She punched in the number and once again heard the notes of the foreign call.

'*Oriste?*' The voice was low and melodious. Pam introduced herself.

'Ah, Detective Inspector, you must be psychic. I have you on my list to call you this afternoon. How very kind of you to call me.'

Pam offered her condolences for the loss of her friend. 'From everything I've discovered about Dr Michaels, she seems to have been an exceptional woman,' she said.

'You're very right, Inspector. Stephanie was a remarkable woman. We miss her very much.'

Is that 'we' her and Mr Leotakis, wondered Pam. Or someone else? Now, how was she going to phrase this next bit?

'I feel that in order to understand this killing, which we now believe is part of some kind of 'vendetta', that it would be helpful for me to talk with Mr Leotakis.'

'We have heard that, too from dear Anna. And yes, Mr Leotakis agrees with you. He thinks that you and he should meet.'

'Thank you,' said Pam. 'That's excellent. There is, however, a problem.'

'A problem?' Eleni sounded as though such things did not enter her life.

'It's that my superiors feel that I should not be talking with Mr Leotakis.' She took a deep breath. This was either going to work or she might lose her job. 'In fact I have been forbidden to talk with him or to go to Crete. I was hoping to go to Dr Michaels' funeral.'

'And so you should, in both regards.' Eleni sounded slightly amused. 'Nikos most certainly wants to meet you. Indeed, he has invited you to dinner tomorrow, so that he does not waste your time during working hours.'

'That's very considerate of him,' replied Pam. 'I shall be in London tomorrow, perhaps we could meet there.'

'That is not necessary,' replied Eleni, firmly. 'Text me the address of where you will be and I will send a car for you.'

'Well, I shall probably be in Putney,' said Pam. 'I'm meeting with Stephanie's ex-husband.'

'Then we can use Farnborough airport, that's very convenient,' Eleni told her. 'It is only forty minutes to Bournemouth and then another fifteen to the house.'

But a long way to get back to Cambridge on Saturday, thought Pam.

'Mr Leotakis will be flying to Crete on Saturday morning,' Eleni continued. 'I am certain that he will want you to accompany him. So it is best if you stay in Dorset tomorrow evening. Then you can stay at his Villa in Crete and we will arrange for the Greek police to liaise with you there.'

'Thank you,' said Pam. How much information did this woman know? She'd talked with Anna, so she'd know that George had disappeared. Did she know about Henry, too?

'I can't tell you how grateful I am...' she began and Eleni laughed.

'You want to find the killer as does Mr Leotakis. There is not conflict, but it is sensible that you come to Crete. Jen and her father will be at the villa, too. I think you will find it agreeable. I will arrange for you to have a cottage on the estate with a sitting room where you can have meetings. It also has a plunge pool which you will find helpful in the heat.'

Pam swallowed and thanked her. The way Eleni delivered information felt as fixed as saying the sun will rise in the East. Murton would find it hard to argue with her. In the meantime, she had to brief her team. While she had a team.

Her phone rang. Murton sounded more irritated than ever.

'When I said that I wanted to see you earlier it was because I'd heard that the coroner had released the body for burial.'

'Yes, Sir. I informed his daughter. I've now heard that the funeral will be on Tuesday'.

'Ah. Well. Since we spoke, I've had a woman on the phone. A Greek... A certain Mrs Apostoli. She was gracious enough to tell me that the Leotakis plane was being made available to our inquiry. News to me, but apparently it's been cleared higher up. And they have also ordered you to go with Mr Leotakis and Dr Michaels' family to Crete on Saturday. Did you know that?'

'Not when we spoke, Sir,' Pam replied. 'Only just now when Mrs Apostoli rang me. She told me that Mr Leotakis had asked me to meet him in Dorset tomorrow evening and fly to Crete with him and the family.'

'So I was told. I am therefore rescinding my previous order.'

That's good of you, she thought, you slippery bastard.

'I do believe that it will be helpful,' she told him, glad he couldn't see her expression. 'I'm sure that right now I will be able to continue my enquiries much more fruitfully in Greece than here.'

An hour later she briefed the team.

'We've done a huge amount in a short time,' she told them. 'I know we've been swamped with calls from everyone and their dog about who they saw on the Monday evening and the Tuesday morning, but we do need to go through them all and see whether there was a witness. Concentrate on the timeline.'

'Do we have any news about the Greek project manager?' asked Dave. 'I've always liked him for the killer. Knew his way about the gallery, knew she'd be there. And did a runner. I'd like to sweat him a bit.'

'Missing the days when you could do your Sweeney act, Dave?' asked Josh.

'And you can fuck off, too.' Dave stomped out of the room and banged the door behind him. Pam raised her eyebrows and looked round the room to see if anyone knew what was eating him.

'He's had a run of losers at the races this week, I think,' said Sue. 'Heard him moaning in the canteen earlier.'

'Amazed he's got the time this week.' Pam knew that Dave like the occasional bet, but if it was becoming a problem, she'd have to deal with it. Christ, she hated that side of her job.

She went through all the suspects who were now in the clear and those who they hadn't been able to interview or print.

'Basically, we're down to two names and a lot of vague conjecture.'

'Can we get the Greek police to take prints of the ones who are now there?' asked Josh.

'I don't know if they do that kind of thing over there. You know, take prints to eliminate people from an enquiry. But I guess I'll find out. I'm flying to Crete on Saturday for Dr Michaels' funeral. And no, before you all get too excited, I can't take anyone with me. Josh is Deputy SIO and he will be taking over in my absence.'

There was a pantomime-worthy chorus of boos. Pam laughed, and went back into her office to brief Josh. He'd do a solid job, she thought. Wouldn't be that long before he got a promotion and would be a SIO himself.

'Suppose you'd like me to email you when we catch chummy?' he asked.

'Yeah, that would be nice. I'll even read it if I can drag myself away from my beach chair.'

'Seriously, though, boss. Be careful. Those stabbings were really nasty.'

'They were. That's the main reason I'm going. To keep watch on Jen. The more I read about this Greek vendetta thing, the more it feels like they go after families. Luckily, she'll be surrounded by family and close friends, and will be staying at Mr Leotakis's villa'.

'Are you going to tell the father that you're concerned?

'From talking to him on the phone I tend to think he'll be telling me. He's not a stupid man.'

'Nor is our killer. He's a thinker.'

'That's what worries me.'

'And you'll be getting to know Mr Leotakis.'

'Seems I don't have any other option. According to his liaison person, Eleni – now there's one powerful woman – I'm also staying with Mr Leotakis, in one of the small guest cottages.'

Josh laughed. 'Does it have its private pool? It does. Tell me, it does.'

Pam blushed. 'Oh shit, I'm never going to live this down, am I? Yes it's got something called a plunge pool.'

Josh laughed as he tried to imagine his boss sitting in a plunge pool. She'd probably have a pile of papers beside her, so she could tell herself she was working. In all the time he'd worked for her, he'd never known her take a proper holiday. Whenever she was forced to take her allowance of days off, she confessed that she'd just stayed at home and slept. She was like a limpet, had to be dragged out of the office or her home to go anywhere. He couldn't remember the number of times she'd backed down from work parties. If there was a drink to celebrate a case, she was always there getting the first drink in. And always the first to leave, begging tiredness, but leaving money on the slate.

Maybe Greece was exactly what she needed. Roberta certainly thought so, as did Barbara, though they came at it from different angles. Barbara thought if she had a life elsewhere, she might stop making Josh work so late and ruining their weekends.

'There is one thing the team want to do' he told her after the briefing. 'You know we're reburying Dr Nichols' cat tomorrow morning. Well, everyone's chipped in and we've bought a little rose bush to plant on the new grave.'

'That is so lovely of you all.' Pam felt tears well up. But why couldn't she have thought of that? What was wrong with her?

'What are you doing later, Pam?' Roberta asked, as she sorted the papers she needed to take with her to Crete. 'Microwave lasagne and box set *Game of Thrones?*'

'*Doctor Foster.*'

'Good choice. So you're free, basically?'

'Yes,' said Pam, tentatively. 'As long as you're not suggesting a late night.'

'No. But I bet if you looked at your legs you'd think they were so white they were virtually blue.'

'What?'

Roberta laughed. 'Prepare to be sprayed,' she said.

'Oh God, you mean... won't that make me all orange?'

'Not if you don't overdo it like the blob in the Oval Office. Since the briefing, I've booked you in for a body massage, and a St Tropez full body session. Followed by a haircut. And then we're going clothes shopping. You're representing all of us, you know.'

'As a detective, not a model,' Pam grumbled. 'I can't afford all that and new clothes.'

'Yes, you can. You hardly pay anything for your dog kennel.'

'Mews cottage.'

'Garden shed.'

'Luxury garden shed.' Pam smiled. 'You're right. I can afford it.'

'Yup,' Roberta said. 'Moreover, it is the general consensus among the female members of your team, that you cannot stay on a Greek island with a billionaire and wear old polo shirts stained with toothpaste.'

'Hummus.'

'And ancient black trousers that could have been bought in the eighties.'

'You're not saying skirts?'

'Dresses. Floaty cool dresses.'

'One has to be black for the funeral.'

'That's okay. Black looks good on a tan. I've looked up the weather forecast. It's about thirty degrees and the sea temperature is over twenty.'

'I won't have time to go swimming.'

'You will. You forget that in Greece the early morning sea is warm. Pam,' she added, 'you're a brilliant detective, but you are allowed a life.'

'Really? Just pray we don't bump into a journalist this afternoon. I can just see it: no new leads, say Cambridge police as lead officer finds time for shopping spree.'

'They seem to have buggered off for the time being. They'll probably be back on Tuesday doing a "one week in and Cambridge police still have no idea who killed famous local archaeologist".'

The following morning Pam packed her new clothes into her new canvas and leather duffel bag. She liked the bag more than the clothes, she decided. It had pockets everywhere and a zipped compartment either end. Perfect to keep sandwiches, she thought, and would also do as a gym bag. She nearly didn't buy it because it was described as a men's travel bag which infuriated her, but decided that it would better to fight the sexism by buying it. Into the case, along with one set of her usual uniform, went a new dark green bathing costume, two cotton sleeveless linen dresses, one blue and one turquoise, a sleeveless black shift dress, a cashmere cardigan and a long scarf-cum-wrap for evenings. She'd never spent so much money on herself in one day. Actually, it was more than she ever spent on herself in a year.

Roberta had been right. She never bought things for herself for pleasure anymore, and she spent less than half her salary each month. She looked at her growing savings which were now enough to buy a small flat, but wasn't sure that she even wanted one. She liked the little kennel she rented. It suited her.

She showered quickly and put on one of her three new pairs of cotton bras and pants and the new short-sleeved navy shirtwaister. Her legs hadn't gone orange or developed tiger streaks, but they were a faint tanned colour and no longer blueish. She looked at herself in the mirror. It was amazing what a good haircut and some new clothes could do. Her hair looked more like the shiny bob Jen had and less like a young Bob Dylan. She slipped on her new Josef Seibel grey sandals, which weren't exactly office, but were comfortable and would be good if she needed to run after someone.

She hoped that wouldn't be happening. Just a quiet funeral, some interviews and then an arrest by the Greek police while she watched. In her dreams.

She decided to drop by the office and have a final word with Josh before going to the station, but when she arrived, she found that he'd gone to Stephanie's house for the reburial of the cat. That was like him, she thought. He'd want to see it was done properly. He was good at those kinds of details.

It was still early, and most of the team wouldn't be there yet. She'd just go to her office and pick up her file and leave quietly before anyone saw her new look. But as she walked down the corridor, she heard voices and laughter. People were in; she felt guilty at leaving them. But it wasn't as though she was going on a holiday, whatever they thought.

'Typical, isn't it? The DI pisses off to Crete and leaves us with the real work.' It was Dave's voice.

'That's what they do isn't it? We do the work and they get the credit.'

She didn't know the voice. Must be one of the civvies.

'Think she'll fuck that darkie cop? Might put a smile on her fat face for once.' Dave again. Somebody laughed.

'If she wasn't so old I'd do her myself,' a civvie replied.

Pam walked into the room.

'DC Butcher, my office now.'

The room went silent as Dave, now scarlet with fury and embarrassment, followed Pam into her office. There had been three civvies in the room, she noted, the one male looked terrified, as well he might. She'd deal with him later. She sat down and pointed to the chair opposite her. Dave remained standing.

'Boss...' he began.

'Shut the fuck up, Dave. I don't want to hear another word out of your mouth today. Now sit down and listen to me.'

He thought about it for a moment and sat down.

'You realise that if I report this, no don't speak, listen to me. If I report this you'll get pulled up before a gross misconduct panel, and you're as likely as not to be dismissed. Pretty sad end to your career, I'd say. I've worked with you for a long time and know that apart from your vile racism, you're a bloody good cop. It's just that something inside you is twisted and wrong. You were also stupid enough to say those words in front of several witnesses, and therefore even if you deny saying them at least one of them will tell the truth. They've got careers to think about.'

Dave looked as though he was about to speak, but changed his mind when he saw how angry Pam was. If only he'd kept his stupid mouth shut, he thought. You couldn't say anything these days. And it was only a bit of banter. Better not to say that, though.

'I could send you on another diversity course, but I don't imagine it will change your mind. I just wish I could find a way of getting you to understand how wrong it is and how fucked up your opinions are. But you are going to ask for a transfer out of my unit. I don't care what excuse you give, but I don't want you on my team anymore. Understood?'

'Yes, boss. I don't know why I said it. I just lost a hell of a lot of money this week.'

'And you've been drinking.'

'That, too.'

'So feeling sorry for yourself, you allow this garbage to come out of your mouth. The trouble is that it's in your head. I don't care what you say about me, but I do very much care that you think it's OK to use words like that. And about a serving officer. Can you imagine what Murton would say?'

'He'd throw the book at me.'

'And he'd be right.' Pam sighed. There had been so many times when things were tough and Dave had helped and even taken a punch swung at her. 'You're a bloody idiot,' she told him. 'You need to sort yourself out. Now fuck off before I change my mind.'

Dave stood up. He almost left without a word and then everything in his head came out at once. 'The trouble with you bloody liberals and politically-correct wankers,' he shouted at her, 'is you can't see the fucking problem even when it's in front of you. Don't stop and search coons, no you won't stop me using those words, because it upsets them, don't keep arresting the Pakis even though they are the ones committing all the crimes. You can't say or do anything now in case you offend someone! No wonder you can't get a decent man to bed you! Who'd want to be lumbered with a cold bitch like you, even if you do scrub up well. I suppose that's for the black DS, or are you after the billionaire?'

'Detective Sergeant Butcher, I am reporting you for gross misconduct. What you have just said will be sent to Superintendent Murton. Now please leave my office.'

Dave slammed the door so hard Pam thought the glass would break. Damn, she was going to miss her train.

She stormed down the corridor to Murton's office where she told him what had just happened, and played him the tape of Dave's speech from her phone. She was still shaking though she tried to hide it.

'I have to ask why you thought of taping that interview?' Murton commented. No commiseration, no comment on what it must have felt like.

'Just a feeling,' said Pam, sighing. 'If he'd apologised and said it was a one-off, I'd have thought of overlooking it and wiped it. He's a good officer otherwise and coming up to retirement age.'

But what made it so much worse, she thought, was the laughter of those who'd been listening earlier. She knew Cambridge had a bad reputation when she'd first joined, but thought it was a things of the past. But here it was. The racism, the sexism. In her unit.

'As for the civvies who were listening earlier and laughing with DC Butcher, I suggest they all go on a diversity course.'

'It's most inconvenient,' said Murton. 'I'll handle it. I don't want this to interfere with this case.'

She was still shaking as she got into the car she'd organised to get her to the station. The bastard, she thought. The bloody bastard! And Murton, too.

Two hours later, having done every relaxation exercise she knew, she got off the Tube at Putney Bridge, and walked along the Embankment where she came to the road where Jen's father lived. It was leafy and quiet and opposite a small park with tennis courts. She listened to the lazy thwack of the balls on the racquets and the laughter of the players. How did you get to be people like that? People who had time on a weekday to play tennis, or could afford it? Paul would say her prejudices were showing again, but it did seem deeply unfair. And yet. Here she was with a bag of new clothes and about to fly to a Greek island. Why couldn't she enjoy that?

The terrace house had clearly been given the architect treatment. Pam could see the connections with the Cambridge house. But this was cosier and more comfortable. She had glimpsed a sitting room with cushion-filled sofas, and the back had been knocked through and extended to create a glass-walled kitchen and dining room.

Colin led her through this into the garden where again cushions featured, this time on a serpentine wall with bricked seating that broke the garden in two. In front of this were several rattan chairs and a large table covered with a canvas awning. Pam could have happily curled up on one of those chairs and snoozed through the day. She saw that the family dog had already decided to do so.

'Sorry about Boots,' said Colin. 'Do you want me to move him?'

'Absolutely not,' said Pam. 'I was just thinking that's what I'd like to do.'

'Can't be an easy case this. So much publicity. We even had the press here for a couple of days, but they gave up yesterday afternoon when there was nobody to talk to and only Caroline and me going out, and we weren't saying anything.'

'Jen hasn't gone out this week?'

'I managed to persuade her not to.'

'Good.'

'You think that she might be in danger?'

'There is a possibility.'

'I've been so worried. She never told me about Skimble, otherwise I'd have gone up to Cambridge back then and brought her here. She can be very like her mother sometimes. Stephanie was extraordinarily stubborn.'

'That's one reason we insisted on driving her here.'

'I thought so. She's been insisting on going to Crete as soon as possible. And I thought she'd be much more vulnerable there. That's why we're so delighted that Mr Leotakis has invited us all.'

'You're flying to Crete tomorrow with Mr Leotakis, too?'

'Yes. Does that mean you are coming as well, Inspector?'

'It does. I'm going down to see Mr Leotakis this evening and then we all go to Crete.'

'That's excellent news. And Jen's godmother and Steph's old friend Popi will be joining us at his villa. I spoke to his... I'm not sure what her role exactly is...'

'General fixer?'

'Yes. Eleni. She said Mr Leotakis lived on a promontory which was guarded twenty-four hours a day.'

What a strange way to live, thought Pam. Always looking over your shoulder. I wonder why he thinks he's in danger. The money? How he got it, perhaps?

'Is Jen upstairs?' she asked, as she sipped her glass of freshly-made lemonade.

'No, she's in Cambridge.'

'I thought you said she hadn't gone out.'

'Not on her own. Your liaison office, Diane picked her up first thing. Jen wanted to be there for the reburial of Skimble. And she also had to pick up her clothes and things for Crete.'

'Diane probably told my deputy.' Pam hoped her smile didn't look as grim as she felt. 'Do you mind if I just give her a ring?'

She dialled the number for the FLO. She turned her back on Colin and found herself staring at a bed of lupins. Her father had liked lupins, she remembered. Her mother didn't. Not surprising, they were far too joyful. The number rang, but Diane didn't answer. Pam felt herself go cold. Should she put out an alert? No. Don't panic. Not yet. She tried to relax her shoulders and rang the number Jen had given her. Jen answered straight away.

'Hello Inspector, how kind of you to call,' said Jen. 'I do want to thank you for the rose bush. It was so nice of you all. And Josh and Roberta came, and they couldn't have been kinder.'

'They're the best,' said Pam, meaning it.

'We're just on our way back now. Diane is paying for the petrol.'

'You're alone in the car?'

'Yes but…'

'Could you do me a favour. Just go in and tell Diane to come back out and have a word with me. Best to stay with her.'

'You sound like my dad. It's not as if I'm in any danger.'

'Better to be safe.'

'OK. Oh, here is Diane. I'll pass her the phone.'

'You left Dr Nichols alone in the car?'

'Sorry, Guv. We're at a small petrol station near Royston. Hold on, I'm just walking away from the car to talk to you. OK. I'm sorry, but I thought it would be safe. There's nobody dodgy here. I've been watching her like a hawk.'

'Just don't leave her alone again and get her back here safely, please.'

'Right. ETA one hour forty minutes depending on London traffic.'

Pam put down the phone. She turned to Colin.

'They're on their way back here. Probably just under two hours.' Pam felt the sweat running down her back.

'Is there something you're not telling me, Inspector?' asked Colin.

'I'm afraid there is. I haven't been able to reveal it for operational reasons, and I don't want it to be leaked to the press, but we do think that in the mind of the killer, the murder was a kind of vendetta, an act of revenge. Revenge for what, we have no idea. Unless you do?'

Colin shook his head thoughtfully.

'No more than I've already told you,' he said.

An hour later, Pam was sitting in the quiet Putney garden listening to a distant blackbird and trying to keep awake. Colin had brought out some bread and cheese for an early lunch that Caroline had prepared, but it seemed she was having a bad day and had gone back to bed. She'd given Pam a wave from the kitchen and it was clear even from that distance how very frail she was.

'Just praying for all our sakes that the disease doesn't turn into a crisis,' Colin had said. 'Not sure this family could take any more bad news right now.' He'd been appalled at the idea the killing of Stephanie had been part of a vendetta, and was now doubly glad that Jen would be shielded by the security system of Mr Leotakis.

'But what happens if you don't catch this madman? he asked. 'Sometimes vendettas go on for years, don't they? At least in Sicily, which is all I know about. Jen has to go back to her teaching in September. She can't be looking over her shoulder indefinitely.'

There was nothing Pam could say about that except words that aimed to soothe and probably just made you look stupid. This case wasn't like any other case her unit had ever worked on and talking with Colin had produced no new leads. Just a few more insights into the complicated mind of Stephanie, which veered from the self-hating, self-destructive drunk to the creative, warm and kind friend. There had to be something in her past that had led to her death, Pam kept thinking. But unless someone had been walking on Sheep's Green and happened to take a photograph of the killer as he left the gallery, the only way she was going to catch him, she now thought, was if he made an attempt to kill Jen.

Colin was right, they couldn't go on protecting Jen for months and certainly not for years. She liked Stephanie's ex-husband; he had the rare ability to make her feel relaxed. Stephanie must have liked that, Pam thought. She could imagine her needing someone calming after the death of her partner. He was wearing a pair of faded jeans and a pale blue shirt, its sleeves rolled up to the elbow, smart without being smart. She was extremely glad to be wearing her new dress and sandals. As if I belonged to their club, she thought. As if I could pass as one of them.

She sighed and prepared for her meeting with the journalist, Chris Brook. When she'd asked Colin for a suitable place nearby, he'd insisted she stay. She'd let both Chris and Eleni know and was delighted that she could now stay here until the car came to take her to the airport.

'I've got work to do in my study and when Jen gets back, she'll probably go to her room,' Colin said. 'She was up with the lark to go to Cambridge this morning. I suppose we'll all be having siestas when we're in Greece.'

Will we? Pam thought. It seemed like the most seductive idea she'd ever heard. She felt her eyes grow heavy and closed them for a moment only to hear voices as Colin showed the journalist into the garden.

Chris Brook was at least thirty years younger than Colin, but had little of his hair. He walked on to the lawn, dropped his shoulder bag and his cycling helmet, and almost fell into the glass of lemonade Pam offered him.

'Fuck, it's hot out there. This is nice, though. Kind of Mr Nichols.'

'Yes,' agreed Pam.

Chris downed two tumblers of lemonade and sat back on the seat.

'Nikos Leotakis,' he said. 'Also known as the Pirate, and at one time wanted for murder in three South American countries.'

CHAPTER 26

'Nikos Leotakis is wanted for murder? Are you joking?'

This changes everything, thought Pam, if this man is a known killer, I'm investigating him, whatever the Prime Minister may say.

'No, I'm not. But you missed the "one time". In all of those countries where there once were people after him, he's now very much a friend.' Chris laughed. 'There aren't any faded 'wanted' posters hanging in dusty sheriff's offices, Inspector. Sorry if that was a poor joke. This is going back a very long way, back to the bad old days of the fifties when a few very bad dictators controlled a lot of Central and South America. We're talking Trujillo in the Dominican Republic, Batista in Cuba, and Pérez Jiménez in Venezuela. The last is particularly key in relation with Leotakis because of all the Venezuelan oil that was being pumped out of the ground and into the building of new cities. This is where Leotakis came when he was twenty and Jiménez was beginning his huge programme of immigration – swamping the indigenous population, in fact. Though, unlike Trujillo, Jiménez didn't want to kill all of them. I could tell….no, another time, I mustn't go off on tangents, however fascinating. Let's stick to the rise and rise of Nikos Leotakis.'

Pam nodded. She was enjoying this, which surprised her. She'd always thought that history didn't interest her, but everything in this case seemed to be about history and she was becoming increasingly engrossed. And this journalist was a good storyteller. Very different from the lecturing manner of Henry Cox.

'Now the thing about South America, of course, is its proximity to the USA, and there wasn't a single bad dictator down there who didn't have American support. And I will go off on a tangent for a moment because this does sort of show how far the Yanks would go to support any government they thought would keep out the Commies. In 1975, they set up a very nasty campaign called Operation Condor, which was precisely that. It aimed to eradicate Soviet influence in the south of South America and used terror and assassinations to do it.'

Chris took a sip of his drink and shook himself slightly as if to rid himself of the things he'd had to read.

'We think around sixty thousand people died because of this, maybe more, and at least half a million were imprisoned, many of them tortured. That's just the background for the Cold War America was fighting in South America. And money was no problem. Dictator or not, if you were keeping the reds out, you'd get whatever you wanted. Of course in Cuba, that also meant Mob money and mass corruption. Now when it comes to shipping billionaires, you usually think of them in bed with dictators, but that's where Nikos differed from the rest. While Onassis and Niarchos and the others fought for supremacy in the Middle East and cosied up to the Arabs, our boy went west. And when it came to a choice between the people and the dictators, he chose the people. The fact that his father had been killed by the Right during the Greek Civil War probably had a bearing on this. Though he's certainly got over his anti-British prejudices now. We were involved in that conflict in Greece, by the way, in case you don't know, Churchill trying to prop up the Right and protect the King. And, incidentally dividing Greece politically and preparing the ground for the Colonels to take over in the sixties. If you're interested, my colleagues Ed Vulliamy and Helena Smith wrote an excellent piece on that about four years ago. Worth reading if you want to understand where a man like Nikos comes from.

'But back to Nikos. I still don't know what he did when he first got to Venezuela, he won't tell me, but he first appears in any documents around 1956, when he was twenty and he married the daughter of a very wealthy landowner and began to work for him. This certainly wasn't a marriage of convenience, because all the people who knew him after Maria died say he was shattered. But it seems that Nikos had got hold of a boat and started moving things around for all kinds of people, and we're talking drugs, weapons, all of that. He got involved with Tito Arias at one point and has some hilarious stories about the ballerina Margot Fonteyn, but I'll leave those to him.

'Anyway, Nikos got rich fast, very fast. He fell in with Frank Sturgis who was running guns down there, including to Cuba. Sturgis then went off to help train Castro's fighters in guerrilla warfare, leaving the gun running to Leotakis. At this time he was being watched very closely by the CIA, so he started to work for them, shipping weapons to the people they wanted to support. Only thing was, several boats and their shipments disappeared. Like Bermuda Triangle disappeared. The Americans still have no idea whether Leotakis was telling the truth when he said they'd capsized in a storm, but they couldn't prove he was lying, and he was still being useful. It's around this time he got the name The Pirate because he stole boats from Trujillo and Batista, and sold them to Guatemalan and Belize fishermen. I think it's almost certain that he was also being funded by Russia.'

'He took money from the Americans *and* the Russians?' asked Pam.

'There's a very old, long-retired CIA agent who could tell you stories about Leotakis that would make a Hollywood scriptwriter drool.'

'You hoping for a film of your book, then?'

'That would be nice. We'll see. I've promised not to

publish until after Nikos dies. Just to protect him. But there are some great stories. The honey boats, for example. I didn't believe that these stories were true until I went to Guatemala and met a delightful old lady who'd actually been one of his gang. She told me that Nikos could sing hawks from the sky; he's still charming, but at twenty? Yes, I can imagine it. The thing is Nikos really likes women. Actually respects them. So when he had a problem, which was how do you get a boat full of armed crooks carrying weapons to stop? His answer was to get a large yacht and fill it with attractive young women who manage to manoeuvre near the boat and then send up a distress signal. So when the crooks all go to have a look at this yacht, they see nothing but semi-clad women. And then they do what you'd expect them to do. They think they'll stop and have a bit of fun. They don't expect the women to have guns, or that they're hiding a couple of fully-armed men: Nikos and Sturgis. One of the stories Sturgis never told.'

'This is true?' Pam couldn't believe what she was hearing.

'As far as I can find out. But in order to repeat the method, Nikos had to make sure there were no survivors. According to my elderly and very charming informant, there were five boats seized in this way, which then ended up in Guatemala and Belize, where they were trying to get rid of their British rulers. Probably Nikos also wanted to give us Brits a bloody nose. Before he became a passionate anglophile. Though that was also down to his second wife, Alison, but much later, of course.

'With the money Nikos got from selling the arms, he then bought an oil tanker from a failing shipping company in Venezuela. You have to remember that around this time, Venezuela was the third largest producer of crude oil in the world, only just less than the whole of the Soviet production. There was a lot of oil to ship – and I'm pretty certain that this is where the Russians helped him. They wanted involvement in South America very badly.'

'This is quite a story,' said Pam. 'He sounds rather

frightening.'

'Except he isn't. He's a gentle and honourable man who I'm very happy to know as a friend. But he's also a man who gets what he wants and that hasn't changed.'

'So he still has enemies?'

Chris sat back and rubbed the back of his neck. He knows something, Pam decided and he's not sure whether to tell me. She sat silently and waited.

'If I tell you this, Inspector, you will be the only person apart from Nikos himself who knows it.'

'I understand. Total discretion.'

'In that case I am going to trust you.' He sat back and looked at Pam for a while. 'Yes, this is your special gift, isn't it? You have an ability to make people let down their guard. I have the feeling that there are a few people in jail who thought you were someone they could confide in.'

'A few,' she admitted. 'People do talk to me. I've never analysed it.'

'Don't,' he urged her. 'In case it disappears.'

'I'm writing a book about Nikos, and with his blessing, but what I'm also doing is trying to find out what his son is up to.'

'His son?'

'Antonio, or Antony, as he now calls himself, was born in 1957 to Nikos's first wife, Maria. Grew up in Venezuela and brought up by Maria's parents after his mother's death. Leotakis kept in touch and paid for his education, but they were never close and Antony never got on with Alison. Antony is the complete opposite of his father. He hates the culture his father nourishes, he loathes England, and he's one of the most wanted criminals in Europe.'

'Why isn't he arrested?'

'Mostly because people don't have enough evidence to extradite him. He lives in Monaco and the Cayman Islands, mostly on his yacht and I think that his father, despite himself, is probably protecting him. Antony owns a large share of Nikos's empire, worth about five hundred million according to Forbes. He doesn't run the businesses – he has people to do that, but he does get a few more millions from people-smuggling rackets. And cocaine, too. Monaco is all sea and snow.'

'What's the relationship between the father and son, then?'

'Mutual dislike. I don't think they've met for the past ten years or more. Nikos certainly didn't go to his son's fiftieth bash last year, which was the kind of ostentatious display of glitz and glamour you used to see around Onassis. Antony hero-worships Ari, by the way, which also annoys his father who loathed the man.'

'It seems that Nikos and Stephanie Michaels were close. Do you think that Antony could have carried out this murder to get at his father?'

Chris sat back and thought for a moment. He rubbed his hand across the back of his neck again.

'If he'd known, and I doubt he did, because Nikos kept it very, very quiet, virtually nobody outside Chiona knew about it, then yes, Antony certainly was capable of it.'

'But would his men have stabbed a cat?' Pam told Chris about Skimble, warning him that it was strictly off the record.

'That sounds exactly like the kind of thing Antony himself would do. We're talking really fucked-up psychopath here. But he never comes to England because we'd almost certainly arrest him.'

'Really nice piece of work,' said Pam. 'Jesus! Isn't there any way of arresting this man and stopping him?'

'Oh, a lot of good people have tried, Inspector. And many of them are now dead. The French, particularly would like to stop him because they're sure he has links with the gangs in Marseille and Toulon, and as for the Greek government...' He paused for a moment. 'I'm not sure, but I get the feeling they're waiting for the old man to die. Antony seems to have bought up some dirty cops, but I know there are a few senior policemen in Athens who would love to grab him if he ventured onto Greek soil. But they don't want to upset Nikos.'

'Antony doesn't live in Crete?'

'No. Hasn't been there for twenty years.'

'And he doesn't know you're investigating him?'

'No, thank God. If he did, to take a phrase from one of my favourite movies, I'd be sleeping with the fishes. If your investigation should find itself drifting towards Antony, that would be a very good moment to drop it. And I really mean that. He's seriously dangerous.'

Chris cycled back to work and Pam tried to balance what she'd heard with the idea of Leotakis as a philanthropist and friend of the Prime Minister. This was not her world, she decided, too rich in every sense. She needed to focus and remember she was investigating a murder. She was helped in this by the arrival of Jen, who wanted to know why she was being guarded as if she were a criminal. Pam tried to make her believe that she could be a future victim. But without explaining the nature of a Greek vendetta and terrifying her, it was difficult.

Despite this, the two women began to enjoy each other's company. Jen admired Pam's haircut and Pam confessed to her shopping spree.

'I think your friend Roberta was absolutely right. We can't stay with a billionaire and wear any old tat. That's why I had to go home and get some nice clothes. Do you like these? She pointed her toe and showed Pam her wedge heeled espadrille. 'Perfect for a yacht, don't you think?'

'We're not going on a yacht, are we?'

'No, but Mr Leotakis does have one, so we might.'

'Did your mother ever talk about Mr Leotakis,' Pam asked.

'A little. I think she became very close to him in the last few years. She'd mention him all the time in relation to what she thought about something or what she'd read. I felt they must be spending a lot of time together. But she never talked about him except to say how kind and thoughtful he was. And seems to be. I mean, it's incredibly kind of him to take us to Crete for Mummy's funeral. I'm not really up to organising anything right now.'

'Unlike Eleni,' Pam replied.

'Yes, that woman is extraordinary. She's always one step ahead. She could run an army.'

'Have you ever met her?'

'No. But I'll tell you who does know her and that's Popi.'

'Your godmother?'

'Yes. Have you talked to her yet?'

'I'm afraid I haven't. But she's going to be at the Villa, isn't she? I thought that would be a good time to talk to her about your mother.'

'They go back a really long time. Her and Henry, though Popi and Henry don't always get along.'

'No?'

'You have to understand that Popi was arrested and tortured by the Junta in 1973. That was the time that Mum got involved with Greek politics. The only time, in fact. Unlike Popi who's been involved with the socialist movement in Greece all her life. And still is, even from her wheelchair. She's quite something. Founded and still helps a major centre for victims of torture and has a constant supply of lost souls she looks after. They all adore her. I think she's got a new one at the moment who helps her about. When I spoke to her earlier this week to tell her about Mum, she said she was helping him find the folder on his family.'

'Folder?' queried Pam.

'Yes. Under the Junta, the Greeks kept huge police folders on everyone. The *fakelos*, it's called. They promised to destroy them, but as Popi has found out, a lot of them are still around. She's helping this boy who wants to know about his grandfather, who was a friend of Popi's. I think his father died recently, which is why Popi is looking after him.

Like I say, lost souls. Popi got to know Stephanie after the Polytechnic massacre.'

'You mentioned that before.'

'It was something that was very important to Mum. She said it was the only time in her life she'd been really scared. But Henry knows all about it, you can ask him.'

'Yes, I very much want to talk to Henry again, I expect he'll be at the funeral.'

'Of course. He was incredibly close to Mum. You've met him?'

'Yes. He said he was at your house the night of the murder.'

'Yes. I'm so cross I didn't know that till later. I'd have gone there.'

'I'm sorry to have to ask this, but when you did get back to the house, was there any sign of his being there?'

'What like an unwashed glass or something? I really can't remember. Diane would know, she was there at the door. Actually I can hardly remember anything about Tuesday morning. It was just a blur. She was there, and then you were there and I was trying not to believe that Mum was dead. And then there were all these yelling journalists and then I escaped here. It still feels like a bad dream. I keep expecting that when we arrive in Crete, Mum will be there in her house. I don't think I'll really believe she's gone until I see her house and it's empty.'

'Did you often stay there at the house?'

'Most years. But actually I used to make excuses to go and stay elsewhere. Often at Popi's. Mum and I always ended up quarrelling if we were together too long. I never felt that Chiona was my home. I'm actually relieved it's not mine.'

'You've heard?' Pam asked.

'Yes. Dad rang the solicitor, and he emailed me a copy of Mum's will. I don't know this Mike, but if he looks after Mum's house, that's fine by me. And I've got my home here, and it's now mine. That's all I wanted. I expect Nikos will tell me about this Mike.'

'I can tell you that he's a policeman who has family in that part of Crete. I think he helped build your mother's new house. He seems an interesting man.'

'Now that's an adjective that tells you a lot and nothing.'

It does, Pam thought. You could use it to describe Nikos Leotakis, too.

'So you don't know anything very much about Nikos?' she asked a little bit later.

'Not from Mum, but there was a good documentary film about Leotakis I saw a few years back. It was at IDFA, that's the International Documentary Film Festival Amsterdam, it's *the* major film festival for new documentaries. There was a sidebar on new films by women from South America, celebrating people like Lourdes Portillo, Natalia Almeda and Marcela Zamora. I'm particularly interested because of the way they film the world without making it about them. That was the subject of my PhD, by the way. About the way that many male documentary directors make the film about them. It was the reason my then boyfriend and I split up because I was also including him.'

'Ouch.'

'Yes. He said he forgave me, but he didn't. Not really.'

'They don't in my opinion.'

'Is that what it's about, Mum's death, somebody who can't forgive?'

'It does look like it. But you were about to tell me about this film on Nikos Leotakis.'

'Yes. He wasn't the main subject of the film, but a few people talked about him. How he helped arm the left-wing groups in Belize, supported them against the British. He didn't sound like your average businessman.'

Probably as far removed from the average as it's possible to be, Pam said to herself.

'Anyway, you're going to meet him this evening, aren't you?' Jen continued. 'You'll get a chance to see Tyneham House. Dad says it's quite something. Used to be a hangout for pirates.'

CHAPTER 27

Tyneham House was certainly something, Pam thought, as the housekeeper, Patricia, walked her through the hall into a domed rotunda from which two matching staircases circled round to a gallery above.

'The former Elizabethan manor house was home to the Bond family who owned Tyneham after acquiring it from the Napiers. But it has been remodelled by Mr Leotakis in the Palladian style of New Wardour Castle. You might have seen that in the film Billy Elliot. The house stood in for the Royal Ballet school.'

Pam supposed that Patricia doing a guidebook number was what most guests expected.

'The reason Napier came here was because of an old friendship with the Welds, who lived in Lulworth Castle, which is about three miles down the road as the crow flies. When they came here, this was the original village of Tyneham, but they found it spoiled their view, so they moved it to where it currently stands. Though as you probably saw, driving through, it is only a ghost village now since it was taken over by the MOD during World War Two. Mr Leotakis managed to persuade the Ministry of Defence to sell him this house in the seventies. It was a complete ruin then, and he rebuilt it.'

Villages moved at the whim of the rich, thought Pam. Not much has changed then. Then Tyneham, now Chiona.

She let the rest of the commentary wash over her as she looked around. The house had two long corridors leading from the circular gallery, which was painted blue and covered with white plasterwork on the walls and the ceiling. Like being inside one of those Wedgewood plates.

The room she was sleeping in was very different. The bottom half was panelled and painted white and the walls were covered with paintings of birds and flowers.

'Every room is different,' Patricia told her, 'and all the roses you see are those grown by Mrs Leotakis. The wallpapers were hand-painted as a present for her thirtieth birthday.'

Richard gave me a box of Black Magic chocolates, which she later found had been donated to the nick, and an absurd and very uncomfortable pair of silk knickers, reflected Pam. Though they turned out to be good for polishing shoes.

'But then this house has always been a place of romance.' Patricia was opening doors to show Pam a wardrobe and a large bathroom with more towels than she had at home. There were also towelling dressing gowns and slippers. A vase on a low white table was filled with sweet peas and there were books on a narrow white bookcase.

'It's not generally known, though it is mentioned in Lord Caston's diary, but this was where Mary Fitzherbert first met the Prince Regent who fell passionately in love with her. She was married to Edward Weld at the time and then, being left penniless when he died, went on to marry Mr Fitzherbert, who also died. And then after again meeting the Prince a couple of years later, in London, she married him.'

'So did she become the Queen?'

'No. Such a sad story. She was a Catholic, so the marriage was invalid. It also hadn't been approved by King George, so the Prince had to marry his cousin Caroline. Though he left everything to Mary in his will. Now,' she turned to face Pam. 'I know it's taken you two and a half hours to get here, so we thought you might just like a cup of tea and a bit of time to rest till dinner. Mr Leotakis will meet you for a drink at seven and I'll give you a tinkle at about twenty to in case you're asleep.'

'That would be lovely,' said Pam, though in fact she couldn't remember ever having been spoiled as she had been today, what with the sandwiches and endless drinks at Colin's house, and the single glass of champagne she'd allowed herself on the plane from Farnborough. In fact she could have got thoroughly pissed since there was also orange juice and champagne in the waiting room at the airport, that was as far removed from plastic chairs at Gatwick as it got. It was all comfortable leather sofas, magazines and newspapers, plus free drinks and nibbles. If you were really rich, she thought, you got given things you could easily afford to buy.

Patricia came back with a pot of tea and small home-made shortbread biscuits.

'I could get used to this,' Pam said as she thanked her.

'Yes, all our guests say that. Except for the ones who live like this every day. Even the PM appreciates life here.'

Pam drank her tea while flipping through a book about the local smugglers. It appeared that smuggling had been rife along this part of the Dorset coast. 'Few people,' wrote the author, 'would be unaware of the smuggling and most would know someone who was involved in bringing ashore illegal brandy and silks.' The world doesn't change, she thought as she undressed, noting that her legs were now a very pleasant honey colour. She had a shower, put on the soft towelling dressing gown, and lay down on the bed. I'll have a quick power nap, she decided. Then I can go through my notes before I meet Mr Leotakis.

Almost immediately, her phone rang. She leapt up. Josh, she thought. Something's happened, but it was Patricia, telling her it was twenty to seven.

Pam found some heated hair tongs in the bathroom, which miraculously brought her hair back under control, put on a touch of foundation and some mascara, then put her blue dress back on. She was ready to meet this extraordinary man.

Nikos Leotakis, she had to admit, did not look like anyone else she had ever met. He was still handsome with short but thick white hair and deeply tanned. He wore a pair of fawn trousers and a white shirt unbuttoned at the neck and a grey cashmere cardigan. But it was his eyes she noticed most. Bright, amused, intelligent, he was a man who didn't miss a thing.

'I'm sorry to drag you down here all the way from Cambridge, Inspector, but it's one of the ways I give in to old age – I rest before a journey.'

'No trouble at all,' said Pam. 'I don't usually get to travel on private planes, and it's wonderful to get a chance to see your house. This view', she added, looking out from gazebo on the small hill on the lawn where they were sitting, over the cliff edge and out to sea, 'you'd never get tired of that.'

'No, I don't,' he agreed. 'Neither here, nor at the Villa Karpathi. No Cretan ever wants to live too far from the sea. This is why I built this little hill. Below is the south west coast path and it would be rather easy for people to wander up into my garden. And I do have some rather good things here, so I had to build a fence. But of course I do not want to sit and look at a fence, so we planted two lines of trees and within them we hide a very strong and tall fence. And thus I build a small hill on my lawn so I can look over the trees and enjoy the view.'

'I did notice the security at the gate lodge as we came in.'

'If I invite a prime minister or a president to stay here I have to ensure that the security is always in place. The same is true of Villa Karpathi in Crete. I was able to acquire the whole promontory and therefore make it secure.'

Does that make one feel more or less safe, she asked herself. He smiled at her. 'I would feel more secure, of course, if I were not rich. And if you are wondering whether I have had death threats. The answer is many times, but not for some years now.'

A waiter, Pam assumed he was a waiter although he might have been something else, as he wore jeans, a black T-shirt and white trainers, brought them a tray of drinks and put it on the table.

'Thank you, Rafael,' said Leotakis. The man smiled and left. 'I may be wrong and assuming too much,' Leotakis continued, 'But I imagined that for our first conversation you would be on duty and therefore not drinking. So these are non-alcoholic Mojitos. The limes are grown here in one of our greenhouses and we grow mint in vast quantities. I do rather have a taste for it. It drives my cooks mad.'

'That was thoughtful, thank you,' said Pam. If this was a charm offensive, he was doing rather well. It was hard not to like the old man. She sipped her drink and decided to let him lead the conversation. Leotakis watched Pam carefully, and she felt she was going through some kind of test. Then he sat back, pressed his fingers together as if in prayer and then began.

'You have to understand that I cared deeply for Stephanie. There's nothing I wouldn't do to bring her back. I miss her company very much. I only knew her for the last five years, but we became close. And if you have heard that, then I assume you must have asked whether Stephanie was killed to hurt me?'

'We have considered it as a possibility.' She hoped he wouldn't be insulted, but he nodded and smiled.

'It is a natural conclusion to make. And, although you may have been instructed not to ask me, I admire your courage in wanting to do so. Now,' he continued, 'regarding whether the murder was done to hurt me, this is an assumption I have had to consider myself. But being so old means that almost all my former enemies are now dead. For the past thirty years my life has been extremely peaceful. You do not get killed for being a philanthropist, I think. A gallery or a museum that is not funded by me may feel disgruntled, but they will not turn to murder. However...' He took Pam's hand and patted it. 'I have made the decision, Inspector, to be frank with you. There is one person who I know could have killed dear Stephanie and that is my son.'

'Antony?'

'Yes. Antony. It makes me very deeply sad that he has become the evil man he is today. I do not use the word lightly. If he were not my son, I would find a way to remove him from this earth, but the gods do not look kindly on filicide.'

The police don't either, she said to herself. He may look like anyone's grandfather, but he clearly isn't.

'Do you think he was behind this killing?' she asked him.

'No. He was not. I do not trust my son,' he continued, 'and I have people embedded in his entourage to prevent the most extreme of his actions. I also know everything that he says online and on his many phones. He never knew about Stephanie. He prefers not to even think about me and for that I am grateful. But I still have to observe him.'

And how many laws is he breaking there, she wondered. Or does he have a private link with a security force?

'Could you tell me about Stephanie?' She felt that they had exhausted the possibility of the son. Though it could be something to discuss with the Greek police. 'I feel I'm not going to be able to track down her killer until I know what it was that he thinks he was avenging,' she continued.

'You can be sure I've thought long and hard about this,' he said. 'If I could imagine anything that Stephanie had done to so enrage a man, I would have told you.'

'Our first thoughts have been about the Chiona treasures,' she replied. 'Whether there were people who felt that she had taken all the credit for a collaborative excavation. The way that she was positioned on the bull, led us in that direction.'

'I have been wondering now if I should remove the statue. It would be terrible if it was seen only as the place of a murder. I have discussed this with Dr Kitson, but we have decided to place a series of pictures of bull-leaping around it, along with information about the Minotaur, and hope that ancient history will distract from recent history.'

'That sounds like a good solution.'

'It was Mark's not mine. I like the boy very much. He will be an excellent director of the gallery.'

'The', not 'my', Pam noted. It has his name but he doesn't feel he controls it. Interesting.

'And I imagined you thought that the publicity about Stephanie and the Chiona treasure had upset someone. That is probably my fault. I was so happy for her. And she was good at publicity. It came naturally to her.'

'We have looked into this, but the archaeologists who might have felt most aggrieved were all still in Crete or Athens at the time of her death. And everyone connected to the Fitzwilliam Museum has been ruled out. The killer left a lot of very clear fingerprints, so it hasn't been hard to eliminate all the staff and those still working on the gallery from our inquiries.'

'Do you have any current leads?'

'I can't really divulge that to you at this stage. After all, you might want to take matters into your own hands.'

'I might. When I was younger, there is no question, I would have killed the man. Today I am more reasonable.'

'I can tell you we have not yet found a clear motive for her death. There have been some leads.'

It should be safe to tell him about the people who weren't possible killers, she decided. She told Leotakis about Kieron James and the man who emailed about the Greek marbles.

'Ah, Adrestia. Yes. I know about him. As do the Greek police. If he attempts to leave the country, he may not find it so easy. He will most certainly not be permitted to leave the country during the period we open the gallery. I do not intend to embarrass or harm the Prince of Wales.'

'We are also keeping an eye on his online activity.'

'I am impressed, Inspector. In a very few days, you have achieved a great deal. And now you would like me to tell you about Stephanie.' Pam smiled and let him speak. Silence was so often a better trigger than questions.

'Stephanie was, in her words, a free spirit. Which meant that she slept with any man she liked whether they were married or not. I can imagine that there are wives in the world who disliked her, but she never tried to break up a marriage. And I don't know of any marriages she did break up. When I knew her she was in her late sixties, but I don't think her behaviour had changed significantly.'

'I have heard a little from Henry Cox.'

'Henry knew her the best. Henry and Popi were her two oldest friends. I do not think she knew her daughter very well. It is…it was a great regret of hers.'

'Do you think Henry hated her?'

'Ah. One of your public school mysteries is Henry. A brilliant mind shut away. He should have found himself a nice young man to look after him. There were passions, I have heard, sometimes consummated, but Henry is too shy. They were not so unalike in some ways, Henry and Stephanie, so naturally they fought. Neither found it easy to mix with people. But I do not think Henry hated her. I don't know. He most certainly dislikes me. He did not want to lose his house. But I don't see him as your killer, he is too English. The theatrical gesture, the writing of the vendetta, none of that sounds in the least like Henry.'

'Unless he wanted us to think that.'

'You think he could be that devious? Oh. I do not know. This feels so much like a Greek death, it comes from the roots of our creation. It doesn't feel like a murder committed by an English gentleman.'

Leotakis sipped his drink and Pam did the same. Sipping drinks and listening to stories, seems to be all I've done today, she thought. Yet eventually I'll hear the story which will unlock this case.

'Are there many stories about Stephanie?' she asked.

'Many,' he replied, 'Her stories were performances, she told me stories to make me love her, but I already loved her.

But she could never accept that, she didn't believe she was worth loving. I think Colin had tried to make her believe that, and from the stories she told me about that time, she had done that teenage behaviour: will you love me if... and the behaviour deteriorates until the lover has had enough. Which proves she is unlovable.

'And so she lives on her own, she takes photographs, she draws artefacts and sometimes she paints – and she had some talent, but never worked at it – she walks in the hillsides and picks wild plants, which she used to dye cotton. And, until her last illness, she allowed every visiting archaeologist into her bed.'

There was no trace of criticism in the way Leotakis described Stephanie's behaviour nor jealousy, though that might be a cover.

'She did her own thing as she would say,' he continued. 'If you want a story about Stephanie I will tell you of how I first met her. We were in the fish restaurant in Chiona. I was with some old friends and Stephanie was, I seem to remember, lunching with two Italians who have a summer house in the village. I noticed them because they were drinking and laughing a lot and Stephanie had a wonderful laugh. She would throw her head back and let her whole body explode with laughter. It was attractive.

'An English family arrived and they were not comfortable there. They were frightened because the tables were so close to the sea. Basically, they were in the wrong place. They ordered a Greek salad and, as you may know, we often sprinkle dried oregano on the feta.

'Oh my goodness, the scream! The woman is shouting that there are dead flies in her salad. Stephanie goes across and tells her it is dried herbs, but the woman says she's leaving, she won't pay to have flies in her food. And Stephanie runs into the kitchen and comes out with a handful of oregano. She throws it all over the woman and tells her to fuck off back to her cosy suburban home, and if she wants to go abroad, learn something about their culture. And then she walks back to her table.'

Pam laughed.

'So Stephanie could be fun, but also unpredictable. She could upset people. I see that, but it doesn't seem to fit in with the idea of a vendetta. Can you tell me something about that.'

'Ah. That I do know. I come originally from the west of Crete and that is where you find still the vendetta. It arises when sheep and cattle are stolen or after a murder or when a woman is raped. It is always families against families.'

'I don't see how this relates to Stephanie.'

'Nor do I. Stephanie was a deeply troubled woman all her life. It is why she drank. Yet at some point in her life she must have done something unforgiveable, which has led to her death, but I do not know what that was. She never told me. And now we will go back to the terrace for dinner and you will go off duty. We will drink wine and discuss more pleasant things.'

Oh God, he'll discover just how boring and ignorant I am, thought Pam. It's going to be a nightmare.

CHAPTER 27

Looking back, Pam found it hard to recall the details of the dinner, or exactly what they'd said or ate, only that she couldn't remember having ever laughed so much or felt so at ease. It might have been the delicious food or the wine, which tasted vaguely like lemon curd on fresh bread, or the soft cashmere wrap that Rafael had magicked up instantly when she shivered in the cooling air.

Leotakis had a knack of drawing out her stories, and making her feel that what she said was important and interesting. He must do this in his work, she realised: charm companies into his control. She'd wanted to feel professional and critical. As a detective in charge of a major murder investigation, she shouldn't be accepting hospitality from a key witness, but it hadn't been her choice anyway, the decision for her to meet him had been made much further up the line. She was merely the beneficiary.

But unlike other people, Richard's friends, for example, Leotakis did not want to make her feel stupid or irrelevant. He made her feel as if she mattered.

'Tell me about this place, March,' he'd said.

'All eels and angels,' she'd replied and wondered where she'd found the phrase. And then he'd called for his tablet so he could see the angels in March church, and had asked her to write down her favourite eel recipe, the one with garlic and rosemary, for his cook. 'Raw eel is poisonous,' she'd warned him and that had led to stories about the Fen Tigers and of feuds and deaths on the fens.

'Sounds very like Crete,' he'd said. 'Like our vendettas.'

And back they'd come. But now he was telling her stories of wild shepherds in mountain villages where guns lay around in kitchen drawers along with tin openers.

'Guns everywhere in Crete. Ancient guns, new guns,' he'd told her.

Later, over coffee in the sitting room, surrounded by paintings which exploded with colour, they talked about childhood. She told him she'd become a police officer because of her father.

'Tell me,' he said, pouring a golden honey liqueur into tiny glasses.

'He was a firefighter; he died in an accident and I wanted to do something that would have made him proud.'

'If he saw you now he would be very proud.' Leotakis patted her hand. Pam felt her eyes pricking. Nobody had ever said that to her before. 'It is very hard to lose a father.'

And that was when he began to tell her about the Second World War and the Civil War that followed. Tales of atrocities and betrayal.

'Life on Crete was hard in those days,' he said. And when the Germans came, they came by parachute. You have to remember I was a small boy and the parachutes weren't just white, the Germans were organisers above all. They had parachutes of different colours for different purposes. Their own personal parachutes were white, as were those for ammunition and weapons. But there were green parachutes for heavy cannons, medical equipment falling down to the ground under pink canopies, while medical officers fell down to earth under yellow parachutes. There were red and mauve and blue parachutes for different ranks of officers and black parachutes for grenades. How can death arrive with so much beauty?

'Although I was still a child, I fought in the hills during the occupation. I saw burning villages and Chania bombed almost to extinction. I lost most of my childhood friends and then I lost my parents in the Civil War. It was in a battle in the Samaria Gorge, where today the tourists leap down the steps not knowing that this was where the local communists were defeated and many partisans who'd fought the Germans were betrayed. Everything I became and everything I am was made on that day.'

'Are you thinking that Stephanie's death was political?'

'It's possible. I don't know how or why, but this kind of death feels political to me. It is because of the way you described how he planned it. A combination of planning and violence. It comes from decades of anger.'

'But where did she come into it?'

'As I say, I have no idea. But the pain of the last war runs through my island. The Civil War divided our nation and that division was continued under the Junta. There are many people who have never come to terms with the past.' He sighed. 'But what has that got to do with my dearest Stephanie? I lie awake trying to think of anything she has told me, but there is nothing.'

He stood up. 'If anyone knows, it will be Henry and Popi. You must ask them.'

'I will.'

'And now, please forgive me if we end this very pleasant evening. We must leave early tomorrow and I am an old man.'

In her room, Pam made a quick call to Josh to catch up on the day, though it seemed that nothing very much had happened. They had found some CCTV cameras along Trumpington Street and Hills Road, and he'd put three constables on to viewing the footage.

'The problem is we don't know who we're looking for. We know George went to the station and so did Henry according to his story.'

'But if you see Henry in Trumpington Street, near the Museum, that totally wipes out his version.'

'Yes. Good point. But a witness would be good.'

'That would be very good. I'm not really sure just what I can achieve in Crete apart from talking with Stephanie's oldest friends and seeing her house.'

'There was absolutely zilch on Stephanie's iPad. Just stuff about the exhibition and a lot of emails telling distant friends she couldn't offer them invitations to the opening. Masses and masses of press stuff. All of which she directed to Mrs Apostoli. Eleni. Seems that she acted as Stephanie's public relations person and all-round fixer.'

'From one conversation, I found Eleni pretty formidable, while Nikos seems...' she tried to find the right word.

'Nikos, is it?' he teased.

She laughed. 'I've had a totally bizarre and wonderful evening, but also a long conversation. I'm pretty certain we don't have to bring Mr Leotakis into our enquiry. He's genuinely distressed by her death.'

'Wouldn't that be a motive?'

'He doesn't think many people knew about them.'

'Maybe Mike could tell you if that's true.'

'Good point. He's been there long enough to pick that up. I'll see him tomorrow; he's coming to join us all for dinner along with the local police major.'

'Major?'

'They have military titles it seems. An inspector is above a colonel, who is above a major, who is above a lieutenant. Sergeants and detectives seem to be a separate species.'

'Oh we are!' Josh laughed. 'You sound really happy, boss. I can't remember the last time I heard you sound so relaxed.'

'Nor can I, Josh. And this is a day that began as my worst ever.'

She told him about Dave and Murton, and some of the pleasure of the evening began to evaporate.

'Just don't think about it,' he told her. 'Enjoy Crete and find the murderer. Then you'll be untouchable.'

After she'd finished the call, she surprised herself by taking a book off the shelf instead of writing up her notes. It was an anthology of poems, and she was about to put it back when she turned a page and saw a poem titled 'The Door.'

'Go and open the door,' she read. She read it once and then again. And then she found she was crying. 'Go and open the door,' she whispered to herself. She'd done that by managing to escape from Richard, but how far had she come? Go and open the door, she read again. 'At least there'll be a draught.'

Is this what poetry was? Just a door that anyone could go through? Just as she'd come through a dinner without feeling a fool. But what was the door she needed to open?

She fell asleep almost immediately and was woken by Patricia with a cup of tea. A large comfortable Mercedes drove them to Bournemouth Airport where they met up with Jen and Colin, and were almost immediately escorted on to the Leotakis jet.

Travelling like this was merely an extension of everyday life, and as private as being at home. Leotakis had a separate compartment on the plane where he had gone to work and rest, and that had allowed Pam and Jen to exchange muted squeals as they examined the luxury of the large jet. There were sofas as well as comfortable chairs and tables that folded out and a cinema screen that dropped down. And a proper shower room and a kitchen where the steward and Rafael, who was travelling with them, brought them hot pastries and croissants and endless fresh coffee and orange juice. Jen and Colin drank champagne, but Pam said she was back on duty, though duty had never felt like this before. She would have loved to have taken a photo to show the team, but felt it would be rude to Mr Leotakis. You don't got into a stranger's house and take pictures of their décor, she told herself. But the plane also had Wi-Fi and once they had taken off, Rafael told her that she could turn on her phone.

Almost immediately, it rang.

'Josh?'

'Sorry to bother you, boss?' Are you in Greece already? Your phone is giving a European ring.'

'I'm on the plane. No. I know about not using phones on planes. This jet has its own rules.'

'Like its owner.' Josh paused and she could hear him moving papers.

'Are you in the office on a Saturday? Barbara is going to want my head on a platter.'

'There's been something.'

'What? Tell me?'

She'd raised her voice and Jen and Colin were staring at her. She smiled at them and gestured that it was all fine.

'I got a constable to check on the post arriving at Stephanie's house…'

'Good thinking, Josh. And something has arrived?'

'It was a letter. All written in capitals, including the address. Inside it just says, "It is not ended."'

Pam looked across where Jen was talking to her father and laughing. She felt cold.

'Where was it sent from?'

'Heraklion, that's the capital of Crete. I got Mike to look at the envelope this morning.'

'Good. But not good. Thanks for this, Josh. I think we'll need to get Mike more involved. Can you ring him and tell him to meet us at the Villa. We'll be there by, oh what was it? Just after one forty-five Greek time, which is eleven forty-five your time.'

'How the hell are you getting there that quickly?'

'No baggage control, and apparently we will be going from the airport to the villa by helicopter.'

'Now I'm seriously jealous.'

'Well, this plane is rather special. It's not one of the ones that they use to go to the races, they tell me. It's a Boeing 737. This is such a different world, Josh. It's hard to get my head round it.'

'Don't get used to it.'

'I won't. I have a dog kennel, as Roberta calls it, waiting for me at home.'

Pam stood up and went to the galley where Rafael and the other steward were sitting on a sofa of their own, drinking coffee.

'Excuse me, Rafael, I need to have a word with Mr Leotakis.'

Rafael got up and disappeared behind the connecting door. Like the rest of the plane, it was painted white. It was all like one of those photographs of Greek islands, blue and white. White walls with abstract blue swirls like waves and white cotton covers on the seats, and sofas with dark blue cushions.

'He has a way of walking, doesn't he?' Pam said to the steward.

'He was the maître d' at one of the best restaurants in Paris. They learn that shimmer there.'

'But he doesn't have the air of a waiter?'

'He's had a few lives since then. He's also Mr Leotakis's bodyguard.'

'Really? How interesting.'

And is he armed? she wondered. Is it having an armed guard beside him that allows Mr Leotakis to be as relaxed as he is? This is a different world from mine. I don't know the rules yet.

Rafael shimmered back through the cabin and told Pam that Mr Leotakis would be happy for him to join her.

The cabin the other side of the door was identical in look to the one they had been sitting in except that it housed a day bed on one side and a large chair and desk on the other.

'Will you excuse me one moment, Pam,' said Leotakis. 'I just need to make a call.'

Pam looked out of the window and saw they were flying over a mountain range, the sun catching the remains of snow below the jagged peaks.

'The Dolomites,' said Leotakis. '*Nai*,' he continued, on the phone, talking fast in Greek.'

Pam wondered where the Dolomites were. They looked remote and strange. She felt so removed from Cambridge and the flat landscape of her childhood she'd talked about that the previous evening, and how she didn't miss hills until she saw them when her parents took her to Dorset for a holiday. 'Near here,' she'd said. 'In fact we went swimming one day in Lulworth cove. After that I missed hills.'

'Yet there you are in Cambridge. I understand about flat spaces,' he told her. 'I once spent two months on the plains in Venezuela fighting the cattle rustlers. This was in the far south east of the country and you can ride for hundreds of miles and all is flat. Then suddenly the Gran Sabana mountains rise up from the earth to the clouds in front of you like a dream. Table mountains. We have a miniature one in Chiona which you will see soon. A single, very small table mountain that just stands beside the harbour, like a slightly flattened pyramid, though once there were battlements on its summit. But the Gran Sabana, ah! If I was not so old I would take you there.'

Pam looked down at this spiky, ragged mountain range and thought that this was dream-like enough. It would do. Maybe one day she would come here on the ground.

Leotakis had finished his call and was watching her.

'Where are the Dolomites?' she asked.

'On the Austrian-Italian border,' he replied. 'You should visit Lake Misurina. It is very beautiful. Now tell me what it is that concerns you.'

'An anonymous letter was sent from Heraklion to Stephanie's house. It arrived this morning. It says, "It is not ended." We've sent it to Forensics, but I think it's quite likely that it comes from our murderer.'

'And you are concerned about Jen?'

'Very. We couldn't stop her coming for her mother's funeral, of course, but I am extremely worried that he will try to kill her.'

'So am I. Tell me what you want?'

'I'll tell her that she mustn't go out anywhere by herself, but it would be good to have some protection if she leaves your villa. Perhaps Mike could come there as an informal bodyguard.'

'That is a good idea. I do have guards at the villa. But it is possible to come close by boat. I will increase the level of security. I will ring Mike now and tell him to go to the villa. Also Stavros.'

'Stavros?'

'Stavros Papadakis. He is the police major I mentioned last night. He is a part of the DDAS, the International Police Cooperation Division. He works in Athens, but his family live in Souda. I will tell him to meet us at the airport. I will ring him now.'

He picked up his phone and pressed a key. 'Eleni, can you ring Major Papadakis and ask him to call me on Viber now. Thank you.' He turned back to Pam. 'He is a very good policeman, based in the National Intelligence Service in Athens, but his family comes from Crete, and he is staying there in preparation to work with you. It has been agreed by your Chief Constable' He smiled. 'I helped speed things up a little.'

His laptop emitted a singing note rising in scale and he clicked on the screen. Pam had to remind herself that this man was over eighty. She had members of her team half his age who were less technically adept.

'Stavros,' said Leotakis, 'I am here with Detective Inspector Gregory and we need to talk with you.'

He beckoned Pam to come over and she leaned over his chair and said 'hello' to the face on the screen.

'We're on the plane, so we may have some interference, Stavros, so forgive us if we seem fuzzy.'

'I can see you both clearly, thank you,' said the Major. He smiled and Pam found herself smiling back. It wasn't that he was good looking like Mike, but there was something warm and reassuring about this man. She felt herself relax; he'd be a good partner to work with.

'The Cambridge police have new evidence that the killer aims to strike again,' she told him.

'And you're thinking that the daughter is in danger.'

'We are.'

'I was wondering, Stavros, whether it might be wise for you to join us today and come with us to the Villa Karpathi,' said Leotakis.

'Good idea, Sir, but I'd like to have my car there, so if that's ok with you, I'll ensure they double the security at the airport. Actually I'll send one of the dogs in to check the helicopter before you go, but I'll drive to Sitia now and meet you there.'

Pam rather liked the way that Stavros managed to do what Leotakis wanted, but in his own way. He clearly wasn't under the old man's thumb. But the idea of dogs made her think of bombs. Would the killer have access to explosives? What kind of man was she looking for? She needed to go to Stephanie's house first and see whether there was any evidence of political involvement.

'Good,' said Leotakis. 'I'll have a guest cottage made ready for you.'

'Thank you,' said Pam. 'I look forward to working with you.'

'Yes,' said Stavros. 'Mr Leotakis has my email address. If there are people you wish to interview, send me their names and I can begin to investigate them in advance.'

'That sounds excellent,' said Pam. 'I have a name. I'll email you the details right away.' She ended the call.

'You have a name?' asked Leotakis.

'A witness, not a suspect,' said Pam.

'You mean George,' Leotakis replied. 'Anna told me he'd run away. You are right to check him and also right to assume he was not the killer. I have worked with him now for over a year and he is not a physical man. But he is good with workmen, he gets the best from them. I thought you might mention him yesterday.'

'I thought that if you suspected him you would have told me,' replied Pam.

'No. You didn't want to tell me anything more than you had to. I understand that. And I forgive you.'

He nodded and Pam took that as her cue to leave. She made her way back into the other cabin and unfolded a table to make a desk. She checked her emails. There was one from Irini with several attachments. Those would be the photographs of the archaeologists; she'd look at them later. An email pinged in from Leotakis with an email for Stavros and she began to prepare her list of names for him.

Top of the list had to be George, the project manager and also the archaeologist, Petros Manoussis. She needed to check his emails. She also wanted to talk with Henry again. Should she tell Stavros that he was MI6? She didn't like keeping work partners in the dark, but she hadn't actually signed the Official Secrets Act. She'd have to think about that. So. Track down George, and go through Stephanie's house. Maybe one or the other would lead her to the killer.

CHAPTER 28

It was one of those perfect, still June mornings. The sea foamed gently on the small beach as if to prove it was the sea and not an endless infinity pool, like the one a few metres from where Mike was standing.

It would be a good day to go snorkelling, fishing, working, talking, walking. Anything. Anything rather than being here, pretending that he could again be a policeman, could protect those he loved from harm.

Mike turned on his heel and walked back into the small, luxurious room near the one that had been allocated to Jen and which would enable him to see whether anyone went in or out of hers.

Mike had only met Jen the last few times she'd come to stay with her mother. The last time was the most memorable. It had started with a dinner by the harbour, with Stephanie at her worst, getting drunker by the minute, and her daughter looking tired and furious and wishing she was a hundred miles away. It had ended with him taking Jen back to the room where he was living and letting her talk through the night. They hadn't made love, although he found her incredibly attractive, but she was the kind of woman who could get under your skin and he was never going to let that happen again.

He wondered how she remembered the night. Or whether she did. She had drunk quite a lot herself, though he knew she didn't make a habit of it. And now he was going to have to protect her from this lunatic.

If he could. And what if he couldn't? What if once again he failed? What if he let down Stephanie who'd helped him so much?

He lay down on the floor and began to do a series of fast, brutal sit-ups until his lungs could no longer supply enough air. Then he threw off his clothes and walked into the shower. He stood there letting the cold water wash over him as the tears poured down his cheeks. Finally, he stopped crying and turned the water to warm until he stopped shivering.

Then he stepped out, dried himself and put on his clothes again. Jeans and a black T-shirt. The kitchen had sent over a pot of coffee, and he poured himself a cup, going through his earlier conversation with Josh, who'd rung him as soon as he'd received the letter.

'Well if it is from the killer – and who else would it be from? Even the worst tabloid journalists wouldn't do this – then it places him here in Crete. The postmark is Heraklion, which is the main city here and about ninety miles from us.'

'Looks as though the boss is in the right place then,' Josh replied. 'I wish I could be there to give her backup.'

'Well she'll have the local police. And I'll do all I can to protect Jen.'

'Thanks, Mike,' Josh smiled. 'That's good to hear.'

He wouldn't say that if he knew about me, thought Mike. He'd tell me to bugger off and get the next plane in himself. Mike tried to concentrate on the letter itself.

'Greek, I'd say, from the wording,' he said. 'We would say, it hasn't ended yet, or it's not over. It is not ended, sounds like the writer isn't writing in his mother tongue.'

'I thought that, too,' said Josh. 'So now it's up to you and the DI to track him down.'

'Not me,' Mike replied. 'I'll just hang around Jen and act as a shield for any passing knife. The DI will be sleuthing with the local cops. I'm glad to say I don't do that anymore.'

'This is such a weird case,' said Josh. 'We're all going through the usual motions of detection, but I'm not sure that any of us believe that they are getting us anywhere.'

'Reminds me of a Western,' Mike replied. 'A stranger comes into town, kills someone and leaves. He's only caught when they send a posse out into the mountains to find out where he is hiding.'

'Sounds like the boss needs a posse then.'

'Yes. And we do have the mountains and plenty of hiding places.' And he'd told Josh the story about George Tzobanakis, the Cretan partisan who had hidden up in the mountains for three decades after the Civil War.

'It's all history isn't it?' Josh observed. 'Everywhere we go with this case people are telling us stories about the past.'

'Probably because a vendetta inevitably has its roots there.'

'If it is a real vendetta and not just a personal grudge,' answered Josh. 'The DI said she had a long conversation with Mr Leotakis and he couldn't think of any event in Stephanie's life that would make a vendetta a possible response.'

And yet it did, they both thought. And now Jen was in danger, too.

Mike walked out of his room towards the helicopter pad and sat on the ground in the shade underneath a cypress tree. Leotakis had planted dozens on this hillside and his gardeners had coaxed them through the storms and the droughts into putting down their roots. It made this small corner of the island feel very different. I wonder whether the Venetians planted cypress here, he thought. He'd seen some in western Crete, but here it was all olives and carobs. The cypress were good at providing privacy, but at the same time they also provided cover for a sniper. Except in this case, there was an impenetrable, alarmed wire fence between the trees keeping everyone off the peninsula. No, the Villa Karpathi was safe. The danger was outside.

Mike forced himself to relax as he waited and very soon

he heard the heavy whirr of the S-76 Sikorsky helicopter. Mike gritted his teeth and tried not to think of the last time he'd heard that sound, only then it was the London Ambulance Service, and it was coming to pick him up. He shook away the memories and stood up. The helicopter landed gently, creating plumes of dust, and as the engines died, two of the staff ran forward to open the doors and greet Leotakis and his guests. Mike stepped forward to join them and found himself facing the DI who looked rather different from his last videocall with her. She'd done something to her hair and the button-through green sleeveless dress looked casual. He hoped she didn't think she was here for a holiday.

She bounded over to him and shook his hand warmly.

'Mike, thank you for coming here to help. Mr Leotakis says we're all meeting for a light informal lunch in a few minutes, but after that I wonder whether you'd come to my room for a briefing. The local police liaison officer will be there, too.'

'Major Stavros Papadakis. I met him earlier. I think he's being taken on a tour of the perimeter fence.'

'Excellent.' She pulled him to one side and dropped her voice. 'I've decided that we won't tell Jen about the new threat. We don't want to panic her and there is no advantage to her knowing.'

Mike nodded. He thought she was probably right, although it would make it slightly harder to stop her from going out if she wanted to.

'See you later then,' Pam said, and turned back to talk with Jen and a tall older man who Mike assumed was Jen's father. No, the DI did not think she was on holiday. And now it was time to meet up with Jen again. Pam was being taken to her room and Jen was looking at the view over the bay. He walked over to greet her.

'Hi, Jen,' he said. 'I'm so sorry about your mother.'

'Mike, I didn't know you'd be here. Thank you. It's still hard to take in. I keep expecting her to drive up and ask where the drinks are.' They began to walk towards the cluster of small cottages where they were all staying. Leotakis called his home the Villa Karpathi, but really it was more like a small village, a dozen small cottages surrounding the larger villa, all within a landscaped garden. He'd been invited here a few times to talk with Nikos, though rarely when Stephanie was staying.

'I find it hard to believe, too.'

'She was just so alive, even though she drove me crazy.' Jen shook her head to stop herself crying. She stopped walking for a moment and looked around her at the villa and the bay beyond it, and the gardens where plumbago and bougainvillea had been trained to climb through the many palm trees.

'Did Mum come here often?'

'Yes. Quite often.'

'Did she... no, I shouldn't be asking that.'

'Was she having a relationship with Mr Leotakis? Yes, if you mean was there a close emotional bond. I certainly saw that. If you're asking about anything else, I never dared ask her, and I certainly wouldn't dare ask Nikos.'

'No. I wouldn't either and quite frankly I'd rather not know. My mother told me far more about her sex life while she was alive than I wanted to hear. But it helps me to understand why he helped her become the star of the Chiona treasure.'

'Yes, it does.'

'And you were close to her, too? I only remember her being very rude to both of us at that dinner.' She blushed slightly and Mike knew she'd forgotten nothing.

'She was a friend, but I don't think I ever really knew her. Not in the way that Henry or Popi did.'

'Popi's arriving this afternoon.'

'That's good.'

'I've been missing her ever since I got the news even though I've been talking to her every day. You know she's retired? She said Alex had to drag her out of her office. They're now living here all the time in their old summer home. Did you know Alex had had a stroke? He's getting better, but not well enough to travel to the funeral. Popi's not great either. But I didn't get that from her, of course. Mr Letotakis told me. He's an old friend of hers, too. She has to use a wheelchair, which she hates. But she's got her current lost soul to act as her carer. You know how she rescues people all the time. She says he wants to find out about his family, so she's helping him. She's always rescuing people, isn't she?'

'She is,' said Mike. Oh yes, and I'm one of them.

'She's just my godmother, but I've always found I could talk to her much more than I could Mum.'

'She's remarkably easy to talk to.'

Mike thought back to a morning two years ago, not long after the incident with the gun on the island. Stephanie had virtually ordered him to go to Popi's, and he went without knowing what to expect.

'Popi is the woman who saved me after Laurent died,' Stephanie told him. 'It's what she does. It's because of what she went through – and no, I'm not going to tell you about that. She will if she wants to.'

So he'd taken the boat to Athens and gone to visit Popi in her old and somewhat crumbling house in Koukaki, where she and her husband Alex were living then. They'd talked for three days and he had told her what he had never told another person, before or afterwards. And knew that she did not judge him as he judged himself.

'Survivor guilt is never recognised as the terrible power it has over you. People destroy themselves because of it and they can destroy others. When you live and those you love die, it is hard. When you live and they die because of you, that is the hardest. Even when it might seem that you didn't have a choice in the matter.'

When Mike returned to Chiona he went over to thank Stephanie. It was the two of them who had saved him, he knew. That was when he stopped drinking and began to lose the weight he'd put on previously. He swam every day and worked and built his boat. The guilt was still there, like a half-dead albatross giving an occasional flap as it hung round his neck, but he could live each day without it killing him.

'I didn't know you knew Popi,' Jen was saying.

'Everyone knows Popi,' said Mike, evading any further questions.

'Dad wants to go over to see Alex. Architect chat I imagine. He's thinking of going after the funeral.'

Stephanie's body was being transported to Crete on Monday, and the funeral, Mike had been told, was on Tuesday morning here at the Karpathi estate in its small chapel. Later, a wake would take place in Chiona, in Stephanie's house, where others could come and play their respects.

'I've been talking about the funeral with Dad,' continued Jen, 'but can I discuss it with you? You knew Mum, probably saw a lot more of her than I did. I'd talk to Henry, but for some reason he's disappeared.'

'So I hear,' he replied.

'It seems he wandered off after spending a night at my house and nobody's seen him since. I do hope nothing's happened to him. Like Popi, he's the other constant in my life.'

'I'm sure he'll turn up for the funeral.'

'He'd bloody better.'

But where was Henry? Mike had checked on his house every day and there was still no sign of him. All Josh had said was that they were keen to speak to him again, which told him nothing. Mike said a temporary goodbye to Jen outside her room. This is like the day before the battle, he thought. When the generals get together and plan. But when it came to battles, you knew who your enemy was. In this case it was as if you were trying to protect yourself from the wind.

Lunch was quiet. Leotakis had gone to his own quarters in the main house and they sat in small groups under a leafy terrace with a view over the garden to the sea. The buffet had enough to feed him for a month, thought Mike, and included all his favourite Greek dishes. He found himself sitting next to Pam, who was trying to hide how excited she was with the food.

'Mr Leotakis got me talking about my interests yesterday evening, and all I could think of was food. Which made me feel really stupid afterwards, though he made it feel as though it was a good thing to have as an interest.' She took a small stuffed vine leaf and dipped it in tzatziki.

'Nothing wrong with food,' Mike said. 'I could eat it every day.'

Pam laughed. Then stopped.

'Oh God, this is so difficult. Is it all right to laugh? I mean the funeral isn't till Tuesday, and yes this is a murder investigation, but it's also the most extraordinary thing I've ever experienced. I've only been abroad once before, to a place in Spain that was all sports bars and English people getting drunk. Might as well have been in Great Yarmouth.'

'Well I've been coming here to stay with my aunt on and off all my life, but stepping in to Nikos's world is always something else. And I don't think you should worry about laughing. It's not as if you can't laugh when you're working.'

'No. We have to. Otherwise we'd go nuts. Do you know what those are?' Pam pointed to a dish of tiny pale green fried parcels.

'Yes. They're stuffed courgette flowers, *kolokythanthoi*. They're stuffed with *mizithra*, which is a local cheese, a bit like ricotta.'

'Oh my goodness, they're delicious.'

'You should try the little pastry things, they're stuffed with spiced meat and that one's a *spanakopita*, it's a miniature spinach and cheese thing.'

'You like our food then?' Pam hadn't seen the newcomer arrive until he spoke.

'Have you met Major Stavros Papadakis?' Mike asked her.

Pam had just that moment bitten into the *spanakopita*

and sent a shower of filo crumbs down her dress. Take a girl from March, she thought. Stavros looked amused.

'We specialise in food to embarrass our guests,' he told her. 'Wait until you've seen our *kourabiedes*. They're small biscuits entirely coated with icing sugar and the moment you bite into them, you send a cloud of sugar all over you and the room. We're inevitably offered them when we go to interview elderly ladies, and it would be rude to refuse. We then cover their furniture with sugar.'

Pam smiled at him gratefully. She finished eating, wiped her hand on the napkin and held it out.

'Detective Inspector Pam Gregory,' she said. 'Nice to meet you.'

'Shall we move to your suite, Inspector?' suggested Stavros. 'I have some information you might want to hear. We can take some pastries and fruit with us.'

He walked over to the table and moments later returned with a platter of pastries covered in honey and nuts and slices of melon, watermelon, and peaches.

'My team would love these,' said Pam, thinking of them working away in their airless, hot city room. 'I'll have to get some to take home.'

They walked through the garden where an invisible irrigation system was sending occasional bursts of water through the grass and around the bushes. Pam had a cottage with a living room as well as a bedroom and bathroom. Its air-conditioning was effective, but also silent and there were three sofas as well as a desk with a solid chair. There was also a large table with chairs around it for guests who wanted to eat in privacy, thought Mike. Although it was near the other cottages, they were hidden by the bushes and it felt comfortably private.

'One moment,' said Stavros. He held up something that looked like a remote control and walked it around the room. Pam looked at Mike in surprise.

'A little gadget I borrowed from a friend in EKAM, that's

our anti-terrorist unit. I used to work there for a while. Our host is well known for his habit of listening to conversations. We are not saying anything that would disturb him, I am sure, but I am sure the Inspector would prefer our briefings to be confidential.'

'Do call me, Pam,' she said. 'While I'm in Greece I'm not really a police officer.'

'And you must call me Stavros, then. That is only right. No,' he added. 'No bugs.'

Pam went over to her bag and pulled out her laptop as well as a large pad of paper.

'I hardly feel I have to ask if there's Wi-Fi here.'

'There is,' Mike told her. 'The code is Emily Bronte. Apparently it was his late wife's favourite rose.'

Pam logged on while Stavros took a notebook out of his pocket.

'Thank you for your email,' he said. 'It was very helpful. I have contacted the parents of George Dimitriakis, and they finally told me he is staying on his grandparents' farm in a mountain village right in the south west part of Crete. In fact it's as far west as we are east, but, nonetheless, I do feel we should go there in person tomorrow. I haven't contacted the grandparents.'

'I agree,' said Pam. 'We don't want George doing a runner again... running off,' she added.

'Doing a runner. I like that expression. Idioms are the hardest things to learn in a language.'

'Your English is amazing,' replied Pam.

'What do you know about George's family?' Mike asked. 'Do you have access to their folders?'

'Folders?' asked Pam. 'Is that like the folders Jen was talking about. The ones the police kept under the Junta.'

'Except, of course, those were destroyed many years ago.' Stavros frowned.

'Apart from all the ones which weren't,' said Mike drily. 'I've always heard that Papandreou never fulfilled his pledge to get the personal files destroyed. I've heard that many were digitised.'

'You don't expect me to comment on that, do you?' said Stavros, coldly.

'But I imagine that, like us, if they've had dealings with the police, there will be records.' Pam wondered at the sudden antipathy between Stavros and Mike. Was it a political thing, or did Stavros disapprove of Mike's presence? Or was it racist?

'Naturally we have records,' Stavros addressed Pam directly. 'But those are not the same as the folders. Why did you mention them?'

'Nothing, said Pam. 'It's just that Jen mentioned that her godmother was helping some young man look for his family records. I wondered what exactly they were.'

'Under the Junta, there were detailed records of anyone who might be thought to be antagonistic to their right-wing government. You have probably seen documentaries about the Stasi in East Germany. These were the same. Everywhere there were police informants in those days. You would find them in shops, in restaurants, and in the kiosks. They would report, for example, if people bought foreign newspapers or made calls abroad. In those days the phones were attached to the kiosks. Add to that the *thyroros*, the person who sat in the door of the apartment block ... what do you call them?'

'Janitor or doormen or concierge,' replied Mike. 'Only really luxury flats have them in England.'

'Well, they were known to tell the police who came and went from the buildings. Happily such a world of surveillance no longer exists.'

'It doesn't need to. We have CCTV,' said Mike.

'Except when it's turned off.' Pam told them about the Cambridge cameras.

'Of course, it would help if we knew who we were looking for,' she added.

'Well, we must start with what we have,' replied Stavros.

'You wanted to see Stephanie's house.'

'Yes,' said Pam. 'Is that okay with you?' she asked Mike.

'Why do you ask him?' asked Stavros. The chill had gone down a few more degrees.

'Because it's now his house,' said Pam. 'Stephanie left it to him in her will.'

'In my head, it's still Stephanie's,' said Mike. 'And Jen's. Of course you can go there. I haven't been there since she died. It didn't feel right.'

'That's good to know,' said Pam, and Stavros nodded.

'I'll stay here and keep an eye on Jen,' said Mike, 'and then we can all talk again later.'

Stavros didn't at all look happy with that idea, thought Pam, but she wasn't sure why.

CHAPTER 29

Sometimes life takes place behind glass; you watch the world around you, but it disappears into a painted backdrop. The view through the window of the school secretary's office, where she sits and hears about her father's death, the sound of Slade singing Merry Christmas music in the Grafton Centre when she's walked out of the house after finding Richard in bed with the woman from across the road.

It was the same now here in Crete. Part of her brain allowed her to see the beautiful occasional burst of purple thyme on the slopes of the rocky hillsides beside the road; another part watched herself, waiting for reality to catch up. Pam had felt like this ever since she climbed aboard the plane in Cambridge; she was not part of this landscape or this life, instead, she was playing the game, making conversation, trying to do what ordinary people did in these kinds of social situations. Travel by private jet? Dine on a candlelit terrace with a dangerous billionaire? Lunch overlooking a sea so blue that she will never be satisfied with any other colour?

The only time she snapped back into herself was when she focused on Stephanie, on trying to solve this bizarre and worrying murder that had sent her on a journey unlike any other, and where she felt frighteningly out of control.

'What do you expect to find in the house?' Stavros asked, swerving the car across the road to avoid a small pickup truck, laden with bags of cement, which had turned into the road in front of them without looking.

'I don't know, but I feel that if the answer's anywhere, it could be there.'

'No pressure then,' he replied and smiled. His earlier hostility seemed to have vanished. She concentrated on the twisting road, glad she wasn't driving. There was a good road to Chiona, now, Stavros told her, built to facilitate transport to the excavations and then for the rebuilding of the village.

'You've been to Chiona?' She needed to know so much, and at the same time differentiate between what was relevant and what was simply a woman's life history.

Stavros explained that he'd come here two days ago, as soon as he'd been assigned to the case, and had looked around the village with Manos, the local police captain. 'You'll like Manos,' he informed her. 'He's a bit like you, a reliable, efficient officer.'

Is that what I am? thought Pam, I've never felt less efficient in my life. She'd also slightly hoped he might see her as her, not just her job, but clearly that was never going to happen.

'Manos speaks good English, too,' Stavros told her. 'I'll arrange a meeting between us. Maybe after the funeral.'

Pam thanked him. Liaison was proving much easier than she'd feared. Stavros was more like a new partner and it made her feel less alone.

'Manos told me how popular Stephanie was, both here and in Sitia. Some of the foreigners who live here are just drunks,' he said, 'but some become family. We love them.'

'Stephanie drank. Perhaps they forgive her because she's made the town richer.'

'Or maybe they did like her. You have a cynical view of us.'

'Not just of you. Of everyone,' Pam admitted.

'That's a little sad. Of course they also liked her because she spoke good Greek.'

'Like your English. How come it's so fluent?'

'Three years at Sussex University reading politics. And three years in Brighton pubs.'

'That sounds like an education.'

Stavros laughed, a deep resonant laugh which made his shoulder shake. He's remembering some fun times, Pam thought. And now he'll ask me where I went to university and he'll think the less of me because I didn't.

'Brighton was fun,' he said. 'It made me a more tolerant person. Crete can be very insular. Before I went to university, I'd never spent time with black people, or people who were openly gay. When they became my friends, my life changed. It was the best kind of education. We have some of the most enlightened laws in this country, and a great deal has changed in the last ten years, but how people feel has not changed so much. If you are a teacher or a doctor in Crete it is probably better that you don't admit to being gay. The older generation in particular, hasn't changed much. And the influx of refugees right now has made it harder for foreigners, especially people of colour.'

Yet that coldness she'd felt earlier with Mike, if it wasn't racist, what was it?

'Look,' said Stavros as they turned another bend. 'There's Palaikastro and beyond it, the little table mountain of Chiona.'

'Oh,' gasped Pam. It was the picture she'd seen come to life.

They drove through Palaikastro. Pam noted the small restaurants and tourist shops. She could imagine stopping here on holiday, it felt designed for that. But Chiona was different. You could see the excavations on the right as you drove down, but the village on the left was private, compact and inward looking. There were no tourist places, only a small café in the centre, and a couple of restaurants, one right on the beach, and one on a piece of rock jutting out into the sea and... and that was where that photograph of Stephanie and Leotakis had been taken, she realised.

Stephanie's house also was private, suggesting nothing from the road. Stavros parked on a sliver of path between it and the neighbouring house. Did Mike say that Stephanie had had a car? She couldn't remember. If so, she'd need to examine it. The local police captain, Manos, would know.

'I don't see a letter box,' said Pam.

'That's because we don't have them. In many villages there's a collection of post boxes in the centre of the village, but they haven't got one here. The post goes to the cafeneion.'

'Can we go there first?'

'Of course. Are you expecting something?'

'Only that if he sent a warning to Jen at her mother's Cambridge house, I wondered whether he'd sent one to her here, too. And maybe one previously. There's certainly nothing in her emails. The only ones she sent in the weeks before she died are work related. The same with her texts, though there were some to Henry. It seems she'd recently had a row with him about something. Unfortunately, we didn't get her bag with her iPad and phone until after I interviewed him and then he buggered off.'

'Irritating.'

'Yes. Two key witnesses ran out in quick succession. My superintendent wasn't impressed.'

'To lose one witness, may be regarded as a misfortune; to lose both looks like carelessness.'

'What?'

'You know. The Oscar Wilde play.'

'Oh that.' She didn't know, of course. Even here, her cultural ignorance marked her out. Richard didn't like theatre, so she hadn't been allowed to go. And her mother thought such trips weren't worth the bother. Her father had taken her to a production of *A Midsummer Night's Dream* in London when she was ten. The fairies had been dressed like punks and it was very rude. They'd laughed, how they'd laughed. And they'd been to a proper restaurant and had burgers and chips. One year before he died. She hadn't been to the theatre since then.

'You suspect this Henry?'

'I don't know. I do want to talk to him. There was a great deal he wasn't telling me. He was spinning me all these stories about meeting Stephanie and her being a cook in Athens, but he was definitely hiding something. Trouble is I was warned off.'

'By a criminal?'

'Oh no.' Pam smiled. 'That would be much easier, I'd simply ignore it. No. A civil servant. An arrogant and rather uncivil civil servant.'

'Are you saying that Henry was an agent?'

'I wasn't told. I was just told to leave him alone.'

'And like a good detective, that made you all the more keen to find out about him?'

'It would be good to get his fingerprints. Just so we could rule him out, for one thing. Then we could go back to concentrating on George. I am thinking more and more that George knows the killer, even if he isn't the killer himself. The architect, Anna, who has known him for many years, says that he's physically short, which would rule him out as the murderer. Our forensic team believe that he would have needed to be over six foot to have been able to lift her on to the bull.'

'But to leave like that. You are right to be suspicious. What was it he said?'

'He saw a ghost.'

'Well, the murderer certainly wasn't spectral.'

'No. He was solid and strong.'

'And he has fingerprints. If there is a letter sent to Stephanie and if the killer has been as casual with his fingerprints on this, as you say he was in Cambridge, we can send the letter to our forensic team and see if he's on our system. Not as good as your Holmes, but we're getting there.'

But now they'd arrived at the cafeneion and it seemed you couldn't go there without having a coffee on the house because, said the owner, who introduced herself as *Kyria*

Maddalena, this is how we welcome the foreign police officer who comes here to find the terrible man who did this to our Stefi.

'How does she know who I am?' asked Pam.

'This is a Cretan village. The information network is unparalleled. What kind of coffee would you like. Cappuccino?'

'Espresso, please.'

The cafeneion was like every picture Pam had ever seen, its paintwork and tables blue and white, the chairs with hard, woven seats. They sat outside, looking down to the sea and up at the looming mountain which actually looked smaller when you were beside it, more like a little hill. Maddalena bustled indoors, making the coffee, digging out the post from a cardboard box on a windowsill. She was small with grey curly hair and wore a shapeless orange dress mostly covered with a large white apron. Stavros told Pam that, in addition to looking after the post for the village, she also baked the bread, together with her husband Pavlos, and pizzas, which their son delivered on his push bike.

As she worked, she called out to Stavros, who laughed. Pam looked at him interrogatively.

'She said she would have brought us a *bougatsa*, but knew we'd just had a large breakfast, so another time. Her daughter cooks for Mr Leotakis,' he added.

'Ah, now we have our information source.'

Maddalena returned to their table with two cups of espresso, glasses of water and a several bundles of letters held together by large rubber bands, which she gave to Pam, who thanked her with the one Greek word she'd learned since coming here, *Efharisto*.

'Most of these I'll give to Jen,' she told Stavros, 'but I just want to check first. I don't want her opening something vile.'

They sipped their coffees in silence while Pam took in what she could see of the village from this central point. The cars had been kept to external roads and slip roads, allowing the lower half of the village to be pedestrianised. The paths were made of small round pebbles which every now and then had been made into mosaics. There were starfish, fish and flowers in white and red patterns, and Pam wondered whether it would be highly unprofessional to take a photograph. Maybe later, she thought. It was an effort to remember that she was meant to be on duty. Anyone looking at her in one of her new dresses and sandals would think her a holiday-maker. Oh, why did she worry about these things all the time? Why couldn't she relax just for a moment and enjoy the coffee, the village and the company of this friendly officer who was doing everything he could to put her at ease?

After they'd downed their coffees and Stavros had argued with Maddalena, who was still refusing to let them pay, Pam found herself giving the old lady a hug. Maddalena smoothed Pam's hair off her face and said something that made Stavros laugh again.

'What?'

'Tell you later.'

Stephanie's house, like all the others in the village, was a single-storey house with shuttered blue-painted windows on the side and the front. Mike had told her that all the villagers had been given an identical plot, which could include a small walled garden and a terrace and looking around, some had chosen this, but Stephanie had not. Her house bent round the external boundaries and therefore looked bigger than the others.

'Do you think she was afraid of something?' asked Pam, or merely wanted privacy?

'The find had brought a lot of media here. She could escape them in a house like this.'

Pam had the keys which had been in Stephanie's handbag, and she opened the door cautiously. This is where I will meet her, here in her home is where I will find out who she is and then, hopefully, why somebody wanted to kill her.

The house was deceptive, just four rooms, built around an open courtyard with large windows looking inwards from all four sides. The courtyard itself had several old wicker sofas covered with soft, multi-coloured throws and cushions, and shaded by strips of canvas painted blue and green and turquoise. Pam thought she'd be happy to sit out there all day. Or for days, come to that.

A solar-controlled fountain bubbled away in a small round pond surrounded by red pebbles. It all felt personal and private. This was her space, thought Pam. It's as if she's still here. She shivered.

'Ghosts?' asked Stavros.

'Just one,' she replied.

She put on her latex gloves and undid the bundles, one at a time, ignoring the official-looking letters, those which were typed and addressed to Dr Michaels, and there it was. Written in red felt pen. Stephanie Michaels, Chiona, Palaikastro, Lassithi. Posted in Heraklion on Thursday. She showed it to Stavros.

'This was posted two days after the murder, on the Thursday.'

'Three days, actually. We found her on the Tuesday, but she was killed on Monday night.' She filled him in on their projected timeline.

'It feels like the controlled behaviour of a terrorist. He is doing what he feels must be done.'

'That is what makes it so very frightening.' She looked at the letter. Who are you? What did Stephanie do to make you so angry? What did Stephanie represent to you? She'd been asking these questions for days, and was no closer to finding an answer. She shook her head and took a deep breath.

'I don't know how you want to play this officially,' she said. 'If it was back home, I'd have the authority to open this, but I'm not a lead detective in this country. So do we take it to Manos, or do you open it?'

'You can open it and I'll film it for our records. He took

out his phone and Pam carefully slit open the envelope. She pulled out the sheet of paper and showed it to the camera. The words this time were written in Greek.

'It's ancient Greek,' said Stavros. 'So a quote.'

'Can you translate it?'

'Yes. I think I've heard it before. It's something like: The block of vengeance stands strong.'

'Revenge again. Vendetta'.

'He is going to attack again. I'll ring Manos and warn him.'

He dialled a number and Pam went into the sitting room.

Hello, Stephanie, she said silently. I'm sorry to impose, but I do have to go through your things and find out who the hell killed you. And I wish I'd met you, though you probably wouldn't have been interested in a Cambridge police officer. The only thing we have in common, really, is your life. And maybe a love of colour and food. Yes, we could have talked about food. You could have shown me how to cook Greek dishes. I'd have liked that.

There were, indeed, many cookbooks, *Salonika, A Family Cookbook* sounded delightful, she thought, as did *Fasting and Feasting*, though she certainly preferred the latter. There was also a new Ottolenghi. She took it off the shelf. 'Happy Christmas, lots of love Jen,' was written inside. So they may have fought, but they were close. She looked around the room, trying to imagine Stephanie within the space. Stavros walked in and for a moment it felt like an intrusion.

'Manos is going to brief the local officers. He agrees with you that Jen is safest at the Villa Karpathi. It's been cleared as a secure venue for the President, he says, so while she's there we shouldn't worry.'

'Do you have an evidence bag?'

Stavros laughed. 'Sorry. No, not my day job.'

'No problem, I have some in my bag.' Pam fished one out and put in the letter and gave it to Stavros. 'Can you send me the film of it for my own files?' she asked.

'Sure.' He tapped in her email and clicked it. 'I think

this does change things,' he turned to her. 'I am certain now we are looking at a Greek. The natural way the letters are formed. I'd swear this was written by a native speaker.'

'It does look that way,' she agreed. 'So we concentrate on George's ghost. Unless the fingerprints from this say different.'

'I'll hand it to Manos tomorrow. He's not on duty this weekend. Then his forensic people can do a fingerprint search.'

'Good,' she said, wishing that he and Manos weren't quite so laid back. But that was unreasonable; it wasn't their murder enquiry, and her team sometimes took weekends off, too, even if she rarely did. She looked around again. Like the courtyard, this was a place to relax with several sofas covered in soft cotton throws. Stephanie's own dyed materials. They looked as if they'd been faded in the sun. One whole wall was filled with shelves. There were books and shards of pottery and a few bottles of whisky and brandy, which were all almost empty.

There was also a pile of notebooks. Pam picked one up and opened it. It seemed to be a diary and notebook. It was dated 2017. There should be a more recent one. There was a table, which Stephanie had used as a desk.

'She wasn't tidy, then' said Stavros.

There were three unwashed coffee cups, an empty wine glass with the dregs of red wine, a scatter of pens, a pair of scissors, a miniature Cretan bull which she'd used as a paperweight, piles of official papers, and underneath these, another notebook. It was similar to the others, with a hard cardboard cover printed with a circle of Greek gods surrounded by helmets and cherubs. Pam passed it to Stavros.

'Haven't seen one like this for years.' He looked at the back.

'International, the best exercise book,' he read out. 'She must have bought them by the dozen, years back.' He handed it back to Pam.

'I'll check the kitchen and you can do her bedroom.'

For what? she thought. What she really wanted to do was to read these notebooks. Somewhere away from here. She opened one that was different from the others. It was a slimmer, black notebook. The writing was different and she knew immediately it had been written by Henry. The tiny italic writing in which he'd written his name, address and email for her. So why was it here? She opened it.

My love, my life, my only love. I killed you. She killed you. I killed you and I will never forgive her.

'Stavros!' she called. 'Come and look at this.'

He came back into the room and as he stood beside her she could smell his skin, salt and lemons and for a split second felt a desire to hold him closer and breathe him in.

'This is Henry's writing. I recognised it. This could be what we're looking for.'

'It could. I've had a quick glance around, but there's nothing that looks out of place or as if someone else has been here.'

'I think these notebooks are where we should start.'

'I agree. So shall we take them back to the Villa? We can study them there and then return them to the house or to her daughter. Whatever you think is best. I feel as though I'm intruding here.'

Pam nodded. Her phone rang. She looked at the sender.

'Hold on,' she said, 'I need to take this.'

She walked back into the courtyard. 'Josh?'

'Boss,' said Josh. 'We've finally got a breakthrough, we've got a witness.'

CHAPTER 30

'So we won't know till later,' Pam sighed. They were back at Villa Karpathi and she had filled him in on the latest news. 'Josh said the woman who's now come forward, was a totally reliable witness. She's been in France for a few days and didn't realise the importance of what she'd seen. But sent a text saying that she had seen someone entering the gallery and was now flying back to England, so her phone would be cut off. Josh has texted her asking her to ring him the moment she lands. So. For the moment, it's back to the notebooks.'

'Yes. But not now.'

'Why not?'

Stavros picked up the note that had been left for her on the table. 'Our invitation from Mr Leotakis for a get-together and swim for those who wish at five-thirty.'

Coming back to the Villa Karpathi from Chiona felt like coming home, if your home had armed bodyguards at a gatehouse, acres of manicured gardens and an infinity pool surrounded by statues of leaping bulls. Pam realised that it was also a place where you obeyed the orders of its owner.

'You don't feel that you can say no to that man, do you?' Pam thought for a moment about how charming he'd been to her the previous evening and how easy it could be to underestimate him. She was glad she'd had the chat with the journalist Chris earlier the previous day.

'Or to Eleni,' Stavros continued.

'She even terrified my superintendent. Have you met her?'

'I don't move in those circles, but I rang a colleague after she called me to tell me that I had been put on this case. Interesting, I thought, that the message came from her first and not one of my superiors. Though they did, of course, endorse it. I was intrigued by her. Rightly so as it turns out. There's quite a dossier on her.'

'One of those famous folders. What are they called?'

'*Fakelos*. No, not those. Just standard records. She often attends events with our leading politicians and therefore has been vetted. She started off working for her husband who ran a travel agency. Then he began doing golf trips for the very rich and she started working with the same clients as a broker for sponsorship. Which was entirely new in Greece back then. We're talking about the early 1980s. She put together the most prestigious arts events and places, the galleries, the museums, with the super rich. Her husband died and she became quite wealthy herself. She's known for being totally discreet. In recent years, she's worked almost exclusively for Leotakis. She has no children or close family.'

'Interesting.'

'She speaks five languages fluently, too. It's interesting to me that with her talents she always chose a position which makes her invisible. There is virtually no photograph of her, and she's never been interviewed.'

'Someone who likes their privacy. Though hardly relevant unless Stephanie upset her and there's no indication of that. And we won't know that without reading the notebooks.'

'We both want to read the notebooks, but we can do it later. Right now I will go to my room and get changed and leave you to do the same. The sea will be perfect. You like swimming?'

'I love it, but I'm really on duty and I shouldn't..'

'Pam,' he interrupted. 'It's Saturday evening. I feel you have been on duty without a break for days. This is not healthy. We can read and talk later. Now, we go and swim.'

She wasn't the first to get to the beach, she was glad to see. Nikos was already there, sitting in a cushioned director chair on a large wooden deck, drinking a small coffee and talking to an elderly woman in a wheelchair Pam hadn't met. There were two or three people already in the bay swimming: Jen and Mike together, Pam noted happily, and Colin. Jen was safe here; it was time to relax. Just have a short swim, and then get back to work.

The bay had been dredged, Nikos had told her the previous evening, and he'd put a boom of buoys across the entrance, with weighted nets, fine enough to keep out jellyfish.

'We don't often get them, but my guests need to know they won't be stung. Mind you, there is a fully-stocked clinic here in case any guest did fall ill.'

Or you, she'd thought. He's thinking of his own age and mortality.

Nikos greeted her and introduced her to the woman in the wheelchair. It was Popi, Stephanie's best friend and Jen's godmother.

Jen had told her a little about Popi on the plane. 'I was never properly baptised, but being a godmother is different in Greece. It's a role that carries great responsibility and the godmother is often the same person who's been the maid of honour at the wedding. Same for the godfather but even more so, he's often the best man or *koumbaros*. That's huge. Traditionally, they even can choose the baby's name. They become pretty much family.'

Although Jen hadn't lived in Greece with her mother, it was clear she was very much bound up in its culture.

'Popi feels like family,' Jen told her.

And now here she was. Pam very much wanted to talk to her, but didn't want to interrupt. But Popi, herself, saw her hesitate.

'Inspector Gregory, come over so I can meet you,' she said. Her English was excellent, although more heavily accented than that of Leotakis or Stavros. Pam wished she had a second language. 'Thank you for coming here to help us. I very much want to talk with you, but not now perhaps. Will you have breakfast with me tomorrow, say eight thirty? Is that too early?'

Pam smiled. Although Popi looked quite stern with very short white hair and piercing dark eyes, her voice and manner were gentle. Jen had told her that she worked as a psychotherapist specialising with those who had suffered torture and trauma, and it was clear instantly that she was very good at her job. Grace and Zofia would love her, Pam thought.

'Eight thirty would be perfect,' she said, noticing a young man who sat behind her. The lost soul who Jen had mentioned.

'Manolis spoils me,' said Popi, noticing her look. 'Brings me everything I need.' She smiled at him, and he gave her an embarrassed, but pleased teenage smile in return. 'We have the same name,' he told Pam. 'Gregory, patron saint of teachers and students.'

'Which is right since he is a student,' said Popi. She turned back to Pam. 'My cottage is the third one after yours. It has a statue of a crane outside it. Sadly appropriate. Stephanie was writing her life as if it were a novel and she'd called it, The Sound of the Crane.'

'Why?' asked Pam. 'Is it a special sound?'

'I think she dug up the reference in some book on mythology. That the sound of the crane is *Yiati? Yiati?* which is 'why' in Greek.'

'So her life asks the question why.'

'Something you must ask a great deal in your work.'

'They used to say that memories come in the wind like the sound of the crane,' added Leotakis. 'Somebody clever once told me that. My wife, I think. Having had no education, I have surrounded myself with wise and beautiful women.' He smiled at Popi.

'This case seems to be tied up with memory,' said Pam. 'Memory and history.'

'Of course, Inspector, Greece is history. Under every stone is blood.'

'In Crete especially,' added Leotakis. 'We specialise in tragedy.'

'Yet for the tourist, it is simply sun and sea. The people don't exist. And when they do it is the caricature. Zorba dancing on the beach,' added Popi.

'They have no idea about Kazantzakis,' said Manolis fiercely. They turned to look at him, surprised. 'Kazantzakis is Crete,' he continued. He begin to recite: 'There is a kind of flame in Crete - let us call it soul – something more powerful than either life or death.'

'Bravo!' said Leotakis.

'Ah the passion of the young,' sighed Popi, as Manolis blushed again. He adores Popi, thought Pam.

'And when did you ever stop being passionate, my dear?' asked Leotakis.

'Never,' laughed Popi. 'Just as I never stop working. Alexandros had to tie me up and carry me to Crete. It was only when I saw how tired he was that I gave in. Do you know he'll be eighty next year? What happens to us? One day we are just getting on with life and then, boum! we are old people. Stephanie used to complain about it when the arthritis was bad. But it didn't stop her working.'

Pam left them and walked over to a chair a little way away, took off the red towelling beach gown she'd found in her wardrobe at the cottage, and dropped it on to a chair. There had been a selection of beach gowns and cotton sarongs with a note to please help yourself. There were also beach towels and more of these here, she saw on a low table. She walked down to the sea, following the line of decking that led almost to the edge. Thank goodness, for Roberta, she thought, imagining how awful it would have been to be here in her old worn costume.

The sea was cool, but not cold, and the sand, imported by Nikos, led down until it was deep enough to swim. She lent forward, let the sea take her weight and kicked forward. It was like silk. She'd never felt anything like this. Why hadn't anyone ever told her that the sea could feel like this? It was pure heaven. She swam out to the line of buoys and then swam alongside them. Jen and Mike had swum over them and were swimming further out and she decided to join then. The small bay made the most perfect sea pool in the world, but she needed to stretch her muscles.

She powered herself forward in a slow, steady crawl when she felt the ripples of another swimmer beside her. She looked up and saw Stavros. She gave a small wave and he waved back and raced out at a speed she had no intention of trying to match. She decided that she'd leave Jen and Mike to themselves and contented herself with swimming parallel to the beach. Then she trod water and looked back.

From the sea it was easy to see the whole shape of the Villa as every part of it faced the water; the main villa, a combination of white walls, glass windows and honey-coloured stone, designed to blend into the hillside and the fourteen cottages that led back towards the gatehouse also looked as if they had been there for centuries. This was not a man who wanted to flaunt his wealth. He used it to make his life perfect, or as perfect as he could. Pam lay on her back and kicked idly. It could never be perfect, though, if the only reason you wouldn't murder your son was that it would defy the gods. Nor could you stop those you loved from dying. Wife, new love. And now new love's child was in danger. Nikos would do anything to protect Jen.

She lay there letting the water lap over her, gazing up at the sky, which was yellowing in a sunset haze while the colour of the hills also began to fade. Time for a drink, she thought and then dinner.

There were, of course, hot showers at the edge of the beach as well as more towels, and nobody seemed in a hurry to go back indoors and change. Could she ever learn to slow her pace to fit this lifestyle?

Nikos was drinking champagne, Mike water – had there been a problem with alcohol, Pam wondered – while Jen and Colin were drinking Bellinis which combined fresh peach juice and champagne, and which clearly had been invented by the gods she decided, after a few sips.

'Actually a bartender in Venice,' said Colin. 'Hemingway's favourite bar.'

Pam smiled politely. It was the same excluding stuff. Refences she'd never get. Stavros watched her as he walked back from the shower to join them all. Something had upset her. He'd seen that look behind her eyes before when he quoted Oscar Wilde. There was a pain there, easily triggered. He felt a sudden desire to make her happy, remove that look.

'Well,' he said to her, taking a beer from a bucket of ice. 'Was that the best swim ever or was I wrong?'

'You were right.'

He sat down beside her and they watched the last of the light fade away in silence. Pam very much liked the fact that he allowed this and didn't spoil the moment.

'A special dinner tonight in honour and to celebrate our dear friend Stephanie,' announced Leotakis a short while later. He got up to go indoors, and Pam approached him as he walked past.

'Would you mind very much if I had dinner in my cottage?' she asked. 'I feel that tonight's dinner should be for those who knew Stephanie.'

'That's very thoughtful of you, my dear,' said Leotakis. 'I'll send one of the waiters to your cottage with a menu and you can choose your dinner.'

Stavros had also stood up as the old man passed.

'If the Inspector has no objection, I'd like to join her for dinner,' he said. 'We have some work to do together.'

'Of course, Major, if the Inspector is happy with that.'

'None at all,' said Pam, happy that she'd be having a quiet dinner with Stavros and not having to take part in a communal dinner where she'd feel an interloper.

She went across to Mike who was watching Jen talking to her father. He's worrying about her, too, she thought. She wanted to tell him about the notebooks and what they'd taken from Stephanie's house. His house.

'I've been thinking about all Stephanie's things,' he told her. 'They must clearly go to Jen, but if she doesn't want the books, I think I will keep them in the house for Stephanie's friends to read when they visit.'

I like these people, thought Pam. I bloody well hope that none of them turn out to be a killer. But he is out there somewhere.

Maybe I can even have dinner without thinking about the murder; I could even allow myself an hour off on a Saturday night. Which led to her having fun with some of the many very luxurious body creams and hair products that Villa Karpathi offered its guests. She made up her face and put on her new turquoise linen dress. She couldn't remember the last time she'd dressed up to have dinner with a man, even if in this case it was only a work meeting. Richard had chosen what she should wear when they went out with his friends and the clothes were never ones she'd have chosen. Too low, too loud, and too tight. Which allowed him to spend the evening making jokes about how fat she was.

She took a bottle of white wine out of the fridge and poured herself a glass. Before leaving Tyneham House, Patricia had packed both the book of poems she'd been reading and the cashmere shawl Rafael had given her when she'd got cold. She'd leave them both here, she couldn't take gifts from Nikos, but she could enjoy them while she was here. She therefore put the shawl round her shoulders, picked up the book and took it outside with the wine.

Stavros arrived a few minutes later. He'd decided, too, that he was off duty and was wearing a crisp white shirt and jeans. He bent over and kissed her lightly on the cheek.

'You look stunning,' he said. 'Blue is definitely your colour.'

Pam was about to say something self-deprecating and then stopped herself. Maybe she did look good. Maybe she was allowed to look good. Stavros looked over her shoulder at the book. 'Poetry, excellent antidote to murder,' he said.

'It was on the shelf at Nikos's Dorset house,' she began, then stopped herself. She was about to apologise, and that was not what she wanted to say. 'There's a poem in here I read yesterday that was about opening doors and it kind of spoke to me. And then I opened the book this evening, and there was a poem which says that although there are terrible things in the world, there's also music. And it made me think that I've always seen it the other way round. So when people talk about music or art, I agree that yes, they're wonderful, but there are also killers and rapists.'

'That doesn't sound like a very healthy view of life.'

'That's exactly what I was considering before you got here. Maybe I have to turn it round. Do you think a poem can do that?'

'Yes,' he said. 'But it's not the poem, it's how you read it, how you place yourself inside it. Sounds like you've already begun the journey.'

'I think this book is about that,' she replied. 'taking you on a journey.'

'That's what writing can do in my opinion. One of these days I'll read you my favourite poem. It's called *Ithaka*.'

'I'd like that.' And it was extraordinary. She meant it. She wanted to hear his favourite poem. She tried to imagine any of her colleagues back in Cambridge having favourite poems and failed. But then, maybe they did and had never told her. Or anyone.

'What would you like to drink?' she asked. 'We seem to have a fridge full of different drinks.'

'I'll have a beer. No don't get up. I'll get it.'

Pam sat down again. I'm on a journey, she thought, and it began with Stephanie. She just didn't know where it would take her.

CHAPTER 31

Somehow Pam managed to spend the whole of dinner without thinking about work. Stavros talked about Brighton, and how lonely he'd been when he first went there and how much he hated the noise and dirt in Athens.

'What can I do? I've got this perfect post which allows me to travel and my HQ is in Athens. I don't have a choice and there are places where you can escape, villages and mountains.' Pam commiserated and told him how she was always glad to get home after spending time in London.

'I love London,' he told her. 'But then when I was there I worked at our Embassy in Holland Park, which is not exactly the roughest part of the city.'

'I hardly know London,' she confessed. 'Though I was working with a team from the Met on a recent case...' and she found herself telling him about the County Lines and how they were exploiting children. And then they talked about their own childhoods, his in a place called Souda, on the west of Crete and, just like she had with Leotakis, Pam found herself explaining what the Fens were, and how strange.

She couldn't remember anyone who was so easy to talk to and who also managed to flirt so gently. This is not the moment to fall for a Greek copper, she told herself sharply, don't let yourself do it. He's probably married.

It turned out he wasn't. He was four years divorced and trying to put his failed marriage behind him.

'Not easy being married to a cop,' she agreed. 'My former husband hated it when I had to do overtime or was late for something, even though he was a cop himself.'

'He should have understood then.'

'He chose not to.'

Sounds a real bastard, thought Stavros, but decided that this wasn't the moment to ask about him.

'That young man with Popi. I can't remember his name, though he said it's the same as mine...'

'Manolis,' said Stavros. 'It's Manolis Grigorakis. I have a list of the guests so I can check them for security,' he added. 'Except for the English. We assume you are really who you say you are and not secret agents.'

Apart from Henry, if he was here, thought Pam. And where was Henry? That was a question that needed an answer.

'Well, Manolis was quoting this writer..' she continued.

'Ah yes. Kazantzakis. Kazantzakis was a great Cretan novelist. He wrote a book called Zorba the Greek which was made into a film. With a Mexican actor called Anthony Quinn. As if there were no great Greek actors in Hollywood. They should have used Cassavetes.'

'You like films?'

'You don't?'

'I haven't seen many. Except on television. By the time I get home from work I'm usually too tired to watch anything that lasts more than thirty minutes.'

'But when you were younger?'

'We weren't that kind of family. My mother didn't approve, and then my husband didn't go to the cinema.'

'You could have gone with friends'.

'I wasn't allowed friends.'

Stavros looked at her with dismay. He'd felt there was something about her, but nothing as bad as this. It wasn't surprising she was so sensitive. And sad she was still so vulnerable.

'I'm not sure why I am telling you this. It's not something I ever tell anyone at home, but here it's as if everything is different.' Pam took a deep breath, 'I had an abusive marriage.'

'Did he…'

'Yes. Mentally and physically. And because he was also a police officer I could never report it. Nobody would have believed me.'

'I'm so sorry.'

'I escaped, thanks to a wonderful woman I knew from work and who's become a very good friend. I do have friends now,' she smiled. 'She's a forensic scientist. She simply took me back to the house where she lives with a lovely psychologist, who's now her wife. Zofia and Grace. Angels the both of them. They hid me and got me a lawyer. And my then work partner also protected me when it got rough. My husband did everything he could to stop me leaving, short of killing me.'

'I'm so sorry.'

'It's almost ten years ago. In fact I'll be celebrating my divorce in two weeks'.

'If you were still here I'd be buying you the champagne. But not tonight.' He smiled at her. 'Shall we work?' he asked.

'The notebooks,' she agreed.

They went back inside and started to examine the notebooks. Popi had been right, it did seem that Stephanie had been writing up her life as a novel. Pam showed Stavros how she'd started.

'She's numbered the notebooks in order.'

'Helpful.'

'So this is the first. Come and read it with me.'

Stavros joined her on the sofa, one arm stretched along its back, so she could feel its warmth and again inhale that smell of lemons. She hated to admit it, but she was finding him increasingly attractive.

If this were a film you'd begin with cockroaches. Of course you don't know that's what they are at first – we're talking pre-credit sequence here – you just see these tendrils, like small filaments of thin wire edging round a cupboard door. Maybe we zoomed into the cupboard first, so we know we're in a small kitchen, dark, narrow, like the end of a corridor. There's a cracked sink made of marble – so this isn't England – and a two-ring stove with a large orange gas bottle beside it. But someone has tried to enliven it. There are travel posters on the wall, white chapels beside improbable indigo seas; the kitchen is by no means squalid. It's clean, the marble sink has been scrubbed, its purple lines trace through the flesh-coloured stone like varicose veins, but the kitchen is empty, it looks hardly used. Then we see the cockroaches.

The tendrils grow in number and slowly, very slowly, at horror-movie pace, the door opens and we see that it's the weight of a dozen cockroaches that's caused it to move; the insects spill into the kitchen. We follow one across the marble-chip floor and on to the wood of the next room. There isn't much furniture in here, either. There's a mattress on the floor, with coloured sheets and pillowcase and a black crochet shawl thrown across the top. A couple of chairs and a table, salvaged from some junk stall, stand on one side, on the other, a bookcase made of planks and bricks. There aren't any posters here, but the occupant has hung scarves and silver ethnic jewellery on hooks. It reminds you of an actor's dressing room. Small signs of occupancy in a transient space.

The cockroach has made it across the floor as far as the bed and dives in between the sheets. Roll credits.

I've always seen that part of my life like a film. It's easier that way. The flat was a basement in Athens and I moved there in September 1973. I'd chosen Athens because an Englishman I'd met on an island told me it was cheap and you could earn enough doing private lessons to survive. And it meant I didn't have to go home and think about the career I didn't want or the boyfriend who'd moved out. It was like putting a blank sheet into the portable typewriter I lugged *around in the belief I was a writer. In my movie the bare walls of the flat are clearly symbolic.*

If I met the Stephanie I was then, I know I wouldn't much like her. I find it hard to believe she's me, the same way I find it hard to reconcile myself today with that slim girl with long, thick dark hair who is smiling out of that photograph I've pinned to the cork board in my study. But I know who she's smiling at and why she looks so happy. She's in love, and you can add all the adverbs you like: hopelessly, totally – truly, madly, deeply. The fact that she hardly knows the man she's in love with, the fact she's naïve and lacking any knowledge of the world where she's chosen to live is irrelevant to her. There she is – Stephanie at twenty-five, sitting on a metal chair outside a cafeneion in Pangrati and smiling at a figure a little to the left of the photographer. She's wearing a faded blue cotton dress and wisps of hair have blown over her cheek. She's so happy it makes you want to smile, but she's so open, this girl, so vulnerable. You want to run up to her and tell her to learn to mask her feelings, feel less strongly. You know this girl is going to get hurt. You can see it straight away. No one can get away with that kind of passion.

Let's get one thing straight. This isn't a romance; it's not a love story, though it is a story about love. It's also a story about betrayal and growing up, but it's not a coming-of-age movie either. I wasn't actually a child, just childish, though I'd have denied it at the time. This is a just a story about a girl abroad, who finds that she has fallen down a different kind of rabbit hole where the rules are not the same as the rules she knew. It's the tale of a witness, the observer of a small piece of someone else's history. But as Henry later told me, there is no innocence in being a witness.

'Henry, so soon,' said Stavros. 'Your instincts were spot on, Pam. He was always involved with her.'

'He knows something,' Pam agreed. It wasn't that she'd wanted Henry to be the killer, but that it had made some kind of sense.

'Why don't you go through Henry's notebook?' she said. 'After all, it does start with what looks very much like a motive for killing Stephanie and I'll go through these and see if I can find out what it is she witnessed.'

'Sounds good,' he agreed. He shifted a bit further down the sofa and picked up Henry's notebook from the table.

'At least we have a date. Autumn 1973.'

'The student uprising at the Polytechnic,' he told her.'

'The Polytechnic! Jen and Henry have both been telling me how important this was to Stephanie. I wasn't listening. Stephanie was involved in some way. Jen said it was something her mother often talked about. And Henry mentioned it. And something else associated with it, which I can't now remember. We have the transcript of my interview with Henry, but I don't feel I can get it till Monday. I've worked my sergeant as hard as myself, and his wife will be furious if I interrupt their Sunday.'

'Yes. I'm sure it can wait,' agreed Stavros, 'though I'm afraid you and I will be working tomorrow. We need to go and track down George the fleeing project manager. Unfortunately, driving there will take us half a day.'

'I'm so glad we actually have the chance to talk with him. I don't believe in ghosts. I want to know who he saw.'

'Yet perhaps there is a ghost stalking this story.'

'Before we set off, I'm having breakfast with Popi'.

'Good. She knows that period of our history.'

'She knows Henry, too. As does Mike. I'll ask him whether Henry has ever said anything and fill him in on what we've discovered this evening.'

'I don't understand why you consult this bodyguard and tell him everything,' Stavros said icily. He glared at Pam. 'He is not police.'

'Actually, he is.' Pam frowned. 'Didn't Eleni tell you?'

'Tell me what?' Stavros had jumped up and was pacing in front of her.

'Before you were assigned to the case, I was instructed to work with Detective Sergeant Mike Paterson who is still with the Metropolitan Police, but happens to be living in Chiona.'

'He's a British police officer? So why does he live here? I am the liaison officer. If he works here I should know.'

'But that's it. He doesn't work here,' explained Pam. She told him the little she knew about Mike.

'Something bad must have gone down. I've no idea what, but he's still on compassionate leave, he hasn't retired. And that just doesn't happen. Even long-term sick leave doesn't go on for years. None of us back home can work it out, and I don't get the feeling it's something he wants to discuss. And then he inherited Stephanie's house which, I think, surprised him. I did ask officially back home whether he was compromised as a translator because of the inheritance, but they said it wasn't a problem because he wasn't a suspect. In any case, he was in Chiona at the time of the murder.'

'I can't believe that nobody told my department. Why didn't it all go through official channels?' Stavros was still outraged.

'I have a strong feeling it was set up by Mr Leotakis. As far as I can see, he doesn't go through official channels. But Mike's been very helpful telling me about Chiona.'

'And now you have me,' said Stavros, sitting down again.

'Yes. Infinitely better. And a proper liaison. It also means that we can leave Jen in Mike's care. Which stops me worrying to an extent. Actually,' she added 'I think Jen's rather keen on him'.

'And this doesn't trouble you?'

'I think it's great. If they get close, he can stick around without Jen getting annoyed. Will be nice for Jen, too. Especially if it lasts. It would mean she'd still be able to go to her mother's house if she wanted to.'

'And this wouldn't upset you at all?' he asked again. Is he implying what I think he's implying, wondered Pam.

'Why? Do you think...?' she laughed. 'No. Mike's not my type,' she said firmly. I do hope that was what he was suggesting, she thought. Otherwise I've just made an utter fool of myself.

'And what is your type?' The anger had disappeared. I didn't imagine it, thought Pam. He was jealous. Fuck me, is that what a decent hairdo can do?

Pam laughed again. 'Notebooks,' she said.

'Slave driver,' he told her, sitting down with Henry's notebook.

After an hour, they stopped, and Pam made herself some herb tea in the kitchenette, to one side of the sitting room. Stavros poured himself a small brandy.

'You must be exhausted,' he said. 'You had a long journey today.'

'Yes. I am a bit. I had a crazy day yesterday and it's just past midnight, British time.'

'So, soon we stop.'

'In a bit. I'm used to reading work late at night.'

'Bad for your sleep. You work too hard.'

'True,' she said. 'So is there anything useful in there?'

'Possibly,' he told her. 'But the fury Henry felt in that extract we read earlier disappeared. This was all about a man called Laurent.'

'Stephanie was engaged to him.'

'And Henry was in love with him.'

'But that doesn't link Henry to the murder at all.'

'No, it doesn't. The rest of the notebook is about his failure to find love and how difficult it was to be gay when he was young.'

'Oh, poor Henry! That's very sad.'

'Isn't it? Life is for living. It has to be.'

'Yes,' she agreed. Open the door, she thought. There are terrible things in the world, but also music.

'Meanwhile,' she told Stavros, 'I found the notebook where Stephanie writes about the Polytechnic. I can see why it was so important to her. Interestingly, she addresses it at the end to Henry.'

'They were clearly close.'

'Yes. I think we have to discount him.'

She passed him the book.

'Have a read,' she said. 'I'm going to read what Stephanie writes about the Chiona treasure.'

Stavros took the notebook from her. 'The Polytechnic. An event that still divides our nation. And a first-person witness.'

CHAPTER 32

Heroes are overrated in my opinion. Agamemnon, Alexander the Great, Hector, Theseus, Achilles. Stuff the lot of them. Survivors. Now they're something else. They have other stories to tell.

Popi, Henry and me. We're all survivors in our way. We lived through the grief and we went on living. It's probably as much as you can ask of anybody. Though I doubt if I'd be brave enough to do it without sucking at my teat of Sitia red. A couple of bottles a day to keep the mind at bay and drift me off towards ... well, I suppose the ferryman, Charon. Not so long before I'll be making that journey. After the exhibition, after I lap up the underserved praise for finding the Chiona treasure and know just how many arrows are out there winging their way to this dead heart.

Henry has his life's work to keep him going, his research into Greek terrorism. Every day he tells me he's getting closer to the centre and, like me, knowing that death only comes once, he ignores the danger.

And Popi. My dearest Popi whom I love like nobody else since Laurent. Popi who still believes she can change the world, one lost child at a time.

My doctor doesn't think much of my chances. Nor do I, but I still feel strong. If I cut down, he tells me I can do the work for the exhibition. But don't stop drinking completely. My body won't take it.

This could be where I write all kinds of crap and say how...

So what do you write when...?

Bugger it! I still haven't written up my Polytechnic notes for Henry. I could do that at the least. Give this to you, my old friend.. Despite that dreadful row we had. You'll probably get over it. You usually do.

I've got notes all over the place. After all it was probably the bravest thing I've ever done, even though it had such a fucked up ending. What it is you always say, Henry? It was Tiananmen Square, sixteen years earlier. But forgotten and ignored by the rest of the world, because the world's television media weren't there and the Americans supported the Junta. Unarmed students facing tanks. It still goes on in other unreported places, I'm sure.

Sorry Henry, about the verbiage above, just ignore it. Old drunk woman in her cups again. Anyhow, you know me. You saw me that day on the bed covered in blood and shit after Laurent died and I lost his baby. You saved my life. But that's another story. That was what you said in the row, wasn't it? Thank you for that.

Am not going down that rabbit hole right now. So, Henry. Here we are. Stephanie's bit about the Polytechnic. And yes, it does matter, I know, because there are still people who don't want to believe what happened at the Polytechnic, who try to make themselves believe that it wasn't as bad as people say, that it's been exaggerated. So before my liver gives out totally, here's a first-person witness.

Polytechnic. November 17th 1973.

You hadn't met me then. I'd just started cooking at Les Bohèmes and I was doing some private teaching and acting at the British Council. That was the gang who introduced me to Les Bohèmes and thus you and my future life. One of my students, Athena, lived on Patission, virtually opposite the Polytechnic. Her parents were doctors and she was alone that night. She saw a neighbour at the window shot by a stray bullet, she saw the tank drive into the students. She was thirteen. But that was her story. You want mine. OK. Here goes.

I'm not there that night, the Friday night, but I've got a lesson with Athena on the Thursday. I get there about two o'clock. Patission Street's heaving with students. Banners and leaflets being handed out everywhere. And they're all shouting slogans. There's a loudspeaker rigged up inside the gates of the Polytechnic and it's playing music. I don't know the songs then but they're the old klephitko songs of the Greek independence, and the Hymn to Liberty and the National Anthem. And Theodorakis. And always the slogans.

And what's so amazing is the carnival-like atmosphere. Students are throwing leaflets into the trolley buses and people are laughing. That's one of the most incredible things. Before, everyone has kept quiet, people don't talk on the buses, but suddenly there's this explosion of voices. When the bus stops at the Polytechnic, which is my stop, I see lots of young people jumping off and joining the students. And the passengers are laughing. Everyone's laughing and talking.

So I teach my lesson, and then Athena and I look out of the window at the scene below. Athena translates for me. Wake up, People, Wake up! Bread! Education! Freedom! Psomi! Paedeia! Eleftheria! Kato Junta - Down with the Junta! It's being said out loud. Out with the fascists!

I know I'm witnessing something extraordinary. But ominous. I look out at the National Museum – it's next door to the Polytechnic and in the street in between are these rows of grey buses full of police. They sit there like, like slugs. Waiting. I watch them and they don't move. I've never ever seen anything so frightening.

And the street is packed solid, everyone singing.

Well. I go home and, on Friday, we've a dress rehearsal of the play on the stage at the Council. The Real Inspector Hound, Tom Stoppard, and I'm playing Mrs Drudge the cockney charlady: 'Lady Muldoon's country residence one morning in early spring.' It's so weird. A country house parody in the middle of all that. And half the cast don't even know what's going on. You know, we're foreigners. Keep your head down and it will all blow over. Some of them talk about the demonstration, that's the word they use. It's as if it's happening somewhere else. I guess it is for them.

I get back late on Friday night. Knackered. I lie down on my mattress in my horrible little basement room on Spiro Mercouri. Dark and damp, but very cheap. Then Dimitri, the student who lives next door, knocks. We share an air vent between our flats. He doesn't have a fridge and often hangs bottles of wine in the vent to cool them. I can see them from my kitchen. I don't much like him, he's fat and spotty and I have to bat him off from time to time. But at midnight he's at my door asking me if I have lipsticks. He speaks English by the way. I ask him what's going on, and he tells me they're using tear gas. Lipstick and Vaseline helps. I lie and said I don't have any. He knows I'm lying. I always wear lipstick. But he goes off.

But, as I say, I'm knackered and I didn't want to get involved. Then I feel dreadful I haven't helped him. I think I hear the sound of guns in the distance, more strange than frightening, and I fall asleep.

A few hours later, Dimitri's back. He sounds scared and there's someone with him. I open the door and they come into my room. This is Andreas, says Dimitri, he's been shot. He needs somewhere to hide. This is when it all starts to feel unreal. As if I've walked into a film.

Andreas tells me he's been one of the organisers of the strike in Patras. He's studying medicine in Bologna and speaks Italian (which as you know, I do, too) so we can talk. He looks terrible, blood all over him, but he says he's not badly injured. The bullet passed through his leg.

He's been shot? What? He needs to go to hospital, I say. What do I know about bullet wounds? He can't, Dimitri tells me, the police are waiting at the hospitals.

But what can I do? I say. I've only got a tube of Savlon. I come from Orpington, and there I am in the middle of the night in this tiny room with a student bleeding all over the floor.

Andreas tells me not to worry. He knows what to do. He just wants some white linen. This really feels more and more like a film. You know, women always have sheets ready for bandages. And I only have the sheets on my bed and they're navy blue and not very clean. But I do have an old white cotton broderie anglaise petticoat which I wear under my Laura Ashley smocks, showing an edge of lace. So I cut it up into strips and soak it in boiling water. Then Dimitri cuts away Andreas's clothing and we use some of the petticoat to wash away the blood. Andreas uses the rest to bandage himself up. I just stand there. There's nothing much I can do. I feel useless. I wash out the bits of petticoat he's used to clean the wound. Then I make some sweet tea. That's what they always say for shock. Drink sweet tea. But neither of them will touch it. Dimitri finds a bottle of ouzo in his flat, and he and Andreas drink that. I'm sure that alcohol isn't the thing to drink, but I don't say anything. They wouldn't have listened anyway. Then I drink the tea, which is horrible. I hate sweet tea. I'd have preferred the ouzo.

And that's it. Andreas lies on my bed and tries to rest. He's taken a handful of aspirins, and I'm not sure about the combination of aspirin and ouzo, but he's OK. He sleeps for a bit and then wakes and wants to hear the news.

Dimitri brings in his radio. What I remember is the call sign, Radio Polytechnic... Radio Polytechnic... the station of the free and fighting students, the voice of the free Greeks in their struggle...

They're translating it for me. The announcements: We need doctors. Then more music and then news: Our brothers have been joined by farmers from Megara. The offices of the Nomarchia of Attica have been seized by construction workers. Then more messages for food, bread, medical supplies and later, of course, much later...Doctors...we are sorry that we cannot receive any more doctors. Two members of the security police with white coats over their uniforms have forced their way inside the building and are using tear gas. Then later still... Please send us priests. And the list of those who died... which grows and grows...

Then the final moments of Radio Polytechnic. They're still playing Theodorakis. Andreas tells me these are laments. Laments for the dead. Then the closing words. A voice cracked with tear gas and hoarse: This is Radio Polytechnic. We say goodbye to you. For the last time. Then static. We twist the dial but there's nothing. Just static. We're all crying.

Dimitri goes back to his own flat and Andreas and I sleep. When it's light we wake and he wants sex. He's a hero. Of course I comply.

Later, I go out to buy food and some more ouzo. I have to be careful that the janitor, you know the guy who sits at the desk inside the door, doesn't see how much I'm carrying back to my flat. Because up to now I've never cooked at home, you see. Only my morning coffee. I eat out every day. At lunch I just have some fruit or a spanakopita, or a sandwich, if I've enough money. So I know it will look odd if I suddenly seem to have started cooking at home the day after the Polytechnic. So I hide the food packages under my jacket.

Andreas is feeling much better. The bullet had just gone through the side of his leg. He lost some blood, but obviously not a dangerous amount. He's been lucky. He's young.

So every day I shop for Andreas and Dimitri and cook; they tell me I'm a rubbish cook, and we listen to the radio. Again I've got that sense of being in a film. The kind that has gallant partisans. I've grown up with these films. My part's sometimes played by an actress called Anna Neagle. She often died in the last reel.

The radio is now all martial music, and the announcement of martial law. A curfew will begin at four. Get some more food, they tell me, everyone will be getting food, it won't

*seem odd. So we pool our extremely limited resources and
I buy rice and tins of tuna and more ouzo. The milk and
yoghurt and bread has all sold out, but I get a packet of rusks
and some eggs.*

*They want the streets clear for the police now because
they'll be coming to arrest everyone, Dimitri tells me. I'm
alone with Andreas in my flat. Then they announce that anyone
discovered harbouring a person not of their immediate family
will be court martialled. That means me. They're going to
arrest me for having Andreas in my flat.*

*I feel frightened and brave all at the same time. But
it's just a movie, isn't it? It can't be real. This kind of thing
doesn't happen to me. There are tanks outside the flat now,
roaring down Spiro Mercouri towards the Hilton.*

*So it goes on for the next few days. I telephone my
mother from a kiosk one morning to say I'm safe. She's
not at all worried. We heard there had been some kind of
demonstration, she said. There always is, isn't there? There's
martial law, I say. They shot students. You do love to make
a drama out of everything, Stephanie, don't you? I ring off.*

*The following Saturday I'm on the stage at the British
Council. It's our delayed first night. All the usual people come.
There's a reception. An elderly woman, dripping jewellery,
congratulates me and I tell her how much I love the play.
Oh you speak English, she cries. She'd found my Cockney
accent impenetrable. My fellow actor Bill and I nick the
British Council cigarettes which have been put out in small
glasses. There's a rumour that the British Ambassador had
rung during the previous week, during the curfew, to ask if
the play was on that evening. No, he was told, there's a seven
pm curfew. I enjoy being on stage. That country house, even
with its fake murders, is so much more real and familiar than
the tanks in the streets, the fear of the knock on the door in
the night.*

*Another story I read in the Athens News says that an
Australian girl who sheltered her fiancé had been given an*

eight-year jail sentence. But the Australian dockers said they'd strike if she wasn't released. I'm sure British dockers won't do that for me. And if the police raid Dimitri's flat – they've already beaten up his girlfriend previously – what's to stop them having a look at the little flat next door? My flat. Where Andreas is still hiding. I'm frightened all the time. But when I walk on to the stage I'm back in England, I feel safe.

When I get back, Dimitri and Andreas are drunk. Andreas tells me that Dimitri misses his girlfriend and I should give him a blow-job to cheer him up. I don't want to. And that's when I see it, the look between them, the friendship, the pleasure. The emotion is between them. I would be only meat. I don't matter. I'm just a foreign girl which means I'm not much better than a whore anyway. I walk away and make a risotto. They tell me it's disgusting. I say it's how I was taught in Italy. Andreas says he doesn't trust Italian food and his mother sends him food parcels. To Italy!

I feel so conflicted. Part of my mind wants to think of Andreas as a hero and part of him thinks he's a spoilt, rather unpleasant young man. Of course both are possible, but how do you react to that? I was too young to know.

The next morning I go to a corner shop to get food again, and I go a bit further because I don't want anyone to see how much I am buying. I've borrowed money from one of the cast during the week. As I get back I see the police van. I shrink into a shop entrance out of sight. They've got Andreas and Dimitri. They hit Andreas as they throw him into the van. I am shaking and crying and furious with him for going into Dimitri's flat. He might have been safe if he'd stayed in mine.

And that was that, Henry. I never saw Andreas again although Popi told me he died later from what they did to him in prison.

I hated him that night for making me feel bad, but I mourned him for the hero he was. I'd done everything I could to protect him, but he was so stupid. He constantly went into Dimitri's flat and they played music loudly. I tried to protect him and I failed. And I've felt guilty ever since. Survivor guilt, Popi's always told me. And what you and she say, there is no innocence in being a witness. But I wish I could have done more. But he was young. We were all young in those days.

Do you feel the same? I know you were stuck at home with bronchitis the night of the 17th? Just listening to Radio Polytechnic. Well, we share that, old friend. We share that at least.

CHAPTER 33

Stavros said very little after he'd finished reading Stephanie's narrative and left shortly afterwards.

So this was the story Stephanie kept coming back to. Pam wasn't surprised. But at the same time she couldn't see how it could possibly relate to her death. The student had died, but it hadn't been her fault, even though she continued to feel guilty. Something was missing. But what? And how did it relate to any of the possible suspects?

She was exhausted; clearly, her brain had long ago stopped functioning. Bed, she said to herself. She took a bottle of water from the fridge, and slid between the cool soft cotton sheets, noticing that this was the most comfortable bed she'd ever slept in. I'll have a swim before breakfast, before anyone else is up, was her last thought.

It's light so it must be morning and she's running, running round and round in this white building. Which has to be the gallery. Yes, it is. And he's got Jen. She's shouting, but no sound's coming out. Richard! It's Richard. Richard's got Jen. Take me, take me instead she's begging him, and he laughs and laughs...

Pam sat up a cold sweat running down her back making her shiver. Well, fuck you, Richard! You do chose your moments. Mind you, he'd always been good at timing, choosing the moment when she was most vulnerable to attack. Why now? Because she'd started thinking about him again? Because she was worried sick about Jen?

But Jen was safe right now, she could worry about her after she left the villa. Now was the time to go and swim away the nightmare. She threw on her bathing costume, already dry on the little line set up on her terrace and picked up a towel.

Irritatingly, she wasn't alone, there was somebody else, swimming far out. It was too dark to see who it was, but they cut through the water as if they'd like to subdue it. Pam stayed within the safe basin and felt the overnight horrors physically leaving her length by length. She managed to get back to her room without speaking to anyone, though had the sensation of being watched as she walked through the garden. She looked round a few times, but there was nobody there. Not a good time to get the jitters, woman, she said to herself. Get a grip.

Popi was alone in her cottage and came forward on crutches to meet Pam. Pam once again thought what a strong and beautiful face she had, the clarity of her grey eyes, the high cheekbones, the warmth of her smile.

'The wheelchair is whole new horror, and I fight it as much as I can,' she said, smiling. 'I've been on these for decades, since the seventies, in fact, and I can still manage for small distances. I don't need help for the bathroom yet, thank the Lord, though dear Alex, that's my husband, he needs help for everything. And thanks to dear Nikos, he has it. I've known Nikos for ages, did I tell you?'

'I can't remember,' said Pam, honestly. 'There was so much to take in yesterday, it's all got fuzzy, apart from a few things.'

'The important ones, I imagine. Come and sit down. They've sent over enough breakfast to feed a family, so we should try to do our best and eat what we can.'

'I'm quite hungry, actually. Had a swim just now and it always makes me eat too much.'

'Too much is a relative term. Eat what you want.' She pushed a plate of croissants towards her. 'So what things do stand out?'

'Stephanie's notebooks. Did she show them to you?'

'She offered to, but then said there wasn't anything in them I hadn't heard a dozen times. Is there anything there that gives you a clue as to why somebody would do this thing to her?'

'No. The only big rows were with Henry.'

'He didn't do it. I know Henry. He's a deeply good man.'

Pam sipped her coffee and nibbled on a croissant while she thought. It was so incongruous, talking about murder and murderers in an idyllic place like this. But then the money to create this estate had come from murder, if the facts Chris Brook had told her were correct. Leotakis had shot boatloads of men in cold blood. And yet he seemed, like Henry, such a good man.

'I feel that you've got a great deal on your mind, Pam. It's alright if I call you that? More than simply arresting Stephanie's killer.'

Pam nodded. 'It's very odd... it's never happened to me before on a case... but the more I investigate it, the more I find myself in Stephanie. I know that must sound mad, I mean I'm just an ordinary policewoman and I've never done anything with my life and I don't know many clever people...'

'Pam,' interrupted Popi, gently, 'I don't get the feeling that you're ordinary in any way.' She smiled. 'You know that Nikos thinks you're special and he's famous for spotting talent.' Pam felt herself glow a little. Did he really think that?

'I have spent so much of my life with very damaged people that I can always recognise one.'

'Oh,' said Pam. 'I never think about this. I mean, I haven't mentioned it for years, but in the last two days I've told two people, Nikos and Stavros. Not the details, but the fact.' The image of the dream seeped back and she shook her head as if to dislodge it. 'I was in a very abusive marriage.'

'And you thought that when you escaped from him, that was that. It was over. Finished.'

'Yes.'

'But of course it wasn't. You still had to remove him from your head.'

'I've never done that.'

'No.' Popi looked at the policewoman thoughtfully. She liked her. Pam was intelligent and attractive, but clearly didn't allow herself to believe that. And her demons were all around her.

'Is your mother still alive?' Popi threw the question out gently.

'Yes. Why?'

'You've never talked to her, have you, about your marriage?'

'No. She'd tell me it was my own fault.'

'Stephanie had a narcissistic mother. I wonder whether you picked that up when you were reading her notebook.'

'Not specifically.'

'Yet Stephanie's neediness certainly was based there. I think her mother was a most unpleasant woman.'

'I got that from the one thing her brother told me.'

'Popi sat back and her eyes widened in amazement. 'Don't tell me you've met the appalling Jeffrey?'

'Only on the phone and, off the record, he was seriously appalling.' She told Popi about the call and they both laughed.

'Oh, poor dear Steph. She was well shot of those two.' Popi sighed and sipped her coffee. Somebody had killed her friend and she couldn't imagine who that could be. And it was going to be hard for this brave young woman who now had her own demons to face.

'You don't have any new ideas on why somebody killed her? No?' Pam shook her head. 'I do wish I could help, but I can't,' Popi continued. 'Stephanie was exasperating, but that was no reason to stab her. There is something much darker here. My advice, Pam, is that you have to look into the shadows. Find the dark moments of Stephanie's life and see who lurks behind them.'

'I'll try,' said Pam. 'Thank you.'

'And when this is all over, we should talk again,' said Popi. 'You should find time for yourself. Time to heal yourself.'

'I'll try,' said Pam again, more out of politeness, than thinking she actually would. 'But I'm afraid they want to dismantle my unit which will mean looking for a new posting. I'll need to get home as soon as I can to try and save it.'

'Well, come back again. I think Crete is good for you.'

'Is there anything I can do before I go?' Pam asked.

'How kind. No I'm fine. I'll stay here for a while and then Manolis can wheel me into the garden. He likes to feel wanted. His father died recently, and he's very lost.'

'I can understand that. My father died when I was young.'

'Stephanie, too. I begin to see where you and she come together. I helped her a great deal over the years.'

'Jen said you collect lost souls.'

Popi laughed. 'I try to heal lost souls. It's rather different.'

Is that how they see me? Pam thought, as she walked back to her cottage. Lost? Am I lost? Is that how my team see me, or is it only here and because I've let my guard down? Well, time to put it back on.

She dressed in her uniform of black trousers with a green polo shirt. And threw a dress and her wash bag into her new travel bag. Stavros had told her they'd probably have to stay overnight in Heraklion. It was a five-hour drive to the village where George's grandparents lived and he had to be in Heraklion on Monday morning. Stephanie was being flown in and he had to sign the papers before she could be put on to the Leotakis yacht to be brought back to the villa for the final time. It made sense to stay there and come back to the villa in the morning.

She made herself an espresso and then turned on her computer and checked her emails. Not many. Murton asking how things were going. Josh, about the witness and Irini. Irini! I didn't open the pictures Irini sent me yesterday. How stupid!

She opened them now and printed out the photographs on the small printer copier that someone had thoughtfully installed on the desk. Stephanie wasn't in any of them. How interesting. The treasure really hadn't been her find. But the credit for the find could make the reputation of the archaeologist who did find it. Someone like Petros Manoussis, the man who found the bull. The man with a perfect alibi.

Irini had written captions on the accompanying emails. Lists of names that meant nothing to her, and pictures of tanned faces smiling at the camera, trowels in hand. They wore faded T-shirts and battered sunhats and baseball caps and looked hot and sweaty and happy. And there he was, Petros Manoussis. Dark haired, with a strong nose, he was wearing shorts and a green T-shirt, patterned with dust and looked as if he'd been laughing the second before the picture was taken. He had his arm round a tall young man who looked a lot like him. Could it be...?

Pam read Irini's note. Petros Manoussis and Christos Manoussis. A son? He had a son?

'Oh my god!' she shouted.

'Has something happened?' Stavros was walking up the path towards the cottage. No white shirt today: it was a police black T-shirt, black trousers and a gun at his waist. Back on duty, too, she thought.

'Come and look at this,' she said. She showed him the picture of the archaeologist's son.

'Revenge for the sake of his father? Is that what you're thinking?'

'Placed on the bull. It does add up. I'll ring Irini,' she added. 'She might know if Christos was in Crete last week. Or whether he studies in England.'

The phone went to voicemail. It was Sunday morning, Pam reminded herself. Pam left a brief message asking Irini to call her.

'I'll ring Josh,' she said.

'Don't forget it's only seven in England, and it's Sunday.'

'Oh God, thank you. Barbara would kill me. That's his wife. I'll have to be patient.'

'Are you any good at that?' He smiled. Don't think about that smile, Pam said to herself while drinking it in. Don't think how much you wanted him to stay last night or the way you held your breath when he kissed you good night. And wanted to kiss him back, but with more than a friendly peck on the cheek.

'You're good at being patient?' he asked again.

'Crap. But this could be it... this could be it.' Finally something that began to make sense. Instead of facing a blank wall, Pam was seeing a narrow opening.

'Are you ready?'

'Yes,' she pointed to her bag.

'Have you put in a sweater?' She looked at him in surprise. The temperature outside was already twenty-five and mounting. It hadn't gone much below twenty-three the previous evening.

'It's a different climate up there in the mountains. Actually it's a different world; you go back in time in some of those villages. They're quite frightening.' He smiled again at her raised eyebrows. 'I'll tell you as we drive.'

'So,' she said as they drove through Sitia and up across a pass in the first line of mountains along the road to Heraklion. 'Tell me about these wild mountain villages.'

Stavros overtook a small car, which pulled into the side to let the large black Suzuki pass. Pam saw an elderly couple, sitting stiffly upright, their eyes fixed ahead of them as if glued in place.

'Here in the east, the crime rate is minimal, but those villages, that's the Crete nobody tells you about in the tourist brochures, although tourists can happily stay there totally unaware of what's going on in the hills around them. It's rather like the wild places you were telling me about last night with people trafficking and guns secretly stored in remote farms. Here it's about major drug cultivation, cannabis specifically, though other drugs, too. It's a bit better now, but ten years ago we realised it was a centre for major crime. There's been talk in Alexandros Avenue – that's where the Police HQ is in Athens – of setting up a major crime unit in Chania just to deal with this. So you have crime and guns. Crete has the highest gun ownership rates in the EU, by the way.'

'Crete?'

'Oh yes. Hard to find a family that doesn't have some ancient firearm, though a few have more recent ones. Leotakis wanted to give you a gun today, by the way. Did he tell you?'

'What? No.' She felt genuinely shocked, both at the idea and the fact he'd mentioned it to Stavros and not to her.

'He wanted to know what my feeling was, officially, as it were, before he approached you.'

'And it was?'

'What you'd expect. You're not licenced to carry firearms in Greece, and if it came out I'd allowed that, my boss would have my head.'

'And if I'd gone along with it, my own boss would have had my head on the block, too.'

'In any case we're going to see an architect who's staying with his grandparents.

'Yes,' Pam agreed, 'It's hardly the OK Corral.'

'No. Not round here and not so much now; there's been a clamp down. But having said that, there are a lot of wild places up there. Take the village of Zoniana. Not a place I'd want to visit in uniform. Now this is just over ten years ago, and things are a lot better now, but there's this cop I know whose brother was caught up in it. It started with a simple stop of a guy in a new Porsche, traffic violation, and then the guy says he's a builder from a tiny village.'

Pam laughed. 'As if...'

'Precisely. The police begin to investigate and it escalates. Before long, you've got a raid on the village. You're talking of a dozen or so vehicles and more than forty armed police officers.'

'Sizeable.'

'You'd think so. But totally inadequate. When they got to Zoniana, they were met with about twenty gunmen with Kalashnikovs. They'd driven into an ambush and in the one-sided battle, several police were injured, one seriously.'

'Jesus!'

'So they turned round and exited swiftly. Cue huge row, voices in Parliament about areas of Crete not within the law. Then they put together an elite group of officers from Athens. Seventy five this time, with proper backup, snipers on the mountainside, helicopters, the lot. Though, of course when they get there, they find that nearly two hundred locals have conveniently disappeared and hundreds of hectares of cannabis plants dug up and shipped out. They grow them among the olive orchards because that camouflages them.'

'It does sound Wild West.'

'There were a number of arrests, though it's likely that the key players are still out there. But what they did find was extraordinary. It wasn't just that they were growing hash. They found huge workshops where they were processing both hash and cocaine. Plus large stores of dynamite and cash machines that had been ripped out of bank walls. And going back to the Porsche-driving builder, he had six million euros in his bank account, and another local man, who said he was a shepherd, had one and a half million euros.'

'Wild and woolly,' laughed Pam. 'Still no laughing matter for the locals who have to put up with the gangsters in their village.'

'No. Hardest for them because they can't say a thing. They know. Of course they know. I mean one of the hash plantations was bang next to the village cemetery with the plants laid out to dry on the gravestones.'

'Somehow I'm relieved that that's not the village we're going to. Both the architect who's known him most of his life, Anna, and the director of the gallery where he was working, said George was a very gentle man. So did Leotakis. My feeling has been that George is frightened in some way.'

'Let's hope we find out why.'

'You don't think Stephanie's death relates to what you were talking about?'

'There are similarities, Pam. The sense of honour and the code of silence. These villages are like those in Sicily because they are remote and the loyalty of the people there is to family and not government.'

'And vendetta,' added Pam, and they both fell silent for a moment.

'Do you think…?'

'I'm not thinking anything,' replied Stavros.

'Just that it seems to feel that we're heading to these western villages for a reason. It's just that I can't see how it ties in with Stephanie.' The longer she spent on the case, the more convinced she was that the answer lay in this island. But in the west? Popi's house was outside Heraklion, but as far as she knew, Stephanie hadn't been further west for decades. She last visited Chania in the seventies, Popi had told her when she said she was going west. This didn't make sense.

Stavros shook his head, and they drove along in silence for a while until he placed his phone into the holder and keyed in his choice. There was silence and then a long chord that seemed to just drift on and on for ever and then, two more chords repeated again and again, and then a simple piano melody, like overhearing a child practising through a window. Again and again the same theme was played, with an orchestra with different instruments, with a piano. Pam thought she'd always associate this journey with those melancholy few notes. It was like a suggestion of a thought, something she couldn't quite touch. Just how she felt about this case.

Pam let her mind wander as they drove on. They now had the sea on their right, and trees and large bushes of pink flowers on the left. Another line of mountains lay ahead and in the distance another lower range ran out in a blur of pale mauve. The sea was a darker blue here, fading into turquoise and then green nearer the shore. Any other time, Pam would have asked to stop and take a photograph.

Stavros must have sensed her thoughts because as they drove round the next bend there was a taverna, on the right, appropriately named the Panorama, with the sign, 'Come and Enjoy the sunset!'

'Coffee?' he suggested

'Please,' she replied.

'Thinking about the idea of the vendetta,' she began. 'That sense of doing something for the sake of your family. It fits the profile of the killing itself, doesn't it?'

'Yes,' he agreed. 'The calm preparations followed by the furious attack.'

'Yes. Yes. But whose family and whose honour is he avenging?'

CHAPTER 34

They sat on the terrace, overlooking the sea, drinking iced coffees and tiny slices of honey cakes the owner had insisted on bringing as soon as she heard that Pam was the police officer who would find the wicked killer of their dearest Stefania. Once again, Pam thought how she had never imagined herself in a place such as this: a semicircle of deep blue sea faced the scatter of white houses of the village below. On the left, a rock lay on the sea like a dozing dinosaur while a single motorboat left a white trail of spray behind it.

'This is exactly the kind of moment that makes me want a cigarette,' said Stavros.

'Yes I get that. I never smoked but there are often moments like...'

She was interrupted by her phone. It was Josh, up early after all. She excused herself to Stavros and got up from the table, walking over to the edge of the balcony, which she leaned against, listening to his familiar voice while at the same time looking out at a most unfamiliar view. It was hard to concentrate on both.

'Good timing, Josh,' she told him. 'We're on our way to interview George, and just stopped for coffee. Want to see the view?'

She flipped the phone and heard Josh groan.

'That's criminal,' he said. 'Do you want to see Cherry Hinton playground?'

'I'll pass,' laughed Pam.

'You think you can bear to come back after all this?'

'How could I keep away from you all?' she joked, but even as she said it, there was a part of her that was asking Josh's question and not finding the same answer. 'So has our witness got back to you?' she added.

'She has. She got back late last night and hadn't turned her phone back on. I mean some people with their phones. I can't imagine that. In any case, she didn't read my message till first thing this morning, but then she did ring me straight away. And it's promising, boss, more than promising. If she's right, we've got a good idea of who the killer is and it's quite different from what we've been thinking.'

'Different how?'

'Younger. She's certain of this, and what's even better is that she knows precisely what the time was when she saw the killer enter the gallery early Monday evening.'

'Always presuming this was the killer, though I agree it seems unlikely that anyone else would go into the gallery just then. There wasn't any reason for them to do so. So talk me through her statement.'

'She'd just finished watching *Pointless,* and always takes the dog for a walk straight after, so she knows it must have been just after six. Which fits our timeline. She said that she'd wondered why a student was going into the gallery as she knew it hadn't opened yet. Definitely young, she said, about the same age as her own son who's nineteen, and with a small backpack.'

'So not George,' said Pam. 'And definitely not Henry. But it could be the son.' She filled Josh in on the discovery that Petros Manoussis had a son.

'I'm waiting to hear whether he's studying in England, but can you ask Stuart to check online and see whether Christos Manoussis is registered at Cambridge University, and if so, get hold of the accommodation people and find out if he's left for the summer vacation. Mind you, he could have checked out of his university lodgings and still stayed in town. He might have friends. Also check his picture against any CCTV.

I'll send it to you now. It's also possible that Christos had a girlfriend and was staying with her. He's a good-looking lad. We don't have a lot to go on, and, irritatingly, most of the students will have gone home before the degree ceremonies. But this is the first clear lead we've got, we need to concentrate on it.'

'Will get on to it. But if it isn't this Christos, it could just be a student. Remind me what it is that Cambridge has thousands of?'

'But not linked to Stephanie Michaels or who can write Greek. This is something close to Stephanie's life. I'd put my career on that; it's personal. So what I want to know is whether it was Christos who George saw, and if so, what's the thing about the ghost? The more I think about it the angrier I get about him running off. His testimony could have saved us days of fruitless work.'

'Give him hell, boss,' said Josh.

'I expect I'll have to be tactful.'

'That's something I wish I was there to see,' he said, laughing. Then she heard him stop laughing suddenly as if a tap had been turned off. 'By the way,' he added, 'Dave's left.'

Dave. She'd temporarily wiped him from her mind. There was only so much room to store worries.

'How? Don't tell me? Murton tells his secretary everything, and she indulges in pillow talk with Paul. Perhaps we should use this as a basic conduit and start sending ideas back up the chain.'

'You may need to. We've heard there's another top brass meeting coming about with talks about readjustments of resources.'

'Cuts you mean.' She thought for a moment. 'If they decide to disband EASOU, which I gather could be on the cards, then it's not just me, it's all of us.'

'Barbara and I are thinking about moving. We could get a much bigger house in Norwich and I could go for DI.'

'I'd back you all the way if you wanted to do that. You'd

be brilliant.'

'You could get a DCI elsewhere.'

'Guess I could. Just not sure if it's what I want. Tied to the office, not out there with the troops. And talking of out there, seems I am heading into the Wild West today. Guns at dawn.'

'You'd better head 'em off at the pass then.'

Pam ended the call and got Stavros up to speed with the news.

'At least we now know that we're not interviewing a potential suspect, that makes it much easier. We can tell George that.'

'I hope so,' he replied. 'If he's there. You do know this may be a wild goose chase.'

'Isn't it always? I don't think certainty ever comes with this job,' she replied.

The rest of the drive was uneventful, though there were many places where Pam would have loved to have stopped and looked at the view or gone for a swim. Halfway between Rethymnon and Chania, Stavros turned off the main road and drove a few miles inland to a small village, which had huge plane trees shading a number of cafes and tavernas. Stavros knew, or was possibly related to, the owner of one of the small hotels, and after a number of hugs and kisses, they were invited into the garden to eat the picnic lunch the chef at the Villa Karpathi had insisted on their taking with them. From the garden there was a view of a line of mountains much higher than any Pam had seen so far.

'They look exactly how I imagined the Misty Mountains to look when I read Lord of the Rings,' said Pam. 'What an idyllic place.'

'Isn't it? I grew up not that far from here, a place called Souda. It's a big navy port, largest natural harbour in the Mediterranean, which has made it very useful over the centuries.'

He talked for a moment about his childhood and then

came back to the case.

'Fill me in on George Dimitriakis from your point of view,' said Stavros, dipping a mint-flavoured meatball into the tzatziki. 'One thing I can tell you is that he doesn't have a police record. Not even a speeding violation.'

'Nothing in those folder things?'

'I don't have access to those. In fact most were destroyed years ago, unless the families were active politically and I think that those were digitised. What do you know about him?'

'Very little, only what Anna Karanaki told me. They were students together in Italy, and they've worked together ever since. Though from the way she talks about him, she does the designing, and gets the name and the credit, and he helps realise her projects.'

'That must be hard,' he began, then stopped and thought. 'Unless it isn't,' he continued. 'Unless he really doesn't have any personal ambition. I do know men like that. Prefer to keep their heads down.'

'Yes. And the opposite of Anna.'

'Who is more like Stephanie?' he asked, noting a theme. 'Wanting the credit.'

'Yes,' she said cautiously. 'Anna definitely enjoys her fame, but Stephanie allowed herself to be credited for things she didn't do. She didn't find the gold bull or indeed most of the treasure. And she never stopped the interviewers from giving her the credit. From what Colin told me on the flight over – he's Jen's father and an architect, too, by the way – Anna really is an architectural star. The new gallery is amazing, and I don't know a thing about architecture. You know it's in the shape of a labyrinth?'

'Yes. There's been a lot about it on the Greek press and on television. And now, of course, after the murder, all the press are out there filming it.'

'Lot of bloody ghouls. That is one of the real joys of being here. To have the press off my back. The last few days were a nightmare.'

'Ghouls?' he questioned the word.

'How do you describe it? Basically the word means a kind of ghost, but it's used to describe people who take pleasure in death... you know the kind of people who slow down when they pass a road accident to see if anyone is injured and not because they want to help. Murder cases bring all the ghouls out, they want the gory details.'

'I understand. They gather and gossip and want all the details. You get them more in Athens than here I think. Here there has been too much bloodshed.'

'And we don't want any more.'

'So that is George. The quiet man behind Anna. Better to relax in her glory than do boring work of your own. Yes, that does make it more understandable. Reflected glory. How old is he? Did you tell me?'

'I can't remember if I did. Early forties, I think. Same as Anna. I've probably got it written down somewhere.'

'Just a bit older than me then.'

'And me.'

'Nonsense, you're clearly not a day over thirty'.

Is he flirting with me, she wondered. Then said it aloud. Smiling.

'No,' he said. 'I wouldn't do that, I'm far too attracted to you to flirt. You have to know there's something there, I felt it the moment we met. Didn't you? I want you very much, Pam, but it will have to wait while we work on this case. Like you, I feel we can't let ourselves be distracted.'

Did I feel it, too? Pam thought back to that meeting. Or the first glimpse of him on the plane. It wasn't that he was obviously good-looking like Mike, though seeing him in those small red Speedos had given her a physical shiver of pleasure, and at dinner last night, yes, in that white shirt and looking at those strong wrists. But surely he's got someone and then I'll just get hurt.

'Don't you have anyone?' she asked.

'Not at the moment. You know what the job is like for relationships. Especially a post like mine when I can be sent anywhere at a moment's notice. I can also be sent abroad to work with other police forces when there's a Greek citizen involved.'

'You can't make domestic plans.'

'No. And so you hook up with fellow cops or nurses. You know.'

'I do. My sergeant, Josh, is married to a nurse, though she's given up her work for the moment to look after the children and she hates it when he does an all-nighter or has to cancel stuff.'

'I was married to an English girl I met in Brighton. Which, yes, is why my English is good. Not just what I learned at university. Clare. She'd been thinking of teaching and then switched to teaching English as foreign language. So she could work in Greece. But it was very hard for her. I was away a lot and she was lonely. She found someone to spend time with. He was a teacher, too. And that was that. Last I heard, they were both teaching in Japan.'

'Did you have children?'

'Luckily not. I couldn't have lost them, too. And you?'

'No. I did get pregnant once. Actually I'd rather not talk about that.'

'I'm so sorry. I didn't want to bring back bad memories.'

'I think I've put my memories in a box. Popi sort of hinted that this morning. I think she may be some kind of witch. Jen thinks so, too.'

'A very special woman. We don't go in for aristocracy and knights and things here in Greece, but we do give out honours to exceptional people and Popi has the Gold Cross in the Order of Honour. She is the woman who always holds the government to account on all sides. A very special person.'

'I'd no idea. I just knew about her as Jen's godmother.'

'You don't know how I envied you your breakfast. Though I have no idea what I'd have said to her.'

'I'm just glad I didn't know all that or I'd have been

tongue-tied.'

'I imagine she wears her fame very lightly.'

'She does. She listens a lot more than she talks. Jen's lucky in having her as a godmother.'

Stavros thought for a moment. 'Yes. That's interesting. Do you know how that came about?'

'No. I've got a couple of the diaries with me to read this evening, so maybe that will come up. You think it could be relevant?'

'Like you, I have no idea what is and isn't relevant in this case.'

'When I was little my father took me for an adventure. He used to do this. Did I tell you he died when I was eleven?'

Stavros shook his head.

'Ah, well it's one of the things I share with Stephanie. A father dying and a bitch of a mother. Anyhow. We used to go on trips together. My mother hated travelling, even in England. And one day he said we were going to go for a special hunt to find the source of the Thames. I think I'd been reading a book at the time about explorers looking for the sources of the Nile. And we ended up in a field in the Cotswolds. And there was nothing there. I think I imagined a spring bubbling out of the earth, but there was a small puddle and a stone sign. And my father laughed and said, "you see: great things can come from nothing".'

'I like your father.'

'You would have done. He was a special person.'

'But this case. It's like that source in reverse. We follow these rivers of ideas and suspects and they all disappear into holes in the ground and there's nothing but a damp puddle.'

'We'll just have to hope that George is a bubbling spring.'

Pam laughed.

'You should do that more often,' he said.

'Yes, I should. She stroked his fingers lightly and then gathered up her bag and the remains of the picnic.

The further they drove, the more the traffic built up until

it became quite busy and they talked very little. Stavros played music and, as soon as he discovered they shared a passion for David Bowie, they listened first to their favourite songs and then took it in turns to suggest the most overlooked songs. Pam couldn't remember when she'd last felt so comfortable in a man's company. Apart from Josh, she couldn't remember the last time she'd actually gone on a journey with another man. Not like this.

After Chania, the main road went inland for a while. After another twenty minutes, they came to a junction and Stavros turned off the road and headed inland going uphill through small villages. The high mountains she had seen earlier had disappeared, but they were still going steadily uphill mile after mile and the hills were a soft green against the hot blue sky.

The colour of the earth in the ground beside the road had gone from the white lime she'd noticed outside Sitia to a red, the colour of raw clay. There were still a few olive groves, but many other trees and it was much greener with many rows of vines.

'Are they any wineries round here?' Pam asked.

'Several,' he replied. 'There's quite a well-known one just before we turned off the road. It's a good area for wine.'

Pam was increasingly glad they weren't going to drive all the way back to Sitia today. This was not a small island. But a lively one, she noticed. As the day grew on, the tavernas alongside the road had become full of people. She mentioned how busy they were to Stavros.

'Everyone goes out for Sunday lunch. Big family occasions. Even in England. Surely?'

'Yes. I suppose so, but I don't think I've ever gone out for a Sunday lunch. Not to a restaurant.'

'You mean since your father died?'

'No, even then. My mother thought restaurants ripped you off, though we must have done once or twice... But I can't remember it.'

'But since. Surely?'

'Richard used to go to the pub to meet his mates on a Sunday. I think they'd eat together. I wasn't invited. He told me it was a good time to act like a wife and clean the house. So I did. I hated Sundays. These days I catch up on sleep and my washing.'

Stavros wanted to stop the car there and then and hug her, but gritted his teeth and imagined just how hard he'd hit this Richard if he ever came across him.

Another twenty minutes of driving and they reached a plateau, and the road began to curve downhill beside a gorge.

'This is Topolia,' Stavros informed her, 'it's famous for its caves.'

She tried to imagine the things she would do here if she was a tourist. She'd stop at the shop selling carvings, which had awnings across the road, and at small roadside stalls selling olive oil and honey. But this was a murder enquiry even though it felt incongruous in this setting. But murder always does, she reminded herself, remembering homes with Christmas trees or holiday postcards on the mantelpiece where she had gone to bring news of death or arrest a suspect. Backgrounds are always deceptive.

They turned right into a narrow road with bushes and trees almost meeting overhead, and then into a tiny lane and there it was, a lone farmhouse. They'd arrived. The question was, was George there?

CHAPTER 35

Stavros parked the car quietly, which was enough to provoke a storm of barking from a mangy dog. Pam was glad to see it was chained even though she hated the practice. An elderly woman came out to find out who had arrived, drying her hands on her apron in a gesture that Pam realised must be the same all over the world.

George's mother was a small dumpy woman, though probably capable of leading donkeys up the mountainside at a rate that would exhaust Pam. She was wearing a floral blouse that tightly covered her solid bust and a differently-patterned floral skirt, with a maroon and blue floral apron on top. Her steel grey hair was pinned up in a tight bun on the back of her head and once she'd got over her initial fear of a visit by a police officer, and understood that the English *kyria* had come all this way to talk with her son, she welcomed them into her spotless house. Each piece of dark wooden furniture had its own, perfectly ironed, white embroidered cloth on it. Pam shuddered inwardly at the amount of work it must take to keep it all looking so pristine.

'She's offering us wine, but I said the English police lady cannot drink wine when she is working, so it will be coffee and probably cake.'

'How much cake do you get to eat when on a job in Crete?' Pam asked, smiling. 'If I stay here any longer I dread to think how fat I'll get'.

'George's Mum clearly eats well,' Stavros replied, quietly, in case George was anywhere near listening.

'If I say something, can you translate?' Pam asked him, as the mother approached their table with a plate of homemade biscuits.

'Of course,' Stavros replied. He switches easily into the formal job, Pam thought. There was a quietness about him as he observed his surroundings and made mental notes; somebody I'd always want on my team, though he probably outranks me. What is a major in UK police ranks, anyway?

'The reason I'm here,' said Pam, deliberately, 'is not only because of the death of Dr Michaels, but because we are very worried about the safety of her daughter. We know your son is not the murderer, but we think he does have information that could lead us to him and therefore protect the daughter of Dr Michaels.'

Stavros translated and she watched the mother's relief when she understood that her son was merely a witness. She went to the foot of the stairs and screamed, 'Yorgos!' and something else Pam didn't understand but imagined was along the lines of 'get down here right now'.

'If he's in the next village, he'll hear that,' she commented and within moments, George did indeed appear, looking both worried and irritated.

'I'm so sorry you've had to come all this way for nothing,' he began and Pam noted that, like Anna, his English was immaculate though his accent was slightly stronger than hers.

'I don't know whether it is for nothing yet,' she replied. 'Can we sit down and talk?'

'Of course, forgive me. My mother has brought you something to drink?

'Yes, and biscuits,' she replied.

'We have the word *philoxenia* which means the love of strangers, but also welcome. But like all Greek concepts, it means a lot more than that. It also means hospitality as an obligation and a duty. It is part of our makeup, who we are.'

'I've noticed it,' Pam replied, politely wondering where

this was going. George wasn't exactly plump like his mother, but he also wasn't skinny. His short, almost black, hair stood upright forming with his carefully trimmed beard, a circle around his face. He also had a gap on his left eyebrow as if he'd hacked at it with a pair of scissors as a child. Maybe he had.

Unlike his mother, who looked dressed for farm or other physical work, he wore a spotless cream shirt over fawn chinos and a pair of polished tan leather loafers. As Stavros said later, George looked as though he was in a bar in Kolonaki, and not in a farmhouse miles away from everywhere.

'We also have the word, *philotimo*,' George continued, 'which again has a lot of meanings including pride in self and family, but also honour. The concept of honour within the family is at the root of who we are.'

'We also have the word honour in English and another, which is principles, which again means many things,' she replied hoping her annoyance didn't show. 'And it is part of our principles that we do not allow innocent young women to die when it is within our power to save them. This is not merely about the death of Stephanie Michaels, whom you may have liked or disliked, but about the immediate threat the killer poses to her daughter.'

'As I said,' repeated George with the same faint smile on his face, 'I'm very sorry you've come all this way for nothing. I am not going to say whether I know anything that could help you or whether I don't. This is, fundamentally a family issue, and it is part of my personal *philotimo* that I cannot betray any member of my family, however remote. And that is all I am going to say, whether you drag me down to a police cell in Heraklion or whatever.'

'Nobody is talking of dragging,' said Stavros in English. 'We are here in a very respectful and polite way merely asking you for assistance. As a Cretan, I am perfectly well aware of the concept of *philotimo* and know, too that there are interpretations of the word that also mean the love and honour of God and your society. Of giving to your society. Not allowing the innocent death of a young woman might very easily be regarded to come within that meaning.'

'That's your interpretation, not mine,' replied George.

'So you won't tell us whether the person you saw on Tuesday morning was Christos Manoussis?'

George looked suddenly confused. Damn, thought Pam. It probably wasn't him.

'I am not saying anything,' said George.

A few minutes later they left. They waited until they'd driven away from the village before they exploded. 'Jesus! shouted Pam, 'I'm not a violent woman, but my God, I wanted to wipe that smug little smile off his fat face.'

'We were extraordinarily tolerant under the circumstances,' said Stavros. 'But there wasn't anything else we could do. We're not in the business of torturing people for information in this country.'

'I'm not going to tell Leotakis about this,' said Pam, thoughtfully. 'I have the feeling it wouldn't take much for him to raise a personal squad of heavies. And they wouldn't play by our rules.'

'Yes, I think you're right. I always have the feeling with that man that he weighs up what you say against what is best for him, and he will do whatever he wants and with no interest in any law.'

'Money,' said Pam, calming down. 'That kind of money. It changes everything.'

'I find it hard to like him when I know how much people suffer in Greece and here in Crete. Since the EC started its whole demand for cuts, and the government began hacking away at people's pensions, the rise in poverty is terrible.'

'That must impact on crime as well.'

'Of course it does. Did you know that almost half of Greek pensioners get something like six hundred euros a month? That's below the official European poverty threshold. Take my mother, for example. She was a primary school teacher till she retired. Now she doesn't have enough money for her medicines unless I help her, which of course I do, as does my sister – she works in Heraklion for a car rental company. But my mother hates taking money from us. It's an impossible situation.'

'I didn't know. You don't get that kind of information in the British press. Or if you do, I miss it.'

'And your mother?'

'My father was a volunteer firefighter, which is the reason I became a police officer, but his real job was as an engineer. It was a family business he'd inherited, and after his death my mother sold it and put the money into a personal pension, year by year. I only found this out when I was on a case and had to check the accounts of the pension company after some money had been stolen. Thankfully not from her account, which was remarkably healthy. Not that she'd ever tell me any of this. We don't really talk.'

'That's so sad.'

'It's better than talking. Anyhow I don't know how we've ended up discussing this.' She paused and looked around her. I never do this, but there's nothing else we have to do today is there?'

'No. Unless you've got any urgent emails or messages.'

'No. Remarkably quiet. I don't feel I really have to worry now until after Stephanie's funeral when Jen moves away from the Villa Karpathi.'

'In which case I think we head for the hotel in Heraklion and dinner. We should be there by about seven, depending on the traffic.'

'Am I allowed to stop and photograph the sunset?'

'You would be if it was earlier, but we can stop for a drink if you want and visit the port of Rethymnon.'

Pam glanced at her watch. It was coming up to four o'clock and she was very glad they weren't driving all the way back to the Villa. 'Maybe another time. I think I'd rather keep going.'

'They have a pool on the hotel roof. We could have a late swim there and then a cocktail.'

'Now that sounds brilliant. Except I left my bathing costume drying at the villa. I had an early morning swim.'

'Wish I'd done the same.'

So the other swimmer hadn't been Stavros. Mike, maybe, or that boy with Popi, what was his name, Manolis. Stavros pulled off the road and took out his phone.

'Unlike the majority of my countrymen, I don't like phoning and driving. I clearly spent too long in England.'

He put the phone on to speaker and Pam heard the hotel answer. Stavros spoke in English, smiling at her, telling the hotel that he was accompanying the Inspector, who would be arriving this evening at around seven, and he believed that Mr Leotakis had reserved rooms for them.

'Indeed, Major, we have two rooms. Mr Leotakis has asked for the Presidential Suite to be made available to Inspector Gregory and we have an executive sea-view room for yourself.'

'I know you have a pool on your roof, can you ensure than we can swim on our arrival? The Inspector has not had any time off duty for a week and I feel that we should do what we can to make her time here feel relaxed.'

'I am sure that will be fine.' With Leotakis's name attached to their booking, Pam was sure that anything would be fine.

'The only problem is,' continued Stavros, 'the Inspector has been working all day, could you please arrange for someone to go to a local shop and buy a swimming costume. Size…'

'Forty,' said Pam having read the labels on her own clothes which included European sizes, and thinking often how much larger it sounded than fourteen.'

'Of course,' said the receptionist, 'any preference of colour?'

'The Inspector says she trusts your own judgement.'

The receptionist laughed and told Stavros that the costume would be put in Pam's suite in time for her arrival. Power, thought Pam, even in a small thing like this; money buys the power to make one's life easy.

'Do you think life should be this easy?' she asked Stavros.

'No,' he said. 'But it is enjoyable to let oneself be corrupted occasionally. Only in this way,' he added ,as Pam's eyebrows shot up. 'I'm not talking about integrity. I wouldn't take Leotakis's hospitality if I thought he was trying to influence your enquiry.'

'Nor would I,' agreed Pam. 'I made that clear to my own boss. But since it seemed that our aims were the same, I've allowed myself to be convinced that he's on our side. Not that I had a lot of choice,' she added. 'He'd also got our Prime Minister on his side from the out. If I'd rebuffed him, I'd have been out, along with my team.'

'So if you are that rich, you can get away with murder,' he said, frowning. 'Just as well that he didn't arrange for Stephanie's death.'

'If he had, I don't think he'd have allowed his new gallery to be polluted. At least that's my argument. If I'm wrong, God help us all, because he'll never get arrested.'

Stavros smiled at her, noting the tension in her shoulders and the worry lines on her forehead. 'I think you are right. I think he was genuinely fond of Stephanie. I also think you should relax more.' He clipped his phone back into its holder and turned the car engine back on. Pam smiled back at him.

'In which case I don't think we need the second bedroom.'

Stavros switched the engine off again and looked at her, seriously. 'Are you sure? I don't do one-night stands, Pam.'

'We've no idea what's ahead, but yes, I am totally sure of this. Surer than I've been of anything for a long time.'

He pulled her to him and she smelled once again that heady scent of salt and lemons.

It was unlike any other kiss she'd ever had, and she would have liked it to last for ever.

'After that I am very tempted to put on the siren and drive to Heraklion in one hour,' he laughed.

'Please don't. We can just enjoy the anticipation.'

He kissed her again gently, then kissed her eyes, one at a time, and she thought that any moment they'd be making love. Which she didn't want to do at the roadside.

'I can calm you down if you wish by talking about George again,' she offered.

He laughed. 'Yes. You're right. The thought of that smug face is a complete anti-aphrodisiac. What are you thinking? I can see you're thinking again and not about me. I ought to be offended, but I'm not.'

'I'm thinking about this whole *philotimo* thing. Who it covers. Is there any way of finding out exactly who his family is? Even cousins?'

'That would be helpful, but I'm not sure where to start with that. It's not my area of expertise.'

' Wouldn't those old police folders help?'

'He nodded. They could if we had them. Yes, we could start there. I'll make a call later. I know someone who's been researching political records.' They drove on. Past so many places where once again she'd have loved to stop if this had been a holiday. There were resorts with huge hotels and long sandy bays.

'Until I came here I'd never actually seen such a blue sea,' she said, as they skirted the coast. 'Not like this, not so intense, not so many shades of blue. Cromer has its moments from a distance, but as soon as you get down to the edge you know it's going to be greyish and sandy. Nothing like the clear sea at the Villa. And it doesn't have that same silky feel either. It actually made me want to skinny dip.'

'I'm sure we can find a place for us to do that if we both find ourselves staying on after the funeral.'

'I've no idea about that yet. I'd like to stay here as long as Jen does, but at least she has Mike to protect her, and I don't see my bosses allowing me the time off. There's probably a new pile of cases waiting for me even now. They won't allow us to spend an indefinite amount of time on this one case. If we run out of immediate suspects to investigate, they'll say we're just wasting our resources.'

'Then you'll just have to enjoy the time you've got. And come back when you have a holiday. I could juggle my own dates so we'd be free the same time.'

Pam thought about a holiday with Stavros. No investigation, just time to get to know him and spend time with him. It sounded almost too good to be true. 'What are the pink and white flowers that are everywhere?' she asked.

'Oleander,' he replied. 'Totally poisonous, every bit of them.'

'That's nice to know,' she said, and let the rest of the journey wash by her. There were more hotels, a marina and then the ferry port. Stephanie looked at a small container parked nearby and laughed.

Stavros looked at her enquiringly.

'Nothing. Just a silly thought. I was looking at that container and it reminded me my friend Zofia says I live in a box the size of a shipping container.'

'What? Is that real?'

'My house is a small sleeping annexe in a garden; I rent it because it's convenient and cheap.'

'But it's a container?'

'I don't know. How big is a container?'

Stavros turned the car across the traffic and parked behind a row of cars, blocking them in. He picked up his phone and keyed in the word.

'It's fourteen point eight square metres,' he told her.

'Feet, please,' she said.

'Very well. Eight feet by twenty feet, that's a small container, a bigger one is forty feet, which makes it a hundred and sixty square feet.'

Well my little place is bigger than that. Maybe a container and a half. She laughed again.

'Now why are you laughing?'

'Because you make it sound so shameful. It's comfortable. I have a sleeping platform and a shower room and a kitchenette and a nice room in one of the best roads in Cambridge. It takes me about eight minutes to walk to work, longer if I stop for a coffee in the café on Christ's Pieces.'

Stavros laughed. 'Let's go inside and see if your presidential suite is bigger than a shipping container.'

Pam realised that they'd arrived. The hotel was directly in front of them. It was an older building, built by lemon exporters in the Twenties, Stavros told her, and it was both luxurious and comfortable. Pam had never stayed anywhere that made her feel so special. Putting on the simple green costume they'd bought for her with a pattern of leaves she might have chosen herself, she went for a swim in the rooftop pool while Stavros stayed in their room, ringing the officer who was investigating folders.

People already dressed for dinner were having drinks in the adjacent bar and, feeling somewhat self-conscious, she only stayed in the pool long enough to unlock the kinks in her shoulders from the drive. Then, putting on the hotel's thick white towelling gown, she took the lift back down to her room. Which was indeed two rooms and marginally bigger than her home.

She walked into the shower feeling self-conscious, and took off her costume there, but a moment later Stavros, similarly naked, joined her and then she didn't feel either self-conscious or embarrassed. They stepped out of the shower, enfolded each other in quantities of fluffy towels, and headed for the bed.

Later that evening, after they'd had dinner on the terrace and after they'd made love again, she'd shown him the poem *Ithaka* which she'd found on her phone, and he read it to her in Greek.

Whatever happens, she thought, as she lay beside him, this is perfect.

CHAPTER 36

Pam must have had her meeting with this architect man, George, by now, thought Mike, looking at his watch. She'd sent him a text saying that they were staying overnight in Heraklion as Stavros was meeting Stephanie's plane in the morning. She hoped that George had managed to shed some light on the whole thing. He'd never known a case that felt as though it should be obvious and which seemed impenetrable.

Tomorrow Stephanie would be brought back to the Villa Karpathi by yacht, and thereafter to a small plot beside the chapel, following Tuesday's service. Even now he found it hard to think of Stephanie dead. Perhaps he never would, and it would just be a memory of her alive that stayed with him, gradually fading.

He found it difficult to stay at the Villa today, perhaps because it had been designed for enjoyment, and he was not in the mood to enjoy anything. Leotakis, obviously, had somewhere private, maybe an office where he could work, but there was nothing Mike could do here. There was a small army of gardeners and any builders would be hired by the housekeeper. It was a luxury cage, and even after a day he was chafing to go home and do something. It seemed that Jen felt the same, and had grumbled at lunchtime that she wasn't allowed to go into Sitia.

'It's Sunday,' said Popi. 'What do you want to do in Sitia that you can't do here?'

'See people,' suggested Jen. 'I know that sounds terrible because I've got you and I haven't seen you for so long...'

'In which case you will spend the afternoon with me telling me your news and pushing me round the garden. I've told Manolis he can enjoy himself today. I don't pay him to look after me after all, and I don't want him to feel exploited.'

'Popi, you'd never exploit anyone!' Jen laughed and Mike agreed.

But that didn't help his problem. There was nothing to stop him going home. Perhaps he could go and see whether Henry had returned, but he didn't. He did some basic exercises, then swam and, later that afternoon, sat on his veranda checking all the Cretan vendetta cases he could find online in case he had missed any. He hadn't. There was nothing that linked Stephanie in any way. He was glad that Leotakis had agreed with him when they'd discussed it a few days previously. He'd worried that his recent lack of police work was showing him up. But Pam had said the same even with the help of their good IT specialist. Stuart, she'd said, was former GCHQ, and she felt he wasn't above digging in places the police usually weren't allowed to dig. She'd kept him informed about the developments since her arrival and he was now investigating the son of the archaeologist who sounded plausible enough, but Mike wasn't convinced. Would he have that much venom? Just because his father hadn't been credited for the Chiona treasure? If so, he was seriously fucked up.

There was something they were all missing, but like the new gallery in Cambridge, it was a labyrinth that led only to an enclosed centre.

Why the bull? he said to himself for the hundredth time. Why place her on the horns of the bull? He pocketed his phone and decided to go and check with Jen. At least he could keep her safe.

Pam had asked Jen to stay within the confines of the villa, but although she was the officer leading the inquiry into Stephanie's death, that didn't give her any authority over

Jen's movements in Greece. Actually she couldn't even forbid Jen in England, Jen knew, though she could advise. And now she'd come up with a request nobody could deny her.

'I know it isn't a custom or anything,' she told Mike as they walked through the garden beside the pool. 'In fact, Dad thinks it's totally weird, but I want to wear something of Mum's at her funeral.'

'One of her dresses?' asked Mike. Jen was wearing a sleeveless, loose stone-coloured dress with big pockets, which stopped just below her knees and was the most casual piece of clothing Mike had seen her in. He couldn't imagine her in any of Stephanie's large flowing multi-coloured skirts.

'No. Shit, no. Wrong style, wrong size. Maybe a scarf or a necklace or something that reminds me of her that I can hold on to during the service.'

It was a reminder to him that while to Leotakis or Pam this was a murder inquiry, it was also a personal bereavement. Jen had lost her mother.

'OK,' said Mike. 'We can do that.'

Although he knew he didn't need to get permission, at least officially, Mike did send a message to Leotakis asking to see him. He was damned if he was going to ask one of his staff, like the Frenchman, Rafael, whom he'd distrusted on sight.

Nikos invited him to come to the main house immediately, and Mike found him sitting in a director's chair in an internal courtyard which had a fountain and was full of roses. A book sat on the table beside him and Mike was somehow not surprised that it was a Greek edition of the essays of Montaigne. If you had everything money could buy, you had time for philosophy.

'Man is finite and truth is infinite,' Leotakis said.

Mike thought about that for a moment and decided he would need a month at least to try and make sense of it. 'Montaigne would have approved of your courtyard as a place of contemplation. It has a somewhat monastic feel about it,' he said instead.

'It does,' Leotakis smiled. 'Although Montaigne himself wrote in a tower, which I wouldn't enjoy at all.' He looked around him, at the bees in the lavender, which had been planted between the rose bushes, and sighed. 'This was Alison's favourite place. She loved the sea and the view from the villa, of course, but there is a sense of peace in this little rose garden that is quite special. The sound of the fountain in particular. Have you ever thought about that? How you get the right sound?'

'No, I haven't,' Mike told him.

'There's an art to it. You don't want it to sound like someone peeing, or a cistern emptying, so you have to get the flow right. Which is why I chose the millstone and the circle of pebbles around it. It's just a gentle bubble of water which never becomes intrusive.'

'I can see why you like being here. It's perfect.'

'Stephanie thought so, too.'

'That's why I wanted to see you. Jen wants to go to her mother's house to pick up something like a scarf or a necklace to wear for the funeral tomorrow. I just thought I'd better check with you before I drive her over.'

'Of course. And thank you for the courtesy.'

'Kindness,' Mike thought, translating the word simultaneously back into English. We've lost the connection between courtesy and kindness in English.

An hour later, he and Jen walked round Stephanie's house, which was still so full of her presence as to be painful for both of them. Jen was near tears, but tried to be practical to help herself deal with her emotions.

'You understand I'm not going to move anything or get rid of any of her things,' Mike told her.

'What about your things? Won't you want to bring them here?'

Mike thought about his bag which contained few books, mostly given to him by Stephanie and a few changes of clothes.

'I don't have any things,' he replied.

'Family things? You don't have any?' She sat down on one of the sofas. 'Sit. Tell me. I can't believe what you've just said.'

'On my father's side, I did once have a carving of a flying fish that his father brought over from Barbados, but it got broken, and after his death my mother threw it out.'

'Your father came from Barbados?'

'His family, yes, but he was born in London. He died when I was seven.' Prostate cancer. Mike had read up on it later and discovered that there was twice the likelihood of people of African descent developing the disease. His father's diet probably hadn't helped either.

'I get my good looks from him though,' he added with a smile.

'What about your mother?' asked Jen. 'Is she still alive?'

Mike shook his head. 'No. She died when I was a student. It was a road rage thing. He forced her off the road.'

'That's terrible.'

'It was. I think it's why I changed subjects at uni. Mum worked in the family deli, but had always wanted me to become a lawyer. But being stubborn I'd done my degree in politics. After she died I did an MA in criminology.'

'But became a cop?'

'One of those much-hated fast track cops, yes.'

'So this was in London?'

'Yes. I had a flat in Battersea, Khyber Road. I chose it because I was lazy. Five minutes walk to Clapham Junction and a direct line to Milton Keynes. My grandparents were still alive then. And I was married then,' he added. He wondered whether Jen had ever been married. He didn't think so. He seemed to reflect Stephanie on more than one boozy evening bewailing the fact that Jen was never going to give her grandchildren.

'Not now?' she asked.

'No. Divorced eight years ago. My grandparents, my mum's parents that is, had a Greek deli. After they died, and after my divorce, there was just Aunt Sofia, so I began to come out here and stay with her.'

'So why join the police?'

'Not sure. Because I saw black kids stopped, and thought I could do better? Or because the man who caused Mum's death was never prosecuted and I thought he should be? Lots of reasons. But I never really fitted. Too rebellious.' He smiled wryly. 'And that's all the questions I'm answering.'

'I'm sorry,' said Jen. 'I didn't mean it to be an interrogation. I was just interested. After all, you know everything about me.'

'Not everything,' he smiled at her. She was so beautiful, but he was not going there. He couldn't allow himself to feel those kinds of emotions again.

'Have you thought what you want to do about your mother's writings?' he asked.

'No,' she said. 'I don't even feel up to reading them yet.'

'You know that Pam has temporarily taken some of her notebooks?'

Jen nodded. 'Yes she told me, or rather asked me in such a way that it was impossible to refuse. She seemed to think there might be something there which could lead her to Mum's killer.'

'I know. We discussed it. But neither of us can think what it is. I've looked at the notebooks, too. She wrote quite well, your mum. I think you'll enjoy reading them one day.'

Jen bit her lip. 'I never took her writing seriously, but she did write a lot. She wrote short stories, too. I think she won a local competition in Cambridge for one of them. If she'd worked at it, she could have been good. But Mum never really worked at anything. Except maybe winning awards for drinking. What really gets me is that she was ill and I didn't know it. Pam went through the details with me so that I didn't hear them for the first time in court.'

'That was kind of her.'

'Yes she is, isn't she? Kind'.

'I suppose she is. I don't really know her. She seems to be getting on very well with that Athenian cop.'

'Do you think?' Jen's face lit up. 'A romance? Oh I rather like that.'

'You don't think it disrespectful?' Mike asked her. He had developed an active dislike of Stavros, but wasn't sure why. It certainly wasn't jealousy; Pam was a pleasant-looking woman, but most definitely not his type. Maybe it was just in response to Stavros's hostility towards him. Racial, he'd decided.

'Disrespectful? Not in the slightest. Mum would have adored it. She was such an old romantic and there was nothing she liked better than matchmaking. She was always doing it.'

Mike felt that there was a personal edge to that and that Stephanie had also tried to find partners for her daughter.

'Did you ever bring your boyfriends here?' he asked. Had Jen known the killer? The thought struck him suddenly. Was that why he'd begun by killing her cat?

'Only one. Tom, Tom Casson. We split up a couple of years ago. He never forgave me for implicitly attacking him in my thesis. Film directors who make the work about them. Which he does.'

'I do dislike films that do that. But the split wasn't acrimonious?'

'No. Not at all. I later discovered in any case he was sleeping with his assistant. He's currently making a film for Channel 4 about seniors having gap years after they retire. He's in Bali, I think, interviewing pensioners who are backpacking and spending their inheritance money. We had lunch before he went off; we're quite good friends these days. The assistant buggered off as soon as she realised just how selfish Tom was. Everything was always about Tom. And he was always squeamish. I couldn't even show him a film if there was blood, in case you were wondering whether he was the killer.'

'Just a passing thought. But I'm certain he's a Greek. Everything about your mother's death feels Cretan.'

'It feels like one of the ancient myths,' agreed Jen. 'Perhaps that's why I can't quite believe it's real. It's only here when I look around and realise Mum won't be coming back.'

This time he gave her a hug, making sure that she didn't interpret it for something else.

'I'm sorry,' said Jen, wiping her face and blowing her nose.

'Don't be. It's an impossible situation. I just wish I could do more. I wish I could work out who on earth killed your mother.'

'And talking about that. Where's Henry? I'm beginning to get worried about him. It's not like him to let Mum down.'

'Do you want to go over to his house to see if he's back?'

'Yes, please. He won't come to the Villa as he can't stand Nikos. There's obviously something there in the past. But then Henry does get these fixations...' She stopped as if aware of what she'd said. 'But not with Mum,' she added.

'It's OK. Didn't Pam tell you? We now know that the killer was young, probably a student, but definitely student-aged. And Henry doesn't have any children.'

Jen laughed. 'I could put money on his not having ever made love to a woman. I think he knew he was gay from his schooldays. It's what first brought him to Greece. I didn't know about the age thing. When did that happen?'

'Only this morning. My understanding of time is all over the place. Pam texted me from the car. So it couldn't have been George, the man they were going to interview, though it seems he may have seen the killer.'

'I'm glad it's not Henry. I've known him all my life; he often stepped in when Mum was being impossible.'

Drunk, Mike thought. Jen hadn't had an easy time with her mother.

'Yes. Let's go over to his,' Jen continued. 'He can help me choose what to pick up for tomorrow. He probably knows her jewellery collection better than I do.'

They locked the door to Stephanie's house and walked down the twisting lane towards Henry's house over the painted cobbles. There were moments when this new village reminded Mike of a film set. It was too perfect. But time would take care of that. Henry's house was just three houses away and it faced the sea directly. They walked round to the front terrace and found the door open.

'Jen. Get back,' hissed Mike. 'Right back, out of sight past that last house.'

'You don't think..'

'Shh,' said Mike, wishing he had a gun or some backup. 'If I'm not out in five minutes, run to the cafeneion and phone the police. Or Nikos.'

Jen backed away, trembling slightly, but as she did, they both heard someone humming and Henry stepped on to the veranda. Jen shot forward and rushed into his arms, almost knocking hm over.

'We thought you might be a burglar,' she said. 'You gave us a terrible fright.'

'I'm not a burglar,' said Henry, cheerfully, nor a killer, though I think the English policewoman has me on her list.'

'Not anymore,' Mike told him. 'A witness has come forward and we know it's someone much younger.'

'That's good news. I didn't like having to ignore the wishes of the Cambridgeshire constabulary, but I had other things on my mind. Even at a time like this,' he said stroking his god-daughter's face. 'Something I had to do and which took me to Paris. I've only been back a few hours.'

'Paris?' asked Jen.

'Yes. Nothing I can discuss now. In fact I shouldn't even be here, I need to go back to London and talk with some old friends there. But I couldn't miss dear Stephanie's funeral. I'd never forgive myself.'

Henry took off his glasses and polished them. His eyes looked tired and red. There was something about him that reminded Mike of a newly hatched chick. Eyes that are always magnified looking disconcertingly small without their protective lenses. and the fluff of white hair.

He was so glad now that Henry wasn't implicated in any way.

'That's why I came over here. I wanted your advice on what piece of Mum's jewellery I should wear at her funeral.'

'That's easy. You should wear the silver trowel pendant that Laurent gave her.'

'Of course. I knew you'd know.' She hugged him again. 'We'll go and get it. It was always her favourite.'

'Yes. She thought a lot about Laurent in recent months.'

'You do, too, don't you Henry?' Jen asked him.

'Jen, my dear, I've thought about Laurent every day for the past forty-one years. Stephanie knew so little about him when he died. I knew a little more. But after his death, I went to France to meet his family. It's strange. I only told your mother about this a year or so back. But it didn't really interest her; she wanted to remember her Laurent, not who he was or anything about him that didn't include her.'

'That kind of fixation is what we're going to find with her killer, isn't it?' said Mike, thoughtfully. Henry had a knack of getting to the point.

'I'm not a psychologist,' said Henry, 'but it would seem so. Someone who is fixated on an event in which Stephanie was involved, and which affected him and for which he blames Stephanie. It is possible that it may be something of which she was unaware. That is the nature of fixations. And now we know it is a young man. So we are looking at history.'

'Something connected with his family,' Mike suggested.

'Yes,' agreed Henry. 'That fits the profile of the killing from what I've heard about it.'

Back at the house, Jen found the small silver trowel, which hung from a silver chain and Mike fastened it around her neck. It was absolutely the right thing. It brought together every part of Stephanie. They went back into the main room where Jen began to look at Stephanie's books.

'First edition Durrell's *Alexandrian Quartet*,' she said looking inside a copy of *Justine*. 'Didn't know she had that.'

'Is it worth anything?'

'I expect so.'

'Well it's yours, of course,' he said quickly. 'You know there's no way I'd want to make money from your mother's inheritance.'

'I do know that,' said Jen, 'and it one of the things I like about you.'

Mike was prevented from replying to this by a soft knock at the door. He opened it and found Manolis standing there.

'Is Jen here?' the young man asked.

Jen stepped forward smiling.' Yes,' she said, 'I'm here. Has something happened to Popi?'

'No, nothing like that,' he said hurriedly. 'It's just that Mrs Filotaki asked whether you wouldn't mind dropping by her cottage this evening before she goes to bed. There's something she would like to ask you.'

'It's probably about the readings for tomorrow,' Jen told Mike.

'Do you want to wait for Mike to drive you back?' Manolis asked her, 'or come back with me now?'

'I don't have to wait,' said Jen smiling at Mike. 'In fact I think he'd rather like a few moments on his own to get to know his new house.' She turned back to Manolis. 'Do you have a car here?'

'Yes,' said Manolis. 'I've got Mrs Filotaki's car. I parked it just up the road.'

'Is that OK?' asked Jen.

'You'll take her straight back to the Villa?' Mike demanded. Should he take Jen back himself? It was only just over six miles and a clear fine evening. They were all chasing shadows.

'Of course,' said Manolis. 'Mrs Filotaki would kill me if anything happened to Jen. And so would you.'

'Yes, I would,' said Mike.

'Nothing's going to happen to me on the road,' said Jen. 'So do I get permission to go back with Manolis? Though it's nice to feel so protected.'

Mike nodded, and she thanked him and laughed. Mike heard her asking Manolis about his studies as she walked away. His turn to be questioned now, he thought. He looked round the room. His house. It would take a long time before he could accept that.

CHAPTER 37

Pam thought she'd fall instantly asleep, but there was something at the back of her mind that was bothering her, a connection that she felt she ought to be making, but that was just out of reach.

It was something she'd heard recently, what was it? Something she already knew about Stephanie. Perhaps she should let herself go to sleep and hope that it would click into place overnight. But it was like a piece of grit under her skin. Something she'd heard, something Grace had said and also Popi.

Then suddenly she knew.

Pam leapt out of bed with a yell waking Stavros who sat up, shocked out of deep sleep, instinctively reaching for his gun until he realised where he was. Pam had thrown on her dressing gown and was chucking her clothes out of her case on to the floor.

'What the hell?' he asked. He looked at the hotel clock beside the bed. It was still only eleven thirty in the evening. They'd gone to bed early, straight after dinner.

'I think I know who the killer is,' Pam told him, scrabbling in her bag for the folder. 'Everyone's been telling me about this ever since my first interview, but I just wasn't listening.'

'Listening to what?'

'Grace said it, Popi said it, there had to have been a trigger. Right?'

'Yes, that makes sense,' he agreed, sitting up and reaching for his own robe.

'And we've been thinking that the trigger was finding the Chiona treasure and getting all that publicity...'

'Well, that would be enough to infuriate anyone who had something against Stephanie.'

'Exactly. And Grace also said that it was like one of those Greek tragedies. It was family. You see the killer wanted to prove to his family that he'd taken revenge on Stephanie for something terrible she'd done. So we kept looking for things she'd done, like stealing the sources of someone's dissertation and getting them thrown out of Cambridge or just getting the credit for the Chiona dig, which she didn't do.'

'Which are pretty bad things.'

'But they didn't result in anyone dying. And this vendetta, as you all keep telling me, is a death for a death. But who did die? That's what I wasn't asking. It was there and I wasn't listening.'

'What was there? Pam you're not making any sense.'

'The Polytechnic. The student she protected who was arrested while she was out and who died. Henry said Stephanie could never forget it. Well what if his family could never forget it? What if it led to a string of suicides? Who is it who's just lost his father and wants to know his family history?'

'Manolis, Popi's young man? You think....'

Pam didn't answer his question. She picked up the phone and rang Mike and at the same time she pulled out one of Stephanie's notebooks and began to rifle through it.

'Mike', she said, the moment he answered the phone. 'Listen, I know this is going to sound very strange but I need you to go to Manolis's room right now and get his folder. I think he's our murderer.'

'What!' Mike shouted, sounding more worried than she expected. 'Manolis! Why? But...Oh holy shit, Pam. I let him take Jen home from Chiona this evening.'

'You let him what? Where is Jen? Is she…'

Mike could hear her questions as he put down the phone and threw on his trousers. 'I'm on my way to Manolis's room right now,' he said as he ran. 'Stay on the line.'

Pam could hear his breathing as he ran. 'Manolis picked up Jen from Chiona this evening,' Pam told Stavros.

Stavros swore. He ran into the bathroom grabbing his clothes with him. Pam also used the time to put on her clothes again. There was a glass of water beside the bed which she drank quickly. She needed a clear head. She needed to keep on top of this. She could hear Mike calling out Manolis's name and then he was back.

'His room's empty. He's not there,' he said. 'He swore he'd bring her back. I'll go and check on Jen.'

'Before you do that,' said Pam. See if Manolis's police folder is still there.'

At least Mike didn't ask why she thought, gratefully. He trusted her. He was back online in a moment.

'Yes. His family folder is still here, I've got it.'

'Oh thank goodness. 'Look up the bit on the great uncle,' she continued, 'the one who was killed after the Polytechnic massacre. Hold on, I'm looking up his name in Stephanie's own account. Yes. It was Andreas. See if his name was Andreas.'

She heard a rustle of papers and sat there biting her knuckles as she waited. If Jen was still alive, they had a chance. If they could find out where Manolis had taken her. If he had taken her and not simply killed her.

'His name was Andreas Grigorakis. He was arrested on the 22nd November 1973.'

'Where? Does it say where?'

'In Pangrati. The street was Spiro Mercouri, from a *garsoniera*, that's a studio flat.'

'Spiro Mercouri. That's Stephanie's flat. It's right here in her own story. Mike, tell me what it says about the informant. There must have been an informant. Was it Stephanie?' This is what she'd been searching for when she couldn't sleep, the connection that had been nudging at the edge of her mind. The guilt that Stephanie felt about the boy who'd been shot after the Polytechnic, and how she kept coming back to it. And both Grace and Popi telling her that there would have been a recent trigger. The death of Manolis's father.

'Stephanie was living in a *garsoniera* in Spiro Mercouri,' she told Stavros. 'The student Stephanie looked after was Manolis's great uncle. And he thinks she was responsible for his death and that of his father. Mike's looking up who it was who did inform the police.'

Pam took a deep breath. The answer to this next question could be the key to how they might still be able to save Jen. Stavros came over to her and took her hand as they both waited.

'This is what he planned,' he said. 'And maybe he even used Popi Filotaki to get close to Jen. He plans and plans and then acts.'

After a long moment, Mike came back to the phone. 'No,' he said. 'It wasn't Stephanie. It says the informant was the *thyrorós*, the janitor. Manolis thinks it's Stephanie, doesn't he? Oh Christ, Pam. You've got it!'

'See if Jen is in her room,' said Pam. 'Oh, and Stavros is ringing Nikos,' she added.

Pam was left in silence again as she heard Stavros talking urgently in Greek to Leotakis, explaining about Manolis. She heard the words she expected to hear, Stephanie's street in Athens, Polytechnic and *thyrorós*.

Almost immediately, Mike was back. 'Jen's not in her room either,' he said. 'He's taken her.'

'Jen's not in her room' Pam told Stavros who passed on the information to Nikos, then ended the call.

'This is now a Greek police case,' he told her. 'This is an abduction. I will ring the Heraklion police and also Manos. This is where we hand over to them.'

'We can't risk Jan's life,' said Pam. 'We mustn't frighten Manolis into killing her.'

'This isn't your case anymore,' said Stavros. 'You have to leave it to us.'

Pam gave him a hard look and dialled Nikos's number. She took the phone on to the balcony. Stavros wasn't even looking at her. He was talking to the local police and giving instructions.

'Pam,' said Leotakis. 'What can I do for you?'

'Can you ring George and make him understand that this is not a matter of honour, but a terrible mistake. I think he knows where Manolis would take Jen.' She gave him the number.

'Yes. And a mistake which also reflects on the family. I will ring him now and then call you back.'

Stavros was still talking on the phone when Nikos called her back.

'You were right. Again,' he said. 'There is an old barn in a village called Anogia. It's where both his grandfather and his father killed themselves.'

'I need to get there,' said Pam. 'I need to talk to him'.

'I think Popi will want to come also,' said Nikos. 'I will go and speak with her and then call you back.'

Pam walked back into the sitting room where Stavros was simultaneously taking and making notes.

'We know where they are,' Pam told him.

'*Perimene ena lepto*,' said Stavros, which Pam now knew meant 'wait a minute'. He turned to Pam looking, she thought, rather irritated by her interruption. 'What?' he asked her. 'How do you know?'

Pam told him and also told him that he needed to hold back the troops.

'We can't just rush in, you know that. We have to save Jen.'

'I'll talk with the police chief here,' he agreed. 'We have the best negotiators in Athens. They were trained for the Olympics.'

'Nikos is telling Popi what has happened. He's going to

ring us back after that.' Pam sighed. 'Popi will be devastated.'

'She'll blame herself for bringing Manolis to the Villa,' he agreed.

'And Mike will be blaming himself for letting Jen go with Manolis,'

'So he should,' said Stavros angrily, 'he should never have let her out of his sight. You told him to look after her.'

'Yes, but he wasn't to know. And I think he'll be beating himself up quite enough without us adding to it.'

She was getting a very strong feeling that she was about to be side-lined while the Greek police took over, and she was damned if she was going to let that happen. She knew it wasn't her case or her country, but Jen had become a friend and she felt responsible for her. *I should have gone back there tonight. This is all my fault for getting distracted. This is my punishment for allowing myself to have fun.*

A few moments later, Nikos rang back.

'George told me that he thought he'd seen Manolis's father, who was his own godfather, hence the loyalty,' he said.

'And he was the ghost,' she said, suddenly understanding it all.

The bond of the koumbaros, they've all been telling me about, thought Pam, *the godfather figure, who's like family. It all makes sense.*

'Popi is here and would like to speak with you,' he added. *He sounded tired,* thought Pam. She'd put her phone on to speaker so that Stavros could also join in.

'Oh Pam,' said Popi. 'I am so sorry. I never thought. And I never asked him where he was last week. He must have gone to England. He studies in England.'

'You just helped him look into his family history.'

'Yes,' Popi agreed. 'I managed to retrieve his *fakelos* for him. He wanted to know about his family. But I don't think he ever opened it.'

'If he had done, he'd have known that Stephanie wasn't responsible for Andreas's death.'

'Yes,' said Popi. 'Stephanie felt responsible, but she wasn't. But Andreas must have thought she'd betrayed him. They must have told his brother. Who later killed himself. As did his son, Manolis's father.'

'Thus triggering the vendetta.'

'When you go there I have to come with you,' Popi continued. 'I think I am the one person Manolis will believe.'

'Can you bring the folder with you?' asked Pam. 'It might help if he sees it.'

'We can't go in heavy-handed,' Stavros said. 'Anogia is one of those villages I was telling you about, Pam. Plus it has a lot of history.'

'I'll speak to the headman in the village so that there is no problem with the villagers,' said Nikos. 'They know me.'

History, thought Pam. As if history mattered now. The only thing that mattered was rescuing Jen and getting to Manolis as fast as they could. However they could. At least they had the resources of Leotakis to help them.

'Right,' said Pam. 'We now know where Jen is and why Manolis took her. We have to make Manolis understand that. I'm going there now. And I'm not taking no for an answer,' she glared at Stavros, who was about to say something.

It was less than a week ago, she thought in amazement, because surely weeks had passed since then, that she was sitting outside a barn in near Cambridge, worrying that Winston would die from drug poisoning because she was waiting for Pell. And he nearly did die. If I wait for the Athens police now, Jen could die. I'm not going to do it.

'Stavros,' said Mike, 'can you hear me?'

'Yes,' he replied, curtly.

'I agree with you that we can't go in with a lot of armed police, but Pam is right, we do need to act quickly. I'm coming too, I've done a lot of hostage training and I'm bringing Kyria Filotaki. She is the one person Manolis might listen to.'

'I will facilitate your transport and talk to the village headman,' said Nikos.

'I'll let the local police know that you are taking pre-emptive action, then,' said Stavros, clearly furious. Pam bit her lip and tried to forget the Stavros she had just spent the past few hours with and concentrate on the man in front of her. 'What's the quickest way for us to get to the village?' she asked him.

'Twenty minutes by helicopter and about half an hour by motorbike if we go through all the red lights.'

'Pam,' she heard the gruff voice of Nikos again. 'How do you want to get there?'

Pam thought for a moment about Stavros driving through red lights and small villages at top speed in the night. They'd be lucky to get there alive. 'Helicopter,' she said. 'We can co-ordinate our arrival time so Stavros and I will arrive about the same time as Mike and Popi.'

'I'll arrange that,' said Nikos.

'Thank you, Pam,' said Popi. 'I will see you there.'

The phone clicked off and Pam and Stavros were left staring at each other. Then Pam rushed to the bathroom and threw up. She then soaked one of the small towels in cold water and wiped her face. She brushed her teeth and gathered her things into her wash bag. Keep praying Jen's still alive, she said to herself as she packed her bag.

She got into Stavros's car and they drove to the airport in around five minutes flat, with his siren screaming. She grabbed hold of the handle above the door as the car swung through the traffic, ignored the traffic lights and was accompanied by the shriek of brakes from all the cars forced to stop suddenly. She'd been right not to choose to go by motorbike. They would never have got to the village alive.

There was a side entrance to the airport and after Stavros showed his police badge, they were let through and he drove around the perimeter to where a small jet and two helicopters were parked. There was a small, comfortable waiting room there with a water fountain and coffee. Pam helped herself to some water and sat down while Stavros stayed outside and talked on his phone.

Her own phone rang a few minutes later. It was Mike again.

'Our helicopter is on its way,' he told her. 'We'll be on board in about five minutes. I'll ring you again then.'

'Thank you,' she said.

'I'm so sorry,' he added. 'I promised you to look after her.'

'Mike, I should have been there, too. We're human. We also trust people. And sometimes we're let down.' She knew she was speaking for herself as well as him, but that didn't make it any easier for either of them. She was impressed by how sensible Mike was and livid at the way Stavros was behaving.

She ended the call with Mike and opened the door. 'Stavros,' she called in her most controlled voice.

'Yes,' he replied, sulkily. Any moment now she was going to slap him.

'It's just occurred to me, I'm not thinking clearly, but we need to have an ambulance waiting in case Jen has been injured. Or just to get her checked over. Can you liaise that with the local forces?'

'Of course,' he said and nodded. She seemed to remember another Stavros who had smiled at her, but he'd clearly gone for good. We're talking to each other like strangers, she thought, sadly. And that's how it ends. She went back indoors and sat down. A few minutes later he opened the door and came inside.

'I've arranged that. And I've now heard from my own commander. The local police are taking my lead on this and coming discreetly to the village but hanging back from the barn itself.'

He sounded slightly more cheerful, Pam saw. Men and their fucking egos, always getting in the bloody way.

After a fifteen-minute wait, he and Pam climbed aboard a small helicopter. Stavros sat in the front with the pilot. And just like that I'm powerless, she thought. My phone won't work in the air and he's got control again. She heard him talking Greek over his headphones, and took out her pad to make written notes while they waited to take off.

There was nothing to write. Get in there and rescue Jen was the only thing she could think of. The rest was simply a matter of whether Manolis believed her and Popi. And how he reacted. She wondered whether he'd have a knife with him and how they could disarm him. This is where I need a taser, she thought, but it was too late for that now and besides, she wouldn't be allowed to use one in Greece. Deep breaths, she said to herself. Just concentrate on breathing and remembering everything you've learned about hostage situations.

After a very long ten-minute wait, the helicopter took off. It followed the coast westwards for a moment and Jen could see the lights of Heraklion and of a ferry boat docked in the harbour. Near there was their hotel, she said to herself, where I had the happiest hours of my life and some of the unhappiest moments. Then the small aircraft swung left and headed towards the darkness of the nearest mountains.

Somewhere down there were Jen and Manolis. But she had no idea whether Jen was still alive or whether the rescue attempt would lead to her death.

CHAPTER 38

'My name is Manolis Grigorakis and if you are watching this film, you will understand the reasons for my actions.

'In Greece we have a word, *timí*, which can mean price or value or honour. We also have the word *timoría*, which now means punishment, but in previous times meant not merely the idea vengeance, but the restoration of honour to the victim. I don't believe you have such a notion in England or understand honour. You look at me and at this woman behind me and you see a murderer. I have heard you describe me as such. What kind of murderer could kill Stephanie? you ask. I will tell you, an honourable man, a man who understands the necessity of purifying the line, and doing his duty to his family.

'Homer tells us in the Odyssey that it is a good thing to have a son who will avenge his father. My father had such a son, and my vengeance will be complete with the death of the daughter you see behind me.'

'No!' exploded a voice behind him. Manolis stopped speaking and turned to Jen, who had managed to use her tongue to push down the scarf he had tied around her mouth. There was blood dripping down her forehead and into her left eye. She'd come round to find herself tied to a chair and knew if she didn't get free, she was never getting out of there.

'You can die slowly or you can die quickly,' Manolis told her. 'But don't interrupt me again.'

Jen nodded and concentrated on trying to move her wrists and loosen the string he'd used to tie her to the chair. Manolis turned back to his laptop and pressed a key again.

'I had contemplated the necessity of killing also the husband, but I see that he is removed from the family and therefore is not culpable,' he continued. 'You may ask how is this woman guilty when she was not born when Stephanie Michaels betrayed my great-uncle. I will tell you. She has the blood of the betrayer in her veins.

'For this is where it begins. It begins with a hero, a hero betrayed. My great uncle Andreas died when he was twenty-four because he was betrayed by Stephanie Michaels. His brother, my grandfather, after whom I am named, killed himself ten years later on November 17th in his memory. And in his memory, my father killed himself this year, thirty-five years later. At his funeral I swore to avenge him, and bring back honour to my family. I have fulfilled my vow.'

CHAPTER 39

The liaison with the village had worked. Pam could see the lights of the football pitch, which had been turned on to give the helicopter a visible landing site. She tried to concentrate on that and not the dark shadows of the mountains, which felt perilously close.

They landed on the pitch with a clatter of rotor blades that sent small tornados of dust spinning into the air. The helicopter then parked in a corner as the second one landed in the centre of the pitch. Stavros leapt out and walked over to an elderly man who'd been waiting beside a clump of trees, beside of the pitch.

Mike jumped out of the second helicopter as soon as he was given permission, and joined them.

'This is Mr Antonidakis, he's the president of the local cultural association, but rather more importantly, the village listens to him,' said Stavros in Greek, so the older man could understand. 'He's talked with Mr Leotakis, and I've explained that we have a very disturbed young man who has taken Stephanie Michaels' daughter hostage. He will ensure that we get the villagers' support. Even here, they have nothing but praise for Stephanie and how she did nothing but bring honour to Crete.'

The man nodded as Stavros spoke and Mike realised that this was going to be very useful. With two helicopters landing in the middle of the night, the whole village was going to wonder what was going on and whether it was a police raid.

'Good thinking, Stavros,' he said and patted him on the shoulder as they made their way back to the helicopters where Pam was now helping Popi into her wheelchair. The sight of Popi completely changed Antonidakis. One moment he had been polite but reserved, but seeing Popi coming to his village changed that in a second.

'Mrs Filotaki, what an honour!' he said. 'Welcome to Anogia!'

'Ah, not the kind of visit I'd have hoped,' she replied, warmly, holding out her hand for him to shake. 'The young woman is my god-daughter.'

Antonidakis crossed himself hurriedly. Mike turned to him.

'We've been told to go to an old barn which is just off the path below the Church of Aghios Dimitrios,' he said. 'You know it?'

Antonidakis nodded. 'I know precisely where you mean. Maria saw a car go down earlier this evening, and we've been wondering why. The barn belonged to Mr Grigorakis, may the good Lord save his soul.' He crossed himself again

'Yes. We know what happened there,' said Stavros. 'That's is what has led to this. His son believed, erroneously, that Stephanie Michaels had been responsible for those deaths. He declared a personal vendetta against her. We're hoping this ends now.'

Mike knew that Stavros's speech was directly aimed at the village gossips and to stop false speculations, but it also would get the village on their side when the police did arrive. Antonidakis looked grim and shook his head. Then he called, 'Panos!' and a teenage boy emerged from behind one of the trees.

'Panos, my grandson, will take you down there,' the village elder told them. He looked quizzically at Pam as if wondering why she was there, and Mike introduced her, telling him that it was she who had solved the case. Antonidakis shook her hand enthusiastically, and she nodded and smiled at him.

'I'll explain on the way,' Mike told her. 'Stavros has just managed to get the village on our side, which is rather important up here.'

Stavros looked slightly surprised and nodded. 'Now, this is what I suggest,' Mike continued, realising he was taking the lead, but for once happy to do that. Old habits, he thought to himself. I used to be good at this.

The idea was to let Manolis know they were there and to allow him to choose which of them he wanted to talk to. Then throw in a phone. 'He left behind everything at the Villa Karpathi,' Mike told Pam as they walked down the stony path, shining torches to show them the way. There were no lights here and the darkness was dense.

'Not just the folder, but his clothes and his phone. As if he didn't expect to come back.'

'Don't like the sound of that at all,' replied Pam. 'In his head, he's got nothing now to lose now. That makes him very dangerous.' She shivered.

'It's a lot colder up here, isn't it?' said Mike. 'It gets lots of snow in winter. People come up here to ski.'

'Yet it's so close to Heraklion,' she said. 'Stavros told me a bit about the history of the village while we were waiting. If Manolis had to choose one village, it's grim he chose this one.'

'It's a village that understands death, certainly,' agreed Mike.

It took five minutes for him, Stavros and Pam to make their way to the barn, with Panos's guidance, but once there they sent Panos back to help his grandfather, who was wheeling Popi down the steep, rocky track, Popi holding a torch to guide them.

They might now call it a barn and maybe use it for storage, but once it had been a home and one that had never been rebuilt. Where the stonework had fallen down it had been patched with wood and stones, but around the edges, the black showed that it had once been burned when the village had been razed in World War Two. This was a living reminder of the War, Mike thought, even more than all the memorials and cemeteries. It shows what people can do to other people. And how important it is to allow reconciliation, otherwise you get hatred passed down the generations. Just as it had been passed to Manolis. The poor deluded boy. He hoped they could get him out alive, too. But Jen first. He realised he was grinding his teeth and tried to relax.

'Mike,' said Pam. 'I think you should be the first one to call Manolis. If he hears Stavros he may think it's the police, and do something rash. And my voice isn't as strong as yours.'

Stavros nodded. I'd do better with a loud hailer, thought Mike looking at the thickness of the walls. But then there were also a lot of holes, so his voice should carry.

'Manolis!' called Mike. 'It's me, Mike Petersen. You need to talk with us. You're making a terrible mistake!'

There was a silence and then a scream. Jen! What was he doing to Jen?

'Manolis! Stop!' he yelled. But the scream was too much for Pam.

'Manolis!' she yelled. 'Stop! Stop and listen to us!' She rushed at the door, which was hardly attached to the wall, and collapsed inwards. Pam leapt over it and Mike and Stavros followed her in. There was still electricity here, and in the dim light he saw Manolis with a phone in one hand and a gun the other, and Jen behind him, blood on her forehead, tied to a broken chair.

'Get back!' shouted Manolis, 'this is not your business.'

'It is my business,' said Pam, no longer shouting. 'This is all a terrible mistake.'

'This is family business,' Manolis replied. He moved towards Jen and Pam ran to try and intercept him. He swivelled round and in one quick movement fired a shot. Pam felt as thought she had been stung by an angry bee, and tottered backwards. She grabbed a fallen beam that was leaning against the wall and held on to it. 'Stephanie was not responsible for the death of Andreas,' she continued.

Stavros drew his gun and aimed it at Manolis only to feel Mike grasp his arm.

'If we fire now, Manolis might still kill Jen or Pam,' he whispered.

'Get out!' Manolis was yelling again. 'You don't know what you're talking about. Get out, or I'll kill you. I'll kill you all.'

'Listen to us,' said Mike calmly. 'Pam is right. Your father's brother was not betrayed by Stephanie. She had tried to save his life.'

'I know what Andreas told his brother, my grandfather. He died because of this woman's mother. And so did my father. I have sworn a vendetta against her. After this death, it is over.'

'You didn't read the folder,' continued Pam who found herself able to talk clearly even though she felt as thought she was floating above the ground. 'It's all in the folder. Please release Jen. She needs medical help.'

'You're saying these words to confuse me. It isn't true. I know what that woman did. I was told it all my life. She was a devil. She deserved to die.'

'Stephanie did everything she could to save Andreas,' Mike told him. 'It was the janitor who betrayed him.'

'Please listen, Manolis,' said Stavros in Greek, moving forward very slowly. 'Now let Jen go and we can talk about Stephanie.'

Manolis wheeled around to face him, and then stopped as another Greek voice began to speak.

'Manolis, listen to us,' it said. Antonidakis wheeled Popi into the barn. The old woman was holding the folder and waved it in the air.

'You never read this, did you Manolis? And after all the trouble I took to find it.'

Manolis's voice faltered. 'I was afraid…' he began.

'If you had read it you would have read that it was the *thyrorós* who betrayed Andreas, as Stephanie always thought.

She was out buying food for Andreas. She also told me he'd gone into the neighbour's flat to play music. She warned him about that, but he was young. As you are. And like you, he didn't listen to her. Stephanie was always devastated that she couldn't protect Andreas, but she didn't betray him. She would not have been my friend if she were such a woman.'

Manolis looked at her in horror.

'Do you believe me, Manolis? You know me. I do not lie about such things.'

'I know. I know you speak the truth always, Mrs Filotaki. Then it is true? It was not Stephanie who…?'

'No. It was the *thyrorós*.'

Mike saw a look of total despair on the young man's face.

'I killed a good woman?' he asked.

'You did,' said Popi. 'You killed my friend and for nothing.'

'I am sorry, said Manolis. 'I am so sorry. Sorry,' he added in English. 'I am very sorry.'

'But my cat,' said Jen, her voice faltering. 'Why did you kill my cat?'

'I thought your mother was there. I was going to talk with her to get her to confess. Then the cat jumped out and… I've always been afraid of cats. Then I was angry because it made me weak and afraid. I'm sorry,' he added. He looked at Jen and then back at Popi. 'I am very sorry.' Then, before any of them could move, he put the gun into his mouth and pressed the trigger.

'Oh fuck,' said Mike, as Popi screamed and Stavros scooped up Pam who was collapsing on to the floor.

'An ambulance!' he shouted. 'We need an ambulance!'

CHAPTER 40

A day and a half later, they were all sitting in the courtyard outside the tiny chapel that Nikos had built at the edge of his property. Refusing all medical advice, Jen and Pam were both there, Jen with a bandage across her head where she'd been first hit by Manolis before he'd bundled her into the boot of the car, and Pam in a wheelchair beside Mike and Stavros.

Since Jen had been rescued, it was Colin who could not stop his tears as he realised just how close his daughter had come to dying in that barn. He'd hugged Mike and Stavros and Pam any number of times and would have hugged Popi, too if she'd allowed it. But Popi was not talking to anyone. She had aged overnight, and was now merely staying for the service before returning home to be with her husband.

Nikos was saying little. Like Popi he, too, had aged with the events of the past two days. He was being supported by Eleni, who had arrived the previous evening. So this was the famous Eleni, Pam thought, seeing a slim elderly woman in grey. She's a woman who tries to look anonymous; she doesn't like being in the limelight. She was helping both Nikos and Popi. What had happened had changed them all.

'There was no way Popi could have known,' Nikos told Pam the previous afternoon. 'We were all looking in different directions. It was you who put the pieces of the puzzle together.'

'I wish I'd done it more quickly,' she replied. 'I could

have prevented Jen's abduction and maybe Manolis's death.'

'I do not think he would have preferred a long time in an English jail,' said Nikos. 'As soon as he realised that he had killed an innocent woman and was not carrying out an honourable family vendetta, his life was over.'

Pam looked around the small congregation. There was Henry holding on to Popi's wheelchair, and Colin holding Jen's hand as if he'd never let it go. Leonard Cohen sang 'Hey, That's No Way To Say Goodbye', and quiet sobs filled the courtyard. Pam brushed her own off her cheeks. It was strange that she missed a woman she'd never known.

While in hospital, she'd spoken on the phone to Josh and to Murton, telling them she'd only been shot in the leg and the bullet had gone right through without doing any major damage. Murton told her he'd already heard from the Palace, and that she was getting the Queen's Police Medal for Gallantry. Nikos had also heard from the Palace, he told her later, and his gallery was now going to open at the end of August. Prince Charles had managed to rearrange his calendar.

'You got shot, boss?' said Josh. 'You weren't joking about the Wild West then.'

'Just a very sad young man,' said Pam. 'We were right to think it was all about family. We just had to find the family.'

Josh began to tell her about some changes with the structure of the team, when she cut him off. 'Sorry,' she said. 'I'm a bit tired for that now.'

It wasn't just the injury that was making her tired, she knew, as she lay back on her bed. She was tired of the whole thing: the internal battles, the fights for promotion, the struggle to prove herself as a woman officer. She was also too tired to deal with Stavros, who'd sat beside her at the hospital. She'd told him she wasn't angry at how he'd behaved, but it had showed her another side of him and she couldn't forget it. She also didn't think she wanted to live in Athens where she didn't know anyone or speak the language. Where he'd have a fulfilling job and she'd have nothing.

'Give me time,' she asked him. And he'd understood. He was here for the funeral, but was taking the night ferry back to Athens.

She'd got sick leave for as long as she needed it, and she was also owed a good amount of back holiday time. She didn't need to go back to England for a while. She wanted to talk with Henry about the history of Crete and go fishing with Mike in his boat. She wouldn't stay at the Villa Karpathi, it was too luxurious for her, but with Mike moving into Stephanie's house there was an empty cottage in Chiona as the owners had decided to go to France for the summer. She might get Nikos to pay for Zofia and Grace to come over.

Here, she thought. I want them here because for the moment I want to stay here.

The music ended and Henry stood up and began to read.

'As you set out for Ithaka
hope your road is a long one,
full of adventure, full of discovery.'

ACKNOWLEDGEMENTS

There is a wonderful beach at Chiona, and two excellent restaurants, but no village and no Minoan palace. That is entirely fictional. But there is a Minoan site just behind the beach at Roussolakkos, and it was while exploring this with the archaeologist Eftychia Anaplioti that I got the idea for this novel. Anything that is correct about the archaeology is thanks to her. Any mistakes are entirely my own. Some of the treasures from Roussolakkos can be found in the excellent small museum in Sitia.

I would also like to apologise to Peterhouse, Cambridge for stealing some of their land to build my fictitious Leotakis Gallery and to those who own land on the promontory above the beach at Karpathiolimnonas, which again my fictitious billionaire has acquired.

My characters move through the Cambridge and Crete I know well, but any errors regarding these places are my own. The additional floors of the Cambridge police station are fictional, as are those who inhabit them and EASOU, which has nothing at all to do with the highly successful Eastern Region Special Operations Unit (ERSOU).

The events of the Polytechnic in 1973, and Stephanie's experiences are not fictional, however, and are based on my own account, written at the time. Like Stephanie, I did protect a student though he, happily, was not arrested or killed.

The life-changing anthology that Pam reads is *Staying*

Alive: Real Poems for Unreal Times, edited by Neil Astley, published by Bloodaxe Books, 2002.

I would like to thank all those who read this manuscript in advance: Trezza Azzopardi, Alexander Gordon Smith, Tony Frost, Madeleine Hutt, David Watkins, Vicky Holtby and above all Alan Pulverness who has edited my work for the past 30 years. They have all helped me avoid all kinds of errors. Also thanks to James Willis and Richard Albary and everyone at Spiffing Covers for their expertise and wonderful design.

Thanks, too, to the Megaron Hotel in Heraklion, and massive thanks to Vicky and to George Belibasakis who have made Portobelis in Sitia my home from home.

A.M. Norwich, 2020.

Coming early next year!

THE LAST TERRORIST

Detective Inspector Pam Gregory has a lot to think about. She is slowly recovering from a bullet wound and dealing with the imminent closure of her department. But her last case had taken her into a new world and made her reassess what she wanted from her life. Now, only a few weeks after its sad outcome, there is another death. Is it merely natural causes, as the police insist, or murder? Pam begins to investigate, and this time finds herself on a darker journey than she could ever imagine.

Check out www.blackcranepress.co.uk for more news and stories!